Books by Michael Bishop

Blooded on Arachne
Eyes of Fire
No Enemy But Time

Published by TIMESCAPE BOOKS

Most Timescape Books are available at special quantity discounts for bulk purchases for sales promotions, premiums or fund raising. Special books or book excerpts can also be created to fit specific needs.

For details write the office of the Vice President of Special Markets, Pocket Books, 1230 Avenue of the Americas, New York, New York 10020.

NO ENEMY
BUT TIME

MICHAEL BISHOP

A TIMESCAPE BOOK
PUBLISHED BY POCKET BOOKS NEW YORK

Quotation from *The Fellowship of the Ring* by J. R. R. Tolkien copyright © 1965 by J. R. R. Tolkien. Reprinted by permission of Houghton Mifflin Company.

Lines from William Butler Yeats's "In Memory of Eva Gore-Booth and Con Markiewicz" from *Collected Poems,* copyright 1933 by Macmillan Publishing Co., Inc., renewed 1961 by Bertha Georgie Yeats. Reprinted with permission of Macmillan Publishing Co., Inc.

Another *Original* publication of TIMESCAPE BOOKS

A Timescape Book published by
POCKET BOOKS, a Simon & Schuster division of
GULF & WESTERN CORPORATION
1230 Avenue of the Americas, New York, N.Y. 10020

Copyright © 1982 by Michael Bishop

Library of Congress Catalog Card Number: 81-18534

ISBN: 0-671-83576-9

First Timescape Books paperback printing April, 1983

10 9 8 7 6 5 4 3 2 1

Also available in a Timescape hardcover edition

Printed in the U.S.A.

To Floyd J. Lasley, Jr.,
Our mild Irish Godfather

Author's Note

As HE HAS on other book-length projects, my editor, David Hartwell, worked very closely with me on the final version of this manuscript. I wish to thank both him and his family for boarding me over the three-day period that he and I devoted to an especially intense scrutiny of my work.

I also owe a great deal to my wife, Jeri Bishop, for her support, encouragement, and suggestions—during both the protracted research that this novel entailed and the many months of actual writing.

No Enemy But Time is a work of fiction. The country Zarakal does not exist on any map, but I imagine its geographic dimensions *roughly* coextensive with those of Kenya. However, the reader may not automatically suppose that Zarakal and Kenya are historically, sociologically, and politically identical. They are not, nor were they intended to be.

Likewise, the protohuman hominid that my characters refer to as *Homo zarakalensis* is a fictional construct. I have created this spurious ancestral human as a means to a particular dramatic and narrative end.

For the most part, however, my paleoanthropological nomenclature conforms to the usage of those scientists currently struggling to solve the riddle of human origins. Although I urge readers not to regard this work as a textbook on hominid evolution, I have not deliberately mis-construed the enormous amounts of data available to those fascinated by the topic.

Debates about classifications and interpretations will undoubt-edly continue to rage. A decade from now, possibly even less, the terms designating *Homo habilis* and *Australopithecus afarensis* may be taxonomic fossils—just as the bones they are intended to identify are virtually all that remain of the small, bipedal creatures who pioneered the frontiers of our humanity so many million years ago.

—Michael Bishop
Pine Mountain, Georgia
June 23, 1981

PROLOGUE

"Next Slide, Please"

I TIME-TRAVELED in spirit long before I did so in bodily fact. Until the moment of my departure, you see, my life had been a slide show of dreams divided one from another by many small darknesses of wakeful dread and anticipation. Sometimes the dreams and the darknesses alternated so rapidly that I was unable to tell them apart. An inability to distinguish between waking and dreaming may be an index of madness, or it may be a gift. After more than thirty years of trying to integrate the two into a coherent pattern, I understand that it is, or was, my gift.

When I was four, my father Hugo brought home a slide projector from the BX at McConnell Air Force Base in Wichita, Kansas. This was a machine with a circular tray for the slides, and if you kept clicking the changer, eventually the same scenes—the same past moments—would flash into fleeting prominence over and over again. In a way, then, each slide wheel was a time machine; and the procession of images on either the wall or the hanging linen sheet was a cyclical tour of bygone days.

To me, though, it was often more fun to have gaps in the tour, empty tray slots that translated into windows of blinding white illumination—for my father, who spoke English with a noticeable Spanish accent, liked to make up silly captions for these vacant squares:

"Moby Deek's backside!"

"Frosty the Snowman at a Koo Kloox Klan rally!"

"A polar bear swimmin' in a vat of vanilla ice cream!"

My sister Anna and I would shout out captions of our own, most of them even more juvenile than Hugo's, and our mother Jeannette, who appreciated continuity, would urge him to get on with the show. She tried to keep the circular trays filled with slides—each one held a hundred—so that there would be relatively few occasions for nonsense. It was not that she lacked a sense of humor, but that for her the wheel of slides represented a living world, a mandala of bright, recapturable experience. Her fun lay in reexperiencing each brilliant epiphany in the show.

After Hugo was transferred from McConnell to Francis E. Warren AFB in Cheyenne, Wyoming, and after Jeannette went to work for one of Cheyenne's daily newspapers as a book columnist and feature writer, our family took fewer photographs. The slide trays still came out on birthdays, holidays, and Jeannette's occasional moments of nostalgia—but once you had endured the programs four or five times, they were as predictable as television situation comedies. "John-John Pointing at Cows" always preceded "Jeannette Hauling John-John Out of Pasture" and always followed "John-John Bundled for October Walk." You could count on this sequence.

From the fleeting darknesses between changer clicks, I began to create my own private "slides." In fact, after my eighth birthday, I usually fell into a light trance whenever the projection equipment was operating; I dropped out of the here-and-now into a past even older than the one flashing by on the wall. Already I was notorious within my family as a dreamer—not the spaced-out, chin-on-fist variety common to most classrooms, but a rare, visionary kind of dreamer—and I am now convinced that Jeannette's apparent fondness for our slide programs was in part a function of her well-meaning desire to tie me to reality. She wanted to reinforce my allegiance to the Monegal family by impressing upon me the indelibility, the vividness, of my tenure among the three of them.

Each slide wheel, as I have said, was a time machine (a time machine with a comfortably circumscribed range), but it was also a yoke to the status quo. By ignoring the Monegal Family Past and investing each moment of darkness between the slides with a freight of private meaning, I was subverting my mother's intentions. I was distancing myself emotionally as well as temporally.

When I was ten, I played a joke that in some ways foreshadowed the principal rebellion of my adolescence.

Hugo, a noncommissioned minion of the Strategic Air Command, had just been sent from Cheyenne to Guam. Even though there were facilities for dependents on the island, he had gone unaccompanied—not only to decrease the length of his tour, but to honor the demands of Anna (who was happy at her current school) and Jeannette (who had begun to earn a respectable paycheck from her reviewing and feature writing). That no one had consulted me about my stake in the matter was no big deal because my dreams were the same wherever I happened to be. I was trying to learn more about them, though, primarily by going to the library and poring over magazines devoted to either travel or natural history. With Hugo absent, in fact, the three of us still in Cheyenne seemed to be riding a dozen centrifugal interests outward from the nuclear heart of the family.

My joke? Well, right before Christmas that year I went to the closet where we kept our slide equipment and removed the boxes containing the trays. Back in my room I spent a good thirty minutes randomly rearranging slides, leaving gaps in the sequence and slotting several transparencies sideways or upsidedown. "John-John Bundled for October Walk" ended up following a topsy-turvy "Jeannette Enjoying Beach at Cádiz," while "Anna Watching Semana Santa Procession in Seville" gave way to a sideways-slotted "Grandfather Rivenbark Checking Out Customers at Old Van Luna Grocery." Then I returned the trays to their boxes and the boxes to their closet shelves.

On Christmas Eve Jeannette told Anna to fetch the slides and set up for another trip into the Monegal Family Past. Anna, now fourteen, obeyed, and we gathered in the dining room. I turned off the lights, Anna clicked her magic changer, and a kind of wacky chaos ensued.

Jeannette's reaction to my vandalism was not what I had expected. After muttering "What the hell" into her cupped hand, she gave me an appraising look, put her fingers into my wiry hair, and pulled my head into the pit of her arm. Although she would not let go, I could tell she was not angry, merely amused by the form my defiance had taken. Anna was the one who got angry. She railed about the time it would take to restore the slides to their sacrosanct order, and she refused to continue the show.

"Damn you, Johnny-boy!" she exclaimed. "You're going to straighten this out yourself. Don't expect any help from *me*."

"Oh, Anna, it's all right," our mother replied. "Go on to the next one."

"But, Mamma, he's mixed them all up."

Jeannette laughed. "But we know what's what, don't we? Let's just run through the lot and enjoy them as they come up."

"You *can't* enjoy them. Somebody who'd never seen them before wouldn't know what was going on. They don't tell a story anymore, they're just bits and pieces of . . . of *one big mess.*"

"But, Anna, the story's in our heads. It won't hurt to show them out of sequence. Let's not worry about some hypothetical somebody who doesn't even know who we are."

"Mamma, *I'm* not going to put them back the way they belong."

"I don't want you to. I'll do it. It won't be hard. They're all numbered, anyway. So let's just go ahead, all right?"

Sullenly, then, Anna showed the slides in all their helter-skelter, heels-over-head, gap-ridden glory, and I was not scolded. And Jeannette had spoken truthfully: the story *was* in our heads.

Each slide evoked its own context. I paid attention to the program—the immutable program implicit even in this crazy shuffling—as I had not paid attention to any of our slides in a very long time. The Monegal Family Experience had taken on new life. My shuffling of images managed to convey nuances that linear sequence could not really communicate. Each click of the changer was a revision and a gloss.

I put my head on my mother's breast believing that she had finally given in to the randomness of "reality." But then I recalled her saying, "They're all numbered, anyway," and I saw in the corner of each cardboard mounting the numerals she had scrupulously, minutely, inked there. These were a hedge against forgetfulness, entropy, chaos—but they seriously undercut my appreciation of my mother's surprising tolerance of my prank. It was easy to be generous of spirit when you could instantly (or at least quickly) reorder the world to your liking. An uncharitable insight on a chilly Christmas Eve in Wyoming.

Later, when I was a teen-ager, I rebelled in a more vehement way against another of Jeannette's ill-advised attempts to impose order on my random experience. And both of us suffered.

CHAPTER ONE

Lolitabu National Park, Zarakal

July 1986 To February 1987

FOR NEARLY EIGHT months Joshua lived in a remote portion of Zarakal's Lolitabu National Park, where an old man of the Wanderobo tribe taught him how to survive without tap water, telephones, or cans of imported tuna. Although hunting was illegal in the country's national parks, President Tharaka granted a special dispensation, for the success of the White Sphinx Project would depend to an alarming extent on Joshua's ability to take care of himself in the Early Pleistocene.

Despite having lived his entire life among the agricultural Kikembu people (Zarakal's largest single ethnic group), Thomas Babington Mubia had never given up the hunting arts of the Wanderobo. In 1934 he had taught a callow Alistair Patrick Blair (today a world-renowned paleoanthropologist) how to catch a duiker barehanded and to dress out its carcass with stone tools chipped into existence on the spot. Now, over half a century later, Blair wanted his old teacher to communicate these same skills to Joshua—for, although considerably slower and not quite so sharp-eyed, Babington had lost none of his basic skills as stalker, slayer, and flint-knapper.

Babington—as everyone who knew him well called him—was tall, sinewy, and grizzled. In polite company he wore khaki shorts, sandals, and any one of a number of different loud sports shirts that Blair had given him, but in the bush he frequently opted for near or total nudity. Welts, scars, wheals, and tubercules pebbled his flesh, in spite of which he appeared in excellent health for a man belonging to *rika ria Ramsay,* an age-grade group that had undergone circumcision during the ascension of Ramsay MacDonald's coalition cabinet in England. For Joshua the old man's incidental bumps and cuts were less troubling than a deliberate vestige of that long-ago circumcision rite.

Ngwati, the Kikembu called it. This was a piece of frayed-looking skin that hung beneath Babington's penis like the pull tab on a Band-Aid wrapper. It hurt Joshua to look at this "small skin." He tried not to let his eyes shift to Babington's crotch, and, for reasons other than Western modesty, he did his darnedest not to shed his shorts or make water within the old man's sight. He was half afraid that to be looked upon naked by Babington would be to acquire *Ngwati* himself.

Until his circumcision Joshua's mentor had attended a mission school run by Blair's Protestant Episcopal parents, and he knew by heart a score of psalms, several of Shakespeare's soliloquies, and most of the poems of Edgar Allan Poe, a great favorite of the old Wanderobo's. Sometimes, in fact, he disconcerted Joshua by standing naked in the night and booming out in a refined British accent whichever of these memory-fixed passages most suited his mood. In July, their first month in the bush, Babington most frequently declaimed the lesser known of two pieces by Poe entitled "To Helen":

"But now, at length, dear Dian sank from sight
Into a western couch of thunder-cloud;
And thou, a ghost, amid the entombing trees
Didst glide away. Only thine eyes remained.
They would not *go—they never yet have gone.*

Lighting my lonely pathway home that night,
They have not left me (as my hopes have) since."

Sitting in the tall acacia in which he and Babington had built a tree house with a stout door, Joshua looked down and asked his mentor if he had ever been married.

"Oh, yes. Four times all at once, but the loveliest and best was Helen Mithaga."

"What happened?"

"During the war, the second one, I walked to Bravanumbi from Makoleni, my home village, and enlisted for service against the evil minions of Hitler in North Africa. I was accepted into a special unit and fought with it for two years. When I returned to Makoleni, three of my wives had divorced me by returning to their families. I was Wanderobo; they were Kikembu. Although Helen was also Kikembu, she had waited.

"We loved each other very much. Later, a year after the war, she was poisoned by a sorcerer who envied me the medals I had won and also my Helen's Elysian beauty. I lost her to the world of spirits, which we call *ngoma*. On nights like this one, dry and clear, I know that she has fixed the eyes of her soul upon me. Therefore, I speak to her everlasting world with another man's poignant words."

This story touched Joshua. He could not regard Babington as a ridiculous figure even when, during the arid month of August, he stood one-footed in the dark and recited,

"Hear the sledges with the bells—
Silver bells!
What a world of merriment their melody foretells!
How they tinkle, tinkle, tinkle,
In the icy air of night! . . ."

Nights were never icy in Lolitabu, which was tucked away in Zarakal's southwestern corner. Instead of bells-on-bobtails you heard elephants trumpeting, hyenas laughing, and maybe even poachers whispering to one another. Babington took pains to insure that Joshua and he never ran afoul of these men, for although some were woebegone amateurs, trying to earn enough money to eat, others were ruthless predators who would kill to avoid detection.

The big cats in the park worried Joshua far more than the poachers did. They did not worry Babington. He would walk the savannah as nonchalantly as a man crossing an empty parking lot. His goal was not to discomfit Joshua, but to school him in the differences among several species of gazelle and antelope, some of which had probably not even evolved by Early Pleistocene times. Joshua tried to listen, but found himself warily eying the lions sprawled under trees on the veldt.

"We do not have an appetizing smell in their nostrils," Babington told Joshua. "The fetor of human beings is repugnant to lions."

"So they will not attack us unless we provoke them?"

Babington pushed a partial plate out of his mouth with his tongue, then drew it back in. "A toothless lion or one gradually losing its sense of smell might be tempted to attack. Who knows?"

"Then why do we come out here without weapons and walk the grasslands like two-legged gods?"

Said Babington pointedly, "That is not how I am walking."

During this extended period in the Zarakali wilderness Joshua dreamed about the distant past no more than once or twice a month, and these dreams were similar in a hazy way to his daily tutorials with Babington. Why had his spirit-traveling episodes given way to more conventional dreaming? Well, in a sense, his survival training with Babington was a waking version of the dreamfaring he had done by himself his entire life. With his eyes wide open, he was isolated between the long-ago landscape of his dreams and the dreams themselves. He stood in the darkness separating the two realities.

· · ·

One day Babington came upon Joshua urinating into a clump of grass not far from their tree house. Joshua was powerless to halt the process and too nonplused to direct it away from his mentor's gaze. At last, the pressure fully discharged, he shook his cock dry, eased it back into his jockey shorts, buttoned up, and turned to go back to the tree house.

"You are not yet a man," the Wanderobo informed him.

Joshua's embarrassment mutated into anger. "It's not the Eighth Wonder of the World, but it gets me by!"

"You have not been bitten by the knife."

It struck Joshua that Babington was talking about circumcision. A young African man who had not undergone this rite was officially still a boy, whatever his age might be.

"But I'm an American, Babington."

"In this enterprise you are an honorary Zarakali, and you are too old to live any longer in the *nyuba.*"

The *nyuba,* Joshua knew, was the circular Kikembu house in which women and young children lived.

"Babington!"

But Babington was adamant. It was unthinkable that any adult male representing all the peoples of Zarakal should proceed with a mission of this consequence—the visiting of the *ngoma* of the spirit world—without first experiencing *irua,* the traditional rite of passage consecrating his arrival at manhood. If Joshua chose not to submit to the knife (which Babington himself would be happy to wield), then Babington would go home to Makoleni and White Sphinx would have to carry on without his blessing.

On a visit to the park in early September, Blair learned of this ultimatum and of Joshua's decision to accede to it—so long as Joshua could impose a condition of his own.

"I don't want a Band-Aid string like Babington's," he told the Great Man. "I think I can put up with the pain and the embarrassment, but you've got to spare me that goddamn little casing pull."

Although less than six feet tall and possessed of a pair of

watery blue eyes whose vision had recently begun to deteriorate (a circumstance insufficient to make him wear glasses), Blair was still an imposing figure. His white mustachios and the sun-baked dome of his forehead and pate gave him the appearance of a walrus that had somehow blustered into the tropics and then peremptorily decided to make the region its home. He seemed to be swaggering even when sitting on the sticky upholstery of a Land Rover's front seat, and his voice had the mellow resonance of a bassoon. In the past ten years his appealing ugly-uncle mug had graced the covers of a dozen news magazines and pupular scientific journals, and for a thirteen-week period three years ago he had been the host of a PBS program about human evolution entitled *Beginnings,* an effort that had rekindled the old controversy between paleoanthropologists and the so-called scientific creationists and that had incidentally served to make Blair's name a household word in even the smallest hamlets in the United States. By now, though, Joshua was used to dealing with the Great Man, and he had no qualms about voicing his complaints about Babington's plans for the circumcision rite.

Blair assured Joshua that educated Kikembu, especially Christians, also regarded *Ngwati* with distaste, and that Babington would not try to make him keep the "small skin" if Joshua were vigorously opposed to it.

"I am," said Joshua, but he neatly parried the Great Man's many well-meaning proposals for sidestepping the circumcision rite altogether. He felt he owed Babington, and he wanted to earn the old man's respect.

Apprised of Joshua's intentions, Babington declared that the ceremony would take place two days hence, in the very grove where he and his protégé had their tree house. Blair then informed Joshua that in order to prove himself he must not show any fear prior to the cutting or cry out in pain during it. Such behavior would result in disgrace for himself and his sponsors. Moreover, to lend the rite legitimacy, Babington had sent messages to several village leaders and asked Blair to invite some of the Kikembu from the outpost village of Nyarati as onlookers. Once the knife glinted, they would applaud Joshua's steadfastness or, if he did not bear up, ridicule his public cowardice.

"Onlookers!"

"It's traditional, I'm afraid. Of what point are the strength and beauty of a leopard if no one ever sees them?"

"Of considerable point, if you're the leopard. Besides, we're not talking about leopards. We're talking about my one and only reproductive organ. Onlookers be damned!"

"They're for purposes of verification, Joshua."

"Maybe Babington ought to circumcise a leopard, Dr. Blair. I'd love to see them verify *that.*"

"Now, now," said Alistair Patrick Blair. "Tsk-tsk."

Joshua spent the night before his *irua* at the park's sprawling Edwardian guest lodge with Blair. At dawn he bathed himself in a tub mounted on cast-iron lion's paws, donned a white linen robe, and, in company with the paleoanthropologist, set off for his rendezvous with Babington aboard a Land Rover driven by a uniformed park attendant.

They arrived in the acacia grove shortly after eight o'clock and found it teeming with young people from Nyarati, both men and women. The women were singing spiritedly, and the boisterous gaiety of the entire crowd seemed out of proportion to its cause, the trimming of an innocent foreskin. Blair pulled off Joshua's robe and pointed him to the spot where the old Wanderobo would perform the surgery.

"You're not to look at Babington, Joshua. Don't try to watch the cutting, either."

"I thought that would be part of proving my manhood."

"No. Rather than being required, it's prohibited."

"Thanks be to Ngai for small mercies."

Naked and shivering, he entered the clearing beneath the tree house, sat down on the matted grass, and averted his face from the ladder that Babington would soon be descending. Blair, his aide, could offer him no physical assistance until the rite was concluded.

The songs of the Kikembu women, the bawdy masculine repartee at his back, and the anxious hiccuping of his heart isolated him from the reality of what was happening. This was not happening to him. Only, of course, it was.

Then Babington was there, kneeling before him with a knife, and Joshua put both fists to the right side of his neck, placed his chin on one fist, and stared out into the savannah. The cutting began. Joshua clenched his teeth and tightened his fists. Doggedly refusing to yip or whimper, he caught sight of a pair of tourist minibuses rolling over the steppe from the vicinity of the guest lodge. That morning while boarding the Land Rover, he recalled, he had seen them parked inside a courtyard next to the lodge. Somehow the tour guide had learned of the approaching ceremony. When the minibuses pulled abreast of the acacia grove, clouds of dust drifting away behind them, Joshua wanted to scream.

The faces in the windows of the two grimy vehicles belonged primarily to astonished Caucasians, many of them elderly women in multicolored head scarves, out-of-fashion pillbox hats, or luxuriant wigs much too youthful for their wearers. The cutting momentarily ceased. Passengers from both vans dismounted at the outer picket of trees and filtered inward to stand behind the swaying and ululating Kikembu women.

"Jesus," Joshua murmured.

"Hush," cautioned Babington. "Or I will deprive you of much future pleasure and many descendants."

A portly, middle-aged tour guide with a florid complexion used a megaphone to make himself heard over the singing and hand-clapping Africans.

The cutting had begun again. Joshua shut out the man's spiel to concentrate on the waves of pain radiating through him from the focus of the knife.

The eyes of the female tourist nearest the guide, Joshua noticed, had grown huge behind her thick-lensed glasses. She was a stout ruin of a women whose magenta head scarf resembled a babushka. Her body appeared to sway in time with those of the svelte, graceful Africans. Her swaying and the guide's ceaseless patter distracted Joshua from the pain of the circumcision rite.

"Finished," Babington announced.

"Don't leave *Ngwati*," Blair countered. "Remove it, please."

Babington snorted his contempt for this command, but swiftly removed the offending string of flesh.

In celebration of the successful *irua*, a chorus of voices echoed through the grove and across the steppe. Now Joshua could look down. He saw blood flowing from him into the grass like water from a spigot. Blair steadied him from behind and wrapped the immaculate white robe around his shoulders.

Now people were dancing as well as singing, extolling the initiate's courage as they wove in and out among the trees in a sinuous daisy chain of bodies. Some of the tourists had joined the conga line, and the two groups, Africans and foreigners, were suddenly beginning to blend. The Kikembu waved their arms in encouragement, and more tourists—sheepish old white people—snaked their way into the celebration.

Joshua, afraid he would faint, held the front of his robe away from his groin to keep from staining the garment. The woman with the magenta scarf approached him from the edge of the grove and addressed him in the flat, Alf Landon accents of a native Kansan.

"I'll give you twenty dollars for that robe."

Joshua gaped.

"Tell him twenty dollars for the robe," the old woman commanded Blair. "Another five if he'll let me take a Polaroid. Our tour guide said to ask before I took a Polaroid."

"Mrs. Givens!" Joshua exclaimed. "Kit Givens from Van Luna, Kansas!" He had last seen the old woman at his grandfather's funeral fourteen years ago, piously occupying a rear pew in the stained-glass, apricot-and-umber ambiance of the First

Methodist Church. She was seventy-two if she was a minute. Her withered cheeks and chin were tinted all the iridescent colors of a mandrill's mask.

"I've never seen him before," Mrs. Givens told Blair, as if sharing a confidence. "I don't know how he could know my name."

"You pulled my hair in my grandfather's grocery when I was a baby."

The old woman rallied. "You're an impudent little nigger. I wouldn't pay you five dollars to mow my yard."

Defiant despite his weakness, Joshua doffed his robe and handed it to Mrs. Givens. "Here. I want you to have this. Take it back to Van Luna—the sooner the better."

Mrs. Givens took the robe from the bleeding man, backed away from him clutching it, and turned again to the paleoanthropologist. "You'll walk me back to the tour bus, please. I've never met this man in my life."

"Of course, Mrs. Givens."

As Blair directed the old woman through the rowdy throng to the bus, Babington helped Joshua climb the ladder into the tree house. Many of the Kikembu from Nyarati had brought banana leaves to the ceremony, and the old Wanderobo had already arranged the leaves into a pallet upon which Joshua could rest without fear of exacerbating his wounds. His penis would not stick to the banana leaves as to linen or other sorts of bedding, and the wounds would therefore heal more readily.

Lying on this pallet, Joshua saw Babington's creased face staring down at him. A face that seemed to have been created in the same way that wind sculpts sand dunes or rain erodes channels into the hardest rock.

"Everyone wants a piece of the sacred," Joshua whispered. "Even if it isn't sacred. Dreaming makes it so, and the dreaming goes on and on until it's a habit."

"Go to sleep, Joshua," the old man said.

· · ·

Three weeks passed before Joshua felt strong enough to resume his survival training. For two nights, despite the antibiotics that Blair had brought to Lolitabu from the hospital at Russell-Tharaka Air Force Base, he was delirious. In his delirium he was visited by the lacerated ghost of his adoptive father, as well as a gnomish Spanish woman who opened her blouse and let him nurse like a baby, a young black infantryman with no head, and the robed figure of Mutesa David Christian Ghazali Tharaka, President of Zarakal. This last visitor, Joshua learned from Babington, had actually been there.

"Why was he here? What did he say?"

Babington handed Joshua an autographed picture of the President. "He said he was very proud of you. You are bridging a chasm between Zarakal's pluralistic tribal beginnings and its modern aspirations. That you, an American black man, submitted to the knife bespeaks the fullness of your commitment to our dream."

"What else did he say?"

"He gave me a photograph, too." Babington pointed at the wall of the tree house, where he had hung another copy of the same photograph. This one bore an inscription to the Wanderobo. Joshua could not see it from where he lay, but he could tell that it had made Babington very happy.

At first it disturbed Joshua that he was taking so long to heal, but Babington explained that he himself had suffered intense pain and then a throbbing tenderness for well over a month after his *irua*. By mid-October, just as his mentor had predicted, they were stalking game again, digging tubers, picking fruit, and diving ever deeper into wilderness lore. Joshua's glans was no longer so sensitive that simply to urinate was to conduct electricity. He was himself again.

Joshua paid attention to Babington's lessons. He learned how to alter his upright silhouette by tying foliage about his waist, how to move on a wily diagonal while stalking game, how to club a sick or wounded animal to death without exhausting himself or making an ugly mess of his kill, and how to eat raw meat, birds' eggs, and insects without nausea or qualm. The time in Lolitabu passed quickly.

The night before Joshua was to return to Russell-Tharaka for additional study—textbook and simulator work, with reviews of the paleontological information he had digested last spring and summer—he awoke and went to the door of the tree house. Babington, silhouetted on the edge of the grove, was reciting from Poe:

> "Yet if hope has flown away
> In a night, or in a day,
> In a vision, or in none,
> Is it therefore the less gone?
> All that we see or seem
> Is but a dream within a dream."

CHAPTER TWO
Into the Dream

"An inability to distinguish between waking and dreaming may be an index of madness, or it may be a gift."

I am in the African country of Zarakal taking part in an experiment—a mission, I ought to call it—that would not be possible without my talent as a dreamer. The American physicist Woodrow Kaprow has just strapped me into an apparatus suspended inside a closed vehicle resembling a windowless omnibus.

This large vehicle rests on the outer edge of an ancient stretch of beach about four hundred feet from the southeastern shore of Lake Kiboko, one of several large lakes in East Africa's Great Rift Valley. We have positioned the omnibus according to Alistair Patrick Blair's calculations. Blair has cautioned Kaprow that Lake Kiboko in Early Pleistocene times had a more extensive surface area than it does today, and that if the omnibus is parked too close to its twentieth-century shore, I am likely to emerge from my next spirit-traveling episode into several feet of tepid, brackish water. *Kiboko,* Blair has reminded us, means hippopotamus, but

crocodiles also cotton to this great lake, and my life would probably be forfeit even if I did not drown. Therefore we have left
ourselves a margin for error.

Outside the sun is rising. It is July, and very hot. Inside,
however, a pair of interlocking rotary blades have begun to spin
just above my outstretched body; the breeze they make evapo-
rates the sweat from my forehead. Kaprow hunches inside a bell-
shaped glass booth punching buttons and flipping switches. I can
see him if I turn my head, but he has asked me to lie completely
still, close my eyes, and concentrate on the recorded human heartbeat drumming in my earphones. The hypnagogic rhythms of this
sound will soothe me toward slumber and induce the kind of
dreaming necessary to shift my body into the Early Pleistocene.

"You're drifting," Kaprow intones. "You're drifting,
Joshua. Drifting . . ."

I am at the eye of a compact hurricane, the toroidal field
generated by the rotors. Waking and dreaming begin to inter-
thread. Although my eyes are closed, my inward vision brings me
images that alternate between a primeval landscape of gazelles
and the twentiety-century interior of the omnibus. Pretty soon
these images are coterminous, and I am in two places at once. In
the throes of dream I drift for nearly two thousand millennia.

At last the rhythm of the heartbeat ceases, and I open my
eyes to find that the rotors above my scaffold have almost stopped
turning. The booth in which Kaprow has monitored my dropback appears to be empty; its transparent hood has taken on a
decidedly smoky cast. The trouble of course is that Kaprow has
remained in humanity's concensus present whereas I have retreated to only Ngai knows precisely what year. (For Ngai pre-
sides over the Kikembu spirit world.) The inside of the omnibus
exists at a set of temporal coordinates different from those of the
remainder of the machine, and my dreaming has been instrumental in affecting this dislocation. Glancing about, bewildered, I apply a tentative forward pressure to the control beside my hand.

This control maneuvers my scaffold up and down on the
pneumatic struts attaching it to the ceiling. Obediently, then, the

scaffold begins to drop through a bay in the floor of the vehicle. The rotors that have half-encircled me remain where they are, like a bird cage that someone has cracked open on the edge of my platform. I am being hatched into a "simulacrum" of our planet's prehistory.

Blair and Kaprow have planned my exit wisely, for when I emerge from the belly of the omnibus I will not descend into a solid mass of rock or find myself forty feet above the surface with no easy way down. No indeed. The ground is only a body length below me. For the present, though, I gaze upward into a column of space furnished with the arcane equipment that has helped me make this transfer. The rest of the omnibus—the tires, the chassis, the body—is utterly invisible, for it exists in material fact only in the final fifth of the twentieth century. Briefings and simulations have not prepared me for the *weirdness* of this effect, and I peer into this hovering hole in the Pleistocene sky like a fretful Alice regretting her introduction to Wonderland.

Although I missed the lake, what sort of splash did I make in that ancient timescape?

Initially, not much. Had there been any sort of fashion-conscious creature there to observe my arrival, though, it would have had to regard me as the Beau Brummell of hominids. Although I was still in harness (on the apparatus that Kaprow called the Backstep Scaffold), I had brought with me not only the clothes on my back but several changes and a small cornucopia of survival items. The point of all this gear was to keep me alive for the duration of my mission, which was supposed to last anywhere from two weeks to a month.

Beyond the bush jacket, bush shorts, and chukkas in which I arrived, here is what I had with me in the way of clothing: three pairs of cotton jockey shorts (Fruit of the Loom); three white, V-necked, cotton undershirts (Hanes); three pairs of white, calf-length tube socks (Gold Cup); and a red bandanna that my sister Anna had given me as a talisman on my eighth birthday. My bush jacket and shorts had come from a safari outfitter in Marakoi, but my chukkas were from the Eddie Bauer firm of Seattle, Washington, U.S.A. They had rubber soles and heels, cushioned scree-guards at the ankles, and uppers of rugged Maple Cuddy leather. Even if they were not exactly designed for East African landscapes and hot weather, I liked the way they felt.

In the way of necessary in-the-field gear I had brought the following: a canteen (Army surplus, government issue); a Swiss Army pocketknife with a lanyard chain (L.L. Bean, Inc., Freeport, Maine); an Eddie Bauer combination stove and survival kit; a shaving bag with a Gillette Track-II razor, a small can of Colgate shaving cream (lime scented), and a collapsible mirror; a first-aid kit with bandages, malaria pills, water-purification tablets, and a modest contingency supply of latex prophylactics; a penlight with a handful of additional batteries (Duracell); a .45-caliber automatic pistol (Colt, government issue); a canvas bandolier with two hundred rounds of ammunition (Army surplus, government issue); a leather holster and belt (Cheyenne Leatherworx; Manitou Springs, Colorado); a combination reduced-print Bible and guide to Pleistocene ecology (the American Geographic Foundation in conjunction with the Gideons); a magnifying glass; thirty feet of heavy-duty nylon rope; and an expensive intertemporal communicator (KaprowKorn Instruments, Ltd.) that almost immediately failed me. Much of this equipment I wore, stowed in my pockets, or carried in a nylon pack strapped to my chest. Once down from the Backstep Scaffold, I would shift this pack to my shoulders.

In addition to my gear I had at least three other things going for me before I jumped from the scaffold to the ground. First, Air Force doctors had immunized me against every conceivable East African disease and several inconceivable ones. Second, I had spent eight months in the Lolitabu National Park with the old Wanderobo warrior Thomas Babington Mubia undergoing wilderness training. And third, I had visited this same untamed epoch thousands of times in my dreams. I could never believe that I might die in this distant realm of *ngoma*, or spirits.

I unfastened my harness, removed my earphones, and pulled away the electrodes taped to my temples and brow. After easing myself to a sitting position, I surveyed the landscape and jumped. The Beau Brummell of hominids debuting in an era of sartorial barbarism. I took my red bandanna from my pocket and tied it about my neck, thinking that surely it imparted to my diminutive figure a dashing, even piratical air. As if anyone here— and I saw no one—gave a damn. Despite being armed, or perhaps because of it, I felt like a paratrooper who has landed miles and miles behind enemy lines.

Beside me, a dazzling turquoise in the morning sun, the lake. It was larger than its twentiety-century self; a brief jog would have carried me into its shallows. The lake's oddest feature today was that, Joshua Kampa aside, it had no constituency. Despite its name, Lake Hippopotamus entertained no boisterous or sunbathing riverhorses. No skittish herds of gazelles or wildebeest braved its open shoreline to slake their thirst, and not a single crocodile knifed through the languid waters looking for breakfast. An eerie emptiness reigned.

Turning to the east, I found that the mosaic habitat of savannah, bush, thornveldt, and gallery forest afforded a similar glimpse of the native wildlife. None. No birds in the sky, and no animals out there among the trees and grasses. The wide, rolling plain was vacant, and the range of gentle, faraway hills over which the sun was now rising looked as uninhabited as the high-lands of the moon. Had the project code-named White Sphinx translated me to primogenial Pangea rather than to preadamite Africa? I was utterly alone. For the first time in my life I did not know whether I was waking or dreaming!

From the breast pocket of my bush jacket I took the hand-held communicator that was supposed to establish instantaneous contact with my colleagues in the twentieth century. A trans-cordion, Kaprow had dubbed it. Its *modus operandi* involved a piezoelectric correspondence among the crystals in the microcir-cuitry of each matched pair. Kaprow had the mate to mine, and, theoretically, all I had to do to communicate with him was type out a message on my instrument's tiny keyboard.

Previous tests, with travelers who had dropped back only a century or two, had shown that the transcordions performed reliably even under adverse weather conditions. Eventually, therefore, Kaprow had convinced himself that the size of the temporal gap separating a pair of transcordions had no bearing at all on their effectiveness. The energy expenditure involved in sending me to the Pleistocene had not permitted us to test this hypothesis in my case, however, and I quickly learned that Woodrow Kaprow, Genius Extraordinaire, had figured wrong. Marconi, Bell, and Edison no doubt had their off days, too.

But for those who collect First Words, Last Words, and/or Pithy Epigrams, here is the first message I fed into my transcordion: *"That's one small leap for a man, one giant step backward for humanity."* It pleased me to be typing rather than speaking this message—because I did not have to fear that radio static would garble my words and perhaps obscure or delete the altogether crucial article in my first clause.

Kaprow did not reply.

Maybe he had not found my opening gambit amusing. I got serious: *"The lake seems to be dead, and the landscape is barren of all life but vegetation. Dr. Blair was right in assuring us that I would be visiting a wetter, more hospitable period, though. The desert of Zarakal's Northwest Frontier District is no desert this morning. It's a big, gone-to-seed golf course with woods, sand traps, water hazards, and overgrown fairways. The absence of wildlife scares me. It's going to be impossible to shoot a hyrax here, much less a birdie or an eagle."*

I gave Kaprow a good five minutes to register and digest this information, but still he did not reply. I grew uneasy. Perhaps the enormous span of time separating the physicist and me *had* affected the transcordions. If it made for a small time lag between sending and receiving, well, that would entail inconvenience, certainly, but not catastrophe. Astronauts, after all, have to cope with this phenomenon. Why not a chrononaut, then?

Walking a few steps along the shore, I keyed this in: *"The past FEELS different, Dr. Kaprow. At least to me. It's not a matter of misaligned geographies or molecules twisted sideways, really. It's even different from my perception of the Early Pleistocene in my spirit-traveling episodes. Let me see if I can explain."*

After clearing the transcordion's display area, I tried to explain: *"When I was small, probably about ten or so, I was thumbing through a science book when I came across a strange photograph. It showed a canary submerged on its perch in an aquarium. The bird was actually in the water, it was wet, and there were guppies and goldfish swimming around it. How neat, I thought, how neat and how weird. It reminded me of my own terrible out-of-placeness in my dreams."*

My display area was nearly full. I cleared it again, knowing that Kaprow's unit was connected to a printout terminal that would preserve my messages on long sheets of computer paper. For portability's sake, of course, my transcordion had no such attachment, and Kaprow was therefore limited to messages of exactly ten lines at sixty-five characters a line. So far, though, he had not said, *"Boo."*

I typed: *"You see, that canary was inside a cubic foot of water sheathed by an oxygen-permeable membrane of laminated silicon. The canary was wet, but it could breathe. It was existing in an alien physical medium. It looked bewildered, but it was existing, Dr. Kaprow, and that's more or less the way I'm experiencing the past. The past feels different, but it's not impossible to breathe and think here . . . Does that give you any idea what the past feels like?"*

This time I waited. Surely, by now, Kaprow would have had time to receive and to respond to at least the first of my messages. I wanted his or Blair's advice about the absence of wildlife. Maybe I had leapt into the wrong past, and maybe our only viable course was to abort the mission.

"That canary was surrounded by FISH," I typed, surveying my creatureless paradise. *"I, on the other hand, am totally alone. And I miss the fish. I miss them because I want the whole Pleistocene, the complete experience of it. I've waited my entire life for this, Dr. Kaprow, and I'm*

willing to wait a great deal longer to make those insidious, beautiful dreams
of mine come true. Do you read me?"

No, I was not going to abort the mission. We had talked
about the possibility of failing to establish or losing transcordion
contact, but always with the tacit understanding that neither of
these dreadful eventualities would befall us. The latter had occupied a bit more of our discussion time—after all, I could drop
the transcordion on a rock or lose it in a stream bed or forfeit it to
an envious and overbearing baboon—but because the transcordion was an instrument capable of withstanding a great deal of
physical abuse, and because I fully understood its value, we had
entertained the possibility of this danger only as a dutiful intellectual exercise.

"DAMN IT, KAPROW! ANSWER ME, PLEASE!"

Our contingency plan was simple. In the event the transcordions failed, I was to assess my situation and either abort or
continue the mission according to my intuitive assessment. If I
opted to go ahead, I was to return the Backstep Scaffold to the
interior of the omnibus (in order not to leave an anomalous hole
in the prehistoric atmosphere) and come back to this lakeshore
site at least once a day. At regular intervals Kaprow or one of his
technicians would lower the scaffold so that I could either reject
the invitation or clamber aboard for a trip back to the twentieth
century. The appointed times for these rendezvous were dawn,
noon, and sunset. Kaprow did not want to leave the scaffold out
at night for fear of retracting into the omnibus's sensitive interior
some rambunctious representative of a Pleistocene primate species. At all costs, it was necessary to avoid monkey fur in the
works. Finally, Kaprow had dictated that I was not to remain
longer than a week without direct transcordion contact.

Reaching over my head, I pushed the control on the scaffold and watched it withdraw upward through the bomb-bay
doors of the omnibus. When these doors swung shut, hermetically
sealing the guts of the time machine from Pleistocene eyes, the sky
was whole again. I stood alone on the lakeshore; half-seen electric

twinklings filled the air around me, like a caroling of microscopic fireflies. This phenomenon lasted only a moment or two. Staring at the place where the hole had been, I reflected that if anyone in the twentieth century successfully broke into the omnibus's equipment hold, the vehicle would either blow apart or lose the temporal pressure sustaining its prehistoric atmosphere. A violent explosion was the more likely of these two events, according to Kaprow, but in either case I would have to live out the remainder of my life in this desolate, primeval setting.

Returning the transcordion to my pocket, I murmured, "I miss the fish."

CHAPTER THREE
Seville, Spain
May 1963

Encarnación Consuela Ocampo, whore and black-marketeer, had decided to take her son out of her dark second-floor apartment for the first time in his life. The child had spent his first winter sequestered in a pair of chilly tiled rooms. Within these walls he had slept, fed, excreted, crawled, babbled, played, caterwauled, and eventually, despite his extreme youth and smallness, learned to walk. By late spring, then, his mother had summoned the courage to take him upstairs into the sun.

Like Cantinflas in a movie comedy currently playing in a theatre near her tenement, Encarnación was an *analfabeto*, an illiterate. To complicate matters, she was also mute. If she had named her child, no one knew that name. Mute, she could not speak it; letterless, she could not write it. The infant, consequently, had grown to toddlerhood in a thunderstorm of nearly continuous silence. Only his own cries, the extraneous noises of the tenement, and the half-heard murmurings of his mother's clients had interrupted it.

Encarnación realized that if her son was ever to have a chance amid the terrible babel of adult life, she must remedy this situation. For too long she had kept him from feeling the afternoon sun on his pert, monkeyish face. That she had deprived him of this blessing, primarily because her neighbors regarded her as a fallen woman and a witch, shamed her deeply. Today she would articulate this shame by attempting to exorcise it.

Hoisting the boy onto her hip, Encarnación steeled herself to the ordeal of carrying him to the roof. Her dirty clothes she had knotted inside one of her cheap, capacious skirts, such as gypsy women wore, and this makeshift laundry bag provided a counterweight to the child. So laden, she left her apartment, walked along the gallery landing, and climbed a set of dingy interior stairs toward the building's concrete wash house.

Expressions of wonder and fear took turns passing across the child's face, but he hung on gamely and did not avert his eyes from a single challenge. Only the angry circle of sun peering down into the stairwell made him blink.

Near the roof Encarnación heard a sound like a single tiny fish frying in a skillet. Emerging into the open, she saw an old woman clad from pate to shoe tops in rusty ebony, all about her the sodden flags of wash day. This person gazed raptly at the Giralda, the tower of the great cathedral of Seville, while peeing into a tin can thrust beneath her concealing skirt.

The arrival of unexpected company startled the *vieja*, but, with a stoop and a whirl dazzling in one so ancient, she withdrew the can from between her legs, made a kind of toasting motion with it, and thereby salvaged both composure and pride.

Encarnación hesitated. Her child, his every didy in need of laundering, was wearing only a stained cotton jersey; and this old woman—hardly a friend, since no one in the building was—hurried forward to examine the boy. After easing her tin can onto the lid of the water drum beside the stairwell entrance, she poked the child with gnarly fingers, all the while gabbling furiously. Although he recoiled from these attentions, the pokes seemed to trouble him less than the spent air spiraling noisily from the *vieja*'s mouth. He had heard Encarnación give vent to many strange sounds, including, most often, tongue clicks meant to warn him away from mischief—but the crone's performance was of a different order, vigorous and patterned. It hypnotized as well as cowed him.

"*Qué alerto,*" declared the old woman, addressing the mother while studying the child. "Is it true that he has never heard the talk of other people? Is it true you have not taken him to the priests for christening? *Por Dios,* Señorita Ocampo, if these accusations are true, you arm those misguided gossips who call you *bruja.* You give them cause to dishonor your name."

Spoken to her face, the word *bruja*—witch—made Encarnación cringe. This calumny, she well knew, derived from her singular appearance and her neighbors' astute surmise that her ancestors were *Moriscos*—that is, Christianized Moors—of uncertain steadfastness in their new faith. Disciples of Mahomet, the Moors had come to Iberia from northern Africa. Yes, but what spiritual allegiance had bound them before their conversion to Islam? Black magic, Encarnación's neighbors would say. Mumbo jumbo. Voodooism. Imbued with misinformation and prejudice, they believed her a stalking horse for Satan. Indeed, the old woman haranguing her on the rooftop now ascribed to her, heartlessly point-blank, an odious personal quality known among Spaniards as *mal ángel,* or negative charm.

"A proper christening would remove this child from the realm of devils. Why do you deny him? To increase your stores of *mal ángel?* Do you wish him to converse only with your titties and the evil spirits of your sins? *Por Dios,* Señorita, it hurts me to ask such things."

Ignoring these impertinences, Encarnación set her child down and brushed past the old woman toward the stone basin in the laundry shed. The *vieja* followed her.

The toddler, meanwhile, hunkered in a wet spot under the flapping clothes, fascinated by the graceful schooling of Seville's pigeons. They careened overhead like scraps of half-charred paper buoyed on erratic updrafts. While Encarnación, heedless of the birds, flooded the basin with cold water and unwrapped her clothes, her son reached heavenward. All his yearning was for the wheeling pigeons.

"How extraordinary, Señorita. Your baby is walking at—what?—seven months? He looks much younger, even though his head is very big. It's the blackness in him, I imagine, this power to walk at so young an age. Do you fear he'll lose this power if you have him christened? Do you believe you must raise him as a *brujito*, a warlock, to insure his survival? Is that your thinking?"

For a brief moment, in the black mirror of the water, the child's mother saw her own unsmiling face. She resembled, even to herself, the bewildered representative of some lost tribe of humanity: sloe-black eyes, a sensuous mouth, and eyebrows growing together above her broad pug nose. In the shadowy water under her hands her swarthiness was emphasized by an even deeper shadow. Many Spaniards considered her a Negro. She shattered her image with a handful of cheap detergent and the limp bludgeon of a diaper.

"Instead, Señorita Ocampo, you are fattening this baby for someone else's feast. You have deprived him of both baptism and the comfort of human speech, and, should you die, no one will stoop to help him. Never mind that he scrambles about your apartment like a Barbary ape. Outside, he will not be able to fend for himself—for at present he is only his selfish mother's *juguete*, a plaything. If you were to suffer a fatal accident or sicken unto death, he too would be doomed. It is wicked of you not to have thought of this."

At the conclusion of this part of the old woman's argument, the child hooted spontaneously and ambled to the railing overlooking the inner courtyard. Encarnación, not seeing him behind her, interrupted her washing to fetch the boy back. To reach him she had to bump the old woman aside, but the contact was less peremptory than she would have liked it to be. This persistent meddling in her affairs was insupportable. It sapped her of energy and self-esteem.

"What of the little one's father? If he knew you had borne

him a child, he would surely wish to rescue it from the folly of such an upbringing. A black man sired this one on you—anyone can see that—but even black men have tongues with which to speak their preferences. You should tell him he has a son."

Encarnación returned to the wash house. The child, emboldened by his most recent adventure, approached the old woman and gripped her stiff skirts. She, in turn, put the tip of one finger in the center of his woolly head and rubbed it around on that spot as if to ward off any evil implicit in his nearness.

"Cruelty and arrogance," the crone continued, still rubbing the boy's head. "It's pride that makes you take on a responsibility of which you are unworthy. Otherwise you would understand that what you do guarantees the ruin—yes, the damnation—of your *brujaco*. Time will undo both your pride and your son. And the shameful occupations you pursue—listen, Señorita, they will kill you before you think."

Her hands and arms dripping, Encarnación whirled about and broke her child's grip on the old woman's skirts. The *vieja* blinked but did not draw back. Although cadaverously skinny, she towered over the young woman, and her height advantage perhaps made her foolhardy. In a moment her mouth was working again, spilling out recriminations, advice, and ominous prophecies.

Encarnación, casting about for an ally, spotted the tin can into which her tormentor had recently emptied her bladder. This she snatched up. Then, shaking the can from side to side before the old woman's astonished face, she circled her prey to cut off her escape down the interior stairs. The crone gasped, covered her eyes with her forearm, and darted beneath a wire supporting the threadbare burden of her family's wash.

"Tenga merced," she cried, ducking beneath a pair of trousers. "Have mercy, Señorita."

The child, hooting, pivoted to keep the action in view. He had forgotten the pigeons, if only for this moment.

The chase continued, and Encarnación permitted the old woman to sweep back beneath the clotheslines and to reach the stairwell. The crone was turning the corner on the first lower landing when Encarnación, upending the can, scored a warm, liquid bull's-eye on the retreating figure's head and shoulders. Screaming and gibbering, her piety altogether flushed from her system, the *vieja* disappeared into the bowels of the building. Her cries echoed clamorously in the tiled enclosure.

CHAPTER FOUR

🖐 *An Ecology of Mirage*

BIRDS, WHEELING BIRDS.

From the western edge of Lake Kiboko, in the lee of the ramparts on that side of the Rift, there lifted a glittering cloud of birds. Cormorants maybe, or kingfishers. They were too far away to identify easily (even with my combination reduced-print Bible and field guide), but in spite of the distance I believed that they were reacting to my presence in their world. Their appearance above the lake legitimized my arrival. In fact, it seemed to me that I had somehow *summoned* these birds into existence.

The past was awakening.

Once, long ago, in another past, my first awakening to my "talent" as a spirit-traveler sprang from a vision of pigeons flying above the rooftops of an ancient city. Birds on the wing invariably provoke this early memory in me, as a taste of madeleine soaked in a decoction of lime flowers always brought to Proust a vivid recollection of his childhood village. A paradox. Nearly two million years before my birth I had been recalling my infancy . . .

Suddenly the lakescape was alive.

Not forty feet away, a crocodile—a moment ago merely a ridge of pebbly earth beside the lake—slithered into the water. Beyond the crocodile, a family of hippopotami, submerged almost to their nostrils, were taking their ease in the weed-grown shallows. These animals were members of the extinct species *H. gorgops*, immediately recognizable by their periscopic eyes . . . Ah, but language plays tricks on me. How could they be extinct when I saw them snorting and yawning like living engines? I, not this family of riverhorses, was the anachronism here.

Never one to surrender without a fight to the fallibility of tomorrow's technology, I took out my transcordion and keyed in this message: *"I'm home, Dr. Kaprow. This is the destination foretold for me in thousands upon thousands of spirit-traveling episodes. It's inhabited, this place, and I'm one of the inhabitants."*

Then I typed, *"Wow."* And waited for a response that never came. And put the transcordion back in my pocket.

Well to the south a small herd of rather shaggy antelopes—they looked overdressed for this latitude—was tentatively approaching the lake. I thumbed past Revelations all the way to Ungulates and confirmed that they were either waterbucks (*Kobus ellipsiprymnus*) or their Early Pleistocene equivalents. A solitary bull with a pair of impressive ringed horns led his harem down to the beach, and even though I had assumed the water to be too brackish for drinking, the cows and several yearlings spread out along the shore and nervously lowered their muzzles.

Overhead, a flight of flamingoes on their way to another Rift Valley lake or maybe another part of this one. They were rose-pink against the lightening sky, gangly and graceful at the same time.

Returning my attention to the waterbucks, I was stunned by the quickness with which death struck a calf that had ventured too far out. A crocodile—maybe even the one I had just seen slither off the beach—lunged from submarine concealment and seized the hapless calf by the throat. As the surviving waterbucks bolted in terror for open country, the croc's viselike jaws dragged the calf into deeper water. Crimson began to marble the turquoise surface of the lake, and although the family of hippos bathing just west of me remained blithely indifferent to the slaughter, I had to turn aside. My survival training with Babington should have inured me to such sights, but until now I had not really believed that the matter-of-fact savagery of African bionomics would prevail in my objectified dream world. I had been wrong, of course, and the rapacity of the crocodile was not only the young waterbuck's comeuppance but mine as well.

Fear had survival value. It could prevent me from falling victim to complacency my first day on the job.

And what, exactly, was my job? In truth, it was twofold. First, to justify further military funding of the White Sphinx Project, I had to satisfy Woody Kaprow's curiosity about the range and effectiveness of his Time Displacement Apparatus. Second, I had to provide the Zarakali government, in the person of its opinionated Minister of Interior, proof that our species' earliest recognizably "human" forebears had lived within yodeling distance of Lake Kiboko, Mount Tharaka, and environs. Alistair Patrick Blair wanted hard evidence supporting his highly controversial theories about human evolution, and he had persuaded his country's Western-educated President that White Sphinx would deliver on this point, with benefits eventually redounding to both the nation's scientific establishment (i.e., by vindicating Blair himself) and its economy (i.e., by encouraging tourism, grants, and additional American aid). As a noncommissioned officer in the United States Air Force, I was the pawn of two governments. My "job" was to make both governments happy.

Specifically, I had to search for protohuman hominids, observe their life styles, and report my findings to my superiors. The transcordion was supposed to bear the brunt of this last obligation, but because it was not working, I would have to commit my observations to memory until I could discharge that duty in person. Blair had suggested that the dropback take place next to Lake Kiboko. His hope had been that I could find a *Homo zarakalensis* welcoming committee gathered about the Backstep Scaffold, but that hope had already gone glimmering. The only two-legged creatures in the vicinity were birds, and they had not yet made a friendly overture.

I strode down from the tuff bordering the lake and hiked eastward into open savannah. The differences between this landscape and its twentieth-century version began to astonish me. Where Zarakal had salt flats and thornveldt, this terrain boasted a well-trodden grass cover, small patches of forest, and a network of half-hidden arroyos feeding into Lake Kiboko from the hills to the west. To the southeast, much taller and mightier than it appears today, Mount Tharaka rose up into the sky like the hunched shoulder of a Titan. Evidence of volcanic activity—calderas, compacted ash, glintings of obsidian—marked the landscape if you looked closely, but on the whole the scene was pastoral, even idyllic. This was the way I remembered it from my previous spirit-traveling, but the surprise of finding my dreams corroborated made me lightheaded, giddy with the deliciousness of *déjà vu.*

Halting, I surveyed the plain. Everywhere my eyes went, life. As earlier at the lake, I felt that I had called this procession of creatures out of temporal limbo by stepping into their element. The richness of racial memory, and my tapping of that richness, had bidden them into being. An egocentric view of the matter but one I could not quite shake. In addition to the waterbucks that had fled Lake Kiboko, I saw gazelles, wildebeest, zebras, and ungainly giraffids with antlers like massive human pelvises. The landscape rippled with spots and stripes, all seemingly suspended in an ecology of mirage.

Only, I had to keep reminding myself, apparently this mirage was real. Although none of Kaprow's dreamfarers had died on their dropbacks, he and his assistants agreed that a dreamfarer *could* easily perish in the territory of an objectified dream.

Babington, the Wanderobo, had told me that I need not fear lions overmuch—but lions, leopards, and the relict population of saber-toothed cats that might inhabit this terrain stayed on my mind, and I was glad for my .45, even if a larger-caliber weapon would have offered more real protection. You make do with what you have, and the logistics of my dropback had dictated our choice of the faithful and familiar Colt. It would easily kill a hyena or a baboon, and if I braced my legs and fired successive shots into the forehead of a charging lion, well, it would probably serve in that situation, too.

"Just don't go walking in a forest of elephant legs," Blair had cautioned me, "and you'll probably be all right."

To make myself less conspicuous, I thought of following Babington's advice and strapping a bit of foliage about my middle, but dismissed the idea because none of the wildlife grazing or browsing within a hundred yards of me seemed especially agitated by my passage. For a moment or two I thought I might be invisible to the animals here, but a small herd of zebras (*Equus grevyi*, today a relatively rare species) blocking my way into a thicket of fig trees dispelled this idiot notion by pricking up their ears, flicking their tails, and stampeding away to the south. Because I was walking into the sun, they had seen me before I saw them, and my presence on the plain had moved them to exercise that immemorial escape clause, flight.

Cautiously I entered the fig-tree glade. No lions or cobras lay in wait, but I did find evidence that it had not always been uninhabited. A small midden of bones and lava-cobble flakes suggested that under one tree a group of tool-using hominids had butchered a small antelope of some kind and feasted on its carcass. Bits of fur snagged on the underbrush or ground into the sandy floor of the stream dissecting the thicket told me that the kill had taken place within the past year or so. I examined the stones scattered about. Obviously imported from elsewhere, they included lumpish core tools and the splinters fractured from them by the industrious bipeds. Hunger had prodded the creatures to this cunning labor, but so cheap and easily duplicable were its products that they had abandoned the implements upon abandoning the glade. I knelt beside the broken rib cage of the antelope and practiced knapping flakes from a polyhedral core tool.

This was something that Blair and Babington had taught me during my eight months in the Lolitabu National Park. The resulting tools—call them awls, or scrapers, or burins—were not so serviceable as the various scissors, toothpicks, tweezers, and corkscrews concealed in the bright red handle of my Swiss Army knife; however, they did not cost me thirty-five bucks, either. One of these tools was sufficiently acute to make an incision (accidental) across the toe of my left chukka boot.

Dutifully I took out my transcordion: *"Firm evidence of hominids only a half hour's walk from the lake, Dr. Blair. Small midden with tool remnants and animal remains. Wish you were here."* And, this time, I put the instrument away without waiting for a reply.

Although not yet noon, it was very hot, and I was sweating feverishly from my work with the lava cobbles. At the eastern edge of the fig-tree thicket I looked across the grasslands at the hills I had seen from the lake. From these hills wooded corridors stretched out into the savannah like the spokes of an enormous shell. Although Blair, the expert, had made many of his hominid-related discoveries in the fossil beds near the lake, I decided that this modest upland region was as likely a habitat for protohumans as any other. I based my decision on my past spirit-traveling and on years of intensive reading to explicate my dreams. If Mary Leakey, Alistair Patrick Blair, and Don Johanson had made no important finds in the uplands, the reason was not that hominids had never lived in them, but that erosion, predators, and volcanism had more successfully obliterated the signs of habitation there. It would take a couple of hours of walking to reach the hills, but I intended to go there. If I wanted to explore the haunts of habilines—that is, representatives of the near-human hominid family known as *Homo habilis,* a species first named and championed by Louis S. B. Leakey—I would have to seek them out and demonstrate for them the full range of my charms and accomplishments.

Ladies and gentlemen, Beau Brummell is on his way.

How would I be received into that unlikely Eden? With open arms or bared bicuspids?

Praying that a pair of furry archangels with incandescent swords and naked backsides would not turn me away, I set off across the savannah. I moved lightly in my chukkas, ignoring the heat. A warthog, its tail inscribing an exclamation mark above the period of its bung, swerved from my path and disappeared backward into its burrow. Wildebeest eyed me warily for a portion of my trek, but returned to cropping grass when they saw that my destination lay elsewhere.

Several times, seeking shade in shallow arroyos or small acacia groves, I paused to rest. At length, however, I entered a tongue of gallery forest extending out of the hills onto the plain, and my adventure among the denizens of Eolithic Zarakal truly began.

CHAPTER FIVE
Seville, Spain
Summer 1963

Two DAYS AFTER Encarnación baptized her meddlesome neighbor with a shower of urine, the old woman's grizzled, potbellied son accosted her on the gallery outside her apartment. This man's name was Dionisio, and he was apparently a pharmacist's superannuated delivery boy. For a grown man with a job he spent a great deal of time around the tenement complex, and Encarnación had often heard the neighborhood children derisively calling his name when he sauntered like a bedraggled peacock through the courtyard. A wastrel, this Dionisio, with a life going the same unpromising direction as her own.

Today he grabbed her by the shoulders and spun her around to face him. His breath partook of a beery perfume, and chest hairs curled out of his shirt like so many popped packing threads. He was a man coming apart with rage; Encarnación half expected to see his shirt disintegrate and his fetid entrails come spilling out.

"Lay a curse on me!" he challenged her, tightening his

grip on her shoulders. "I spit on your sorcery and your pride. How would you like to go over this rail, eh? How many would then gather to piss on your broken corpse?"

Dionisio began slapping Encarnación about. As he pummeled her, he treated her to an obscene catalogue of her faults. Finally, he delivered a stunning blow to her temple, caught her in his arms, and threw her to the gallery floor.

"But I'm not going to be imprisoned or killed for the pleasure of ending your sluttish life, you bitch. *That* would make you laugh from the grave, wouldn't it? *That* would give you a voice with which to mock us. I know how you think."

Squinting past the hematoma blooming beside her eye, Encarnación saw Dionisio's chubby fingers unbuttoning his pants. Then her consciousness began filtering away. She heard a humiliating sibilance and felt an acrid warmth spreading through her skirts. Then she saw, heard, and felt nothing.

That night Encarnación Consuela Ocampo determined to do two things: to take up other lodgings and to wean her son. Long after the radios had been turned off and the run-amok children scolded into bed, she left the tenement carrying a bag of clothes and household items. The child had his usual place on her hip, and he rode wide-eyed through narrow alleys, past padlocked storefronts and bodegas. A milky sprawl of stars was visible overhead.

Their new residence was a condemned building not far from the mouth of Leoncillos Street. A row of timbers braced against the curb propped the façade of this derelict upright, and warning placards, which Encarnación could not read, stood in the building's ground-floor fenestrae. She entered the foyer and, with an American-made bobby pin, sprang the lock on the ornate grate screening the stairs. Her son and her other burdens she then carried up three flights of steps to the empty sitting room of a desolate flat. Here she deposited all her belongings but the child.

Before dawn she made three more trips through the labyrinthine alleys to their old apartment, never once abandoning her son in either place. Much of what she toted back to the condemned building was black-market merchandise, including nearly two dozen cartons of American cigarettes, a cache of wristwatches (Timex, Bulova, etc.), and several small electrical kitchen appliances. Once or twice, exhausted, she permitted the boy to pick his way over the cobblestones beside her, and he kept up remarkably well.

A month went by. The boy began drinking from a plastic cup that Encarnación bought for him in a department store called Gallerías Preciados, not far from the Calle de las Sierpes, Seville's famous pedestrian thoroughfare. The milk—genuine *leche de vaca*— she purchased from vendors who rode their battered motorized carts past her building several times a day. She also bought oranges from fruit stalls in the neighborhood and gave her child the juice. Because she was purposely denying him her nipples, she tried to compensate by introducing him to such effervescent soft drinks as Coca-Cola and Fanta, which might not be good for him but which he greedily enjoyed. This strategy worked very well. They boy soon ceased pestering her to present her breasts.

Another decision loomed for Encarnación. One day the city's blue-collar henchmen would come to the building with a wrecking ball. What would happen after that? Her removal from the tenement complex had ruined her livelihood as a black-marketeer and prostitute, and what money she made nowadays came chiefly from doing errands for the owner of a nearby bodega and selling to his out-at-the-elbow customers the remainders of her cigarette and wristwatch inventories. If she should die, no one would appear to rescue her baby. And if she lived, she would have to find more lucrative work before the wrecking ball turned them out into the streets.

Her son was her joy and her martyrdom. Ever since their run-in with Dionisio's mother, however, he had begun to change. First he had ceased vocalizing, almost as if aware that silence was the best means of preserving their squatters' rights in the condemned building. Although he listened to the people jabbering on the sidewalk below their boarded balcony casements, he never tried to attract their attention with a hoot or a squeal. On trips into the streets on shopping errands he habitually fixed his gaze on the lips of every speaking passerby or salesperson, but, Encarnación noticed, he did not attempt to emulate the sounds these people made. His fascination with the sequential sound patterns of human speech was entirely passive, and his mother began to fear that, having recognized her muteness, his infant mind had opted to achieve a similar state in himself.

The second change was in some ways even more worrisome. The child dreamed. These dreams, during which his eyelids flickered and his body thrashed, seemed to be especially vivid and captivating for one so young. Midnight horror shows. Morphean fantods. When his eyelids ceased jumping and his body lay perfectly still, the whites of his eyes showing like crescents of hardboiled egg, Encarnación would panic and try to rouse him. Although he always came out of these swoons, they never failed to frighten her. She was afraid that her treatment of her son had mentally unbalanced him and that she had ruined his life forever. The final revenge of the *vieja* who had tormented her on the tenement rooftop was the accuracy of her analysis of the boy's chances as an adult. Encarnación felt that she had doomed her son.

The highway to Santa Clara, the American housing area on the outskirts of Seville, was wide and desolate, the surrounding landscape forbidding under the summer moon. Encarnación, not without suffering and doubt, had made up her mind to brave the edge of this highway on foot.

Carrying her son, she crossed the final bridge before the jungle of minor industries flanking the highway on the south. Traffic was light but daunting, most demoralizingly so when the gigantic automobiles of American military personnel came whooshing by. Off to Encarnación's right the spooky amber of the Cruz del Campo sign gleamed above the dark superstructure of the brewery. No one stopped to offer her and her child a ride, and she did not attempt to solicit one. She was prepared to walk the entire distance.

To rest her arms, however, she soon set the boy down. Delighted, he trotted out ahead of her. Even barefoot, he looked quite handsome, for Encarnación had dressed him in a striped jersey and a pair of navy-blue shorts. She hurried to catch up with him, took his hand in hers, and counted his tiny steps in order not to have to think about the implications of what she was doing. Shortly—all too soon—the American enclave emerged from the oppressive dark.

Santa Clara reposed in the arid Andalusian countryside like an oasis of elms, neat stucco houses, and towering, shepherd's-crook street lamps. At the housing area's unguarded entrance these lamps cast overlapping circles of green-white radiance, blotting out the color of the lawns and imparting an oily sheen to the asphalt streets. Insects whirred in the grass, and music issued from an open doorway somewhere along the nearer of two parallel drives. In defiance of the panic building in her, Encarnación picked up her son and headed straight into this displaced American suburb. She had no clear idea what she was going to do, but she felt confident that her instincts were right. She knew a little about Americans.

Chance intervened.

A gaggle of teen-age girls approached Encarnación along the drive, gossiping and gesticulating as they came. They had on toreador pants or tight-fitting shorts, clothes that few Spanish girls would ever wear. Despite the heat the tallest of the five girls sported a crimson jacket with leather circlets around its shoulders and a huge felt hieroglyph on its left breast. Encarnación halted, weighing her options and hoping to calm the beating of her heart.

"Hey, look!" one of the girls exclaimed. "What're they doing here?"

"Somebody's maid, I'll bet, looking for a ride home."

"What about the kid?"

In a moment Encarnación was surrounded by these teen-agers, even the shortest of whom dwarfed her. They had apparently taken her child for either her little brother or a babysitting charge, and he charmed them by reaching out toward them with grimy fingers. Their banter was jolly, Encarnación decided, and she was especially reassured by the manner of the freckle-faced Amazon in the garish letter jacket. The letter jacket itself reassured her, ugly as it was.

"Hey, he's cute. *Really* cute. He looks a lot like Lucky James Bledsoe."

"Yeah, he really does."

Then all the girls laughed, and the one in the letter jacket asked Encarnación, in tremulous Spanish, if she could hold the little boy. *"Con su permiso, por favor."* Encarnación yielded her son to this request, and he immediately clutched his new protectress's red-gold hair and twisted it experimentally in his fingers.

"Ouch," the Amazon cried, pulling her head back and laughing.

Whereupon another girl attempted to snatch the boy away from her. A mock battle for the right to hold him ensued, and he was swung from side to side as the girl in the letter jacket sought to retain custody.

Encarnación, deadening her instincts, began to back away. When she reached the edge of the circle of light cast by the street lamp, she turned around and ran, darting between a pair of single-story duplexes and disappearing into the shadows. Only then did the girls realize what she had done, and only then did her son break his self-imposed silence and screech in outraged bafflement.

"Hey, you can't do that!" shouted the Amazon after his fleeing mother. *"Vuélvase*—come back! Come back here!"

The intruder was gone, vanished into blackness.

"Looks like you've inherited a little brother, Pam."

The girls huddled together in the tree-lined drive. Raucous in the heavy stillness of the evening, the lyrics of a popular song reverberated from a nearby house:

"I'm with the crowd,
I'm with the party crowd—
Cool and cocky and keen.
Music's growlin' hot and loud.
Yeah, we're proud
It's a crazy scene . . ."

"Gee, what am I supposed to do now?" Shifting the screeching child to her other arm, the girl searched her friends' shocked faces for an answer.

On the roof of the condemned building across from Leoncillos Street, Encarnación knelt beside the iron railing and brought great gouts of air up from her lungs. These she expelled painfully through her mouth and nostrils, her head hanging forward. The sound thus made was a resonant, unsteady keening, and she kept this up until her strength was gone and dawn began to glimmer in the east.

 CHAPTER SIX
Helen

I saw my first hominids—if not habilines—only a few minutes after I entered a strip of forest wedging into the savannah from the eastern hills. These creatures were the kind that in a dream diary of my youth I had always indicated by the symbol of a human hand with a set of blunt teeth in the palm. *Australopithecus robustus* in the argot of taxonomists, although I had not learned the impressive ten-dollar Latin words until I was eleven or twelve and had given up my diary in favor of tape cassettes.

"Johnny," Jeannette had told me, handing me the portable recording unit my father had bought for me in Guam, "keep your diary with this. Use it to record your dreams. Recording them will be easier than writing them down. When you're older, Johnny, you'll have your 'spirit-traveling episodes' on tape."

I had taken my mother's advice.

Now—fifteen years later, or two million years earlier—I found myself watching several representatives of *A. robustus* (black-hands-with-teeth) in an East African thicket, and the invaluable lessons of my boyhood whirred through my head like the garbled output of a tape on high-speed reverse.

Heavily built creatures with wide faces and massive jaws, the australopithecines had been grubbing for insects and foraging desiccated fruit. There were five altogether, four of whom, apparently hearing me approach, beat a swift retreat into denser foliage. The remaining hominid was a male, his penis a mere nub in the Brillo pad of his pubic hair, his scrotum as round and intricately puckered as a rotten grapefruit. A pronounced crest ran fore and aft over his skull, like the wedge of a Mohawk haircut.

Fascinated, I decided to reveal my presence.

Despite my six-inch height advantage—he was probably about four feet, nine inches tall—for nearly a minute the male stood his ground, aggrievedly eying me and making rumbling noises in his throat and chest. He was covering the escape of the others, who had already completely disappeared. Then, having accomplished his purpose and satisfied the demands of honor, he too turned and gimped away into the undergrowth.

My heart was hiccuping in my chest. On my first day in the Pleistocene I had encountered specimens of an extinct hominid family—not extinct, however, but alive. Alive! Indeed, I was the first human being ever to lay eyes on an upright-walking primate that was not itself a human being, for the australopithecines have been extinct throughout the entire history of *Homo sapiens.* The significance of our brief encounter was staggering, and for a moment after the male's departure I was at a loss to comprehend the full meaning—the unbelievable *wonderfulness*—of what had already befallen me. Indeed, Blair would have agreed to stand before a firing squad for a face-to-face confrontation with a burly member of *A. robustus.* I stared into the undergrowth after my unsociable hominid acquaintance.

I was still not alone. From the branches of the surrounding trees a throng of bandit-faced monkeys, probably vervets, had watched my run-in with the australopithecines. Ill-tempered elves in black-face, they leapt about excitedly, scolding and anathematizing me. I had chased off their big bipedal cousins. Moreover, *I* was like nothing they had ever seen before.

"Quiet down, fellas," I told them. "You'd better get used to this turn of events. *A. robustus* is going the way of five-cent cigars, 33-rpm records, and Cadillac convertibles."

Startled by my voice, the vervets quieted: I got no more response from them than I had from Woody Kaprow over the transcordion. If *A. robustus* had not survived, I asked myself, what were *my* chances?

Kaprow had not permitted me to drink or eat for twelve hours before my dropback, and although I had been running all morning on will power and adrenalin, I had just about depleted my reservoirs of both. Besides, the sun told me that it was lunchtime. Not wishing to shoot a vervet—though their manners did not really warrant clemency—I gathered leaves from several different kinds of acacias and made myself a dry, unappetizing salad. I found water trickling through the mulch cover in the glade and drank long and hard to dislodge the pulpy residue of leaves sticking to my teeth. The meal was not very satisfactory, but I was not yet ready either to kill an antelope or to exploit the limited resources of my survival kit.

Not far away, through the clustering foliage of my temporary hideout, I saw a baobab. *The Tree Where Man Was Born.* In fact, I had seen three or four baobabs while crossing the savannah, but this one was close enough to study, admire, and approach. The baobab is an exclusively African tree, with a bole like the leg of an elephant trousered in baggy sailcloth and branches like enormous, naked nerve endings. Leopards often use them for their headquarters. A Sambusai legend has it that an evil spirit pulled the first baobab out of the ground and replanted it upsidedown, thus transposing its roots and its branches. Even so, an edible fruit grows high in the baobab, and if I could find a few, I would augment my lunch with some of these hard-shelled, woody delicacies, known to many Africans as "monkey bread."

After determining that no leopard was present, I climbed

the tree, using the numerous nodules and indentations about the trunk. I ate in its branches, confident that my .45 could fend off any intruder. Had the vervets in the acacia grove possessed automatic pistols, I reflected, they might have already stripped the tree of its burden of monkey bread.

When I came down from the baobab and hiked deeper into the forest strip, sweat began to pour off me. My Right Guard had long since failed, and I was beginning to tire. After shedding my backpack and slinging my epaulet of nylon rope down beside it, I slumped to the ground for a breather. A tree trunk was at my back, and although the savannah was visible through the foliage to the southwest, I had no real apprehension of the carnivores out there. I was at risk certainly, but I was also so rare a creature that, simply by being a rarity, I felt I generated a kind of armor about myself. I rested my hands on my stomach, closed my eyes, and felt myself drifting . . . drifting . . . drifting into dreamland . . .

Drifting into dreamland.

If you adopt a literal interpretation of this phrase, a metaphysical puzzle presents itself.

My *bodily* venture into the distant past took place six years ago, when I was twenty-five. For the preceding quarter of a century, however, my every fourth or fifth dream had been a special one, an instance of what I had referred to, even as a child, as "spirit-traveling." During these clairvoyant special dreams I visited, willy-nilly, the primeval landscapes of organic evolution in East Africa. Always a detached observer, I witnessed scenes that were commonplace in context but beautiful, bizarre, or frightening to one who had no waking experience or knowledge of such events. I had bucolic dreams in which hundreds of antelopes grazed in the somnolent heat of the savannah; horrifying dreams in which doglike animals tore the throats out of young or enfeebled gazelles and even devoured their own wounded; oddly poignant dreams in which naked quasi-people fed, cradled, or romped with their mischievous, monkeylike infants; and on and on. My spirit-traveling ranged across nearly the entire spectrum of Early Pleistocene life east of the Great Rift Valley. Some holographic kernel in my collective unconscious opened up these vistas for me, and I tracked them in my sleep like the stylus on a seismograph recording the earth's most subtle crustal movements.

Occasionally, although not often, events from our own era would become illogically commingled with my spirit-traveling. In the summer of 1969, for instance, not long after the first moon landing, I dreamed a prehistoric landscape into which a pair of astronauts in helmets and hulking white pressure suits emerged from a delicate lunar module. A volcano—probably Mount Tharaka—was erupting not far from their lander, and the air was filled with drifting ash. I could see the astronauts' boots making herringbone patterns in the layers of buoyant soot blanketing the veldt. A pack of ragged hyenas, enormous creatures, came jog-trotting through the clouds of volcanic debris toward the men. While one of the astronauts performed dreamy, slow-motion jumping jacks, his partner dispersed the hyenas by jabbing a stiff American flag at them . . .

Most of my spirit-traveling episodes, though, were pure, untainted by anachronism. Long before Kaprow's White Sphinx Project, in fact, I had familiarized myself with dinotheres, giant baboons, australopithecines, and most of their extinct fellow travelers. Such creatures, after all, were the aboriginal denizens of my dreams, and I knew them by their behavior and their anatomy if not by their multisyllabic scientific names, which I learned only later through study. Simply by drifting into dreamland, I had become an expert natural historian—minus the diplomas, the degrees, the publications, and the terminology—at an age when most kids still believe in the reality of Santa Claus and the Tooth Fairy.

This, then, is the metaphysical puzzle I am trying to pose: What sort of dreams must come to those who, through the dire expedient of time-travel, have drifted into the objectified territory of their subconscious, a "dreamland" that is no longer a dream but a palpable place? The answer is simple and perhaps not all that surprising. Such people will begin to dream about their native present, across the entire span of their lives before their actual bodily displacement into the past. They must relive their infancy, childhood, adolescence, and youth through the agency of spirit-traveling; and they must witness this procession of events at random, as if it were a slide program shuffled out of obvious sequence.

Sitting in a grove of acacia trees, two million years before my birth, I must have dreamed of my real mother and Spain, of Jacqueline Tru and the Mekong Restaurant, of President Tharaka and the Weightlessness Simulation Incline, of Mrs. Givens and Van Luna, Kansas. I do not recall exactly which of these dreams I dreamed that first day (for undoubtedly some of these dreams came later), but the upshot of all my dreaming was that every episode came to generate its own context and to coexist with every other—so that each moment I lived was a reenactment of every moment that had preceded it. I became my own history. I became myself.

Someone touched me. I opened my eyes and saw her. Acting on its own, my hand went to my hip and unbuttoned the flap on my .45's leather holster. The lady who had prompted this reaction—by every appearance a protohuman creature—retreated a step or two into the shade of the acacias, but did not bolt like the skittish australopithecines I had met earlier. My stomach flip-flopped, and I tried to get to my feet.

She watched me. How, two million and six years after our first meeting, to describe her? Well, even as my forefinger fumbled for my automatic's trigger, I noticed that she had uncanny self-reliance and poise. The fact that she was carrying a hefty club in one fist underscored this observation, but did not occasion it. She appeared to be about four inches shy of five feet tall and too lithe of build to throw her weight around effectively—a diminutive, sinewy Black Beauty. Her beauty was to me

*Like those Nicean barks of yore
That gently, o'er a perfumed sea,
The weary, way-worn wanderer bore
To his own native shore . . .*

This poem crossed my mind, I think, because Babington had recited it repeatedly during our last two or three weeks together in the Lolitabu National Park. From the first, then, I called the creature who had awakened me in the prehistoric woods Helen—not so much after the Helen of Homeric legend as after the enduring passion of an old Wanderobo warrior who had once been married to a woman by that name. This distinction is important, for although I recognized the individuality of Helen Habiline's beauty almost from the outset, I saw it in an African rather than a Western European context.

She appeared to be clad in the creation of a horny furrier. A girdle of fur covered her lower abdomen and loins, but her breasts and upper thighs were so lightly haired that the ebony smoothness of her flesh shone through. The hair on her head was hyacinth, wiry, and flyaway, almost as if she had grabbed an uncombed fright wig from a department store mannikin—but her eyes sparkled like ripe black olives and her nose was fierce and generous. Her everted upper lip curled backward over a set of prodigious uppers, teeth like unpainted casino dice. In brief, her face and figure commanded my attention, focused my admiration and awe.

The heat of the day and the suety animal smell of Helen told me that I was not dreaming. There was precedent for what was happening to us, too, for I recalled that on the only occasion that Lemuel Gulliver permits himself to go skinnydipping in the land of the Houyhnhnms, a female Yahoo throws herself lustfully into the water after him. Although Helen was less brash than that libidinous Yahoo and I more modestly attired than the startled Gulliver, our meeting otherwise seemed to parallel that of our fictional counterparts.

Helen scrutinized my clothes with intent interest—from the red bandanna about my neck to the rubber-soled chukkas encasing my feet. When she cocked her head to one side, I had the unnerving impression that, with an effort of superhabiline concentration, she was mentally disrobing me. What kind of body did I have under the strategically arrayed skins cloaking my back and loins? Although she had never met a fop before, Helen clearly understood that my togs were accessories rather than outlandish extensions of my person. She tried to see through them to me.

I took off my bandanna and held it out to her. "Here. If you want it, it's yours."

Her eyes widened at the sound of my voice, but she did not accept the bandanna, merely studied the way it dangled between my fingers. Then she retreated another step or two.

"Joshua Kampa at your service. I've come in peace for all mankind. Womankind too, as far as that goes."

At this point Helen raised her club, showed me her enviably powerful teeth, and erected the short hairs on her shoulders and upper arms. This response nonplused and frightened me. I gestured placatingly with the bandanna, but she pivoted, glanced at me over one muscular shoulder, and, imparting a pretty swivel to her steatopygic fanny, stalked eastward through the undergrowth. A ridge of dark fur ran down her spine to the small of her back, but there was only enough hair about her anus to defend her when she sat upon the ground.

Helen was indisputably a member of the hominid species for which I had once invented the black-hand-with-eye symbol for use in my dream diary. A representative, in other words, of the species that paleoanthropologists call either *Australopithecus habilis* or *Homo habilis*. Alistair Patrick Blair preferred the former term because he had pinned his hopes of winning the earliest-near-human-ever-discovered sweepstakes to the coccyx of a dubious creature called *Homo zarakalensis*. To my mind, though, Helen had to be considered human, and the term I preferred then—and still prefer today—is *Homo habilis.*

The specimens of *A. robustus* who had fled from me earlier *were* mere apes by comparison to Helen. The fact that she had come out exploring on her own also told me something about her character; i.e., that she possessed a degree of independence typical of many well-adjusted, adult human beings. She did not mind taking acceptable risks; she did not mind acting, upon occasion, entirely on her own. A baboon, an australopithecine, or even a chimp would never have ventured so far afield without at least one confederate nearby for moral support.

Looked at in another light, however, Helen's independence argued *against* her categorization as an advanced hominid. Our immediate ancestors, Blair had taught me, were gregarious creatures, craving companionship and the approval of their peers. A loner among such buddy-buddy primates would have been an aberration, for her people would have lived in a social unit where the ethos of a loner could contribute only uncertainty and disruption. This chain of reasoning led me to conclude that Helen was indeed an aberration among her kind, but probably in a positive rather than a pejorative way. Judged against the standard of her fellow habilines, she was more rather than less human. She had her eye on the angels.

Why was she out alone? Two possible reasons presented themselves. First, maybe she had got fed up with the demands of habiline togetherness and retreated to the woods to commune with her—dare I propose it?—soul. Second, maybe she had struck off by herself on a mission meant to benefit her entire group, in which case she would have been a patriot rather than a misanthrope, and hence an aberration with a certain grimy social cachet. If this second hypothesis proved out, why, Helen and I had something significant in common.

I struck off in the direction she had gone.

Within a mile I came to a clearing in the gallery forest, where woods and savannah abutted each other on the slope of a hill. Between two fingers of forest, at the point of a V-shaped web of grass, a modest hominid culture flourished. To my astonishment, on my first day I had found a bona fide habiline "village." Three crude dwellings—with stone bases, curved sapling supports, and haphazard thatchings of brush—occupied this little nook, and I gaped at them like a man who has stumbled upon a McDonald's at the summit of a remote Himalayan mountain. None of these structures would keep out a heavy rain or deflect a howling wind, but they were clearly capable of providing shade during the day and a sense of womblike security at night.

Damn my broken transcordion. Here was confirmation that the habilines had built shelters similar to those of contemporary hunter-gatherers in the Kalahari and elsewhere, but I could not report the finding.

I named this village Helensburgh.

Having arrived just ahead of me, Helen hooted to announce her return, and through the holes in the haystack huts I saw dark bodies responding to her oddly musical call. Several females and children spilled out into the V-shaped clearing from the huts, while others appeared from the edges of the woods. Because of my impeded view at the edge of the gallery forest and the habilines' incessant movement, I could only estimate the number of creatures that turned out to welcome or waylay their prodigal Amazon. Fourteen or fifteen, it seemed to me. Helen had status among these people. What kind of status, however, I could not yet say.

My next surprise was that she towered over the adults in the village by as many inches as I towered over her. Standing among them, she might have been the queen of a race of delicate pygmies. All her subjects, though, were matrons, ingénues, or children, some of these last so small and downy that they resembled teddy bears or upright vervet monkeys. A couple of the younger women clutched infants in their arms. This was civilization of a kind, a civilization in miniature, and I hung back to keep from disrupting its workings. Having just named the village Helensburgh, I decided that Helen's people needed a name, too, something descriptive but far less formal than *Homo habilis*. As members of the family Hominidae (of which all-conquering *Homo sapiens* is today the only surviving species), they led me willy-nilly to the nickname Minids.

During my childhood in Kansas and Wyoming, people speaking to my mother about me would often say, "Why, Jeannette, he's no bigger than a minute." I was still small, but Helen's diminutive people were even smaller, and I relished the idea of confronting all my mother's old friends with the news that, yes, I was finally bigger than a Minid. For the first time in my life, in fact, I was *tall*.

The Minids quickly disabused me of the notion that Helen was their queen. After ascertaining her identity, one grizzled matron waved an arm at Helen (revealing a ridge of hair from her armpit to the underside of her wrist), chattered high-pitched imprecations, and furiously shook her head and mouth. Bored, the children eventually wandered away, while the two mothers with infants sat down on the grass to poke and dandle them. Helen endured this scolding for two or three minutes, occasionally glancing at the gallery forest with a vacant expression, but finally tired of the game and lifted her club over the old woman's shoulder to signal her weariness. Even though this gesture looked as much like a salute as a threat, the harridan ducked her head, turned sideways, and, bending deeply, exposed the enlarged *labia minora* of her genital region, a pink satin slipper.

Rather indifferently Helen touched her club to the old woman's tail bone, forgiving and dismissing her with the same gesture. Then she ambled off to another section of the clearing. Here she squatted and relieved herself. No one paid her any further mind, and the object of her parodic knighting went chattering back into her hut as if nothing had happened. By briefly assuming what primate ethnologists call the presentation posture, the harridan had both truckled to and appeased Helen. She had also underscored the ambiguity of Helen's status among the Minids, for Helen was a female whom the other adult females treated both as a wayward sister (the scolding) and as an unattached adolescent male with formidable physical strength but no real community standing (the presentation posture). It was entirely possible that Helen had forgotten me the moment her back was turned, and that her disregard of my presence had enabled me to follow her back to Helensburgh. I did not like to think that her endocranial volume was so slight that it denied even a few out-of-the-way brain cells to a memory of me, but I could not ignore this possibility. Maybe I was nothing to her because I had literally made no impression on her understanding. A painful hypothesis.

Inwardly denying it, I watched her and the other habiline villagers go lackadaisically about their business—which seemed to consist primarily of half-hearted foraging and vigorous loafing.

The Minids—a band of approximately twenty-five, if I counted in the adult males who were probably out scavenging or hunting—had their capital at the overlap of two of the habitats of the East African mosaic: savannah and gallery forest. Because bush country, hills, and lakeshore territories also lay close by, the Minids were well situated to exploit a number of different food sources and survival modes. Still, I had not expected to find half of such a band taking its ease at midday without a single sentry.

Eventually I decided to withdraw from the encampment. If the males came back and found me ogling their women and children, I might find my visit to the Pleistocene cut short by their intolerance and outrage. At this early stage in my explorations it was best to avoid arousing either suspicions or tempers. Moving from tree to tree, then, I renegotiated the path that I had followed to Helensburgh—but I had gone no more than thirty or forty yards when I spotted a small, hairy figure approaching the village from farther down the path.

My counterpart halted and glowered at me like an offended policeman or teacher. It—he—was a Minid, with beady eyes, protruding lips, and a receding chin from which waggled a sparse, reddish-black goatee. Although he was several inches shy of five feet, he was clearly an adult and a lankily muscular one whose small size did little to calm my fears of him. At length I took a cautious step forward and nodded apologetically at the habiline, who, keeping me in his sights, began to creep around me in a cunning arc. My principal concern was that he might be leading the other males home.

"Listen," I began, "I'm sorry. It's just that—"

From several feet away he lofted a globule of saliva and hit me squarely on the chin. Then, while I was wiping my face with the back of my hand, he scampered into the village screeching and chattering and calling down the wrath of Ngai. A terrible hubbub broke out among the encampment's denizens, and I fled, my legs churning and my fancy indelicately conjuring up a dozen different ways to die at the hands of these protohuman creatures. Soon enough, however, I realized that they were not following me and that the Minid I had just encountered was probably their appointed sentry. I had caught him taking an unauthorized and ill-advised break, and each of us had scared the gibbering bejesus out of the other.

For a long time, then, I stood on the edge of the vast savannah trying to recover my wind and quiet the thunderous pounding of my heart. These things done, I began to laugh, and my laughter doubled me over into a self-protective crouch, and in this crouch, still laughing, I made myself consider what I must do next.

CHAPTER SEVEN

Morón de la Frontera

July 1963

COLONEL ROLAND UNGER, the vice commander of the SAC Reflex Base near Morón de la Frontera, approximately thirty miles southeast of Seville, reminded Jeannette Monegal of Douglas MacArthur whittled down to about two-thirds scale. In the light coming through his office windows from the flight line, the hair on his forearms sparkled like aluminum filings and his shoes radiated a dazzling ebony shine. He stood beside his desk in crisp summer khakis, staring bemusedly at the tiny, dark-skinned child who was pushing his coaster chair into a cabinet on which stood the official photographs of the President of the United States, the Secretary of Defense, the Secretary of the Air Force, the Joint Chiefs of Staff, and the local base commander. The child seemed to be determined to topple these photographs, but Colonel Unger made no move to hinder or distract him.

"I am *not* a social worker," he told the people who had requested this audience. "None of us was sent out here to see to the daily needs of displaced Spanish nationals. Orphans just aren't our line."

"What if they're part American?" Jeannette asked. She and her husband, Staff Sergeant Hugo Monegal, had kept the abandoned child in their quarters in Santa Clara for the past five days, and the point of this interview was to make him a permanent member of their family. She had never wanted anything else quite so passionately, and her commitment to her goal both surprised and pleased her.

To the Monegals' left sat Major Carl Hollis, who, as an agent of military intelligence, routinely wore civilian clothes. Today he had attired himself in cotton ducks and a seersucker sports jacket with blue and white stripes. He had a neat brown moustache, threaded with strands of amber, and a pair of mirror-lensed sunglasses that he was dangling nervously from his right hand. Colonel Unger had invited him to the interview, and Jeannette was uncertain whether to regard him as an ally or an official marplot.

"Look at him, sir," Hollis encouraged the colonel. "The kid's as red, white, and blue as Willie Mays, if you know what I mean."

Colonel Unger replied, "He also happens to have been born to a Spanish mother, in a Spanish city, and it's the mother's nationality that traditionally decides these things. We're on pretty shaky ground here. You can't just arbitrarily take custody of a bona fide *Sevillano*, Major Hollis."

"Maybe not *de jure*, sir, but *de facto* we've already done it. The mother handed him over to Drew Blanchard's kid, Pam, and I'd lay odds he's an indiscretion of Lucky James Bledsoc's. That's Master Sergeant Lavoy Bledsoe's son, sir, and they've already rotated stateside to a base in Alabama."

"You think we should get in touch with the Bledsoes?"

"Jesus, no," said Hollis, leaning forward earnestly. "They probably don't even know about little 'Say Hey' there."

"John-John," Hugo Monegal interjected, touching his

wife's hand. He was a man of thirty-two, a Panamanian who had entered the employ of the U.S. government in the Canal Zone. Later he had come to the United States to attend Wichita State University, from which he had dropped out to join the Air Force. In that same year, 1957, he had married Jeannette Rivenbark of Van Luna, Kansas, thereby acquiring, in addition to a handsome and headstrong wife, his American citizenship. "John-John" was the first phrase he had spoken aloud since the initial introductions, and Jeannette watched the way the officers' eyes gravitated to her husband, grudgingly, as if he had burped or let wind.

"We've been calling him John-John," she said, hurrying to Hugo's assistance. "For President Kennedy and the late Pope John. He had to have a name. You can't go around every day calling an active kid like this one 'Hey, you.' Or 'Say Hey,' either."

"We want to keep him," Hugo added. "What you wish to keep you have to name."

"You mean you want to adopt him?" Colonel Unger asked.

"We want him to be ours," said the sergeant. "I don' really know about this adoptin' business, though." Because Hugo spoke Spanish fluently—"an accident of birth," he sometimes joked—the Air Force had sought to coopt this skill by assigning him to installations in Spain. He and Jeannette had already pulled one two-year tour at the rotating SAC unit in Saragosa and were now very close to concluding their second Iberian assignment.

John-John, still struggling with the coaster chair, managed to knock the Secretary of the Air Force off the empty liquor cabinet. Colonel Unger retrieved the secretary's portrait and returned it to its place.

"Don't you have any children of your own?"

"Only Anna," Jeannette responded. "She's five. We didn't intend to have any more until we saw John-John."

"Pamela brought the baby to our quarters," Hugo explained, "because she thought we could maybe, you know, talk to him. He listens very good, but he is still too small to talk in any language."

"He's just on the verge of being a feral child," Hollis told the colonel, "if we can deduce anything about his condition from what we know about his background. His mother was a mute, a woman deeply involved in black-market dealings and prostitution. We lost complete track of her about six weeks ago. The city police arrested her for creating a public disturbance the morning after she gave her baby to Pam—she was in a condemned building, making a godawful hiccuping racket on the roof—but they released her without prejudice before noon, and we haven't seen hide nor hair of her since. Before she deserted her tenement apartment, though, she kept that boy"—nodding at John-John—"locked up inside it both night and day. The isolation, coupled with his mother's muteness, can't have been good for him."

"What did you just call him?" Jeannette asked. "A feral child?"

"Right," said Hollis.

"And what is *that*, exactly?"

"Well, it means a wild child, a child raised by animals. Back in the 1920s there was a famous pair in India called the Wolf Children of Midnapore. A couple of young girls abandoned in the jungle and supposedly suckled by wolves. An Anglican missionary named Singh captured them and carried them back to the orphanage he directed. Tried like rip to make human beings of them, but they ran on all fours, ate like dogs, showed their teeth, and occasionally bayed at the moon. One of them died within the year, but the other progressed well enough to wear a dress and attend church services. She never did learn to speak more than fifty words, though, and that in nine years, Mrs. Monegal."

"Maybe the Reverend Mr. Singh's mother was frightened by the ghost of Rudyard Kipling then, Major Hollis."

"Ma'am?"

Jeannette was wearing a chocolate-colored dress with a

nunnish white bib. Hollis, she could see, had adjudged her, on this fragile basis and the fact that she was married to a noncom, a demure do-gooder whose mind reposed in her husband's calloused fist. He had certainly not expected her to challenge his stupid anecdote with sarcasm.

"Are you trying to tell us, Major Hollis, that from henceforward John-John should be known as the Wolf Boy of Andalusia?"

Hollis blinked, then put on his sunglasses. "I just meant to point out that he's been disadvantaged by living with a mother who couldn't talk. Maybe 'feral child' was a bad choice of words. Call it 'social isolation,' if we have to stick a label on it. The upshot is that he's going to have trouble learning to speak, adjusting to human society. Kids raised in isolation by uncaring or handicapped parents often end up irreversible retardates. It's entirely possible—"

"Where do you get all these words, Major Hollis?"

"Ma'am?"

"John-John's mother wasn't an uncaring parent. Except for her handicap—her muteness—she took beautiful care of this child."

"She did, did she? Then why didn't she try to expose him to people who didn't share her handicap?"

"What do you think she finally did? She gave John-John to Pamela Blanchard, one of his father's people. It wasn't hard to see that the folks in Santa Clara enjoyed certain material advantages over her own circumstances. That was pretty damn brave, if you ask me, and Hugo and I would like to honor that bravery by . . . by adopting him."

"Going into any family situation is going to be a big change for him," Hollis appealed to Colonel Unger, who did not reply.

"He's already made the transition," Jeannette declared. "He doesn't pee on the drapes or tear live chickens apart with his bare hands. As for learning to talk, he'll make it. He's not a year yet—you can tell by looking at him—but he's already walking.

Most kids his age aren't even *thinking* about walking. Anna didn't begin until she was a year."

Nudged by the back of the coaster chair, the photograph of President Kennedy toppled to the rug. With the toes of his brand-new Buster Brown shoes overlapping the cheap gilt frame, John-John tried to prise the commander in chief off the carpet. Colonel Unger, mulling certain troublesome legalities, ignored his struggle.

"What do you suggest?" he asked Hollis.

"There's no official alternative to yielding him to the Spanish authorities."

"What would happen then?"

"Into a charitable institution of some kind, I'd imagine, probably a church-run orphanage."

"With what chances for adoption?"

"As I said, the kid has a Willie Mays profile. Spanish girls date Negro enlisted men, but usually—if you want my opinion—in the hope of bagging American husbands and ending up in the Land of Levis and Lincoln Continentals. I don't really see the denizens of Seville banging on the orphanage door for the right to take John-John home."

"He belongs with his mother," Colonel Unger observed.

"Who has completely disappeared, sir."

"Why didn't you arrest her when you knew where she lived and had her dead to rights on that black-marketeering business?"

"Miss Ocampo was really just small potatoes, sir. We wanted the people who were buying from her, then reselling the stuff at higher prices in other parts of the country."

"Did you get them?"

"No, sir. Not yet, that is." Hollis looked uneasy.

"Which brings us back to square one. Still, the boy's at least partly one of ours and the Monegals want to give him a home."

As if reporting a vivid daydream, Hugo said, "If we had a birth certificate showin' that John-John was delivered at the clinic in San Pablo, why, it would be easy to take him stateside with us this November. Very easy."

"That's something we could do, a birth certificate," said Hollis.

"Why don't you do it, then?"

"We will," Hollis said, gesturing abruptly at the Monegals with his sunglasses. "Of course, they'll still appear to be toting someone else's kid out of the country."

"My hair is as curly as his," said Hugo Monegal, "and my eyes are as black. A mestizo somewhere in the family past showin' up in this *niño*. Who would challenge my fathership of John-John, my own wife's baby?" He smiled shyly at Jeannette. "This is a virtuous woman, Major Hollis."

"God," murmured the virtuous woman.

CHAPTER EIGHT
Aubade

AFTER MY RUN-IN with the Minid sentry, I walked back toward Lake Kiboko, venturing quite often into the savannah bordering the forest strip to the south. Other bands of habilines must be about, I told myself, as well as other specimens of *A. robustus* and surely a few of their ancestral cousins, *A. africanus.* It was impossible to know in what proportions to expect these three primate species to be coinhabiting the landscape, and because I saw only gazelles, antelopes, zebras, and a distant pride of lions, I was not likely to solve this problem in a single afternoon.

My transcordion did not work, and in the event of its failure Kaprow had advised me to return to the omnibus and signal my well-being by commanding the Backstep Scaffold to retract. However, I could not command what I could not see, and although at the lakeside the sun was dropping toward the violet ramparts of the western Rift, Kaprow and his cohorts had still not extruded the scaffold through the bomb-bay doors of the omnibus. The twilight sky was entire. I wanted a plug to be pushed out of it, exposing the copper and chromium viscera of our time machine—but what I wanted and what I got were two different things.

Because sunset traditionally marks a hair-trigger truce at an African watering site, I found that many large animals—elephants, rhinos, giraffids—were clustering out of the dusk to drink. Knowing that my .45 would be next to useless against most of these beasts, I nevertheless drew it. My vantage above the lake gave me a degree of safety, for the invasion was occurring on either side of my small promontory of tuff—but the scaffold still did not descend, and a hairy elephantine creature not sixty feet away had begun to writhe his trunk at me, as if my smell offended him. There were trumpetings and snorts from other visitors to the lake, too, and the precariousness of my position would increase as the darkness thickened.

"I'm waiting," I tapped out on my transcordion. *"It's sunset, and I'm waiting. Please drop the scaffold."*

No reply in my transcordion's display window. No miraculous lambent parting of the Pleistocene air.

Had White Sphinx stranded me in this place? I had no one to talk to here, no one to tell my troubles to. Even Kaprow and Blair, my liaisons to another reality, had tuned me out. A lost cog in the pitiless organic machinery of the veldt, I told the varieties of my fear the way a nun tells her rosary beads.

"This is getting you nowhere, Kampa."

I clambered down from the lakeside promontory to the plain, where I spent the last twenty minutes before nightfall gathering brushwood, antelope chips, and stegodon patties for a fire. The malicious lavender sunset pitched over into darkness about the time I was piling this fuel at the base of a kopje, a broad outcropping of granite on the steppe, about a half mile from the lake, where I hoped to avoid the gathering animals. I lit the brushwood and dried animal droppings with a match from my Eddie Bauer stove-cum-survival-kit, then scooted high up onto the outcropping to enjoy my bonfire. Nocturnal predators would be instinctively wary of the blaze, and there was no way for them to leap up behind me from the plain. Plenty of fuel and an impregnable position—I was set for the night. Although I finally realized that I had eaten only once that day, my fatigue disciplined my hunger pangs and I abstained from a brief hunting trip into the savannah.

It was a long night, almost interminable. I could not let myself drift off into a deep sleep—into dreams of my own far-future past—for fear the fire would go out. My kopje was a life-boat in an ocean of grass, and once the lantern in its prow was extinguished, strange creatures from the pelagic prairie would crawl aboard to devour me. I dozed, but always with an ear to the dangers of the night. Unless you have camped out in the bush, you have never heard such an eerie racket: the quarreling of hyraxes, the hose-pipe bleating of pachyderms, the madman laughter of hyenas. I huddled on my rock, trying to convince myself that this night was no different from the ones I had spent with Babington in Lolitabu.

The lesson did not take. At length I had recourse to my reduced-print Bible and field guide. With penlight and magnifying glass I spent an hour or so reading the Old Testament by the erratic fire flicker. Although I could not keep my mind on the words, this activity helped pass the time, and when I finally ran across a passage in Proverbs that spoke to my heart, I committed it to memory and repeated it as a mantra until the frail breaking of dawn.

"The conies are but a feeble folk, yet make they their houses in the rocks . . ."

The world quieted while I was repeating this passage, and I realized that I had lived almost an entire twenty-four-hour period in the Early Pleistocene. I had made prehistory. None of Kaprow's other volunteers had ever gone back even a thousandth as far, and only the physicist himself had remained longer on a single dropback than I had already been on mine. It struck me that there ought to be a party hat, a magnum of champagne (a domestic variety would do nicely), and a bullroarer in my survival kit. There wasn't even a pineapple Danish. To celebrate my accomplishment, I would have to hunt up my own breakfast and down it with gusto.

That was when I heard an otherworldly singing reverberating over the steppe, like the cries of disembodied saints. It came from the hills to the east, the general vicinity of Helensburgh. I got to my feet and cocked my head to listen to it. A wordless canticle of untrained habiline voices greeting the dawn. An aubade, call it. It was heartbreakingly fervid, not sweet or pristine, but rough-edged and full of raw conviction. An anthem.

The habilines—humanity's ancestors—were singing.

After ten or fifteen minutes the singing stopped. Although I should have returned to the lake, I kept waiting for it to resume. Yesterday, apparently, I had arrived too late to hear it. The impression this singing left on me—a kind of awe, a tingling in the nerve ends—took a while to wear off. Eventually, though, it gave way to the engines of appetite, my nagging hunger.

I kicked the remains of my fire off the kopje, stamped them down to keep them from starting a grass fire, and headed for a stand of fig trees to the east. In the red-oat grass bordering this glade a flock of guinea fowl strutted. To test my survival skills, I took the time to trap one of these birds noiselessly, after the fashion of the !Kung, and by stealth and patience managed to accomplish this feat without scaring off the entire flock until my trap had actually sprung. Even Babington could not have done better.

Using fingers and pocketknife, as the old Wanderobo had taught me, I plucked, dismembered, and cleaned the bird, then fell to and devoured its flesh raw. My time in Lolitabu had prepared me for this primitive approach, and I actively enjoyed my meal, the first real one since my arrival. A dry rivercourse divided the fig thicket, but I found water by scooping out a hole in the arroyo's sandy bottom and watching underground moisture seep slowly into view. Down on my hands and knees, spurning the use of my water-purification tablets, I drank directly from the stream bed, then washed the sticky blood of the guinea fowl from my face and fingers.

After that I sponged myself down with yesterday's T-shirt and dug into my shaving bag for my toothbrush, razor, and blades. In retrospect much of this attention to dress and cleanliness seems ridiculous to me, but in spite of my survival training I had not yet broken completely free of the twentieth century. My most sinful indulgence that morning was changing my underwear. This feat (although detailing it may invite ridicule) I accomplished without taking off my chukkas, for it seemed imperative to me to be able to run if danger threatened. I had trained barefoot with Babington, but I still did not trust myself to negotiate a landscape littered with acacia thorns. Keeping my shoes on meant stretching the elastic around the leg holes of my briefs, but that was a lesser evil than having to flee a leopard in my stocking feet. Actually, I was more worried about having only two packages of Fruit of the Looms left in my pack, and I devoted a good ten minutes to washing out yesterday's pair in the stream bed. These I placed on a euphorbia bush to dry.

I probably should have spent my sunrise on the shores of Lake Kiboko. If Kaprow had dropped the scaffold to me at dawn, I had not been there to witness the event or to confirm for him the fact of my continuing existence. However, I could not convince myself that I had missed anything, and the singing of the habilines was a phenomenon worth at least another day in the Pleistocene. Our contingency plan, along with our matched set of transcordions, had temporarily broken down. White Sphinx would find a way to retrieve me, surely, but for the moment I had to hold my own.

As I fetched my Fruit of the Looms from the euphorbia on the edge of the glade, I saw marching single-file across the savannah, north-northeast toward Helensburgh, a pack of hyenas. Prodigious creatures, they were good, if frightening, examples of the extinct Pleistocene megafauna. I froze, hoping that some of the laughter I had heard intermittently all night—the nerve-racking cachinnations of brigands—had signified a successful hunt.

I counted fifteen slope-backed hyenas in all, each of the eleven adults as big as the biggest male lion. It being July, the wind was blowing gently from the southwest, from the hyenas to me, and upon it I could smell the unmistakable tang of carrion. The animals' coarse, yellow-brown pelts were marbled with interlocking swirls of black, and their unlovely faces bespoke the smugness of—Ngai be praised—satiety. That, in them, was a condition I could gratefully stomach.

Alistair Patrick Blair often said of hyenas, "I wish the bloody buggers had never been born." This giant variety—although he had obviously never had the chance to see one—he especially detested. Their great crime, in his eyes, was their nearly wholesale disposal of the bones of their two-legged contemporaries. By this indiscriminate feeding behavior they had eradicated from the fossil record an invaluable store of information about human origins. *My* distaste for hyenas was less lofty: they killed as well as scavenged, and they stank.

When the hyenas had gone, I gathered up my gear, including my freshly laundered shorts, and struck off into the bush to establish a home base much closer to Helensburgh.

Once, that second morning, I thought I saw bipedal creatures roaming the veldt to the north, as if stalking prey, but the heat haze and the intervening herds of antelope may have played tricks on my vision.

A short time later I arrived at the head of the Minids' V-shaped clearing and squatted like a breakwater between the fingers of forest pointing into the savannah. The Minids saw me at once, and three or four children who had been tumbling in front of the huts together stopped to watch what I was doing. An elderly male hooted to his younger compatriots in alarm. Struggling to control the pounding of my heart, I dug nonchalantly at the grass. I examined individual sprigs, turned over rocks, sniffed my fingers appraisingly.

Quite by accident, a fortunate one, I discovered a scorpion. It lifted its stinger and moved on me in immemorial scorpion fashion. Meanwhile, I knew, the Minids had formed an attack group of their own and were advancing on me with upraised clubs. Deliberately ignoring the habilines, I made a show of rapidly striking the scorpion with my knuckles—a technique much beloved of baboons—until the odious little beastie was so dazed that a flick of my finger capsized it to its back. Next, I removed the stinger, along with the poison sac, and killed the scorpion with a squeeze.

By this time every Minid in Helensburgh was watching me. In fact, Helen had joined the males in their cautious war party. I saw her, club in hand, tiptoeing toward me along the left-hand side of the clearing. The males were spread out in a sagging U, moving slowly but methodically forward. I tried not to betray my nervousness.

Making an involuntary moue, I put the best face I could on the eating of the scorpion. The idea was to demonstrate to my bipedal brethren that, all appearances to the contrary aside, I was one of them, a bona fide grass-grubbing, arachnid-crunching, down-to-earth habiline. Further, if permitted to, I could contribute to their food-gathering industry, as witness my success in finding the scorpion.

Nothing doing.

The menfolk closed on me more menacingly, the hair on their shoulders erect. Helen's intentions appeared no more friendly than those of her male counterparts. She fell in behind a *macho hombre* with a tangled black beard and the astonishing tonsorial discrepancy of a Thin Man mustache. This dude, the largest in the band, was almost certainly the Minids' *alpha* Romeo, for which reason I had already mentally dubbed him Alfie. Helen, however, had at least an inch in height on him, and it was interesting to note that she had not waited for his okay to join their assault group, a fearsome juggernaut of nationalistic feeling.

The taste of scorpion acrid on my palate, I stood up. I

raised my hands. Because I was taller than the herbivorous australopithecines with whom they shared a portion of the bush-and-savannah habitat, the Minids stopped. Further, I was as nimble on my feet as the habilines. Come the crunch, fear and adrenalin fueling me to victory in spite of my chukka boots, I felt sure I could do a Jesse Owens on even their fleetest and most tenacious sprinter. For now, though, I spread my arms and showed them I was holding neither club nor stone.

The habilines, renewing their approach, stalked to within fifteen or twenty feet of me, perilously near. Reluctantly, I unsnapped my holster, drew my pistol, and pointed it skyward. A single warning shot would probably send them scrambling for cover, but it would also set back my hopes of cementing a relationship of mutual acceptance and trust. In the face of this dilemma I began to talk, spilling out the Pledge of Allegiance, the Preamble to the Constitution, the entire text of a Crest toothpaste commercial, several nursery rhymes, and the lyrics to a goldie-oldie popular song, all in soothing, confidence-inspiring tones that I hoped would resolve the crisis in my favor. For a moment or two they listened attentively, then flashed one another a series of significant looks whose meaning—*"Attack!"*—I somehow intuited.

Desperate, I began to sing. I sang in a rich, lilting tenor, and I sang with feeling:

"A day ago,
I had a lovely row to hoe.
Where did it go?
Oh, all has changed, and rearranged,
From but a single day ago . . ."

The sound of this plaintive melody spilling from my lips gave my attackers pause. Or maybe it was not so much the music itself—a simple ditty, heartfelt and direct—as the sheer unexpectedness of my singing it for them. Singing was even better than eating scorpions as a proof of my habilinity! Although virtually spellbound through the second refrain, my audience then began to tire of my performance. Exchanging a series of rapid glances and gestures, they resumed closing in on me. Their faces made it easy to decide what to do for an encore.

I fired my pistol.

The effect was dramatic. Three of the males fell to the ground as if I had poleaxed them, two others ran into the woods, and a sixth beshat himself and dove sideways with his arms over his head. Still in front of me, dazedly crouching, were Helen and the steadfast Alfie. In Helensburgh itself a pandemonium of shrieks and gibbering had broken out among the women and children, but this died away quickly as they hurried for shelter. With their menfolk routed, however, who would defend them? I was cutting a decidedly Genghis Khanish figure, but my assumption of this autocratic role gave me no pleasure. I had probably blown my chance of achieving a workable detente with the Minids.

Extending one hand, I took a step or two toward Helen and Alfie. They backed away. The remaining habiline males rolled over, leapt up, and hightailed it for the huts, there to make a stand if I chose to pursue them. The fellow who had lost control of his bowels oared himself backward over the grass, scraping fecal matter from his derrière, while the warriors who had run into the forest returned to see what was happening. A brave people. My pistol shot had signaled a shift in the balance of power in almost the way the explosion of an atomic device over Hiroshima had signaled a similar alteration between the Allies and the Japanese. At least, however, I had fired a warning—I had plenty of bullets.

"I'm not going to do it again," I assured Helen and Alfie. "That was to save my life."

But they, too, withdrew to the huts, where, among a congregation of fuddled, uncertain faces, they stared at me as if I were Death Incarnate. When I made no move to press my advantage, two or three of the males began gesticulating with their clubs, hooting belligerently, and indulging in ridiculous swagger, their hackles lifted along their shoulders and their chests puffed out.

In the thicket to my right, however, a young Minid male was scrutinizing me with almost chilling calm. He had large, limpid eyes and a professorial dignity. He and Alfie seemed more dangerous foes than the vainglorious gasbags dancing about before the huts, and I decided to get out of Helensburgh to avoid having to shed anyone's blood.

"Goodbye," I told them. "Look for me to make this up to you. All in all, I'm not such a bad dude. Goodbye . . ."

Oh, all has changed, and rearranged,
From but a single day ago . . .

CHAPTER NINE

Van Luna,
Kansas
October 1964

LYING IN BED one night, Anna and John-John long since tucked in
and told "sweet dreams" in the other bedroom, Jeannette tried to
explain her ambivalent feelings about her home town to Hugo,
who was smoking a cigarette and desultorily following a George
Raft and Ida Lupino late movie on the portable TV that sat on
the chest of drawers. His cigarette smoke curled eerily in the mirror behind the set.

Hugo stubbed the cigarette in a glass ashtray with a SAC
emblem in the bottom. "I am now gettin' serious, *mujer.* I am now
ready to tell you what the trouble is."

"Yes?"

"The trouble is that Van Luna is not real."

"Not real?"

"I said that, yes. Not real. Instead, Van Luna is like a
spotless laboratory chamber, very clean. Good air, sweet water,
pretty white mice for its population. Stick a little brown mouse in,

and what's the big difference? The white mice stay pretty, and the brown mouse gets fed and sniffed at just like everybody else. It isn't real, Van Luna. It's just like a laboratory chamber with little food and water bins."

Jeannette pulled herself away from Hugo, drew up her knees, and took the ashtray from his hands. "Little food and water bins? What are you talking about? My father has faced economic reality every day of his life in this town. It's done things to him, too. *That isn't real?*"

"Are we talkin' about John-John or your father?" Hugo let his eyes drift back to the TV screen, where Ida Lupino was testifying, animatedly, before a packed courtroom.

"Look, you know the reality of supporting a family on a noncom's pay. That's why you've moonlighted at the store. Are you trying to tell me that sort of thing isn't real?"

"Not me."

"And the competition's beginning to get him down. It's twisted him—my own father—into *stinginess,* of all things."

"Van Luna is very real for your father," Hugo acknowledged.

"But it's not real for you, is that what you're saying?"

"Of course it's real for me, Jeanie. You were askin' me—I think—about John-John and these people because his skin is black. You've changed the subject out from under me." He tapped a cigarette from a Marlboro flip-top box, lit it like George Raft, and waggled the burning tip under Jeannette's nose. "You don' listen, *mujer.* You listen sideways, anyway. So I'm gonna repeat this only once: The problem you've discovered is that for John-John—not for me or you or Mr. Rivenbark or Mrs. What's-her-face—*Van Luna is not real.* If you like to worry about that, Jeanie, go ahead, please. Worry up a storm."

Jeannette handed the ashtray back to Hugo, then moved closer and put her chin back on his shoulder. "Do you think we should move into Wichita, then?"

"What for?"

"So that he'd have someplace real to live. A borderline neighborhood, not too run-down. That sort of thing."

"Hell no. That would be crazy."

"But I'm trying to—"

"But nothin', Jeanie. The best place for kids to grow up is a place that ain' too goddamn real. In Bogotá, you know, I've seen the little orphan boys—the *gamines*—runnin' in packs, sleepin' in the streets under newspapers. And Zaragoza, and Sevilla, and other such realities. Screw 'em. You want to take John-John to Mississippi, maybe?"

"I don't want to take him anyplace. I was just—"

"Good." He jabbed his cigarette toward the television set. "Look at that Ida Lupino. She's a real bitch in this one, eh?"

Later, well after midnight, Jeannette went into the children's room to check on them.

A night light glowed in the tiny room. This was a clown with a bulbous nose and a pair of round, upraised fists. Outward from the bedside table on which he stood, his hands and nose shed a circle of pale orange light, a fuzzy nimbus. Anna lay half out of her covers on her trundle bed, while across the room from her, still in a crib, John-John sprawled with one tiny hand extended backwards through the spindles. Jeannette rearranged Anna's bedding before approaching the boy. She found him in the throes of dream.

Supine, his head seeming to pivot on the knob of bone at the back of his skull, John-John was making a gentle, gargling noise. His eyelids had fallen back, like the eyelids concealing the bright marble eyes of a Madame Alexander doll. Half hidden from view, however, John-John's eyeballs jiggled from side to side in the upper portions of the sockets, their faintly muddy whites pulsing in time. Jeannette had witnessed this strange phenomenon dozens of times since bringing John-John home from Spain, but it never failed to disconcert her.

"Dear God," she murmured.

The Air Force doctors at the McConnell dispensary, to whom she had taken the child about both his slowness in learning to speak and these uncanny nocturnal fits, always assured her that John-John was perfectly healthy. He had an especially vivid dream life, perhaps, but the fact that his eyelids rolled back did not imply that he was suffering from epilepsy, petit mal, or any other nervous disorder. In fact, the vividness of his dream life might well be inhibiting—temporarily—his development of certain postinfantile speech patterns. The dreams were a substitute—a *temporary* substitute—for language development. Besides, Jeannette was supposed to keep in mind that he was not yet two, and that he was probably still adjusting to his transfer from a Spanish- to an English-speaking culture, and that in every other respect he seemed to be completely normal. The doctors, of course, had never had to confront the spectacle of his jiggling eyeballs and pulsing whites at one o'clock in the morning. They did not have to square this upsetting image of the child with their picture of the quick, active, curious kid scooting about their dispensary. Nor did they have to worry very much about the enigma of his first eight or nine months . . .

"What's the matter, Jeanie?"

She turned and saw Hugo in the doorway, his boxer shorts ballooned about his hips and another cigarette burning in his fingers. "He's doing it again," she told him.

"It's okay. He always stops."

"I don't like it." She gripped the edge of the crib. "I can't stand it, in fact. It scares the hell out of me."

"He's dreamin'. The doctors have told you. Why do you get so"—he gestured with the cigarette—"so *histérica?*"

"Because I'm a mother!" Anna stirred in her bed and, whispering, Jeannette asked, "What the hell does he have to dream about? And why do his eyes have to come open like that?"

"Maybe he's not really asleep, eh? Maybe he likes to watch you get riled up like this."

"Tell me, for God's sake, what he's dreaming about."

"Puppy dogs, and ridin' in his stroller, and eatin' ice cream. Who knows, Jeanie, who knows?"

"It's none of those things."

"What do you want me to say, then? He's dreamin' of his real mother, of España and poverty? You like that better?"

"I don't like any of this." She began to cry.

Hugo, his cigarette between his lips movie-gangster-fashion, came into the room and embraced her. "It's all right, Jeanie. We can wake him up if you want to."

"No. I won't do that. Let him dream."

It hurt her to watch him, though. The *real* John-John—the lower hemispheres of his eyeballs fluttering, his delicate fingers spastically grasping air—seemed miles and miles away, trapped in an eddy of experience forever beyond her knowledge or comprehension. At such times he was utterly lost to Jeannette, and she wanted to be closer, closer, closer. His dreaming was a barrier to closeness, the dream-racked body he left behind an accusation and a taunt.

Finally, averting her eyes from the child, Jeannette permitted Hugo to lead her back to bed.

The next day she took John-John for a walk through several old neighborhoods to Anna's elementary school, where the girl was a first-grader. The playground here was a sloping gravel lot, sparsely tufted with grass and cockleburs, enclosed on three sides by a hurricane fence and on the east by the school itself. They left the stroller at home now, and John-John, so eager was he to see the children at recess, trotted the whole last block. Bundled in a nylon parka and a pair of blue corduroy pants, he reminded Jeannette of a penguin sashaying across an ice field. No ice, though; just thousands upon thousands of crinkly fallen leaves. These whirled around him as he ran.

They reached the softball backstop and the solitary set of bleachers at the west end of the playground. John-John waddled to the fence just as a fourth- or fifth-grade boy came running up to retrieve a foul tip, and Jeannette sat down on the first bleacher level.

"Hi," the boy said, speaking over John-John's head to Jeannette. "He's cute. What's his name?"

Jeannette told him. Almost a year after Kennedy's assassination, in the middle of Kansas, her son's name had no special significance for the boy.

"Is he yours?"

"Mine and my husband's. He's Anna Monegal's little brother. Do you know Anna?"

"No." The boy let John-John hold the softball through the fence. When John-John dropped it, the boy picked it up and returned it to his hands. "You like this softball, fella? Do you? One of these days you'll be *some* player, I bet."

John-John pinned the ball against the other side of the backstop.

"Don't he talk yet?" The boy's teammates were demanding that he return the ball, but he ignored them. When Jeannette confessed that John-John had not begun to talk yet, he said, "You talk to *him*, don't you?"

"All the time."

"Do you read to him, too? Read aloud, I mean."

Who was this kid, anyway? The Grand Inquisitor? "He's a little young for that yet. We look at picture books together, though."

"Throw us the ball, Donnie! Throw the stupid ball!"

Donnie gently removed the ball from John-John's hands, whirled about and threw it wildly into the infield. Then, turning back to Jeannette, he said, "You ought to read to him out of real books. He'll listen to you. That's what my mother used to do with me, even before I could talk. The whole first year after I was born she used to read me 'Tiger, tiger, burning bright' every night. I could say the whole poem—every line—before I even went to school," he bragged.

"You like poetry, huh?"

"Come on, Donnie! Hurry up!"

"Not so much. I don't know what it means, a lot. I can say it, but I still don't know what it means. I like softball better." Through the fence he gave John-John an amiable poke in the gut. " 'Bye. Nice to meetcha, John-John."

He sauntered off. John-John remained at the fence, hypnotized by the activity. Jeannette, her hands in her coat pockets, searched the playground for Anna, but could not find her before the bell signaling the end of recess sent the school's entire student population scrambling up the slope toward the building.

On impulse she led John-John up the leaf-strewn sidewalk, past the school, and eventually into a low-income housing development with a single unpaved road dead-ending on the edge of an open field. Eight miles away, over a rolling stretch of prairie dotted with cottonwoods, lay Udall, Kansas. The blacktop from Wichita, Highway 15, cut a clean diagonal toward that almost mythical little town. During Jeannette's senior year in high school, nine years ago, a tornado had completely flattened Udall, killing more than sixty people and distributing kaboodles of outlandish debris all over the countryside.

As they walked into the open field, Jeannette told John-John the story. She embellished the account with colorful details. The farmer who had described the twister as sounding like a thousand jets and looking like a big oil slush. The telephone operator who had died at her switchboard. The man who had been thrown up a tree alive. John-John, his mother noted, appeared to be hanging on every word, as if she were promulgating some obvious but deliciously entertaining lie. Too, the rhythms of her voice had seduced him.

"Today that town looks one-hundred-percent, brand-spanking new," she concluded. "You'd never know it had once been wiped off the map as surely as Neanderthals and woolly mammoths."

They stood in the autumn turkey grass together, silent again. A meadowlark flew up from the ground cover, inscribed a parabola on the pale October sky. Jeannette began to feel vulnerable, exposed, as if their uprightness in this place invited either ridicule from the conventional folks in the houses behind them or attack from the cavemen and pachyderms hidden in the bushes beyond the arroyo dividing this small expanse of cow pasture. Crazy thoughts, but the wind was blowing and the world seemed big and hostile.

Now that her tornado story was over, John-John's interest shifted elsewhere. He took off downhill, toward the gully. He was fast, too. To keep her dress out of the snagging thistles and shrub branches, she grabbed it up by the hem, then plunged down the meadow after him. By seizing his wrist, she halted his single-minded assault on the dry flood bed. The boy strained against her grip. He pointed and made unintelligible noises in his throat.

Phrygian, Hugo facetiously called these vocalizations. We've got a kid who speaks Phrygian. That, according to a friend of his in the library at McConnell, had once been thought the first language ever spoken by human beings . . .

Beyond the arroyo were five or six white-faced heifers placidly chewing their cuds. Despite their bulk, Jeannette had not seen them until just now. Like rhinoceroses or giraffes, they were browsing on the shrubbery that had partly concealed them, stripping the year's last leaves from their branches. It was weird, this sudden apparition of cattle. Even weirder that they were browsing rather than cropping grass. It almost seemed that John-John had summoned them into existence by pointing at them.

"Cows," Jeannette said distractedly. "Cows."

"Cao," John-John said, still pointing.

Startled, Jeannette knelt in front of the boy and gripped his shoulders so that she was blocking his view. "That's right," she said eagerly. "That's right—*cow!* The word is *cow!*"

He pulled to the right, not interested in his mother's efforts to reinforce his accomplishment.

Brushing a strand of wayward hair from her face, Jeannette stood up. Let him see the goddamn cows, for God's sake!

She felt lighthearted and proud. Phrygian, hell! *Cao* was English, no matter how broadly inflected. A good Anglo-Saxon English word. By uttering this single word he had vindicated her faith in his potential. Even though many children did not speak until well after their second birthday, that "feral child" business of Major So-and-so in Colonel Unger's office had bugged her for better than a year. She had secretly begun to suspect that John-John's unmonitored infancy in Seville had taken an insidious toll on his capacity to pick up language. This suspicion, in turn, had riddled her with guilt, because otherwise he was an alert and vivacious child.

"Cow," she said, laughing. *"Cao, cao, cao."*

"I don't believe it, *mujer.*"

"It's true—he spoke."

"To a herd of cows?"

"Not *to* them, Hugo. He just saw them and he—"

"He said *cow,* Daddy!"

They were sitting in the kitchen at a table with a Formica top, part of the dinette set that Hugo had bought last Christmas through the McConnell Base Exchange. John-John was in an aluminum high chair with a yellow plastic tray. With a spoon in his right hand and the greasy fingers of his left, he was eating overdone hamburger granules. His mouth was smeared with mustard.

Hugo addressed Anna with mock stateliness: " 'Four score and seven years ago,' John-John told the cows, 'our fathers brought forth on this continent a new *nación,* conceived in *libertad* and dedicated to—' How does the rest of it go, *niña?"*

"Daddy!"

"He really did speak," Jeannette insisted. "Not Phrygian, either."

"Then I think we should be havin' steak instead of hamburger." Hugo lifted a piece of hamburger patty on his fork tines.

"John-John, this is *cao*, too. You see this? You're eatin' *cao*, Juanito, all the time eatin' those big sleepy creatures with those big brown eyes. Say *cao* for me, pretty please."

The boy, scattering bits of hamburger on the linoleum, pointed in the direction that Jeannette had taken him on his walk that morning. Toward the elementary school. Toward Udall.

"And at the playground a little boy named Donnie told me I ought to read to John-John—not just alphabet and picture books. Real books, difficult things. I'm going to start doing that, too."

"When?" Hugo asked warily.

"Right after his bath. Why don't you and Anna get the dishes?"

"Why don' I wear high heels and lipstick?" Hugo retorted. But he and Anna did what Jeannette had asked.

Jeannette, meanwhile, supervised John-John's bath, diapered him, shoehorned him into his terry-cloth pajamas, and stood him up in his crib. He folded his arms over the crib's top railing and watched his mother jockey a rocking chair into place beside him. Although he was old enough to climb out of the crib, Jeannette had taught him that doing so at bedtime would cost him. Two or three evenings a week he made a break for it, anyway.

Tonight, however, Jeannette's continued presence in his and Anna's room kept this impulse in check. As his mother removed a garish paperback from the pocket of her sunflower-print apron, he looked on with mounting curiosity. Then Jeannette sat down in the rocking chair and opened the book and began to read: " '*When Mr. Bilbo Baggins of Bag End announced that he would shortly be celebrating his eleventy-first birthday with a party of special magnificence, there was much talk and excitement in Hobbiton. . . .*' "

CHAPTER TEN
Fruit of the Looms

OUR CONTINGENCY PLAN demanded that I be present at lakeside every sunrise and sunset for the possible extrusion of the Backstep Scaffold, a stipulation that cut down my range and frustrated my efforts to observe Helen's people. This demand was doubly difficult to observe because the scaffold did not appear. Nevertheless, after missing my first sunrise assignation, for the entire week afterward I honored my end of the bargain and showed up at lakeside even when irritably certain that my colleagues in the twentieth century would fail me again. Still, I did not believe I was permanently stranded. Kaprow and his assistants were experiencing Technological Difficulties, bugs that they would undoubtedly overcome in time, and time was Kaprow's private bailiwick.

In fact, I began to believe that maybe my apprehension of time differed in some significant way from that of my White Sphinx colleagues. Maybe, because of the sheer temporal distance of my dropback, my sunrises and sunsets no longer corresponded to theirs. Eventually, I decided, Kaprow would figure that out, and the scaffold would appear—seemingly out of thin air—exactly when it was supposed to. In the meantime, though, I would abandon the lake to give the habilines my full attention, returning at the end of another week to see if I had surmised correctly. After all, getting to know the protohumans was what I had come for.

For the next couple of days after this decision, then, I mounted dogged forays on the Minids to press my suit. They did not react well. Although they no longer tried to drive me away, they would not tolerate my presence closer than forty or fifty yards from the huts. To make me keep my distance they hurled figs, mongongo nuts, berries, tubers, clumps of dirt, and stones. I had hoped to make inroads on their concerted resistance by plying two or three of the younger habilines with sugar cubes and gum sticks from my survival gear, but the children would not let me approach them, and the mothers of the Minid teddy bears were extremely conscientious about keeping them close to hand.

On the third morning, I arrived in the clearing between the fingers of gallery forest to find empty huts. The Minids had moved, had relocated Helensburgh elsewhere in the mosaic of interlocking East African habitats. Momentarily I panicked. I had driven them from their capital, and it might not be easy to find them again. This fear passed. The morning after I had fired my pistol into the air—the morning after I had entertained them with a soulful rendition of "A Day Ago"—the Minids had again greeted the sunrise by singing. Their wordless chorale, awakening me, had echoed over woods and veldt like the spirit of thunder or earthquake.

To find where the Minids had relocated their village, all I would have to do was listen for their next reverent aubade. They sang, I had decided, not only to express feelings that they could not otherwise articulate, but also to inform other habiline bands of their whereabouts—not as an irrevocable claim on territory, but as a social courtesy and a means of keeping the communication channels open. In fact, I had heard faint habiline singing from the far northern shore of Lake Kiboko and also from the vicinity of Mount Tharaka to the southeast. I was certain, too, that habiline ears were much better than mine, that they apprehended these faint dawn concerts as powerful surgings of emotion. Although the singing of one habiline band probably alternated with that of another, up to now all I had been able to hear clearly were the voices of the nearby Minids. If they had not moved too far off, I would hear them singing again tomorrow. They would not sever their polyphonic alliance with others of their kind merely to be forever shut of Joshua Kampa.

I was right.

The next morning I heard the Minids chorusing their raw benedictions of the dawn. By following these sounds I tracked them to a site about two miles from their former encampment, where they had reestablished Helensburgh (I could not give it any other name) on a grassy hillside overlooking the vast checkerboard of savannah, thornveldt, and forest strips fronting Mount Tharaka. A citadel, this community.

Its chief disadvantage from my point of view, and one that genuinely fretted me, was that I could not approach the new capital except by walking exposed on the open grassland below. A battlement of granite boulders partly blocked my view of the haystack hovels behind it, and there was not a tree within sixty or seventy feet. The Minids themselves were arrayed across the southwestern face of the hillside like spectators at a high-school football game, but when they caught sight of me, they scampered to their battlement and treated me to a torrent of stones and taunts.

So. Their singing had led me to them again, but their placement on the hillside thwarted easy access, and I was no better off than I had been before their move. They had hardened their position, in fact. A cunning and fearless leopard might be able to get to them, but I never would. That most Pleistocene leopards had too fine an instinct for self-preservation to make the attempt was not lost on me, either. I returned to my headquarters feeling lower than Lake Kiboko in an epoch of protracted drought.

· · ·

I am not going to detail here the piddling hardships I suffered (dysentery is not a pretty topic), or the dangers I passed (not all of them in my stool), or the fabulous menagerie of quadrupeds, serpents, and birds that I either befriended or ate (if not the one before the other). Nor am I going to recount my daily chores in the acacia thicket, from washing clothes to gathering firewood to burying my garbage (which last task I scrupulously performed to discourage the visits of a host of four-legged trash collectors, most notably the giant hyenas). Instead, I want to tell you what I learned of the Minids while still trying to gain admittance to their clannish hearts.

First, I found that between, say, ten in the morning and the hour before sunset, the males and the famales often went their separate ways. Blessed or encumbered with children, the women—on days not expressly devoted to dawdling—occupied themselves accumulating berries, birds' eggs, beetle larvae, scorpions, melons, and other easily portable foodstuffs, all of which they carried in crude bark trays or unsewn animal skins. One of the older females had a vessel so expertly woven that I wondered if some unsung chrononaut had dropped back in time to give it to her, whereupon I realized that her "basket" was in fact a weaverbird nest that she or her husband had stolen from an acacia tree. (Necessity is often the mother of light fingers instead of invention.) With their children in tow and an armed male nearby to harry the kids back into the woods if danger threatened, the women skirted the edges of the savannah. To benchmark their progress through the bush, and to maintain contact with one another, they babbled, cooed, and scatsang as they foraged. Usually they gave way in silence to a herd of elephants or a pride of lions or a pack of giant hyenas. If, however, the interlopers were lesser hyenas, baboons, wild dogs, or robust australopithecines, the women were as capable as their male counterparts of raising a diversionary ruckus or a spirited defense of their foraging domains.

Three or four times I contrived to tail the womenfolk, but I was no more welcome a tagalong than a flasher on an outing of Camp Fire Girls. Once aware of my presence, they invariably shrieked and hurled things at me. The stain imparted to my bush shorts by the albumin of a well-thrown guinea fowl's egg remained set in the fabric to the day I gave them up for lost.

Helen never went on these excursions. She had no child, and the womenfolk, though generally tolerant of her, were uneasy when she was about. Instead, Helen went hunting with the males.

These hunts took place on the savannah, where, if ever I climbed off my belly, I was unable to disguise myself effectively. I saw either a great deal or almost nothing. It did become clear to me, though, that the Minids not only tolerated Helen among them but frequently put her in a position to deliver the *coup de grâce* after a well-coordinated stalk. Under my astonished gaze she battered down a warthog and a duiker. Often good for two or three days' eating, these kills released the Minids from the burdensome need, if not the nagging desire, to hunt—so that I sometimes had nothing to do but sit in my tree and reread Genesis. The Minids, meanwhile, stayed in New Helensburgh and feasted.

What progress was I making? Very little, it seemed. The best construction I could place on my relationship with the habilines was that I was no longer a stranger to them.

I recognized by sight each one of the adult Minids. In addition to christening the band's obvious head honcho Alfie, I had assigned the following monickers to its menfolk: Ham, Jomo, Genly, Malcolm, Roosevelt, and Fred. Ham and Jomo were the two oldest Minids, if their creased faces and salt-and-pepper manes were reliable indices of age. Genly was the habiline who had given me so intense a scrutiny after the fateful pistol-shot incident, while Roosevelt was the unfortunate soul whose sphincter muscle had betrayed him. Malcolm, he of the red-black goatee and pencil-point eyes, had served as sentry the day I discovered the original Helensburgh, and Fred was the youngest of the hunters, a hobbit with a permanently dislocated jaw and a wide gap in his front teeth—as if in bygone days he had run afoul of one of his elders' more emphatic fits of pique.

The ladies I named in this wise: Dilsey, Guinevere, Emily, Miss Jane, Odetta, and Nicole. Dilsey and Guinevere were the consorts of, respectively, Ham and Jomo. Guinevere was the harridan who had given Helen such an extended tongue-lashing on my first afternoon as a spy. Since that time I had developed a more favorable opinion of her. In fact, I had even begun to suspect that she was Helen's mother. Emily, Genly's wife, struck me as the inveterate sexpot among the distaff Minids, a lady with a roving eye and a wandering backside. She was Alfie's favorite, although he too apparently appreciated a carnal smorgasbord. Miss Jane, Odetta, and Nicole had made a single distinctive impression on me: they were excellent mothers, tenacious in their children's defense, amiably feisty in their dealings with the menfolk.

As for the children, I had not yet familiarized myself with all of them beyond the point of assigning names. The oldest among them, probably Dilsey's offspring, was an adolescent male whom I called Mister Pibb. Thereafter the children, toddlers, and babies got mixed up in my mind, but the names I eventually wrote on the genealogy page of my reduced-print Bible and field guide included Jocelyn, Groucho, Duchess, Bonzo, Pebbles, Zippy, Gipper, and A.P.B.

A.P.B. was Fred and Nicole's baby. His initials stood alternately for Alistair Patrick Blair and All Points Bulletin, the latter earned by the shrillness of his demands to be given suck.

Twenty-three habilines in all (for I had been counting the Minids). I was their first cousin, two million years removed, come home for a visit, and they refused to acknowledge me. I was also beginning to wonder if I had become a nonentity to my colleagues in the dream territory of the twentieth century. Perhaps, for them, I had never existed . . .

I, Joshua Kampa, was extinct on my feet. The invisible man, another country's native son, cut off from his roots in the primeval Kane'an. A has-been, a may-one-day-be, a dreamfaring dodo bird, and I might have to stay.

Two days running at the end of a week, I returned to Lake

Kiboko to see if Kaprow had lowered the Backstep Scaffold for
me, and it still did not descend. But I was beginning to feel a part
of both the Pleistocene and the habilines to whose band I now
wanted to be admitted for more than solely scientific reasons. And
at length I managed a minor breakthrough with Roosevelt, the
young male who had reacted to my pistol shot by soiling himself.
He did not lack courage in more commonplace bush-country situations. In fact, at catching birds and tracking small game such as
hyraxes and hares, he seemed to me one of the most adept of all
the habilines. Often, in the early evening, he did not scruple to
carry out solitary hunting expeditions—as much for his own private pleasure as for the trophies he might bring home. For safety's
sake he kept these outings brief and did not venture very far from
New Helensburgh, but by persistent observation I learned of his
penchant for such trips and determined to act upon my knowledge by shadowing him.

Alert to my clumsy trailing tactics, Roosevelt usually made
sure that I got no closer than sixty or seventy yards. On at least
four occasions, after spotting me he gave up the hunt and sauntered home with a kind of wounded dignity. I was forever associ-
ated in his mind with loud noises and the terrible humiliation of
independently functioning bowels. However, the terrain came to
my rescue. The veldt below New Helensburgh abounded in
kopjes, those granite outcroppings showing either bare rock or an
austere covering of scrub. I began using them as blinds, as the
Minids and other predators habitually did, and it is to a kopje
and my own improving stealth that I owe my first successful tête-
à-tête with Roosevelt.

Roosevelt had just caught a hare by a technique that
Babington had tried to teach me in Lolitabu, a technique I had
not yet mastered. It involves observing a spring hare's half-cocked
ears as you run behind it in full pursuit. As soon as the hare
flattens its ears against its neck, you jump to either the right or the
left and open your hands for a possible capture. The flattening of
the ears is an infallible sign that the hare is going to "jink," or
turn, and by jumping to one side you give yourself a fifty-fifty

chance of intercepting it. On this occasion Roosevelt's intuitive leap to the right proved correct, and the hare forfeited its life to the Minid's quick and brutal hands. I witnessed the denoument of this primal drama from the slope of a barren kopje overlooking the plain.

Carrying the dead hare by one of its hind legs, Roosevelt approached my outcropping and squatted just beneath me in the lee of its overhang. He had decided to eat his catch in solitude rather than carry it back to camp, where the others would expect and probably receive placatory allotments of the carcass. Although Odetta, his consort, probably deserved the consideration of a rabbity drumstick, I did not half blame Roosevelt. He had taken the risk and he had won the prize.

I peered down on him with respect and great excitement. Roosevelt, ignorant of my presence, knapped some sharp flakes from a lava cobble and began to perform deft surgery on the limp underside of the hare. The singlemindedness with which he was dismembering his dinner suggested that unless I revealed myself, he would never awaken to the fact that he was being watched. Sheer youthful carelessness on his part, but a break for Joshua Kampa.

Carefully, then, I got to my feet and balanced on the edge of the kopje. The sun was sinking toward Lake Kiboko, and my shadow fell behind me to the east, out of Roosevelt's line of sight. Catching my breath, I leapt as far out into the savannah as I could and twisted about in midair so as to be facing Roosevelt when I landed. My backpack banged my shoulder blades as, instantly crouching and spreading my arms to prevent the Minid's escape, I hit the ground. Roosevelt shrieked and dropped the mangled hare. Unfortunately, he also dropped the contents of his lower intestines.

Dear Ngai, I thought. Not again.

I let my backpack slide into the grass behind me and tore off my T-shirt by way of a hasty peace offering. After demonstrating how it might be used to clean one's backside, I thrust the undershirt toward Roosevelt with many solicitous murmurs and smiles. He regarded the garment with the utmost suspicion and attempted to sidle past me to the right—but I stayed with him, and he seemed to understand that he would have to grapple with me to win his escape. Consequently, he showed me his teeth—his tongue—his liver-colored throat—while the hair along his shoulders and upper arms crackled erect and undulated in the faint twilight breeze. My height advantage seemed irrelevant. I did not want to fight him.

"Take the T-shirt," I intoned sweetly. "Please take the T-shirt, Roosevelt."

Against all my expectations, he did, snatching it from my hand as if retrieving something that had belonged to him in the first place. He then set about a swift, comprehensive clean-up campaign, never taking his eyes from my face. A moment later the soiled T-shirt was lying in a wad at my feet and Roosevelt was sidling along the face of the kopje to the left. I moved with him. Our clumsy little waltz was getting neither one of us anywhere. We halted.

What now? Roosevelt's beetle-browed expression appeared to inquire.

From the thigh pocket of my bush shorts I removed my last unwrapped package of Fruit of the Loom cotton briefs and nimbly extracted them from the plastic. Like a matador displaying his cape, I shook them out. They were clean and bright, so seductive that a week ago I had almost broken down and changed into them as a means of combating my can't-get-started-with-you-habiline blues. Now I was glad I had not. The briefs had a waistband of resilient elastic completely encircled by a single golden thread. I posed behind them so that Roosevelt could see how they were supposed to be worn.

Roosevelt's mamma had not raised a blockhead. He quickly made the necessary notional leap and snatched the briefs away. Then he retreated to the southern end of the kopje's overhang to fondle and examine them. Warily eyeing me as I gestured encouragement, he stood on one foot long enough to insert the other through the garment's leg opening, then hurriedly switched feet and completed the job, shinnying the briefs up his lean thighs and over the hairy knot of his genitalia. *Voilà!* A habiline in immaculate Fruit of the Looms.

I was misty-eyed. "Jesus, Roosevelt," I told him; "Jesus, you really look *nice.*"

Still leery, he swaggered back toward me and retrieved the gutted hare. This, without ceremony, he gave into my hands, apparently in exchange for the underwear. Before I could assure him that there were no strings attached to my gift—beyond the heretofore badly frayed hope that it might establish my trustworthiness as an ally—Roosevelt had darted off across the darkening savannah in the direction of New Helensburgh.

I hunkered in the shelter of the kopje to eat the remains of the hare, pleased with myself for not having pointed out to Roosevelt that he had donned my resplendent briefs backwards.

It had not rained since my arrival in the Pleistocene. Obviously it had been dry for quite some time. Recently, however, this lack of rain had provoked the migration of many herd animals—gazelles, wildebeest, zebras, and several species of protoantelope—out of the area. Although the food-gathering techniques of the Minid females probably accounted for two thirds of what the band actually ate, the absence of meat on the hoof would eventually work real hardships on Helen's people, primarily by depriving them of a vital supply of protein. Mongongo nuts were rare in this part of Africa; and if the smaller game animals—guinea fowl, hares, warthogs, monkeys, hyraxes, and water birds—followed the example of the ungulates, why, the Minids would soon be facing the ghastly specter of Famine.

And so would I.

The prospect excited as well as disturbed me. A change for the worse in hunting conditions might prove my best opportunity since the Great Fruit of the Loom Giveaway of winning friends and influencing habilines.

After giving Roosevelt the briefs, I detected among all the hunters a heightened willingness to tolerate me on their trail, as if I embodied a queer sort of sartorial example and maybe even a source of further handouts. It perplexed me that Roosevelt did not wear the briefs—I could not help wondering what he had done with them—and that these hunts usually went badly, but at least I had been granted the right to spectate. A genuine concession. Helen, across a hundred or more yards of savannah, would sometimes turn and fix me with a stare, neither hostile nor admonitory, that would make me tremble in my chukkas. I do not know exactly why I trembled, but the impetus might have been simple gratitude. A pariah often interprets the bone flung into his face as nourishment rather than rebuke.

But, as I said, these latest hunts seldom concluded successfully. Even though I tried to keep a low profile, my presence on the veldt handicapped the Minids. Nevertheless, the most compelling factor in their slow undoing was the drought. After the zebras, Tommies, wildebeest, et al., withdrew in populations numbering in the several thousands, an exodus of lions, leopards, cheetahs, and mangy canids ensued. Soon the Minids and I were sharing our homeland with game too big to dispatch easily (giraffids, quasi-elephants, hippos) and territorial competitors like the hyenas and those awesome baboons called *Simopithecus jonathani* that reminded me of agile gorillas. Only a few robust australopithecines remained in the area, sad-sack shamblers who provoked in me—on our increasingly rare encounters—a disquieting blend of pity and guilt. They were vegetarians, who, I knew, sometimes fell victim to the omnivorous cunning of their cousins. Most of them had probably deserted the gallery forest not so much because of the drought as because of the habilines' merciless depredations.

Helen's people, I might reiterate, were not the only protohumans in the area. At least three other bands of comparable size roamed the mosaic of habitats bordering Lake Kiboko on the east. I had heard them singing in the mornings; and on three or four occasions, taking particular care not to reveal myself, I had actually seen the hunters of one of these bands—the Lakeys, I called them—conferring on the plain with Alfie or other representatives of the Minids.

Indeed, a few days later the Lakeys and the Minids had engaged in a seemingly spontaneous fiesta in a river strip of fig trees about halfway between Lake Kiboko and New Helensburgh. Such get-togethers, I understood, provided an essential social outlet for the habilines. A randy young male might well find a nubile *femme fatale* among the unattached ingénues of the other band. Depending on circumstances, he would either return with her to his own people or remain with his bride as an adoptive son of his in-laws. As yet, however, I had witnessed no marriages and could not predict which of these two likely patterns would prevail. Mister Pibb was the only Minid even remotely close to marrying age, but he had not asserted himself during the shindy with the Lakeys, so nothing but chatter and good-natured wrestling had come of that meeting.

In addition to the Lakeys and the Minids, I had evidence—in the form of haunting morning songs and an occasional distant sighting of strange bipeds—that two other bands of habilines lived relatively near. One of these had colonized a wooded flank of Mount Tharaka to the southeast, while the other had established an amorphous principality somewhere in the opposite direction (a region today given over to Zarakal's chronic border disputes with Ethiopia and Somalia). The tacit understanding among all these bands was that they fared better as maverick units than as partners in even a semiformal alliance. The availability of edible plants and the disposition of game across the plains did not permit the mounting of a grandiose habiline republic, especially in seasons of drought.

United (beyond a certain ecologically determined limit) you fell. Divided (into autonomous bands of fewer than thirty) you stood. For which reason Alfie the Minid did not aspire to be Alexander the Great.

During this fallow period the Minids compounded their problems by missing several kills and allowing a pair of aggressive lionesses to drive them off another. It struck me that I could improve my status by demonstrating my talents as a breadwinner. I would make my reluctant cousins a present of an animal large enough to keep them well fed and sassy for two or three days. To that end, I went out one morning before dawn, before the ritualistic choiring of habilines, and walked in the cool half-dark all the way to the edge of Lake Kiboko. By the time I arrived the sun was rising, marbling the eastern horizon with delicate rose and salmon. The lake itself was a vast looking glass of turquoise.

I drew my .45 and crouched on a lava flow above the southeastern shore.

At which moment, glancing sidelong, I saw that the Backstep Scaffold from Kaprow's omnibus was hanging in space like a mechanical variation on the Old Hindu Rope Trick. My pulse quickened, and I leapt to my feet. Here, if I wanted it, was rescue. Even after all this time, Blair and Kaprow had not forgotten me. They had solved their Technological Difficulties. Peering upward, I approached the scaffold, startled anew by the window into deliverance. I was tempted, too. It would be so easy to chin myself into position, strap myself in, push the control retracting the scaffold, and dream myself back into the bosom of a world of double-digit inflation and percale bed sheets. Who could say, in fact, whether I would ever get another chance?

I took out my transcordion and keyed in the following message: *I am fine, surviving quite well. Have made contact with a band of local hominids*—Homo habilis, *I believe—and am gradually winning acceptance. Intend to pursue these observations for several more weeks. Very necessary if we are to learn anything. If possible, will return at weekly intervals, starting from today. Cannot afford wasting time traipsing back and forth. Listen:* SCAFFOLD NOT HERE EVERY DAY! *Please don't forget me. I will be back. Best, J."*

Then I put the instrument on the scaffold, and boosted the platform back into its spacious aerial womb. The sky was whole again, and I had reduced my morning's various options to one. Quite a significant one. I felt better for having done so, too. My entire life had pointed to this mission, and I was not about to abort it simply because a drought was threatening my habiline cohorts and me with hard times—especially now that I knew I could, with a little luck, get home.

I resumed my vigil at lakeside. Fifteen minutes later I shot a small, lone antelope of a species unknown to both me and my field guide—the creature had a copper-colored pelt and graceful, corkscrewing horns—and dragged it away from the water's edge to prevent its being purloined by a crocodile. After gutting the antelope, I hoisted its lolling carcass to my back. My plan was to carry it over the intervening grasslands to New Helensburgh, lay it sacramentally before the Minids' citadel, and thereby earn their undying gratitude and respect. This was a heroic scenario, but because I had fully envisioned it, I expected it to work.

The trip back to New Helensburgh, however, did not go as I had foreseen. As I staggered along, the body of the dead antelope grew progressively stiffer and heavier. Also, as part of my revolving alert for hyenas, wild dogs, and other potential dacoits, I made myself turn about in a circle every thirty or forty yards. Unhappily, about two hours into my journey, just as I was beginning to believe in my ultimate if not my immediate success, my conscientiousness paid off in a sighting. Some distance off, sharkishly patrolling the steppe, a pack of giant hyenas trotted toward me from the northeast.

"Oh, shit," I murmured aloud. "Oh, holy shit."

I dropped the antelope carcass *(Aepyceros whazzus)* and unholstered my Colt *(Equus fatalis)*. Unbalanced by the sudden removal of so much dead weight, however, I fumbled the pistol to the ground, where it fired a muffled shot into the dust and kicked over onto its side. The noise halted the hyenas in their tracks, but only briefly. As soon as I had retrieved the .45 and pointed it shakily in their direction, they were already advancing again, con-

tracting from a file of animals into an ugly, loping wedge. Only
six bullets remained in my eight-clip, and although Roy Rogers
or Hopalong Cassidy might have found that number sufficient, it
would fall about ten shy of what I needed to survive this onslaught. I sighted along the pistol's muzzle, pulled the trigger,
and—

   Click.

   I had not slid a fresh clip into the butt of the .45 that
morning. Further, under prevailing circumstances I was going to
have a hard time extracting the old clip and feeding in a substitute. A single bandolier crossed my torso, and I hurried to
squeeze seven or eight cartridges out of its canvas loops into my
hands. I was shaking so badly that a couple of these fell into the
grass at my feet. Looking up, I saw the lead hyena. Its mouth was
as big as one of the Carlsbad Caverns; its shallow panting breaths
seemed to be coming in perfect synchrony with my heartbeats.

   The hyena jumped. Scattering bullets everywhere, I struck
the creature a desperate blow to the head with the butt of my
pistol. A froth of saliva showered up into my vision, and I fell
backward over the little buck I had killed. The hyena rolled away
from me unconscious.

   Dazed, I struggled to my feet again. A second and a third
hyena, intimidated, went around me—but their remaining comrades had just crested a gentle swelling in the plain, and it did not
seem likely that, in light of their overwhelming numerical advantage, they would all prove such cowards. I dug into my pocket for
the Swiss Army knife, not even daring to think what good it
might do.

   If I should die before I wake,
   I pray Ngai my soul to take . . .

Whereupon, so help me, the cavalry arrived.

   Leaping, ululating, brandishing their clubs, the Minids
scurried into my field of vision from the east. Alfie and Helen
were in the vanguard of this unexpected counterattack, and Alfie,

bless him, had girded up his loins in the same pair of Fruit of the Loom that Roosevelt had snatched from my hand days and days ago. Whether Roosevelt had relinquished the briefs willingly I had no idea—but the sight of that hairy habiline modeling those dirty jockey shorts while laying waste about him with his stave—well, it cheered my twentieth-century soul.

All the Minids—Jomo, Ham, Genly, Malcolm, Roosevelt, and Helen—performed admirably, swinging their clubs so spiritedly that the hyenas, for all their size, were beset, bashed, brained, and bested. Moreover, throughout this abbreviated combat my rescuers kept up a demoralizing stream of hoots, yodels, and yawps.

Those hyenas that could tucked tail and ran. Four or five others crawled away with crushed skulls. I, altogether overcome, crumpled to the ground, a collapse that could have spelled an end to White Sphinx—except that the Minids, when they came forward to finish off the hyena that I had knocked unconscious, treated me not as an odious interloper but as a fellow habiline.

A fellow habiline in rather indifferent standing, perhaps, but undeniably a comrade and band member.

Hunkering nearby, Jomo and Malcolm banged the dead hyena's massive head against the ground, fingered its nostrils and eyelids, and mumbled in their scraggly beards. Genly, squatting beside the antelope, was deeply curious about the bullet hole behind the buck's right ear. While Roosevelt kept popping up from his crouch to survey the savannah, Ham, Alfie, and Helen lackadaisically cut away strips of meat from the open belly of my kill. I had never, without a pistol in hand, been this close to the Minids as a group before, and I wondered that they did not take more interest in me. Only Helen occasionally made eye contact, and I could not tell whether she was finding fault with my appearance or trying to index me in her mental catalogue file of bipedal neighbors. Somehow, as she had known all along, I was not quite right. I was, and I was not, one of their own.

I gave her a smile—that ancient, self-serving primate signal of one's own inoffensiveness—and lay back on the ground. I had accomplished my design. All it had required was weeks of effort, a bribe of inexpensive underwear, a drought, a foolhardy hunting expedition, and a posture of absolute helplessness in the face of an attack by giant hyenas.

Helen sidled near.

Into my hand she placed a collop of antelope meat. I accepted this and looked into her eyes, which were red-rimmed and haggard—but beautiful for all that. Then I cast a glance at my slaughtered prey, the antelope, and a reminiscent queasiness flooded through me. (Bambi.) Embarrassed, memory-choked, I averted my head and closed my eyes.

CHAPTER ELEVEN

Cheyenne, Wyoming
1969–70

HUGO WAS STATIONED at Francis E. Warren Air Force Base, and Jeannette, who had refrained from seeking salaried employment while Anna and John-John were preschoolers, had recently taken a part-time position as a feature writer for a local newspaper, the *Herald-Plainsman.* Hugo did not approve of her working, but because the money she earned was genuinely useful, at times almost a godsend, she had no intention of sacrificing her job to his wounded machismo. Besides, she enjoyed writing for the paper, even if Hugo, ambiguously tongue-in-cheek, would sometimes acknowledge one of her columns by crooning, Caruso-fashion, "Hark, the *Herald-Plainsman* sings . . ."

The Griers, from whom the Monegals had been renting their remodeled basement apartment for nearly three years, were a saltily robust couple in late middle age. They lived directly overhead, but with a porch entrance set regally above the sunken, half-hidden door by which the Monegals must go in and out. The house itself was a mint-green stucco affair with dark-green shutters. Pete Grier did the heavy yard work, while his wife Lily took care of the decorative gardening about the porch. They were decidedly idiosyncratic people, but the Monegals had almost come to regard them as family.

Lily Grier, a woman of Slavic extraction, wore her iron-gray hair in bangs and her lower body in heavy, pleated trousers. Her face had the off-white color and the noncommital expression of a frozen Swanson's chicken pot pie—except when she smiled, for her teeth, all her own, were beautiful. She had been raised on a cattle ranch in Colorado, and her favorite interjections were "shit" and "goddamn." Nevertheless, the presentation of an unexpected gift or a stray kitten's mewlings would reduce her to tears. She was taller than Hugo, and weighed more, and had an abiding, paranoid faith that Pete took advantage of every trip to the drug store or the post office to cheat on her. If that were so, Hugo told Jeannette, Pete undoubtedly packed the Fastest Gun in the West.

A whip-thin, red-haired man with forearms like Popeye's and the beginnings of a paunch under his belt, Pete had made his living driving heavy machinery. He still owned a small yellow bulldozer, which he kept in a collapsing wooden shed in the tiny back yard. Two or three times a year, at some rancher's request, he would dig a cattle pond or a drainage ditch, demanding his payment in cash to avoid having to mention the transaction on his income-tax forms. At the same time, however, he was an avid defender of his country's greatness, a patriot. The American military was the world's last best hope for the defeat and eradication of communism. Both he and Lily regarded the deployment around Cheyenne of intercontinental ballistic missiles in underground silos as tangible proof of their own and their neighbors' faith.

Indeed, the Griers' unflinching patriotism—at least in defense-related matters—had probably contributed to their readiness to rent to the Monegals. Hugo, after all, was a man with a dubious accent, and John-John's complexion suggested the radical politics of Huey Newton, Eldridge Cleaver, and H. Rap

Brown. Fortunately, he was only five when the Monegals moved from Van Luna, Kansas, to Cheyenne. Even at that age, though, the boy was beginning to realize that the Griers were the sort of people who sometimes, with sinister innocence, sprinkled their private conversations with racial epithets. But Hugo, house hunting in the autumn of 1967, had won them over with his Latin charm and military bearing, and they had taken pity on his need. The upstairs/downstairs arrangement proved workable from the start, and neither family regretted its association with the other.

At the end of July, at the height of Wyoming's arid, short-lived summer, no one could escape the aura of blossoming spectacle attendant upon the coming of Cheyenne Frontier Days, a Wild West festival of parades, honky-tonking, and butt-busting rodeo events, all seemingly sanctified by the fragrance of fresh manure. It would be a long winter, and no one wanted to greet it without having celebrated as fiercely as possible the rollicking High Noon of July.

This year Jeannette's parents, Bill and Peggy, flew in from Wichita to experience a portion of the flapdoodle with the Monegals. Besides, it had been nearly two years since they had seen their grandchildren. Pete and Lily put the Rivenbarks in a tiny guest bedroom upstairs, and Jeannette was startled by how well the two couples got along. Peggy, after all, hated bad language and shrank from those who used it; she had fallen away from churchgoing of late, but she still prayed silently several times a day and demanded a heartfelt grace before every meal. Without much diluting the cattle-ranch flavor of her speech, however, Lily endeared herself to Jeannette's mother by her exuberance and her unstinting hospitality. Bill and Pete, meanwhile, hit if off like old World War II buddies. In fact, they had both been Navy men, Bill a sailor aboard the U.S.S. *Saratoga* and Pete a Seabee in the South Pacific. Within only two or three days the couples had cemented a gratifyingly cozy relationship. Privately, Peggy told Jeannette that once she and Bill returned to Van Luna, she would rest easier knowing that her children and grandchildren were under the wing of people as big-hearted and caring as the Griers.

No one could deny that Pete, as well as Lily, was going out of his way to ensure that both their downstairs tenants and their upstairs guests enjoyed Frontier Days to the fullest. He gave the Rivenbarks free rodeo tickets and made arrangements with a friend in a local men's civic club for Anna and John-John to be in the parade that traditionally opened the festitivites. The parade's hallmark was the passing in procession of nearly every sort of transportation that the early pioneers had used in traversing or settling the Great Plains: horses, covered wagons, traps and buggies, steam-driven locomotives, old-timey automobiles, and so on. Pete himself had not attended a parade in four or five years, but he would certainly go to see how the young Monegals fared if they chose to accept his friend's invitation.

"What do we have to do?" Anna asked.

"Just ride," Pete told her. "Just ride, honey."

On the morning of the parade Anna was assigned to the front seat of a remodeled Stanley Steamer, a replica of the 1906 automobile whose top speed was nearly thirty miles per hour. Dressed in her frilly Sunday-school best, Anna waved to the crowd as her goggled and dust-coated driver eased the old vehicle along the tree-lined avenues not far from the city hall.

John-John rode on a Plains Indian travois behind a spotted pony surmounted by a dark-haired man in buckskins who said he was Richard Standing Elk, a Cheyenne now living in Portland, Oregon. According to Pete, he managed a small Ford dealership there. Richard Standing Elk's impatient pony had to clop-clop along at the pace of the parade.

Immediately in front of Richard and John-John, the flame-red caboose of a train on rubber tires wobbled from side to side. Behind the travois, meanwhile, marched a phalanx of American Indians in magnificent headdresses and beaded moccasins. Most of these men strode the street with an aloof dignity, but a few pounded tomtoms, shook lances, and danced—colorful eddies of activity in the otherwise placid stream.

"Look at the Indian!" someone shouted. "Look at the Indian on the rawhide sled!"

"What Indian? I don't see no Indian!"

"He's takin' a magic-carpet ride!"

"That's no Indian *I've* ever seen before!"

"He's a Blackfoot, a genuine Blackfoot!"

"Here comes the Blackfoot!" went the shout up the line of spectators. "Get ready for the Blackfoot!"

John-John waved, unperturbed, and a good number of people waved back, grinning as if he were a fine joke on them as well as on himself. The *hi-ya, ho-ya* of the tomtomming, dancing Indians behind the travois seemed to him a kind of good-natured complimentary laughter. John-John kept waving. Periodically he would crane his head around to watch the twitchy hindquarters of Richard Standing Elk's pony, to study the design on the buffalo-skin shield tied high up on its butt. The ride aboard the sledge was a herky-jerky, stop-and-go business, but he never once thought about jumping off and walking. He was having too much fun.

"The Blackfoot! Here comes the Blackfoot!"

Afterward, when the Griers, the Rivenbarks, and the Monegals had all reunited with both Anna and John-John, Hugo took the boy aside and asked him if he had minded the shouts of the people along the route.

"No."

"Good. It didn' mean anythin', you know."

"I know."

"You're a very wise fellow, Juanito. Sometimes I think you're six goin' on sixty." And he led the boy back to the Griers and the other members of the family.

One afternoon when John-John was seven, he found Pete Grier and his adoptive father in the back yard making plans for a hunting trip. His sister Anna, then twelve, was languidly pumping herself back and forth in the swing that Pete had hung in the maple near a neighbor's fence. Ignoring her, John-John climbed into the bed of Pete's pickup truck, a battered red GM with a gun rack across the rear window, to watch Pete struggling with a screwdriver to mount a spotlight on the vehicle's cab. The enthusiasm of the men's talk seemed premature, for it was nearly four months until either deer or elk season. Gesturing with the screwdriver, Pete described a stretch of hilly territory not too far from Cheyenne where it would be easy to sight, hypnotize, and drop a pretty little whitetail deer. A hatrack, he emphasized; not a doe. One helluva hatrack.

"Hypnotize?" Hugo wondered aloud.

Pete patted the spotlight, glanced over his shoulder, and winked at John-John. "You like deer meat, don't you, Johnny? Missed not havin' any over the winter, I'll bet."

The previous autumn Pete and Hugo had gone on a three-day hunting expedition in the vicinity of Eight Mile Lakes, a trip that Lily had permitted only because straight-arrow Hugo had ridden along as a watchdog. The men had come home bruised, flatulent, and empty-handed, and Pete's disappointment over their failure still ran deep. An entire winter without venison.

"I want to go too!" shouted Anna from across the yard. She jumped from the swing and came trotting across the dappled grass to the pickup's tailgate. In jeans, sneakers, and a green University of Wyoming sweatshirt she looked like a fragile ballerina kidnapped from her dance troupe and disguised by her abductors in urban-cowgirl garb. "I want to go too," she repeated, more sedately.

"Go where?" Hugo demanded.

"Poaching. With you and Pete and John-John."

Hugo made up some sort of story for Jeannette, and at seven o'clock that evening Pete drove him and the kids out State Highway 211 toward Federal on the way to Horse Creek. Anna and

John-John rode in the back, huddled against each other under a musty patchwork quilt. Beneath them was an army blanket that Anna had folded double and anchored in place with a fishing-tackle box and a Styrofoam cooler laden with Pepsi-Cola cans, a jar of mayonnaise, a loaf of bread, and a package of bologna. The sky over this desert of tufted flatness was so big that it seemed to tent the world. Twilight edged over into dusk, and the air slip-streaming around the cab of the truck grew chillier and chillier. When stars began to wink palely in the dusk, pinpoints of sequin dazzle in the Wyoming Big Top, Anna fetched a package of Fritos from under the quilt and shoved it under John-John's nose.

"Here, have some!" she cried.

John-John stuffed himself. Corn chips bulged his cheeks, poked brittle ends against his tongue and palate. Their saltiness summoned his saliva, and he ground the baked corn meal to a gritty paste on the crowns of his hindmost teeth. Anna, laughing, thrust the package at him again, urged him to take more. They fed each other. Finally, the truck whirring west-by-north under a milkweed scatter of stars, they began lifting corn chips out of the sack and flinging them into the roar of the back-blasting wind.

Corn chips flew kamikaze missions into the night. They struck the tailgate and scuttled back and forth across the corrugated loadbed like tiny autumn leaves. They sailplaned and loop-de-looped.

Wearying of this game, Anna began brushing Frito crumbs onto her lips, leaning over her brother, and depositing them on his mouth with her tongue. This was so funny that they sputtered in each other's faces, unable to get serious again. Mock-kiss followed mock-kiss, corn-chip debris granulating on their mouths, sticking to their fingers, transferring like sticky pollen to their clothes. Their hilarity increased, and they rocked from side to side in each other's arms.

Thump, thump, thump.

Craning their heads, they saw Hugo gesturing angrily at them from the cab of the truck. He was rapping on the window glass and staring apoplectically sidelong, his face grotesque. The truck rumbled onto the shoulder of the highway and ground to a bumpy halt.

A moment later Hugo put his hands on the sideboard and subjected the children to a powerful scolding, the gist of which dealt with the unseemliness of sultry displays of affection between brothers and sisters. Anna, aggrieved, protested that they were only "messing around," but Hugo cut short her argument by banging on the side of the truck and resuming his lecture. Pete Grier, after easing himself out of the cab and leaning over the opposite gunwale, observed that kids seemed to be "starting younger every year."

"Criminy!" Anna exclaimed, outraged. "Boy, do you guys ever have sick minds!"

Before Hugo could lay into Anna for this impertinence, a set of headlights flashed into view behind them and bore steadily up the highway toward Pete's truck. When this vehicle pulled abreast of them, they could see that it belonged to the state highway patrol. Pete cursed under his breath.

"Everything all right?" called the trooper, leaning toward his passenger window. "Need a lift or a tow truck?"

"No, no," Hugo replied. "Jus' had to get my kids settled. We're doin' jus' fine."

The trooper went on his way, having defused Hugo's anger by scaring him to death

To give the partrol car time to draw off toward Chugwater, Anna made sandwiches for Pete and Hugo. Neither she nor John-John could eat another bite, but they each downed a soft drink and washed off their hands in the ice water in the bottom of the Styrofoam cooler. Eventually, Pete again felt brave enough to put their poaching operation back on Go, and they forsook the highway's shoulder for the highway itself. John-John watched the corn chips dancing on the loadbed.

The truck bounced over a cattle guard and turned onto a rutted access road blockaded by a barbed-wire gate. Pete opened the gate, Hugo drove the truck through, and Pete returned to the driver's seat. John-John and Anna felt the metal beneath them vibrating as the pickup, tilting first to one side and then the other, climbed an easy grade through empty pasturage.

"Where are we?" Anna called.

Pete kicked open his door, leaned out, and flicked on the spotlight he had installed that afternoon. Its beam swept the top of the opposite ridge and immediately struck fire from a pair of distant eyes. They shone like amber matchheads there. The animal to which the eyes belonged stood unmoving, transfixed, in the trembling circle of the beam. An adolescent buck, by the look of the knobby points on its head. It was so still, so statuesque, that John-John tried to believe that a taxidermist had already mounted the creature.

Aloud he said, "I hope it isn't real."

"Of course it's real," Hugo responded, sotto voce. "What do you think, maybe it's a piece of cardboard?"

Pete took his rifle from the cab of the truck, drew it out of its zippered scabbard, and sighted over the top of the half-open door. The deer gave a high, off-balance bound that carried it out of sight beyond the ridge top, whereupon the report of Pete's rifle—so sudden it made Anna and John-John jump—echoed across the prairie like a thunderclap. John-John cried out, but Hugo reached over the truck's sideboard and held his hand over the boy's mouth until the night was quiet again.

"You missed him," he told Pete.

" 'Fraid not. He was dead when he jumped. Let's go see."

Doors slammed shut, and the truck bumped through a narrow draw and labored to the top of the ridge from which the deer had leapt. Pete cautioned the Monegals against stepping on loose stones, cactus clumps, and live rattlesnakes, then led them down the far side of the ridge with his flashlight. John-John, hoping that Pete had missed and his deer had gone pogo-sticking into the open wilderness, struggled along behind the men. Twenty or thirty yards down the slope Pete directed the flashlight beam under the dry skirt of a piñon tree and got back the glitter of a glassy eye. Anna turned aside, but John-John stared at the shadowy carcass in disbelief.

"I'm gonna gut this little Billy Buck," Pete informed Hugo. "You can cut off the legs and head. There's a bone saw in the truck, under the seat. We need to finish up and skeedaddle before anyone spots us."

Heedless of cacti, stones, and rattlesnakes, John-John bolted back up the ridge. Wind scoured his mouth and eye sockets. He hurled himself headlong over the rear tire well of the pickup and crawled to the quilt crumpled on the floor near the cab. He cocooned himself in this, curled up like a shrimp, and began to cry.

Anna reached him a minute or two later, coaxed him upright, and held him against her as the men went about the business of preparing the deer's body for the trip home. The door to the truck's cab opened once or twice during this work, but John-John paid no attention to what was going on. When Hugo and Pete emerged from the darkness for good, they were swinging the gutted, dismembered carcass between them like a bloody hammock. They laid it out in the rear of the truck on a painter's dropcloth, then covered it with another piece of stiff canvas that Pete conscientiously lashed down with ropes.

By John-John's imperfect reckoning, the trip back to Cheyenne took twice as long as the trip out. He and Anna had a grisly fellow passenger in the loadbed, and this passenger reminded him of the otherworldly carnage of his dreams. For the first time in his life, thanks to Hugo and Pete, he understood a few of the implications of that carnage. The implications frightened him.

CHAPTER TWELVE

Among the Minids

EXHAUSTED AND SHAKEN, I returned to New Helensburgh with the habilines. The trip back included a detour through the acacia grove where I had made my headquarters. Here I picked up much of the gear—rope, jacket, shaving bag, and so on—that I had not carried to Lake Kiboko with me. (Malcolm and Roosevelt were toting the uneaten portions of my kill.) I had explained the need for this side trip by improvising finger lingo, snatches of pidgin Phrygian (an ignorant king having once decided that Phrygian was the oldest human language), and a range of facial tics and tremors that would have done Mary Pickford proud. These ploys, in combination, had persuaded the Minids to follow me to the place where I had stowed my gear, for, to communicate with one another, they were themselves dependent on hand signals, vocalizations, and a subtle repertoire of eye movements. While gathering my belongings together I was especially conscious of how much information they appeared to be able to transmit through glances, blinks, and brow furrowings. They could "whisper behind my back" without having to face away from me.

Once in New Helensburgh itself, a wide ledge on a hillside overlooking the steppe, I had to contend with the curiosity of the children and the mistrustfulness of their mothers. The male habilines had ceased to regard me as a threat, but the women did not want me touching their offspring, bribing them with sugar cubes, entertaining them with the narrow beam of my penlight. That the children—especially Malcolm and Miss Jane's little imp, the Gipper—*enjoyed* being terrified by this strange instrument, and came back again and again to have their minds teased and their pupils shrunken, did not soften this maternal hostility. I was not allowed to enter any of the four clumsy huts on the ledge, or to partake of the women's food stores, or to wander too near when Odetta took her toddler Pebbles up to the hilltop for walking lessons, which always occurred under the vigilant gaze of Fred, Roosevelt, or Malcolm.

In short, I was a second-class citizen. My sophisticated wardrobe aside, I was the Minids' resident nigger, only begrudgingly better than a baboon or an australopithecine. The role was not altogether unfamiliar.

My survival kit contained a six-foot tube tent and a windscreen. I pitched the tent and erected the windscreen about thirty feet from the citadel's main thoroughfare. A dwelling of bright yellow plastic, the tent invited—yea, demanded—the curiosity and admiration of the Minid children, who liked to play inside it whenever I left it untended even for the duration of a whiz in the weeds. On my third day as a semihonorary habiline, in fact, I returned from emptying my bladder to find Jocelyn, Groucho, and Zippy entangled in twenty feet of fishing line. My Bible-cum-field guide, meanwhile, lay three quarters of the way down the slope, its pages riffling in the breeze like the wings of lazily mating moths. I had to cut the young Minids free with my pocketknife, thus ruining the fishing line, while Groucho kept baring his teeth and screeching. After releasing the children I looked outside my tube tent to find it surrounded by fretful Minid hunters as well as their wives. Thereafter, despite the inconvenience, I rolled up the tube tent every morning and redeployed it in the evenings when I was ready for bed. My knapsack became a permanent daytime fixture between my shoulder blades because I did not dare leave it anywhere else. Quasimodo Kampa.

If I fit into the Minid band at all, it was because of Helen. She took a special interest in me, I think, because I simultaneously mirrored and magnified her own predicament vis-à-vis her conspecifics. Granted, she had once joined the hunters in attacking me, but her participation had probably resulted not so much from a fear or a mistrust of me as from her own innate allegiance to her people—even if her lot among them was decidedly peculiar. I had ceased to be a complete outsider to the habilines because their own outsider-in-residence had chosen to acknowledge my existence. We were two of a kind, Helen and I. Our similarities transcended even the gross and arbitrary dictates of taxonomy.

Helen's status among the Minids derived from two unusual conditions. The first was her size, which made her either equal or superior to her male counterparts in speed and strength. She could outrun even Alfie, and although he might have been able to overpower her physically—a dubious speculation at best—he tended to avoid situations pitting him head to head against Helen or any other habiline. He ruled by force of personality, the hint of intimidation. If Helen submitted unquestioningly to his preeminence, she may have done so because her speed and strength did not yet give her a psychological antidote to the social dictates of gender. A big, strong, swift-footed, and cunning female was still a female.

The second circumstance determining Helen's status among the Minids was her barrenness. She had no child. She showed no signs of ever conceiving one. In fact, she stood outside the more or less formal pair-bonding relationships structuring the habiline band. Undoubtedly she had had paramours among the males. Alfie had almost certainly plucked from her the fresh gardenia of her maidenhood, for his chieftaincy of the Minids gave him carnal access to almost every female who had attained menarche. Those exempt from his lust included Dilsey (probably his mother) and, among the younger women, both Miss Jane and Odetta (perhaps his sisters). But if Helen had coupled with Alfie or any of the other hunters, she had apparently never conceived. Her breasts were high and small, her loins lithe and undisfigured.

At present, whatever her sexual behavior in the past, she seemed to avoid engaging in amorous dalliance with the males. In view of her vigor and appetite in other areas of physical indulgence—running, killing, eating, excreting, climbing, and roughhousing with the Minid children—this scruple puzzled me. Had her barrenness, exiling her from the tender domestic concerns and the friendship of female habilines, inflicted upon her an aversion to the woman's role in the sex act? Well, possibly. She ran with the males, and cocks of a feather may sometimes celebrate the joys of treading their jennies.

Together, Helen's size and barrenness permitted her to fashion, within a social structure predicated on cooperation, a life style of surprising autonomy. It would be false to argue that she had the best of both worlds (male and female), for only Guinevere and Emily on the distaff side ever treated her with affection; whereas among the hunters she had achieved "equality" not as another competent comrade but as a potent secret weapon (the bipedal equivalent of a Remington 30.06) against the merciless enemy Hunger. Still, being childless, she came and went pretty much as she chose; and, although Roosevelt or Alfie might occasionally go on solitary hunts, Helen was the only Minid who regularly ventured well beyond the citadel for longer than an hour or two.

Once, in fact, Helen disappeared for an entire afternoon, and I worked myself into a lather imagining that she had fallen to predators. She returned a little before sunset carrying a baboon infant, still alive, which she cuddled and unintelligibly wooed for several hours. How Helen was able to cull the baby from its troop without sustaining a scratch or setting off a riotous chase over the grassland, I cannot guess—but somehow she had managed. For most of the evening, the other Minids—with the exception of the children—kept their distance. Finally, however, Alfie sauntered into the little creature's field of vision, frightening it so badly that it bit Helen. This incident ended Helen's brief tenure as madonna, for Alfie, after fussing for a moment over her wound, insisted that she relinquish her baby to Jomo. Jomo and Malcolm carried the infant baboon into the darkness, and that was the last any of the rest of us ever saw it. I derived some consolation from the fact that it did not come back to us in bloody sections.

Helen liked me for my oddness, I think. In my own way, I was as peculiar a Minid as she—tall enough to discomfit Alfie, sufficiently fleet and steadfast to run at her side without lapsing, and enough of an inveterate loner to chafe under the sometimes onerous burden of habiline togetherness. For these and other reasons she would occasionally tolerate my company on one of her private foraging expeditions. The benefit to me was twofold. I got out of New Helensburgh without having to follow the men, and I learned some clever food-gathering techniques that made it possible for the Minids to remain where they were when drought seemed to demand that they pull up stakes for a happier hunting ground.

Here is one such technique:

Over a stretch of savannah from which the snow-clad peak of Mount Tharaka rose skyward like a colossal, milky diamond, Helen led me into a glade of whistling thorns. Inside this copse she took pains to move as silently as she could. Although less adept at such stealth, I took pains to follow her example. I soon realized that she was searching for bird nests lodged in the thorny branches of the shrubs. I did not understand how we were going to be able to grab any birds, though.

A thought hit me. "Eggs?" I asked Helen. *"Huevos?"* I made an egglike circle with my thumb and forefinger, then made a show of extracting this sign from between my legs. Helen merely curled her upper lip back in negation and maybe disgust.

By creeping up beneath a nest, squinting long and hard at its bottom, and then snatching from it a fine, fat mouse—which she deftly squeezed to death while withdrawing her hand—Helen demonstrated what our task was and how to proceed with it. Empty nests permitted light to pass through them. Nests sheltering mice, however, appeared tightly woven from the bottom. If you reached into a twiggy domicile through which no light shone, your reward was usually a rodent.

We crept through the whistling thorns evaluating every nest we chanced upon, and at the end of an hour we had five furry mice for our pains. I cached them in the enormous, snapdown pockets of my bush shorts, which were now so frayed and seam-worn they hung upon me like an overelaborate breechclout. Twilight sifted through the thorn bushes, for we had begun this outing quite late; and the coming of darkness, which my newfound avidity for mouse snatching had pretty much disguised from me, was suddenly plain. Helen was still not ready to go—despite the fact that the darkness was going to invalidate our method of discovering occupied nests. Although I tried to hasten our departure from the thicket, she continued to tarry.

The problem was that for Helen this thicket was an irresistible supermarket of tree mice. In early starlight, because her vision was so much keener than mine, she managed to sniggle two more of the hapless rodents. My pockets bulging, my brain bugling retreat, I could not persuade her to leave off hunting. Maybe the only way to win her over was to let her get her fill.

I found my penlight in my pocket, under a warm, bleeding mouse, and showed Helen how to operate the gizmo. She handled it with such enthusiasm and skill that she could have prolonged our hunt almost indefinitely, spotlighting nests and nabbing any occupants. However, the sight of that tiny beam stabbing upward through the thorn branches reminded me of another spotlight, a spotlight seventeen years into my twentiety-century past, and I grabbed the penlight from Helen's hand and brusquely returned it to my pocket.

Helen's astonishingly luminous eyes said, "Indian giver," but she did not try to reclaim the instrument. Because it was now too dark to mouseknap by the Helen Habiline Method, she reluctantly gave up her sport and led me back to the Minid citadel.

Among the hunters Genly was Alfie's sole rival for undisputed leadership of the band. However, he was a rival who had apparently failed to achieve victory in some pivotal past confrontation. As a result, Genly bore a deep scar on one forearm (habiline teeth marks, if I was any judge) and carried himself with a kind of saintly diffidence. He had redirected his aggressive instincts into the hunt, during which he could sometimes behave so belligerently—battering a warthog to death, driving a troop of baboons out of an attractive foraging area, snapping the neck of a colobus monkey with his teeth—that even Vince Lombardi would have quailed before such meanness. On these occasions, gentle Genly unloosed scads of repressed hostilities, bees out of a jostled hive, and Alfie would glance nervously sidelong, bemused by the intensity of his former rival's rage.

In New Helensburgh, on the other hand, Genly was deferential, glad to be of use. He never pushed for his share of any kill toted among us by another, never withheld so much as a wishbone from the importunate little beggars clamoring for a bite of his guinea fowl. You could easily wonder how he stayed alive on so little food. In fact, the vertebrae of his spine looked like broken wingnuts, and his face was more haggard than his comrades', with a hint of sagittal crest running like an embossed central part in his frowzy hair. While watching the others eat or handing an antelope thighbone over to a youngster, he would sometimes rub a finger along this crest, as if absentmindedly trying to press it flat. An endearing gesture. It made me think that he was trying to assist the hit-and-miss laborings of evolution.

The foremost indignity of Genly's life sprang from the control that Alfie exerted over his relationship with Emily, his bond partner. Wolves and whippoorwills establish essentially steadfast pair bonds; so did the majority of habilines, but Alfie, unlike all the other Minid males, rotated among a series of pallet partners. His favorite, as I have mentioned, was Emily, Genly's "wife."

Emily was a lanky lady with atavistically prehensile toes and skin the deep blue color of ripe plums. Frequently she would forsake the bosom of her family to live in Alfie's windbreak mansion. She did this so often that her allegiance to Genly began to seem a function of Alfie's whim rather than of her own free will and devotion. She came each time Alfie summoned her and departed each time he dismissed her—so that I could hardly blame her if she no longer knew her own mind.

Not long after my arrival among the Minids, Genly turned to me for solace, the innocent solace arising naturally between people who must make do in the emotional hinterlands of pariahhood. Almost, he was a male Helen. Not quite, though, because when Emily returned to him, he melted back into the habiline status quo and became just another adult hunter—whereas Helen and I were never that smoothly folded into the aspic of Minid society. Often, then, Genly came to me seeking either comfort or diversion, and I tried to oblige him.

He wanted little enough, really. A chance to fondle or heft certain of my twentieth-century artifacts was enough to transport him from his problems. I gave him, for instance, the penlight. He shone it into his eyes and ears, played its beam across the faces of the children as he had seen me do, poked it into snake holes and warthog burrows, and exhausted its batteries within a mere three days. I took the penlight back and gave him my magnifying glass. He accepted this new plaything, lifted it to his eye, and, after "reading" a few pages of the tiny book I had also handed him, returned both items and stared meaningfully at my pistol.

Startled, I shook my head. "Cain and Abel are still a few centuries up the line, Genly. Murdering Alfie isn't going to solve your personal problems." (In retrospect, however, I wonder. . .)

Genly put his hand on the butt of the automatic, forcing

me to twist aside from him and spread my fingers across his chest as a friendly caution. Disturbingly, he did not take his eyes from the weapon.

"Veddy dangerous," I told him. "Pull trigger. Go boom. You recall this effect, no?"

My pre-Phrygian patois did not impress Genly. He raised his eyes and leveled at me a long, disarming stare.

Well, not quite disarming, for I refused to yield the Colt and finally distracted him by jockeying a new set of batteries into the penlight and directing its beam through the thatching of one of the nearby huts.

Alone among the habilines, however, Genly displayed no fear of the pistol. Even though I tried to keep it holstered and had not used it since shooting the copper-colored antelope at the lake, even Helen eyed it warily. Alfie, too, remembered what my .45 had done. I felt sure that his present laissez-faire attitude toward me owed a great deal to enlightened self-interest. He was far from stupid (even if he did not yet understand the benefits of occasionally washing the briefs he had taken from Roosevelt), and insofar as my weapon went, at least, the other Minids had adopted his policy of Leave Well Enough Alone. All, that is, but Genly.

I began to believe—naïvely, as it happened—that a new demonstration of the Colt's power would deepen the other habilines' awe of my weapon and convert even the persistent Genly to this respectful attitude. I decided to use the pistol the next time we went stalking on the plains. The fact that the males' last several hunts had been only middling successes, and that scavenging during this period had not been very profitable, either, gave me an additional excuse for unholstering the .45 again. Genly must learn to respect the Colt, and the Minids, me included, deserved the psychological boost of a kill larger than hyrax, hare, or guinea hen. We had gone a long time without.

The day after my little talk with Genly (while Emily was still shacking up with Alfie), I shot a giant suid—a devastatingly ugly warthog—at almost the full extent of my pistol's effective range.

During the stalk the habilines closed in on this bygone beast by *looking* one another to the places where each hunter ought to be. Depending on eye contact and discreet head bobs, they made very little use of hand signals. Eventually, without its ever having seen them, they half encircled the animal in a copse of whistling thorns, convincing me that it would be unnecessary and maybe even counterproductive to break out my .45. Then, however, Fred and Roosevelt, who had been engaged since dawn in a kind of frisky one-upmanship, destroyed the element of surprise by bursting into the copse from the north and flushing the warthog into the open before their fellow hunters had completely closed their dragnet.

Therefore, when the suid, lifting its tail, attempted to vamoose, I planted my feet, took aim, and fired. The noise scattered a flock of migrating swallows from the whistling thorns and momentarily confounded the Minids, who dropped to the ground or darted to the cover of the shrubbery. Although the fear of loud noises is supposedly innate, a carryover from the automatic fears of our reptilian forebears, Genly merely winced and crouched. A moment later he was at my side, his jittery attention focused not on the dead warthog across the savannah but on the smoking barrel of my gun.

"You're hopeless," I told him.

Was it possible that Genly had a hearing impairment? Other than his immunity to noise-induced panic, I had no real evidence for this theory, but life among the habilines would not have been impossible for a deaf person, merely exceedingly difficult. Sight, smell, and the more subtle tactile senses might have compensated for an auditory deficiency. In any case, Genly was not wholly deaf.

"Boom," I said, holstering the pistol and fastening the snap.

We got the pig home by means of a crude travois that I improvised from branches, my open bush jacket, and a couple of pieces of nylon rope. My marksmanship with the .45 and my ingenuity in assembling the travois—a feat of on-the-spot engineering that I had craftily premeditated—gave the Minids a great deal to think about. You could see their thinkers thinking, whirring toward better mousetraps and self-propelled family vehicles and maybe even unspoken unified field theories. As Genly and I dragged my makeshift sledge and its savory burden back toward New Helensburgh, I felt that Alfie and the others had finally concluded that I, Joshua Kampa, was . . . a Credit to All Hominidae. I basked in their (probably illusory) esteem and wished that Helen were there to witness my moment of self-justifying triumph. Helen, however, had remained with the womenfolk that morning, probably with the intention of going off later and plundering our populous paradise of tree mice.

Her absence did not badly cramp my enjoyment of the moment. Little aware of what was to come, I strutted and strained in harness.

That evening we partied. The warthog was dragged, shoved, boosted, and kneed up the slope of the hill to the flat, grassy summit above New Helensburgh. In that spot all the Minids gathered to partake of the dead animal's flesh. Excitement ran through these creatures—indeed, through me too—like surgings of electricity, the elemental élan vital. Our gamboling on that gentle rampart was spontaneous and joyful. The hunters made an initial show of nonchalance, but this gave way to undignified chases and hide-and-go-seek games with Mister Pibb, Jocelyn, Groucho, Bonzo, et al., and only Helen seemed to be having any success resisting the general frolic.

Alfie had bequeathed to me the honor of butchering the suid for dinner; I did so with never an appeal to habiline flake tools, relying instead on my Swiss Army knife to slit, slice, and dismember. This hard work kept my inward ebullience on an outward simmer. Once I had finished cutting, Alfie indicated that I was to have the first substantial bite and the opportunity to parcel out allotments as I saw fit. At social gatherings like this one, habiline etiquette demanded that whoever had made the kill receive the proper due, even if the successful hunter were a youth, a female, an outlander, or, like me, an exotic freak of nature. Alfie was abiding by this tradition, this natural morality, and I played my part by distributing meat to all those brave enough to come and get some.

At first even Ham and Jomo hung back, afraid to approach me. After they had come forward to take generous servings from my hands, however, the children and some of the women clustered near, too. No one disputed my right to serve, or squabbled with me or any other partygoer about the size of our portions, or sought to secure seconds before everyone else had taken firsts. I nibbled as I worked, twilight giving the veldt beneath us the beautiful antique dinge of an old painting.

By this time, though, flies—miniature fighter aircraft with hairy landing struts and faceted double cockpits for eyes—were buzzing about with annoying persistence, and the redness of the warthog's flesh had begun to alarm me. Against the entire thrust of my survival training with Babington, I suddenly feared contracting either a pest-borne viral disease or the worm-communicated agonies of trichinosis. Dizziness descending, I stopped nibbling, stopped dispensing cold cuts.

"Brothers," I cried. "Sisters," I added. "How would you like to top off this party with a taste sensation nonpareil?"

The Minids gaped at me. They seemed to regard my rare verbal outbursts as staunch Anglicans might view the babblings of a Pentecostal ecstatic. That is, as unseemly lapses. Ironically, their own bursts of amelodic song at sunrise or other unpredictable moments of emotional overload were inarticulate analogues of my recourse to speech. The Minids did not recognize this similarity, of course; and, at the time, neither did I.

"Brothers, sisters, gather round. For the first time in the history of the prehuman race, I offer you the chance of a lifetime. You ain't seen nothing like what I'm about to lay on you this evenin' . . ."

And so on.

Unraveling this tawdry spiel, I got my nausea under control, waved merrily at the circling flies, and spitted the remainder of our warthog on a stick. There was not a lot of fuel lying about the hillside, but I gathered what I could find—dry grass, twigs, some underbrush—and flicked a match into the pile. The flare-up so astonished the Minids that they gasped and fell back. The sinuous flicker of the fire imparted an iridescent oiliness to the dark eyes and skins of the habilines, who, recovering, crept forward again. Still talking, still spouting poppycock, I thrust the haunch of the suid into the flames and held it there until the popping of its skin and the outrush of a delectable fragrance had overwhelmed our entire company.

"There," I said. "There's the first-time-ever smell of roast pig. Ain't it sweet, though? Ain't it sweet?"

The fire drove the Minids back, but the aroma enticed them closer; not one of them seemed to have a good idea which impulse to obey. For want of fuel, unfortunately, my fire was going out, and the sparks drifting up into the African twilight were like evanescent stars, forming and dying at the same time. I had driven off the pesky flies, but the meat was still red, empurpled by thickening blood and the advent of early-evening darkness. I had to keep the fire going if I wanted this pig to cook, and the only way to keep the fire going was to add more fuel to the tiny conflagration at my feet.

"Here we go," I crooned. "Here we go now. Gonna barbecue up some ribs for every little Minid . . ."

I began nudging the heart of my fire across the hilltop to the ledge of eroded boulders overlooking New Helensburgh. I charred the toe of one of my chukkas doing this, but the habilines, fuddled, parted to give me passage, then closed again and followed me to the lip of the granite wall. Directly below me was one of the four habiline huts. Crying "Banzai!" I kicked the pitiful remains of my fire over the ledge and onto the topknot of dry grass roofing that shelter. The hut ignited almost at once, sending a shower of sparks back up the hillside and illuminating our citadel, no doubt, for miles across the outlying steppe.

Several of the Minids began singing, pouring out arias of praise or lamentation to the youthful night. Your heart would have leapt or broken to hear them, and mine, I think, did both. In my hands, though, was the stick on which I had spitted the remaining meat, and I lifted this load into the air with both hands, presenting it to Ngai, Who dwells on Mount Tharaka. The fitful singing of the habilines faded in my ears.

"Preheat to four hundred fifty degrees!" I shouted. "Then roast until a tender cinnamon brown throughout and bubbling with natural juices! Serve with pineapple slices, parsley sprigs, and side dishes of fresh spinach salad!"

I hurled the warthog haunch into the burning hut, where it collapsed a section of thatching and disappeared into an angry roar of flames. The smell of the roasting meat was heavenly. The habilines left off lamenting the ruin of the hut to peer down into the conflagration. I half expected to see the soul of that poor suid ascending to the realm of spirits on blistered pig's feet. Helen, who had crowded forward, was suddenly at my elbow.

"You don't *have* to roast the rafters with the repast," I announced to all and sundry. "But it's a time-honored technique. Invented by a Chinese nitwit descended, I assume, from Peking man. Read all about it. Read all about it in . . . in 'A Dissertation on Roast Lamb' by one Charles Pigg—for of all the delicacies in the entire *mundus edibilis,* my friends, this one is the *princeps.* Hallelujah. Step right up, brothers, sisters; step right up for a succulent taste of heaven . . ."

The fire did not spread to the other huts. Twenty or thirty minutes later, when the ashes were smoldering and a few acacia boughs crumbling into crimson coals, I worked my way down the hillside to New Helensburgh with Alfie, Helen, Genly, Emily, Mister Pibb, and several of the smaller children. With a stick I rolled the burnt warthog haunch out of the ashes and onto a rock to cool. Later, I gave a taste to everyone who wanted one. The habilines all appeared to enjoy what they ate, but I have since begun to doubt if their taste buds were sufficiently developed to permit fine discriminations. A pity, if true. Why were our ancestors so late to harness the random lightning to the cooking of their foods? Perhaps because they had no incentive in their mouths . . .

Following dinner the Minids wrestled, raced, and cut capers, the curmudgeons along with the kiddies. There was not much order to these postprandial festivities, only enthusiasm and a high level of tolerance for juvenile mischief, no matter how old the perpetrators. I had recovered from both my dizziness and my irrational fears of coming down sick. And although the bloated feeling that springs from overindulgence now plagued me, I bore it stoically. I did not care if I ever returned to the present. The moon, looking little or no different from the way it looks today, spilled its ghostly lantern sheen across the vast savannah. The Minids and I were Children of Eve together, Sons and Daughters of the Dawn. With Genly and Roosevelt as sentries, we lay down like siblings on the hilltop.

I was happy; supremely, unconditionally happy.

But I dreamt that night, a dream of my adolescence many thousands upon thousands of years into the future of the planet. No Alka Seltzer in the Pleistocene, you see, not even in the first-aid kit of an Air Force chrononaut . . .

CHAPTER THIRTEEN
Van Luna, Kansas
April 1964

As soon as winter had given way to the uncertain balminess of a prairie spring, Jeannette began to take Anna and John-John on walks from their house on Franklin Street to Van Luna's old-fashioned business district: two rows of faded brick buildings facing each other across a wide, cobblestone street. Van Luna was her home town, the community in which she had first begun to formulate a philosophy about the way the world worked, and it was good to be back. Her burly father Bill had found them a small clapboard house to rent, and, having flown home from Spain in early November, the Monegals had moved into it only a week before President Kennedy's assassination.

Lots of service families lived in Van Luna, in housing developments that had sprung up on the northern side of town. Air Force brats were as commonplace as roofing tar and ten-penny nails. Every morning their fathers drove the blacktop between their ticky-tacky suburban tract houses and McConnell Air Force Base on Wichita's southeast side, and every evening, honorable executors of the SAC slogan "Peace Is Our Profession," they returned via the same stretch of highway. The Monegals, however, lived in an older neighborhood, relatively near the sleepy heart of the town. Although less financially secure than the families of the officers commuting from the tract houses, they were content with their lot. Serene in its welcome predictability, no more complicated than an iron doorstop, for the most part this was a happy period in their lives.

On their outings to the business district Anna would push her adopted brother in a squeaky stroller with a red-and-white-striped visor, while Jeannette brought up the rear pointing out flowers, meadowlarks, squirrels, even fire hydrants and lamp posts—anything at all to provide an excuse for her chatter, which she believed crucial to his development of verbal skills. (He was well past one now, and still not talking). After descending through the park behind the Pix Theatre and the barbershop, they would cross the cobblestone street to Rivenbark's Grocery. On an elevated concrete walk in front of the grocery, a pair of stubble-chinned retired farmers would be sitting on a railway bench swapping lies and lackadaisically ogling the street traffic. By Jeannette's second or third such visit to her daddy's store, they had assimilated John-John and determined that he was not a threat to civic order—not, at least, an immediate one. Jeannete, after performing the usual obligatory greeting ceremonies with these old men, would lift the boy from his stroller and shoo Anna into the store ahead of her.

"Hey, Daddy," Jeannette would call, going past the checkout counter, "I've come to get some stuff for supper."

"Help yourself," Bill Rivenbark would reply, wiping his hands on an apron stained with produce spills and marking ink. "Your money's as good as anybody's, baby."

And she and the children would shop.

One afternoon Jeannette seated John-John backward in a shopping cart and pushed it up an aisle after Anna. Excited by so much bounty, the girl had skipped over the grimy softwood floor to the shelves of breakfast cereal and the small wire racks containing packets of Kool-Aid. (Yesterday morning Jeannette had found her in the kitchen over a bowl of Cocoa Puffs and a jelly jar brimming with a sweetened, artificially flavored drink the color of thin antifreeze.)

"Anna!" Jeannette said. "Anna, we have plenty of those things!"

At the end of the aisle appeared another shopping cart, its operator a fiftyish woman who had hidden her hair in a bright blue scarf and fairly effectively concealed her ample figure in a turquoise chemise. This woman smiled at Anna—a long-legged child with perfect skin and Natalie Wood eyes—and turned to remove a canned item from the shelf across from the cereals. When she saw John-John, however, she stayed her hand and studied the boy quizzically. Then she backed her cart out of the aisle and headed for a frozen-food locker out of Jeannette's field of vision. Jeannette could hear one of the locker's glass windows sliding in its aluminum grooves.

Strange, she thought, suddenly uneasy. Very strange.

It grew stranger. Right there in Rivenbark's Grocery the woman in the blue scarf initiated a game of Cops and Robbers. She made a point of following Jeannette and the children up and down the high-ceilinged old store's several aisles, pausing when they paused, trundling when they trundled. This game continued right up to the moment that Jeannette wheeled her cart into her daddy's checkout lane. Bill was not behind the register, however, and the woman came cruising up behind Jeannette as if, by some unlikely coincidence, they had concluded their shopping at the same time.

"You're Bill's daughter, aren't you? Bill and Peggy's little girl, Jeannette?"

"Yes, ma'am."

"I'm Mrs. Givens."

"Pleased to meet you," Jeannette said, extending her hand.

Mrs. Givens ignored the proffered hand. "You met me when you were younger, four or five times. I know you."

"Oh. Well, I—"

"What kind of husband did you marry?"

"Ma'am?"

Quite gracefully for one so big-boned and meaty, Mrs. Givens squeezed past her shopping cart and slipped her hand into John-John's hair. Her fingers twisted the nap; not viciously, but not sympathetically, either. "What kind of hair do you call this?" she asked, leveling an inquisitorial stare at Jeannette.

"Hey," said Anna, "get your hands off my brother."

Jeannette was too taken aback to speak.

"What kind of hair do you call this?" Mrs. Givens insisted, closing her hand on a tuft above the child's left temple. John-John's eyes were as big as horehound jawbreakers. He yanked his head aside without dislodging the woman's grip.

This movement prompted Jeannette to strike. She slapped the other woman's wrist so stingingly that John-John was freed. "I call it head hair!" she raged. "I call it head hair because it grows on his head. If it grew on his elbow, I'd call it elbow hair. Listen, what's the matter with you? You've gotta be—" She stopped, her heart doing somersaults and her hand trembling.

Bill Rivenbark slipped in behind the checkout counter, flustered. Mrs. Givens, ignoring his arrival, unknotted her blue scarf and swept it from her head in a single dramatic motion.

"It's not hair like this," she told them quietly. "Or like yours, Jeannette. Or like your little girl's." She looked at the grocery's proprietor. "It's not hair like yours, either, Bill."

"Listen, Kit, why don't you change places with Jeannette and let me check you out."

"I don't want what's in this basket."

"Yes, you do," Bill told her. "You certainly do."

"I don't want what's in the basket and I probably won't be coming in here again." She made an elaborate circuit around the other checkout counter and pushed her way through the dingy screen door with the Wonder Bread placard mounted in its upper half.

"Did you see what she did? Did you hear her? *God*, Daddy, it was unbelievable!"

Bill Rivenbark shook his head, then began ringing up the items in Jeannette's basket. He usually deducted five percent from the total of each bill, an amount not a great deal larger than the sales tax.

"Daddy, I'm sorry, I really **am**. Scratch one customer, I guess."

"Her? Hell, Jeanie, good riddance."

But his restrained manner, his attention to the prices on the canned goods and packaged meats moving under his hands, made her realize that the possibility of losing Mrs. Givens's business disturbed him. He did not want it to—he was ashamed that it did—but he could not conceal the fact that he was upset, both by the silly woman's defection and by his own inability to support his daughter without compromise. Jeannette was embarrassed for him. Various threats to his livelihood—inflation, new competitors on the outskirts of town—had made a coward of him, or at the very least a tightwad; and this was especially galling when she considered that, to demonstrate her filial loyalty, she had forbidden Hugo to shop at the base commissary, where the food prices, even after her father's grudging discount, were a great deal less expensive. Maybe the problem wasn't entirely mercantile. Maybe her father, for the same reason Mrs. Givens had made a fuss about John-John's hair, found it hard to accept the boy as his grandson.

Appalled, Jeannette grabbed up the groceries Bill Rivenbark had absent-mindedly sacked and broke for the door.

"What's the matter, Mamma?"

She turned to face Anna. "I don't know, child. Here. You put the groceries in the stroller while I fetch John-John." She gave Anna the sack, lifted John-John out of the shopping cart, and, giving her father a wan smile, backed out of the store onto the elevated sidewalk. What was the matter with people? Why were they so frightened of one another? When would it end?

One of the old men on the bench said, "Say, Wesley, you think John-John's ever gonna get as tall as that nigger over at the state university?"

"What're you talkin' about? He ain't been over there in four or five years, that nigger."

Jeannette, busy maneuvering the stroller down the steps to the street, glanced over her shoulder at the farmers. " 'What're you talkin' about?' is a helluva good question. Do you senile old coots have any idea what you're talking about? What you're *really* talking about?" She banged the stroller the remainder of the way down and had Anna wedge the groceries into the seat beside John-John.

"Wilt," said Wesley's companion. "Wilt the Stilt."

"Nah," said Wesley, tugging at his sweat-stained felt hat. "Bill's grandbaby ain't ever gonna get that big. He's a runt, John-John is, but we might could put him at shortstop for the Dodgers."

"Call him Pee Wee Monegal."

"Yeah, he's already big enough to play for 'em."

"The Dodgers?"

"Hell, yes, the Dodgers. 'Bout the right hue, too."

Delighted with this repartee, the old men laughed together, cackling like crazy people.

"Jesus," Jeannette said under her breath.

"What's the matter, Mamma?"

"Nothing. Let's go home. I've got to get supper on."

Crossing the carrot-colored cobbles of Main Street to the empty stucco carcass of the Pix Theatre, Jeannette looked back and saw her father's portly silhouette in the grocery's doorway. He seemed to be a prisoner behind the rusty mesh of the screen.

CHAPTER·FOURTEEN
A Death

But man is a noble animal, splendid in ashes, and pompous in the grave, solemnizing nativities and deaths with equal lustre, nor omitting ceremonies of bravery in the infamy of his nature.

—*Sir Thomas Browne*

THE NIGHT EXPLODED. I ascended from my dream to find Genly stretched out on the hilltop not more than five or six feet away. My pistol was not in my holster but wrapped about two of the unfortunate habiline's fingers. I crawled to him in the dark—the moon had long since gone down and discovered that although he had shot himself through the lungs, he was still conscious, still painfully breathing. His black eyes, tiny pools of ink in a cadaverous face, stared up at me with neither recrimination nor recognition. As I eased the .45 out of his limp hand, I made a clumsy attempt to read his pulse.

Curiosity killed this cat, I thought.

Another portion of me replied, Curiosity and your own goddamn stupidity, Kampa.

I could have cried. What restrained me was my terror of the Minids, who scrambled from their hovels or crept cautiously toward me from their resting places on the cold hillside. They encircled me and their dying comrade, but did not venture beyond an imaginary barrier about ten feet away. Helen and Emily were the only exceptions to this superstitious timidity. Without waiting to assess the others' reactions they glided like wraiths to my side and knelt with me over Genly's prostrate form. Although I expected moans and teeth-gnashing from them, their behavior, despite their bewilderment, was exemplary, low-keyed and seemly—as if they understood that an unrestrained outpouring of grief or rage would further traumatize the dying male.

At last, when Emily put her lips to her husband's furrowed forehead, I did cry. The habilines apparently had no tears—not for emotions, anyway—and their dry-eyed faces ringing us about seemed a shadow-gallery of gargoyles and carven masks. I was a stranger here. Then the faithless lady lifted Genly's hand and with a kind of reminiscent tenderness held it between her thighs. Genly shifted his gaze, and a froth of blood bubbled at the corner of his mouth.

"Genly, Genly, I'm sorry—"

I do not remember *all* that went through my mind then or shortly afterwards, but my foremost thought was that Genly was suffering. I ought to put the .45 to his temple and pull the trigger.

Technologically disadvantaged, the Minids did not understand the mechanical operation of firearms. Few of them, however, doubted that my automatic was a potent death-dealer. Even Genly in his curiosity and presumption had understood that much; he had simply not counted on dealing that fatal card to himself. So when I raised the Colt to his head, the Minids grunted their disapproval even as they cowered away into the darkness.

Beside me, Emily put one lank, hairy arm around her husband's head, while Helen, angry, made insistent chittering noises and jostled my gun hand. I engaged the pistol's safety and backed away.

"He can't recover, Helen. There's no way Genly's ever going to be well again. You've got to let me *ease* him along, ladies. All I want to do is *ease* him along."

Helen ceased chittering and stared at me. Under the implications of that stare, I withered. Shot down by an Eolithic princess who popped the heads of tree mice between her fingers and performed most of her excretory functions in public. Even though I believed then, and still believe today, that Genly deserved the merciful blitz of a bullet to the brain, I withered. Emily and Helen were holding out for life when the choice was not between life and death, but between a quick death and a needlessly protracted one. Because they would not let me shoot Genly, he would have to modulate by painful degrees toward his inevitable dying. That process was not one I was going to be able to watch.

"Listen, Helen—"

When she jostled my hand again, I stood up, removed the clip from my pistol, scattered cartridges right and left, and held the weapon before me like a defanged cobra, a creature no less hateful for having been rendered harmless. The night was chilly, probably no more than fifty-five degrees Fahrenheit; and, half-naked to the stars, I was a candidate for either pneumonia or hypothermia. I wanted a good warm, woolen blanket and a bottle of whiskey or ouzo. My tears were streaming, and I tried to staunch them with my forearms and the back of my wrist.

Goddamn rod, I thought. You've turned poor Genly into his own assassin. You've made me an accomplice . . .

I stumbled away from the dying habiline and the two Minid women. The other members of the band, wearing expressions of imbecilic incomprehension, reeled back to let me by, and I began circling a small section of the hilltop, winding my body about itself the way a discus thrower does. At last I caught myself up and hurled my pistol out over the savannah toward Mount Tharaka. It spun away into the night like a stone from a catapult. I was rid of it. This knowledge frightened as well as relieved me. For the sake of a quixotic scruple I had set my entire life at risk. Did Genly, or anyone else, give a damn . . . ?

Genly was a hardy soul. Although he finally fell unconscious, he took all night to die. Considering the nature of his wound, my first-aid kit (a grab bag of bandages, painkillers, and placebos) was powerless to aid or ease him, and I made no second attempt to intervene. Afraid to go too far afield as well as to remain too close at hand, I spent that night hiking up and down the hillside and along its serpentine parapets of stone. At dawn I returned and found only Emily still keeping vigil.

By this time Genly had begun to resemble the mummy that death would make of him. His skin was taut on his bones, his hair brittle and lackluster. When he died, Emily, who knew, made a blood-clabbering keening sound, her head thrown back and her cry half the howl of a canid and half the desperate threnody of a human being. All the Minids came out to listen, and to watch, and to feel the fingers of mutability grapple at the mortal handles of their hearts. One of their own was dead.

Ceremony?

Yes, there was ceremony. To have witnessed it, Alistair Patrick Blair would have given up his post in President Tharaka's cabinet. To have prevented its cause, I would have foregone the chance to give flesh to my dreams. These were sacrifices that neither Blair nor I had the option of making, however, and the ceremony commemorating Genly's passage from death to some uncertain transcorporal realm took place in my presence rather than the paleontologist's.

First, the Minids knew that they must remove the corpse from their city. If they did not, the smell of decomposition would summon vultures, hyenas, and other carrion eaters. Second, the habilines remembered Genly as he had once been. In mourning the rigid, unblinking state into which he had lapsed they also mourned their own mortality. Conscious, or preconscious, our protohuman ancestors suffered an acute *tristesse* that could only have derived from an intuition of the inevitability of death: "One day Genly's fate will be mine. What does this mean?"

Not long after sunrise, the women spread out across the steppe and gathered the wild sisal called *ol duvai* by the Maasai of Kenya and Tanzania as well as by their Sambusai cousins in Zarakal. Later the women anointed Genly's body with the juices of this plant, a natural antiseptic and painkiller. They covered him from head to foot and canted his corpse onto its side in order to reach every part of him. Wherefore medicine for a dead man? Did they wish to spare him the unknown agonies awaiting the newly dead deeper in the domain of nonexistence?

But the females had played out their role. Genly's body hair was gummy with sisal juice, his brow a piece of parchment spread with mucilage. Now the males moved in, and I with them. Fortunately no one sought to prohibit or discourage my involvement. As the youngest hunters, Roosevelt and Fred bore the brunt of transporting Genly's corpse down the hillside to the savannah, but the rest of us helped when the going got particularly treacherous. Beneath New Helensburgh the Minids rested briefly, girding themselves for a trek to the southeast—in the direction of Mount Tharaka, the throne of their world.

The travois on which we had brought the warthog back to our citadel lay at the base of the hill. I signaled to the habilines that, if we still had a good distance to go, Genly should be laid upon the travois. After debating this matter with glances and subtle eye narrowings, the Minids agreed to my suggestion. I insisted on gripping the forward poles of the sledge and dragging my dead friend's body to wherever his compatriots wished it to go. Again no one gainsaid me. The other Minids, carrying staves or clubs, acted as outriders; and for approximately three miles we trudged in disorderly procession across the grasslands to a solitary baobab.

Here, to my surprise, Alfie, Malcolm, Roosevelt, and Fred struggled to install the corpse in the tree, as high among the great rootlike branches as they could lodge it without risking their own lives. Exempt from this labor by virtue of age, past service, or (in my case) fatigue, Jomo, Ham, and I looked on. We made ourselves useful by surveying the surrounding countryside for enemies, predatory gatecrashers. At last poor Genly sat slumped in a niche of baobab boughs, and the other Minids, sticky with sisal balm, cascaded to the ground one after another to offer their heartfelt obeisance to the corpse. I expected singing, but there was none until all the Minids except Ham had retreated to a patch of bush nearly a hundred yards from the tree. I withdrew with the majority, but I kept thinking that if a lion or a saber-tooth or even a pack of wild dogs caught Ham out there alone, he would soon join Genly in the problematical Never-Never Land of Habiline Heaven.

Then Ham began to sing. His tired old throat gave out a rasping keen that went on and on, focusing the implicit meaning of the entire veldt on the baobab beneath which he stood. I shuddered to hear his song, shuddered to think that I might actually understand the immemorial impulse giving rise to such homage. Then Ham stopped singing and came sauntering toward us on his bandy legs, a naked, defenseless gnome paradoxically dwindling in stature the farther behind him he left the baobab—as if the reality of his person paled before the ideal embodied in his lofty, sour song.

I then expected the Minids to set out for New Helensburgh, to take back to their women confirmation of Genly's tree burial. From dust to dust, from treetop to treetop. But even as the day drew on past noon, we remained in our blind of scrub plants and gall acacias. To stop the throbbing in my temples, I sat down and hung my head between my knees. Roosevelt and Fred paced back and forth in the undergrowth, heedless of the heat, impatient for a break in our vigil. Excitedly they signaled this break themselves by hooting softly and crowding forward to the edge of the thicket.

Beneath the baobab there had appeared a leopard, a long, handsome animal with caved-in flanks and sapphire-bright eyes. Although primarily a nocturnal hunter, this leopard—respectfully contemptuous of the dangers posed by the afternoon activity of its cousins, the lions—was answering Ham's midday summons. It glanced about the landscape, gave a tentative growl, then flowed up the trunk of the baobab with the grace of a python. Here it took possession of Genly with its teeth.

Alfie, I saw, was pleased. So were the other Minids. Involuntarily the corners of their lips had lifted into placatory smiles.

Alfie was thumping the end of his stave against the ground as if applauding the leopard's arrival. Dear Ngai, I thought, they *want* their comrade's corpse to be eaten by this creature. And indeed they did. We watched the big cat tear away a portion of the dead man's flank and bolt this down as a hungry dog gobbles down a can of Alpo. It now occurred to me that the women had anointed Genly's body with the juice of *ol dwai* to inure it to the brutal depredations of the leopard. Further, by sacrificing his corpse to this handsome animal, the Minids denied it to the vultures and the hyenas. Hence the pleasure they took in what was for me a grisly interlude in the funeral ceremony.

Finally, knowing that Genly was "safe," we returned to the Minid citadel. I dragged the travois behind me, feeling the kind of cosmic estrangement that used to succeed my childhood spirit-traveling episodes. No one had eaten that day, and no one would eat again until the next. This fast was yet another element in the habilines' communal reaction to death, but my discovery of these various elements—ones that many contemporary paleo-anthropologists have either dismissed as nonsense or hedged about with qualifiers—gave me no sense of accomplishment, no exhilarating shot in the arm. The series of rituals that allowed the Minids to come to terms with Genly's passing induced in me a profound shock. From the total sum of deaths suffered by human beings since the beginning of our species, I reflected, we had no right to subtract those of *Homo neanderthalus, Homo erectus,* or *Homo habilis.* How many more collateral species should we add? Was there, in fact, any legitimate cut-off point?

How strange to think that a creature dead these two million years had fears and aspirations akin to my own. *Akin*—a very appropriate word.

Back in New Helensburgh I set myself a task of penance and atonement. I gathered saplings, dry grass, and stones with which to build a hut to replace the one I had destroyed by fire. In fact, I accumulated and laid by enough materials to construct a second hut for myself. My preparatory labor kept me toiling up and down the slopes of the hill until evening, when I began the actual work on the huts themselves.

Quickly and surely I erected the wall and ceiling supports, then covered them with a much thicker weave of dry grasses than the Minids usually employed. This enterprise, which surprised and fascinated the habilines, kept my mind off Genly's death—without, however, dispelling my nagging subliminal awareness of it—and I began to cherish the idea of retiring to the warm, dry interior of my hut for a long nap. I wanted privacy, but I did not want to abandon New Helensburgh to acquire it. By moonrise I had finished both structures, and I crept into mine like a creature intent on plunging itself into the oblivion of a hard, hibernal sleep.

I could not sleep. Genly had died because of my carelessness, and the anarchic gaiety of the previous evening arose in my memory to taunt me by way of contrast. From blithe giddiness to black despair in less than twenty-four hours. The Stone Age, it seemed to me, had an adamantine heart. Outside, the Minids were softly singing their loss, each dirge creating its own context of grief, eight or nine separate voices with nothing in common but an otherwise inexpressible melancholy. Like Ham's song that afternoon, this phenomenon had no precedent in my experience among the protohumans, and I felt even more a disruptive force, an intruder.

A silhouette suddenly appeared in my low doorway. It was Helen, her flyaway hair a halo against the lingering crimson of the sunset. I had not seen her since that morning. She was no respector of thresholds, and mine was probably too new to merit any special consideration *as* a threshold. What was mine was willy-nilly hers, apparently, and she seemed to have concluded that this new hut could easily accommodate both of us. She squeezed inside, walked to me on all fours, and touched my forehead like a confessor bestowing absolution on a penitent.

Something cold and hard fell against my knee. I reached down, picked it up, and realized that it was my Colt automatic.

Slyly canting her head, Helen leaned back and studied my face. Her eyes were smoky marbles in a bust of discolored lapis lazuli, and I regarded her at that moment as an angel of transcendent apehood, a woman well ahead of her time.

"You're liable to need that," she said.

Of course she had said nothing at all, but in my despair I half believed that she *had* spoken, and I felt with absolute certainty that all I needed to survive this out-of-sequence period of my life was Helen herself. To that end, reading my thoughts, she had come to me of her own accord.

CHAPTER FIFTEEN

Eglin Air Force Base, Florida

Spring 1976

On Friday afternoon Hugo came into his family's Capehart housing unit and found John-John sprawled across a chair reading an omnibus volume of John Collier short stories. The boy acknowledged him with a nod but went quickly back to his book. Nobody else was at home.

Anna was attending Agnes Scott College in Atlanta, and Jeannette, since mid-April, had been living on Long Island with the family of her editor at the Vireo Press. She was doing full-scale revisions on a manuscript that had been assembled in February, a collection of semiserious book columns she had written for the *Herald-Plainsman* and then for a small syndicate with outlets in both the Sunbelt and the Rocky Mountain region. Her purpose now was to polish, update, and citify these columns so that they would appeal to Eastern urbanites as well as the easygoing, down-home sophisticates who had comprised their first audience. Hugo had wanted Jeannette to do this work at home, but when her editor invited her to New York for consultations on the necessary changes, he had not been able to bring himself to forbid the trip. Anyway, he had never had that kind of power.

"Come on Johnny, let's take a little vacation this weekend. You up to goin' for a ride?"

"A vacation? Where?"

"Through the pine woods of northern Flo-REE-dah. Maybe over to Silver Springs, too. We'll go for a cruise on a glass-bottom boat and watch the pretty mermaids in the ballet."

John put down his book and grimaced.

"We're goin', *hijo mío.* I'm tired of all this jackass creative bachin' we been doin' and ready for somethin' new, okay?" Supper, if he bothered to fix it, would be either hot dogs or frozen TV dinners. "Go pack some stuff, Johnny. Twenty minutes, okay?"

The boy grudgingly obeyed. Hugo, in his own room, threw several items into an overnight bag and changed into sports clothes. He found the meerschaum pipe that Pete Grier, four years ago, had given him as a going-away present just prior to his departure for an unaccompanied tour of duty on Guam. That tour, with Jeannette and the kids remaining in Cheyenne, had marked a critical watershed in the Monegals' married life, their first protracted separation. There were lots of bad memories about his part in the bombardment of Cambodia, too, including playing father confessor to a young navigator who had accidentally obliterated a friendly village by failing to throw a switch locked on the village's targeting beacon. The kid's B-52 had "boxed" the place with bombs . . . It was a good pipe, though, well broken in and comforting.

An hour away from Eglin, driving east, they saw the first of the garish billboards advertising Ritki's Gift & Souvenir Emporium. The signs were spaced at mile intervals, amid the exotic vegetable architecture of kudzu, and each one promised the out-of-state vacationer a variety of marvels. Papaya juice. Porcelain figurines. Fudge divinity. And a free "animal ranch."

When the complex itself hove into view (a pair of single-story, whitewashed buildings with tile roofs and heavy Spanish beamwork), Hugo swung off the highway into the gravel parking lot. Behind the larger of the two buildings was a bamboo stockade—a fortress projecting into the pines—and behind the stockade loomed a densely forested hill. Despite its being Friday evening, Hugo's green-gold Dodge Dart was one of only about four cars in the immense parking area.

"You want some papaya juice, don' you, Johnny?"

"No, sir. Not really."

"Well, I do. Come on." Hugo gestured the teen-ager out of the car with his pipe and led him toward a gangway beside the main building. A huge red arrow on the wall directed father and son to a turnstile, which squeaked as they pushed through. Inside the stockade a metal rack containing peanuts caught Hugo's eyes, and he dropped a quarter into the coin box and handed John-John one of the small brown paper bags. "You can feed the animals, okay? Maybe cheer you up."

They strolled between a pair of green metal rails describing a mazelike path through the compound. Gravel crunched underfoot, and the glassy twitterings of caged birds reverberated in the hush of the evening. Hugo halted John-John briefly before a wire-fronted cage in which a coyote lay, its tail immersed in its own water trough. Elsewhere peacocks strutted, a pair of llamas nibbled hay, rattlesnakes coiled in dirty glass display cases, a burro drowsed, and a slew of half- and three-quarter-grown alligators, like the victims of some bizarre massacre, lay sprawled atop one another in a scum-filled concrete basin. Hugo was utterly heedless of the stench, but eventually, to his son's relief, he tired of the coyote's listless behavior and ambled away over the gravel to another small green cage.

RHESUS MONKEYS *(MUCACA MULATTA)* COMMON TO INDIA LIKE PEANUTS BUT MAY BITE

Here two monkeys occupied a cramped ledge, one a shy female and the other a male with one leg dangling into space. The male lay prone, the neon-bright callosities of his buttocks exposed. Hugo told John-John to give the female a peanut, but her stare seemed to disconcert the boy, as did the casual posture of her mate, and he yielded the bag to his father.

"What's the matter?"

"They're prisoners, Papa. I feel guilty standing here. They're like furry little people who've been put in jail for no good reason at all."

"It's no worse for them than the others."

"It's worse."

"Okay, okay, *está peor,* Johnny." He chewed his pipe stem, dug in the paper bag. "Maybe a peanut'll make this little lady feel better, what do you think?"

Hugo extended a peanut through the wire mesh, but the female moved so suddenly to accept it that he was startled and dropped it into the bottom compartment of the cage. Undismayed, the rhesus dropped from the wooden ledge, retrieved the offering, and faced away to crack and eat it. Hugo, laughing, flicked another peanut through the screen.

"Look, Johnny, *tiene hambre.* She's hungry."

The sound of cracking shells aroused the male, who promptly sat up, hiding his bruised-looking derrière beneath him and noncommittally working his muzzle. Balanced on the edge of his perch, he put his small, delicately fashioned hand through the wire—but stared off into another section of the compound, as if too proud to acknowledge to either himself or anyone else that he was begging.

"Ven aquí," Hugo urged the loftily uninterested rhesus. "Come get your *cacahuate,* eh?"

Haughtily the monkey turned his head and looked at Hugo. Attention fully engaged, he reached ever farther toward the Monegals, leaning against the wire so that his hairy shoulder was outlined in the mesh. His upsettingly human fingers closed on the peanut—then, deliberately, let it fall into the gravel at Hugo's feet. This disdain for the offering, John-John could see, had struck his father as an insult, one more slight in a chain of slights initiated by Jeannette's steady progress toward a career independent of the Monegal family unit. How else explain Hugo's reaction to an event of no objective magnitude whatever?

"What's the matter with you?" he shouted at the rhesus. "They feed you so good you can turn up your nose at a nice plump peanut?"

He bent to puck up the peanut. Swiftly—so swiftly that John-John scarcely had time to blink—the male rhesus grabbed the bowl of Hugo's meerschaum pipe and wrenched it from his mouth. Shielding the stolen pipe with his body, the monkey retreated to the back of the cage and, casting guarded glances over his shoulder at the two human beings, proceeded to bang the pipe against the sleeping ledge.

"Hijo de puta!" Hugo exclaimed, grievously hurt by the creature's duplicity. He threw himself against the cage and reached through the wire for a handful of reddish-brown rhesus hair.

"Papa! Papa, *don't!"*

The male spun about madly, sprang forward in a rage, and drove Hugo back. Mouth wide open, the rhesus displayed a set of glistening yellow fangs and a liver-colored throat. The female shied into a corner, but her mate, growling, clung to the wire mesh and taunted the human beings, who were in embarrassed terror of him. John-John glanced about the compound to see if anyone else had observed the rhesus's attack and their clumsy withdrawal. No one had.

"Goddamn little gook!" Hugo exclaimed in English, echoing the abusive language of men who have served in remote corners of the world. "Give me back my *pipa!* My pipe, you thief!"

Unimpressed, the rhesus disengaged his hands and feet from the wire and leapt back to his plank, where he sat on his haunches chewing the pipe's briar stem until, audibly, it splintered. Hugo's favorite pipe, a comfort and a crutch from the days he had manfully struggled to give up cigarettes.

"We'll tell them inside," John-John suggested. "We'll tell the manager what's happened."

But Hugo flung the bag of peanuts aside and stalked angrily through the gravel toward the compound's exit. The boy followed. They passed other cages, other animals, an aviary, a small stable with ponies, and turned a final corner to find themselves facing another sign and a second turnstile.

IF YOU HAVE ENJOYED RITKI'S ANIMAL RANCH
PLEASE MAKE A DONATION TOWARD FEEDING
THE ANIMALS

To leave the stockade, it now became clear, they would have to go through the souvenir-cluttered emporium of the main building. Intimidated, Hugo pushed a dollar through the window of the donations booth, murmured a greeting at the bored woman inside, and shoved John-John through the turnstile and into the gift shop. The sickeningly sweet smells of peanut brittle and pralines assailed them, and Hugo stumbled toward the door like a man who has narrowly survived a mugging. John-John apologetically stumbled after.

The Monegals drove until dark, then found a second-rate motel consisting of ten or twelve separate cabins where they stopped for the night. Hugo left John-John sitting on the bed watching television and returned about twenty minutes later with a pair of barbecued-pork sandwiches wrapped in translucent wax paper. At eleven he made his son turn off the television and go to bed. Then, like a paid hospital orderly, he sat in a cheap, imitation-leather chair opposite the bed, cleaning his fingernails with a penknife in the faint illumination coming through the cabin's only window.

John-John awoke convinced that the rhesus from Ritki's was perched on the chest of drawers near the cabin's bathroom. His father was not in bed with him, and when he hitched himself into a sitting position against the headboard, he saw that somebody or something was indeed staring across the room at him. His stomach dropped, but he did not cry out. Instead, his hand crept through the darkness to turn on the floor lamp next to the sagging bed.

Click!

In the electric light's yellow glare John-John saw a mirror in which his own dark face was reflected. The expression on the face betrayed his fear.

Hugo was gone. Further, the Dodge Dart was not in the parking lot outside the cabin. Benumbed by this inexplicable desertion, John-John stood in the open doorway staring at the small, swordfish-shaped neon sign burning red and violet above the motel's office building. He stood there for a long time, watching automobiles go by on the highway and waiting for one that looked like the Dart. He felt no panic, for he believed implicitly that Hugo would return for him.

Eventually a Florida state trooper arrived at the motel. He came to John-John with Hugo's room key and the news that his father had just had a serious automobile accident several miles to the west.

Later, after Hugo had died without recovering consciousness, the Monegals were able to reconstruct the sequence of events culminating in the accident. John-John and the state police were instrumental in providing the details that made this story cohere.

Possessed by a desire for vengeance, Hugo had waited for John-John to fall asleep. At last convinced that the boy was dozing, or perhaps even spirit-traveling, he had left the motel and driven back along the highway toward Ritki's Gift & Souvenir Emporium. Before reaching the compound, however, he turned onto a side road, a mere red-clay gash in the pine forest, and parked. Darkness and clustering foliage concealed the car.

Carrying the Remington 30.6 he had bought in Wyoming for his hunting trips and poaching expeditions with Pete Grier, Hugo climbed the little hill behind the animal ranch. At the top of the hill, crouching beneath the fanlike branches of the trees, he had a clear moonlit view of the cage containing the rhesus monkeys. He took a sighting and fired. One of the monkeys—ironically, the female—slammed into the back of the cage, almost as if it had been thrown against a wall, and the entire compound erupted in a hysterical chirping, howling, and braying.

As Hugo stumbled back down the hill, a battery of klieg lights flashed on, illuminating the entire complex and a formidable swatch of highway.

John-John's father fled the scene, obviously intending to return to the motel, but driving recklessly fast. Three or four miles from Ritki's he was intercepted by a trooper going in the opposite direction. The trooper braked, wrestled his car about, and set off after the Dart at high speed, siren and tires screaming. The night came alive with the spooky, peacocklike cries and the revolving blue strobes of one willful machine prodding another to the brink of self-annihilation. Even when the superior horsepower of the state vehicle had plainly decided the outcome of their contest, Hugo kept gunning the accelerator. The result was that the Dart capsized, fired one rear tire off its rim into the woods, and pinned Hugo beneath the steering column and the spectacularly dimpled roof.

Back from her sabbatical in New York, Jeannette was waiting for John-John when he finally got home. Anna was there, too, as distraught as he had ever seen her. By this time Hugo was slowly, painstakingly dying, and no one knew what to say to anybody else to alter, disguise, or soften this fact. It was not Jeannette's fault, John-John knew. No, of course not; it was definitely not his mother's fault. But from that moment he began withdrawing from Jeannette; and later, when it seemed to him that she had taken steps to sacrifice him to her ambition, he did not find it difficult to close the door on his life with the Monegals and to run away from home.

CHAPTER SIXTEEN

Habiline Reflections

THE EVENING THAT Helen returned my pistol I was as nervous as a seventeen-year-old virgin. My confusion had a simple source: I did not know what mode of approach and receptivity must prevail between us. This confusion, baldly stated, has certain humorous overtones that I did not fully appreciate at the time.

Pair bonding, as I believe I have shown, was a common feature of the habiline life style. Although the resident cock of the wadi, or alpha male, might with impunity coerce somebody else's cutie into his clutches, he usually had a favorite among these rotating concubines. In Alfie's case, of course, this was Emily, and after Genly's death she became his permanent live-in.

Observing this, I decided that Alfie had had designs upon Emily from the beginning, but that his status among the Minids and his uneasy relationship with Genly had not permitted him to surrender to out-and-out monogamy. To have done so would have been to risk another serious run-in with his only real rival among the men, for Genly was not so cowed as he sometimes contrived to appear. Therefore, not only to reaffirm his preeminence in the band but also to minimize the chances of a savage knock-down-drag-out with Genly, Alfie had had to bestow his affections upon Guinevere and Nicole as well as Emily.

Inadvertently, then, I had helped provide Alfie with an escape from the prison of his own power. He no longer had to lord it over the wives of Jomo and Fred in order to underscore his chieftancy, for Jomo was too old and Fred too young to represent genuine threats to his leadership. Variety being a much-sought-after spice, Alfie did not completely forgo the company of other ladies while establishing a household with Emily, but his philandering took on a decidedly illicit cast, occurring out of doors and catch-as-catch-can rather than by invitation in the sacrosanct confines of his hut. He was a changed and seemingly happier man.

So was I, albeit a confused one, too. Wherefore my confusion?

First, without deliberately engaging in voyeurism, I had seen plenty. The habilines were an uninhibited people. Their natural rhythms, if you will pardon a phrase with an unhappy history, had an immediate outlet in their personal relationships. Couples coupled when coupling called. Ordinarily they sought privacy in which to answer this summons, but not always. Anyone with eyes would eventually learn that Minid males pressed their suits from behind and that, in order to facilitate disengagement should a dinothere come dithering along or a porcupine prickling past, partners often remained upright. Although I, too, placed a premium on survival, these approaches were not my style.

Second, they were not invariably the Minids' style, either. Sometimes a couple disappeared into a strip of forest, where in a half-hidden bower they lay side by side on plaitings of savannah grass and rocked in each other's arms like children afraid of the dark. (I had once stepped on Malcolm and Miss Jane so disposed.) Was this a nocturne of love or merely a melody of mutual consolation? I did not know, but I had a hunch that among the Minids now, eyes had more to say to them than rump or pubic promontories. Granted, they could still find pleasure in the backward amorousness favored even today by Kalahari Bushmen, but their options seemed to be increasing, their tastes growing more catholic. Slowly, however; very slowly.

Third, dispite all I had witnessed and surmised, I did not yet know if habiline women enjoyed a state of constant sexual receptivity or if they were the love slaves of an estrous cycle. Had Alfie invited Emily, Guinevere, and Nicole in and out of his hut in solitary heats because no other arrangement afforded him the unadulterated pleasure of their company? Or did he, requiring a brief recuperative respite as surely as the next man, order these entries and withdrawals in accordance with a tyrannical cycle of his own? Among chimpanzees the females develop cumbersome sexual swellings to signal their readiness to mate ("pink ladies," Jane Goodall once called the possessors of these fragrant passion flowers), but habiline women, naked under their long and scanty hair, were fortunate in never having to flaunt such gaudy carnal corsages.

I, meanwhile, was unfortunate in having no clue to Helen's designs, if any, on my person. After setting my pistol aside, I drew her to me. Although stronger than I, with hands capable of ripping apart the rib cage of a hippopotamus carcass, Helen did not resist. Her head nuzzled my armpit, and we lay back together on the grasses of my pallet. I think she was listening to my heartbeat, which was bongoing calypso rhythms in the constricted drum of my chest. She listened for a long time. The singing of the melancholy habilines ceased, and the sunset glow on the horizon beyond New Helensburgh gave way to a lustrous eggplant color and a dot-to-dot patterning of stars. Soon Helen was asleep. Putting my uncertainty about her intentions on hold, I too finally slept.

At dawn I awoke to find Helen staring down at me with those bright, smoky eyes. All my previous doubts and apprehensions came surging back. What did she want of me? What did I want of her? How were we to bridge the chasms of anatomy, angst, and animality separating us? A gray light filtered into my hut through the gaps in its thatching, and it seemed to me that Helen and I were tree mice, primed for some rapacious giant's lightning grab.

"What?" I asked Helen. "What do we—?"

Helen lowered her eyes, meaningfully rather than demurely. Her gaze came to rest on my tattered bush shorts. If I could pass the physical, I would qualify in her estimation as a suitable husband. Since coming among the Minids—as, initially, with Babington at Lolitabu—I had been guarded about my biological functions, and to date Helen had had no assurance that I was not as neuter as a Kewpie doll under my Fruit of the Looms. Although I cannot ordinarily do business under the eyes of strangers, Helen was no longer a stranger, and with trembling fingers I moved to allay her doubts.

First, though, I unknotted the red bandanna about my throat and showed it to Helen. She remembered it from our first meeting, when I had attempted to win her over with a bauble and she had spurned the offer by raising both her hackles and her club. This morning, though, the offer charmed her, and she allowed me to tie the bandanna around her neck as a betrothal gift. Indeed, it constituted her entire trousseau. The moment lengthened, and I will never forget the way she looked as we shared it.

Even with my shorts off, I was not entirely a Minid. My mind kept tracking back and forth, sorting data, printing unflattering labels on my natural appetites: *bestial, perverse, reprehensible, depraved.* My parents, bless their souls, would have been appalled by my yearnings, and an old country boy like our Wyoming landlord Pete Grier would have seen more poetry in a farm boy's hasty violation of an indifferent heifer than in my adult attraction to the willing Helen Habiline.

Helpless to prevent what was going to occur, I tried to make a concession to both Good Sense and Conscience. In so doing I confused Helen about the exact nature of my masculinity.

Naked and erect, I rolled aside from Helen, grabbed a foil-wrapped condom from my first-aid kit, and fumbled the ring of folded latex out of its packaging. Then I unrolled the condom's milky second skin over the instrument of our impending union and turned to face my bride. Helen was taken aback. So was I. My sincerity was suddenly suspect, even to myself. Despite the deep affection and healthy lust that the Minid woman had engendered in me, my recourse to a prophylactic declared that I had certain nagging doubts that annulled the purity of my passion. Was I afraid that I might impregnate Helen? No. All the available evidence suggested that she was barren. No, I was not thinking of Helen. The specter of venereal disease, age-old scourge of the promiscuous and the incontinent, had struck from my subconscious and I had grabbed for my first-aid kit. Now, I was momentarily unmanned by the pettiness of my behavior. Helen looked at me wide-eyed. I was a melting Tootsie Roll in a casing of wrinkled liquid latex.

"You probably think I've got to perform lickety-damn-split-quick or I can't do anything at all," I told her, embarrassed.

Cautiously Helen reached out and touched the ring of my condom. She had undoubtedly seen the everted skins of snakes cast on the ground or caught in the forks of trees, but undoubtedly none of the males of her acquaintance had ever reversed the ecdysial process in this priapic particular. Soon her curiosity overcame her fear, and she drew her finger around the ring. Flash-freezing my ardor and unwrinkling my second skin, I saluted, greatly startling her.

"Give me a minute, Helen—I'll take it off."

This was easier promised than performed. Electrolysis, I swear, plucks hair less painfully. But I managed.

Off, the prophylactic still fascinated Helen. She took it from my hands and lifted it over her head as if it were one of those repulsive delicacies favored by the French. She refrained, thank Ngai, from popping it into her mouth, and I took it back. Inspired by the notion that our get-together was a celebration as well as a solemn rite, I inflated the condom's pale skin to the size of a bowling ball and tied it off at the ring as my mother had once tied off party balloons. *Electronically Tested for Reliability* read a legend near the ring. Buoyant, my condom and I demonstrated the innate risibility of tumescence.

Helen's eyes grew wider. Her bottom lip dropped. Then she snapped her mouth shut and reached for the balloon. However, she must have scraped its taut skin with a fingernail, for the next thing I heard was an ear-splitting *P*O*P*!* and Helen's involuntary cry of distress. I went down almost as fast as my condom.

Terrified, Helen rolled away to the wall, clutching her knees and biting her lovely deep-purple lip. Tossing aside the illegible postscript of my French letter, I hurried to apply to her forehead the frank of my consoling kiss. Before Helen could respond, Jomo and Alfie burst uninvited into the hut.

"Jesus!" I exclaimed.

Then I saw their faces. Jomo and Alfie were reacting to the report of the punctured condom, and their bleak expectation— another habiline shot dead—Helen's huddled form seemed all too neatly to fulfill. I struggled to pull the lady upright and myself together.

"It wasn't the pistol, brothers. We popped a balloon. Nothing to worry about. Only a balloon . . ."

Talking soothingly to Helen, I got her to a sitting position. Jomo and Alfie squatted in front of her, looking glances of silent inquiry into her eyes, and she replied by looking back at them the answers they seemed to want. The crisis was past. Helen was alive and well.

The men, noticing my nakedness, scrutinized me skeptically. If they persisted in their contemplation, I reflected, my plumbing would be on the fritz for a week. What I had neither intimidated nor impressed them. After looking at each other with the open-mouthed "play faces" common to young chimpanzees and the children of Kalahari Bushmen, they left the hut and

apparently reported what they had seen to their compatriots outside. A moment later, the Minids were serenading the dawn sky
with a hoarse, many-throated aubade.

I returned to Helen. We settled back on my pallet in each
other's arms. As the strands of untutored habiline singing gradually unraveled into silence, my bride let me coax her round. I let
her coax me round, too. Genly was dead, but we were alive, and
the difference was crucial. With the echoes of twentieth-century
disapproval dying in my mind, I embraced Helen, put my lips to
her brow, and somehow succeeded in joining with her on an elemental level that only a few weeks ago would have struck even me
as unthinkable.

Physiologically, I concluded, Helen enjoyed a state of continuous
sexual receptivity. However, she also experienced ups and downs
of appetite that probably stemmed from her menstrual cycle, for
in this female particular she was almost wholly human. We accommodated each other's needs, and if Helen occasionally withheld herself for several days, these bouts of protracted abstinence
eventually worked to purge me of passion—much in the way that
a lengthy fast inevitably undermines hunger. Together again, re-
discovering the pleasure of the act, we fed on each other like
starving carrion birds. Nor did I ever again insult my lady by
producing a condom and thereby reminding her of how close I
had come to bursting the promise of our romance.

Through discreet observation I confirmed that Helen was
different from most of the habiline womenfolk in the disposition
of her sexual organs. Whereas Dilsey, Guinevere, Emily, and all
the rest had labia set almost directly beneath their anuses, Helen's
genital flower bloomed in a more forward location. This placement made it possible for us to consummate our mutual lusts face
to face, the technique we preferred above all others. The other
Minids, with some infrequent exceptions, as I have noted, usually
mated after the fashion of mandrills and mangy australopithe-

cines—but Helen was a human being in my sight, and our love was not bestial but sublime. I insist upon this point because there are so many people whose prejudices force them to deny what to me was self-evident from the moment of our first coupling.

(Later, of course, I had other, even better, proof of Helen's humanity—but I do not wish to run ahead of my story.)

In the intervals between each rush of passion, Helen and I carried on as friends and companions. Our sense of oneness seldom permitted us to leave the other's sight. I deloused her, and she fed me berries and tree mice. We scavenged, hunted, and foraged together. Side by side, we wandered the veldt and gallery forests. In Ngai's eyes, at least, we were surely husband and wife.

I did not empedestal Helen, though. She had faults that I am not ashamed or embarrassed to record. For one thing, she sometimes stank. Her hair would become matted with grease or coated with dust, and the lack of water in the area made it difficult to remedy these problems. Once, under the pretext of play, I enticed my bride into the last remaining wallow of a rivercourse not far from New Helensburgh and there applied a piece of pumice stone to her back and belly. Afterward she smelled better, and behaved coquettishly, and gibbered at me her girlish gratitude. She did not like to be dirty.

A second fault here springs to mind. Helen could launch one-sided prattlefests, but she could not really talk to me. Although she was hardly to be blamed for this failing, I had begun to miss the sterling inanities of human conversation. I would have given two years' pay and perquisites to hear from her pretty lips a single "Hot enough for you?" or "Have a nice day." Instead I got tuneless scatsinging and a great deal of murmurous blather.

I decided that Helen must learn to speak. During my in-depth training for White Sphinx at Russell-Tharaka Air Force Base, Blair had introduced me to some of the current research on animal vocalization, and my understanding of this subject led me to conclude that Helen's Babelesque cries and whispers were limbic in origin. That is, they had very little to do with the neurology of human speech, which flows like a river of light from the neocortical headwaters of Broca's and Wernicke's regions. Researchers can prod a rhesus monkey to spill its entire reservoir of natural calls by flooding current into electrodes sunk like spigots in the limbic lobes. So primed, the monkeys babble indiscriminately.

By contrast, Helen's prating was uniform in its emotional content and uncoerced, but "primitive" in that it rose from brain tissue older than those from which human speech pours forth, limpid and sustaining. (When, of course, it is not turbid and constipating.) I wondered if Helen had the cerebral wherewithal to learn what I had resolved to teach her. And concluded that she must, not merely because endocasts of hominid brains have given proof of their incipient Broca's areas but also because my habilines possessed a repertoire of sounds so far beyond that of beasts that even I could not satisfactorily ape it.

Human beings have had reasonable success teaching rudimentary American Sign Language to chimpanzees and gorillas. However, I did not know this system, and the gestural language of the Minids already contained subtleties and refinements too nice for my apprehension. Even so, they *best* "talked" among themselves using facial expressions and eye movements, the way wolves are said to reveal a full gamut of canine strategies and desires. Likewise the Minids. A squint or a blink could apprise another in the band of the whereabouts of nearby vegetables. A puckering of mouth or brow could provide a telling gloss on this communication. Both text and gloss, unfortunately, were in an alphabet almost opaque to me, and although I did come to understand a little of Helen's eye language, I made up my mind to teach her English.

I started with pronouns. Pronouns befuddle and exasperate. As in an old Tarzan movie or Abbot and Costello routine, pronouns deny or misconstrue themselves as soon as the instructor thumps his chest or nods pupilward. "I," I said, pointing at myself: "I, I, I." Although Helen could say this word, she pronounced it like the preface to a bloodcurdling hunting cry. No matter. My heart leapt. Of course, when I tried to teach her the word's semantic value, to demonstrate that she had encompassed the concept, she poked me repeatedly in the chest with her gnarled thumb, all the while murmuring, *"Ai, Ai, Ai."* It took me a day to undo the damage, a feat I managed only with superhuman patience and the artful deployment of my shaving mirror.

We named, enunciated, and made meaningful moues in my hand-held mirror. Helen, to her credit, did not lose interest. Because I had not shaved since moving into New Helensburgh, she had never seen my mirror before. It was a circle of glass in an aluminum frame, and she immersed herself in its silver flatteries as a swan immerses itself in water. Each word I shaped was a new excuse to go gliding on her own reflection. Sometimes, indeed, she got so far from our mutual purpose that I despaired of pulling her back. She liked the way she looked, and she had never mistaken her image in the glass for that of a two-dimensional stranger trapped inside the mirror's imprisoning frame.

Helen—as if I required further evidence of the fact—was *self-aware*. My mirror, a miracle, had simply given her a chance to walk on the waters of her self-awareness. I tried to get her to say the word.

"Mwah," she responded. *"Mwah."*

Because she could not simultaneously hold the mirror and preen in its tiny window, she made me hold it for her. Repeating her disappointing approximation of "mirror," she loosened the bandanna I had tied about her neck and lifted it over her nose and lips. For a brief moment, then, she was an Islamic lady proclaiming the privilege and the pain of purdah. Then, hoisting it upward, Helen transformed the bandanna into a blindfold, through whose misaligned threads she disingenuously peered at herself. Up and down the bandanna went, becoming in the process a mammy scarf, a pair of earmuffs, and even a masquerader's polka-dotted domino.

"Say 'bandanna,' " I urged my bride. " 'Ban-DAN-nuh.' "

"Bwaduh," Helen said.

At that moment, trying to keep her bobbing face in the glass, I imagined myself the progenitor of an Ur-Swahili dialect whose descendant tongues would one day be spoken in Kenya, Uganda, Tanzania, and Zarakal. *Mwah* and *bwaduh*—along with *Ai, mai,* and *yooh*—were precious little upon which to base such a fantasy, I realize, but it seemed to me then that Helen and I were making progress. Frustratingly slow progress, but progress nevertheless. I did not want to give up too soon.

According to Jeannette, I had not spoken *my* first recognizable word until I was well past two. Helen was far older than two, of course, but she had been exposed to bits and pieces of a comprehensive linguistic system only intermittently since my arrival. With our auspicious beginning (five "words" in as many days) as a base, given ten or twelve years Helen might well acquire a real oratorical competence.

By the afternoon of our fifth day of language lessons Helen's five-word vocabulary seemed a historic accomplishment. I had not tried to teach her either my name or hers for fear she would ascribe to each an encompassing generic connotation, Joshua becoming "man" and Helen "woman." Too, I had begun to feel a trifle guilty about having bestowed upon her the name of Thomas Babington Mubia's favorite wife. Or maybe about the fact that for most Westerners this name apotheosizes a standard of feminine beauty having nothing to do with my lady's primeval negritude. Our earliest vocabularies corrupt, and what I had learned in the household of Jeannette Rivenbark Monegal had of course influenced—i.e., corrupted—my vision of the world. As for my first name, believing that Helen would be unable to pronounce it, I never spoke it aloud for her.

"Mai mwah," said Helen when we broke for late-afternoon communion with the other Minids on the fifth day. *"Mai mwah."*

She had the mirror—*her* mirror, she had just called it—and before I could retrieve it from her, she left our hut to clamber along a winding parapet of stone to the hilltop where the other Minids were gathered. The old man Jomo was sitting in the shade of the only tree up there, a fig tree, while his consort Guinevere searched his back for lice.

Helen shoved the mirror under Jomo's nose. This act affected him as if she had peeled off his rubbery face and slapped him with it. He reared back, threw an arm around Guinevere, and stared at Helen aghast. I tried to grab the mirror away from Helen, but she murmured, *"Mai mwah,"* and rebuffed me. Jomo, recovering, eased the mirror from Helen's hand and bemusedly ogled his own flat features. Guinevere peered over his shoulder.

Other Minids began to gather, adults and children alike. Now that he no longer feared it, Jomo was jealous of his new possession. He had trouble ignoring the press of curious onlookers, many of whom squatted behind or to one side of him and extended their hands palm upward in patient entreaty. I stood aside and watched. Everyone wanted a moment with the mirror. Possession being nine-tenths of the law, no one moved to snatch the mirror from Jomo, but no one ceased begging, either. Even Alfie had squeezed into a forward position beneath the fig tree.

A slippery portion of himself in hand, Jomo devoured this delicacy while the others appealed to his better instincts for a taste of the same. How could he continue to refuse such a well-mannered plea? In fact, he could not. At last Jomo turned aside from Alfie and surrendered the mirror to his aged comrade Ham, who hunkered with his back to the tree trunk.

To demonstrate to himself the plastic amiability of the goon in the glass, Ham grabbed his nose, blinked his eyes, and tugged his earlobes. A dozen palms wobbled within a foot of his face, stoically demanding their turns, and finally Ham, like Jomo before him, gave in to community pressure. He passed the shaving mirror to Dilsey.

Despite his status as chieftain, Alfie was temporarily odd man out, for Dilsey handed the glass to Odetta, who relinquished it to her toddler manchild Zippy, who grew bored in a matter of seconds and let it slip into the clutches of the effervescent adolescent Mister Pibb, who yielded it to Roosevelt, who, perhaps in remembrance of our previous exchange of gifts, passed the fragile compact to me. Alfie, by now, was looking on with a lugubriousness that almost corralled my sympathy. However, I tore my gaze away, cried, "Wait here—I'll be right back," and hurried down the hillside to my hut. A moment later I was back among the Minids with an aerosol bomb of Colgate lime-scented shaving cream.

The habilines watched awe-stricken as I meringued my face with the shaving cream and then mischievously flicked lather hither and yon to witness their reactions. Horrified to see the lower half of my face foaming away, Bonzo and Gipper covered their eyes while the other youngsters gaped like spectators at an automobile wreck. Malcolm and Ham nervously palpated their own cheeks and chins to assure themselves the phenomenon was not contagious. Gibbering or singing, the womenfolk huddled against their mates for warmth or consolation. Helen, however, withdrew a good twenty feet, squatted on her heels, and put her arms around her knees.

Alfie sidled near. He extended his palm, a plea for my attention. I lifted the can of shaving cream and squirted a ball of foam into Alfie's hand. He flinched but did not scuttle for safety.

Sniff, sniff.

The pungent scent of limes. This implied, even for a habiline, edibility. Seduced by the fragrance, Alfie tasted.

Pfaugh!

He spat out the offending foam and wiped his hand on the ground. Then his palm came up again, and I willingly gave him the aerosol bomb.

Suspiciously delighted, Alfie located the trigger atop the can and spilled into being between his feet a shin-high marshmallow monument. His thumb came up, and he and the Minids contemplated the result. Everyone was impressed, even the architect. He carried the can to the fig tree and put an epaulet of foam on Emily's shoulder. When she fled from his ministrations, scolding him for decorating her, Alfie turned on Daddy Ham and bearded the old man with a snowy dab. Guinevere knocked the can from Alfie's grasp and kicked it between his legs to Malcolm, who, fielding it as gracefully as Maury Wills sucking up a grounder on the second hop, underhanded it to Fred. Fred festooned Mister Pibb with a rope of foam and vaulted into the fig tree. Alfie, Roosevelt, and Mister Pibb pursued him aloft. While the remaining Minids hooted at these inept brachiators, I went to Helen, lifted her to her feet, and led her back down the hillside to our tent.

By this diversion I had saved my mirror.

Looking over my shoulder, I saw the branches of the fig tree dripping with boas of evocative whiteness, almost as if it had snowed in this arid equatorial region of prehistoric Zarakal. A moment later the Minids came charging into New Helensburgh after us, releasing fluorocarbons into the Pleistocene atmosphere and plastering the cracks in our hut with shaving cream.

All that night the odor of decaying limes hung in the air, scenting our citadel, and in the morning the lumps of lather decorating our huts had taken on the honeycombed appearance of bleached and abandoned wasp nests. As for the can of shaving cream, I found it a day of two later in the branches of a small euphorbia bush at the bottom of the hill. Just as I had led Genly into accidental suicide, I had led his compatriots into the temptations of littering and aerosol warfare. *C'est la vie.*

Helen and I kept up our language lessons. The mirror, which earlier had enabled me to confirm the forward placement of her reproductive organs, continued to prove a valuable aid. Unfortunately, its principal value lay in maintaining Helen's interest, for she could not properly shape the words I tried to teach her, and her acquisition of an English vocabulary had stalled at ten or eleven words. *Love,* if you do not count pronouns, was the only abstract term among this number, but whether she recognized its possibilities as a verb, too, I am not yet ready to declare. She could parrot a sentence I had taught her containing this word, however, and I have often consoled myself on melancholy nights by pretending that she knew exactly what she was doing.

The sentence?

Why, "I love you," of course. I do not record it as Helen actually pronounced it because such a transcription would give the sentence a comic cast. Although I am not totally without humor regarding my relationship with Helen, in this instance I do not like to provoke your laughter. All of us cherish certain memories, and Helen's distinctive phrasing of the words "I love you" is one of mine.

CHAPTER SEVENTEEN

Pensacola, Florida

July 1985

JOSHUA CAREERED THROUGH five o'clock traffic on his battered red Kawasaki, leaning first this way and then that, the beach a stinging blur of whiteness to his left and, when too many automobiles and campers blocked the asphalt, the sandy right-hand shoulder of the highway his private corridor to Pensacola. He was dirty, sweat- and paint-stained, but if he tried to stop by the trailer for a change of clothes and a bite to eat, he would probably miss Blair's arrival at the auditorium. He had to get there not merely in time to hear the Great Man's opening remarks, but early enough to waylay him outside the building and let him know that Blair was not the only expert on East African Pleistocene ecology in the Florida panhandle. Joshua Kampa—a.k.a. John-John Monegal—was another, an expert with no formal training but a great deal of eyewitness experience. Indeed, he had convinced himself that his entire previous life had been pointing him toward this meeting with Blair.

Alistair Patrick Blair, the noted hominid paleontologist from the African state of Zarakal.

Weaving in and out of traffic, Joshua repeated the name almost as if it were an incantation, a mantra: Ali*stair* Patrick *Blair,* Ali*stair* Patrick *Blair,* Ali*stair* Patrick *Blair* . . . By repeating the name to himself he convinced himself of the reality of the man's visit and of the inevitability of his meeting Blair. The chant emptied his mind of every distraction, every possible impediment to his goal. The Kawasaki, at the bidding of some implacable Higher Power, was directing itself to Pensacola . . .

Three days ago Joshua had read in the *News-Journal* that Blair was going to speak tonight at one of the local high schools. To raise funds for his researches at Lake Kiboko in the Northwest Frontier District of Zarakal, he was in the United States under the auspices of the American Geographic Foundation for a series of public lectures. This stop in Pensacola, a city not on his original itinerary, was reputedly owing to his friendship with an American military man who had once visited the Lake Kiboko digs with a contingent from the United States embassy in Marakoi, Zarakal's capital. Whatever the rationale, Alistair Patrick Blair was in northern Florida, almost within shouting distance even now, and soon he and Joshua would be face to face on the walkway outside the auditorium.

After all, how often did a world-renowned authority on human evolution—not to mention Zarakal's only white cabinet minister—condescend to show his slides and deliver his spiel to an audience of Escambia Countians? Never before, the paper had said. Blair had visited Miami before, but never Pensacola, and Joshua shot toward this rendezvous like a madman.

For twelve years, ever since he had begun to record his spirit-traveling episodes on tape, Joshua had read and thoroughly digested every book about Pleistocene East Africa, paleoanthropological research, and human taxonomy that he could lay his hands on. In most of these tomes Blair was mentioned as the coequal of all the most prominent fossil hunters and cataloguers to emerge after World War I, and only last year the Great Man had consolidated this position, at least in popular terms, by being the host of the controversial television series *Beginnings*. Who better than Alistair Patrick Blair, then, to answer Joshua's questions, the questions of one who had actually visited the temporal landscapes that Blair's work attempted to reconstruct? Why, no one. No one but the Zarakali paleoanthropologist was likely to confirm the legitimacy of Joshua's dreams.

He arrived at the school nearly an hour ahead of time and sat on his bike at a point on the broad, palm-lined boulevard from which he could clearly see both of the doors by which Blair would be likely to enter the auditorium. His plan would be foiled only if the Great Man was already inside. Surely that was not possible. Blair's time was too valuable to spend exercising his vocal cords with local school officials in an unair-conditioned building. He would arrive from elsewhere, probably under escort.

The school's parking lot began to fill, and people in loose-fitting summer clothes clustered in groups beneath the breezeway fronting the auditorium. Joshua's digital watch said 7:43. Seventeen more minutes. Twilight was congealing. From the pocket of his fatigue pants Joshua removed a small note pad. On its topmost sheet he wrote his name, address, and telephone number. Then, beneath the telephone number, he drew a tiny, five-fingered hand and blackened its interior—except for a stylized eye in the very center of the palm—with hurried crosshatchings. A signature from his childhood, one that he believed altogether appropriate to his impending encounter with Alistair Patrick Blair. He tore the sheet from the note pad, wiped his sweaty hands on his ribbed T-shirt, and folded his message to the paleontologist with care. Many of the people arriving at the school for Blair's talk stared at him, and he suddenly understood why.

A gnomish black man in dirty clothes sitting on a Japanese-made motor bike and fluttering a piece of paper between his fingers as if to dry it. He did not look very much like your typical paleontology buff, and his presence near the school was probably vaguely threatening to some of these people. A security guard in the auditorium's breezeway—a heavyset black man—kept giving him the eye, too.

Five minutes later an old Cadillac convertible—a species of automobile so rare these days that Joshua could hardly believe this one existed—pulled up to the auditorium's side door. Even in the thickening dusk, Blair was a recognizable figure in the convertible's back seat. Joshua knew him by his high, tanned forehead; his dramatic white mustachios; and, his trademark on tour, a loose-fitting cotton shirt embroidered with tribal designs. Joshua kicked his bike to life and gunned it across the boulevard to the sidewalk parallel to the parked Cadillac. He put himself between the convertible and the steps leading up to the auditorium's side door.

"Excuse me, sir. Excuse me, Dr. Blair. I've got to talk to you."

The other man in the back seat—an Air Force colonel in a wrinkled summer uniform—half rose to scrutinize Joshua. "If you've got a ticket, young man, you can—"

"I'm going to buy one at the door."

"Good. That's the way to do it. You can hear Dr. Blair talk without presuming upon his time out here."

"But I—"

"Come on, now. Move that contraption. He's got a program to deliver, and you're holding us up."

Joshua pulled away from the convertible, stationed his bike under one of the palms lining the sidewalk, and darted back through the crowd to intercept the paleontologist on his way into the building. Before anyone could screen him off from Blair or scold him for his unmannerliness, he thrust his message into the Great Man's hand and hurried back down the steps to the sidewalk.

"Don't throw that away!" he called. "Keep it, sir! Keep it!"

Blair glanced down at him curiously, touched his brow with the slip of folded paper, and, to the admonitory murmurs of the Air Force colonel and a second escort in civilian clothes, disappeared through the door at the top of the steps.

Inside, Joshua took up a position against the auditorium's eastern wall. His heart was pounding. Blair and his companions had probably believed him a political activist, possibly one of the opponents of the controversial arrangement whereby the United States had funded, built, and acquired access to a pair of modern military facilities on Zarakali soil, a naval base at Bravanumbi on the Indian Ocean and an air base in the desert interior. Global politics was not on Joshua's mind, however; he wanted to survive the evening and exchange a few words in private with the paleontologist. He was beginning to be sorry that he had not taken the time to change clothes and eat. Most of those in the metal folding chairs on the auditorium's hardwood floor—during the school year, a basketball court—were either pointedly ignoring him or trying to figure out where he had stowed his broom.

Eventually, Blair, the Air Force colonel, and several other people filed onto the stage, and an official with the American Geographic Foundation—an attractive woman in a multicolored summer dress—took the lectern to introduce the Great Man, who stared at his knees or whispered with the colonel throughout her remarks. When she had concluded, the audience applauded warmly and Blair sauntered forward with outstretched arms and an engaging smile. He was in his early seventies, but still vigorous, still a glutton for adulation and work. The stage had been carefully set before his arrival, with props and portable movie screen, and he stalked back and forth along its apron as he reeled off an informal prologue to his program.

For better than twenty minutes, his bald pate shining, his mustachios sweat-dampened and bedraggled, Blair held forth on the differences between his assessments of recent African finds and the assessments of his chief on-the-scene rivals in paleoanthropological research, the Leakeys of Kenya. He and the Leakeys were good friends, he confided, but he liked to rib them for their excesses of enthusiasm. They liked to rib him, too. Blair and the Leakeys were members of one big, opinionated, and diverse family, the clan of hominid paleontologists.

"Although some of our colleagues in other fields have violently disputed the fact, hominid paleontologists are likewise members of another important family. *Homo sapiens* it's called."

This drew a laugh. Joshua laughed along with everybody else, and Blair, encouraged, moved on to the next segment of his performance. The highlight of this segment was an eloquent apostrophe to a plaster replica of the skull of a hominid that Blair, amid much controversy, had named *Homo zarakalensis*. He had discovered the original of this skull two years ago in his Koboko digs, and his frequently ridiculed claim was that *Homo zarakalensis*, or Zarakali Man, represented a distinct form of hominid immediately ancestral to *Homo erectus*, the form that had mutated gradually into the first bona-fide representatives of *Homo sapiens*. In other words, Zarakali Man, an ancient inhabitant of Blair's own country, was the earliest hominid deserving the unscientific description "human." The Leakeys believed that *H. zarakalensis*—a term that Richard invariably placed in quotes as well as italics—actually belonged to the species already known as *Homo habilis*. Indeed, Richard Leakey had argued persuasively that Blair had created an entire species out of a shattered cranium, a jigger of Irish whiskey, and a dash of Zarakali chauvinism. If so, Blair was hardly the first. Paleoanthropologists were congenitally media-oriented.

Now, like Hamlet in the churchyard scene, Blair was flourishing a plaster-of-Paris death's-head and addressing it feelingly:

"Alas, poor Richard!
Thy skull has lain enearth'd three million years,
And several trifling centuries besides.
Thou wast a fellow of finite braininess,
But sufficiently sharp to o'ershadow quite
The brilliant Leakeys' well-beloved *habilis*,
Whom we now perceive to have been a jilt,
And no thoughtful precursor of ourselves,

No germ for genius, no model for Rodin—
But merely, this *habilis,* an upright ape
Of the australopithecine kind."

The Great Man paused, stared into the vacant sockets of the skull, and then began to declaim again, his deep bass voice resonating in the old auditorium like the singing of the sea:

"O Richard, Richard, thou numbskull namesake
Of my late lamented colleague's single-minded son,
Thou hast shaken from our shaken family tree
Not only habilines but southern apes
Of both the robust and the gracile sorts.
And though an ape by any other name
Must needs make a monkey of our nomenclature,
I here proclaim thee, chopfallen Richard,
By which I mean this skull and not thy brother
Leakey of the Koobi Fora lava beds,
Our foremost father in the man-ape line,
Preceding *H. erectus* on the upswing
To our sapient selves. Alas, poor Richard!
Habilis is deposed as well as dead!
In the long-lived, bony ruins of this cold brainbox,
Long live the successor, Zarakali Man!"

Showmanship. Even though this pseudo-Shakespearean rant could not have made perfect sense to everyone there, it inspired intermittent laughter and finally a cascade of applause.

Blair kissed the skull on its brow, replaced it tenderly on the table from which he had first picked it up, and signaled for the dousing of the auditorium's lights. He then narrated a colorful and comprehensive slide program interspersing panoramic shots of the Lake Kiboko digs with close-ups of recent fossil discoveries, the native wildlife, and many of his assistants at the site. He confessed that much of the work at even a fruitful paleoanthropological site was downright boring, and that he was not one of those people who actively enjoyed roaming the lava beds in temperatures of 102° F. In addition, he no longer had the patience for the painstaking work of cleaning a fossil discovery still perilously *in situ*. Younger hands were steadier than his.

Next—something Joshua had not expected—a series of slides devoted to the paintings of a prominent Zarakali artist's fastidious reconstructions of Pleistocene animals. Despite the heat, Joshua began to shiver. It was strange realizing that this artist, working from bone fragments and imaginative taxidermal hunch, had attempted to objectify the persistent subject matter of his dreams. How accurately had she accomplished the task? Indeed, had she accomplished it at all? Joshua was the only one on hand, not excepting Alistair Patrick Blair, who would be able to tell.

"First slide, please."

There jumped onto the screen a fanciful genus of sheep or buffalo called *Pelorovis olduvaiensis*. It had enormous curling horns that measured, according to Blair, ten feet from tip to tip. Joshua had read about this animal, but he had never encountered it during his recurring thalamic jaunts into the Pleistocene and so could reach no conclusion about the accuracy of its depiction. He felt lightheaded, though, as if he had surrendered the burden of those horns to the creature in the painting.

"Next slide."

This one was *Hippopotamus gorgops*, with its projecting brow ridges and periscopic eyes. Joshua recognized it from his dreams, and the artist had expertly rendered the goggle-eyed strabismus typical of this hippo's entire clan.

More slides followed. Giraffes with headgear reminiscent of the antlers of North American moose. Giant baboons, giant warthogs, giant hyenas. Primitive elephants known as *Dinotherium*, with abbreviated trunks and backward-curving tusks. If the paintings of these animals fell short of total accuracy—and sometimes they did—they usually failed by misrepresenting some aspect of the skin or fur: color, texture, markings, length. Wholly understandable errors. All in all, Joshua was astonished by the artist's clairvoyance.

"Next slide."

Several slope-backed animals with manes and horselike

snouts appeared on the screen. The artist had made the manes dark brown and the bodies that luminous tawny color peculiar to African lions. The creatures all had moderately long necks, and Blair, after executing a hammy double take, invited everyone to tell him what these unlikely quadrupeds actually were. "Giraffes!" some people shouted. "Antelopes!" others called. "A kind of horse!" a child's voice cried.

Blair, dimly visible beside the screen, raised his hand. "Well, they *are* a variety of ungulate—that's a vegetarian mammal with hooves—as are all the animals you've just named. But take a closer look at these hippogriffic camelopards. No one seems to have remarked their most distinctive and perhaps oddest feature."

"Claws," Joshua said to himself. Someone in the rear of the auditorium emphatically shouted the word.

"Right you are." Blair stepped into the ray of the slide projector and tapped the feet of one of the animals rippling on the screen. "Very good. Of course, no one has yet put a name to our . . . our camelopardian hippogriffs. What's the matter? Doesn't anyone out there wish to rescue these poor fellows from anonymity if not extinction? They must have a name, you know."

Joshua said, "They're chalicotheres." He pronounced the word clearly and correctly, KAL-uh-koh-THERZ. A lovely word, Joshua had always thought. His saying it took Blair by surprise.

"Ah, a full-fledged paleontologist in attendance," the Great Man said, peering into the twilight grayness of the hall. "Or perhaps a crossword addict."

The audience laughed.

"No, no, I don't mean to joke. Who among you has done his homework, pray? That industrious and discerning soul deserves his own name spoken aloud. It would be fitting, I think, if he announced it for himself. Come on, then, speak up."

Joshua said, "My name, address, and telephone number are in your pocket, sir."

Discomfited by this intelligence and perhaps by his memory of the young man who had accosted him outside the hall, Blair was unable to find Joshua. "Sounds as if our expert handed me a bill of lading, doesn't it?" The audience chuckled only tentatively at this riposte, and the Great Man turned back to the screen. Joshua noted that he was patting a trouser pocket, as if trying to reassure himself that he still had that address slip on his person. He seemed to fear that it had mutated into something unpleasant, like a hernia or a hand grenade.

"Chalicothere means 'fossil beast,'" Blair gingerly resumed, facing the hall again. "I used to know a little ditty about the creature. 'T went, I believe, something like this:

"The chalicothere, that vulgar beast,
Applied his toes to Nature's feast,
Et with élan but not-iquette,
So fell to Darwin's dread brochette.
To spare yourself a like retreat,
Eat with your fork and not your feet."

This was well received. Blair had overcome a moment of perplexity by falling back on a show-biz schtick that had undoubtedly served him well in the past. It consigned the voice of Joshua Kampa to oblivion and permitted an effortless segue into pure lecture:

"Baron Cuvier, the father of modern paleontology, held that any animal with teeth shaped like the chalicothere's and showing wear patterns indicative of vegetarianism—well, he said that any animal of that sort must certainly have hooves. The operative word here, of course, is 'must,' for it ultimately betrayed the poor Baron to the profligacy and the unpredictability of Mother Nature.

"Cuvier died in 1832. The discovery, soon thereafter, of the remains of a chalicothere proved him dead—D.E.A.D.—wrong. Here was a herbivore with monstrous claws on its feet, and no one could satisfactorily explain what the creature used them for. A standard speculation is that the chalicothere dug roots and tubers out of the ground with its nails and so occupied an ecological niche quite distinct from that of most of its fellow ungulates."

"It also ate flesh," Joshua said quite loudly.

"Oh, my goodness," Blair murmured. At his insistent beckoning the lights were turned back on, and, shielding his eyes, he scanned the floor for his kibitzer. "That, I'm afraid, is quite a ridiculous assumption."

"It's a simple statement of fact."

Blair, having finally found Joshua, dropped his hand from his brow and addressed the young man expert to upstart. "The microwear patterns on the chalicothere teeth available to us for examination don't support that 'simple statement of fact.' "

"Then maybe you've got the wrong damn chalicothere teeth, sir. I've seen them scavenging, using their claws as a civet or a hyena might."

"*Seen* them?" The Great Man was broadly incredulous.

Joshua wrapped his arms around his middle, like a patient in a straitjacket. A photographer from the *News-Journal* rose from one of the metal folding chairs, crept forward from the front, and exploded a flash bulb in his eyes. From other angles the man took other photographs.

"Yes, sir," Joshua said, blinking, an audible quaver in his voice. "What I mean is—" He had erred, saying that aloud, but he did not want to back down. The crowd, he could feel, was against him. Having one of the few black faces in the hall did little to endear him to Blair's outraged partisans, but challenging the Great Man in public was the more heinous offense. Joshua could feel their stares going through him like unmetered dosages of radiation. A crazy nigger had interrupted their soirée. "All I'm saying," he resumed, feeling the heat, "is that the chalicothere isn't quite what you people with your microscopes and calipers have imagined it. That's all I'm saying. Is that such an unspeakable heresy?"

"Sit down!" a man in the middle of the auditorium shouted. "Shut your mouth and sit down!" A low murmuring of approval greeted this suggestion. When Joshua refused to budge, however, the murmurs turned into catcalls.

"No insults or abuse!" Blair roared from the stage. "Insults and abuse are to be reserved for scientists attempting to sort out the implications of conflicting theories! This young man and I are scientists, and we are quite capable of insulting and abusing each other without your impertinent assistance!"

Grudgingly the hall quieted.

"Perhaps I should note," Blair continued, the voice of Sweet Reason, "that many East African peoples, members of several different modern tribes, have legends about a creature called the 'Nandi bear.' It's not supposed to be so large as the animals depicted here," tapping the overilluminated images on the screen, "but it has the same downward-sloping back and, according to legend, eats flesh as well as vegetation. I've always felt there is a connection between the Nandi bear and these prehistoric creatures. It is a fact, I'm afraid, that we'll never know everything there is to know about animals that are extinct."

"They're the wrong color, too," Joshua persisted, indicating the chalicotheres on the screen. "You never see them that corny lion color. They're beautifully striped. Brown over beige in wavery Vs that point toward their butts."

"Can't we get him out of here?" another voice called, and the undercurrent of grumbling erupted into jeers and boos. Although Blair might choose to be sweet and forbearing, these people had paid three dollars apiece to listen to *his* lecture, not that of some no-name pygmy with delusions of paleoanthropological infallibility. Joshua did not blame them for wanting him out, but he was powerless to silence himself. These several hours in Pensacola were supposed to mark a turning point in his life, a turning point long deferred, and he was not going to surrender to their hostility.

"And another thing, Dr. Blair, *Homo zarakalensis* is a figment of your imagination, just as Richard Leakey says." Joshua could see that the security guard who had been standing at the rear of the hall was now strolling down the aisle toward him. "*Zarakalensis* is a habiline, just like the hominids discovered by Louis Leakey's son at Koobi Fora in Kenya. You know this yourself, sir."

The booing intensified, and the security guard, the same imposing black man who had eyed him earlier, took him by the arm. "That's enough," he said quietly. "I think you've had your say." His grip a remorseless shackle, the guard led Joshua out of the auditorium to the goosestepping cadence of hand clapping.

"Not only does the young man see into the past," Blair called out to the audience, apparently attempting to quiet it again, "he also sees into the minds of ancient monuments like myself!"

Those were the last of Blair's words that Joshua heard that night.

CHAPTER EIGHTEEN

In A Season of Drought

ONE MORNING WE awoke to find Alfie dismantling his hut, scattering the supports and thatching to the wind. Ham and Jomo, witnessing this activity, attempted to follow suit, but Alfie prevented them. Although he was jealous of his own hut, he apparently wanted to leave a few dwellings intact as decoys. These would give both predators and other house-hunting hominids pause, suggesting to foe and friend alike that the original builders might soon be back to occupy their dwellings. By this stratagem, Alfie seemed to imply, we would get a jump on at least some of our competitors.

It was time to follow the example of the tree mice, the zebras, the gazelles, the wildebeest, and all of Ngai's other children. No rain had fallen here in at least four or five months, and only mongoose, hyraxes, naked mole rats, lizards, grasshoppers, and snakes were going to find this area of the veldt hospitable to their life styles. We had best bid New Helensburgh adieu.

We set out. I had not thought of returning to Lake Kiboko

for weeks, but I *had* seriously considered going the whole hominid and shedding my remaining clothes. However, my bush shorts and chukkas still seemed indispensable. The pockets of the former accommodated many useful items and my scuffed boots had been on my feet so long that I had lost the calluses acquired during my survival training. Along with my shorts and shoes, I wore my .45 in its unornamented holster. My bush jacket was stretched taut across a makeshift travois, upon which I dragged my backpack, my bandolier, and a crude antelope-skin kaross of melons, tubers, nuts, and berries that Helen and I had gathered over the past several days. But because I did not want to renounce my entire past to achieve the disadvantaged innocence of our Pleistocene ancestors, I kept my pants on.

A carefully considered, but ultimately rash, decision.

We moved in good order, the men encircling the women and children. Despite her recent pair bonding with me, Helen continued to play a masculine role. Like Alfie, Jomo, and Fred, she brandished a hefty acacia stave. Malcolm, Roosevelt, and Ham carried lovingly polished antelope bones for clubs, while I, relying on my pistol and the others' martial skills, pulled my travois as if I were a member of the women's itinerant sorority.

Once, far out on the savannah, I turned and looked back at New Helensburgh. Despite the distance I saw a number of two-legged beings swarming over the hillside and along the battlement in front of our abandoned huts. I pointed out these figures to Helen. She cocked her head to one side and for a good half-minute studied their activity. No one else seemed interested, and we moved on. At regular intervals, though, I would glance back at the hillside. Eventually the tiny apparitions scurrying about there came down into the grasslands and completely disappeared from view. I had the distinct, unsettling feeling that the creatures were following us.

We reached the baobab in which we had installed Genly. Ham sang a long, plaintive note in remembrance, frightening several of the children, but we discovered no sign of either our dead comrade or the leopard that had devoured his remains. I worried that in response to Ham's call the leopard would return, thinking that we had brought it another offering. The other Minids apparently shared this fear, for we did not shelter under the baobab but continued our southeasterly trek toward the mountain.

That evening, then, I found myself reciting in my head—with alterations dictated by circumstance—a poem I had first composed in Fort Walton Beach, Florida, after an especially vivid spirit-traveling episode. At the time I had been working during the day for Tom Hubbard's Gulf Coast Coating, Inc., doing research on the Pleistocene at the public library in the evenings, and dreaming my singular dreams every fourth or fifth night. I was nineteen when I wrote the poem, and I never showed it to anyone, not even Big Gene Curtiss, my trailer mate.

Now, though, I decided to speak it aloud to the Minids, who sat or lay among the fig trees and acacias bordering the little gully where we had stopped. "This is called 'For the Habilines Who Have Won My Heart,' " I told them, and I walked back and forth along the bank, declaiming my 2,000,007-year-old poem almost as if I were Alistair Patrick Blair putting on his Richard Burton act at an American Geographic fund raiser. In my own defense, though, I projected my very soul into the words, and the Minids listened to me with rapt self-extinction:

"Your mothers drop you in the dust of unnamed basins.
Your sires rove like jackals on the periphery of extinction.
How I came to be among you is anybody's guess.

Your sun is a gazelle's heart held throbbingly aloft.
You are learning how to pick apart its ventricles.
Scavengers, you speak to me only of your appetites.

Heedless, I ask you of Pangea and its postmitotic progeny.
Laurasia and Gondwanaland are orphans to your understanding.
The incontinence of Africa sculpts you to its needs.

Language begins to sprout in the left brains of the females.
The males poach dexterous insights from the dead savannahs.
Birth remains a labor insusceptible to practical division.

The tools you make resemble plectra for uninvented lutes.
My pocketknife is a triumph no less complex than television.
What percussive music rings above the barren of our rivercourse.

My awe goes ghosting at our austere communal feasts.
Together we break crayfish and suck the slip of birds' eggs.
Our most lovely artifact is a fragile group compassion.

What you make of me is what the millennia have made.
My sophistication is a fossil from the future's coldest stratum.
Am I the last anachronism of what you move toward?"

Yes, a rapt and scary self-extinction. There was no applause when I finished, but no one had heckled or walked out on
me, either, and when I sat down beside Helen to pass the coming
night, she put her arm around my shoulders and huddled near.

Dawn elicited no reverent hymns from the lips of the habilines.
Groggy, we puttered about trying to forage up breakfast and get
our blood moving. We found grubs, a scorpion or two, some desiccated fruit, and a few tiny rock lobsters in the eroded banks of the
rivercourse. Although I missed the singing, I knew that this morning we did not want to give away our position or proclaim this
poor place our temporary capital. We were in transit, and our
rootlessness had affected us all with a subtle sadness.

A holdover complication from yesterday still worried me.
Behind us to the northeast, a mysterious band of two-legged creatures continued to dog our heels. Squinting into the sunrise, I
could barely discern them moving through the thorn scrub, so like
ghosts floating cool and transparent in the haze of mirage were
they. Helen saw them too. As we marched she continually peered
over her shoulder to catch a glimpse of the phantoms, but they
had melted into the landscape and there was little hope of that. I

soon ceased to fear the apparitions, but I never did get over the whispering nag of their presence. They were definitely there, and they were definitely following us.

A little before noon Roosevelt halted and made a strange pawing gesture with his arm. All the other Minids halted too, and a series of significant glances, mostly opaque to me, flew about among the hunters. Ahead of us was a cluster of trees—like an immense green umbrella on a desert of dry grass—and Roosevelt led us toward this copse until the two strange animals laboring in its shade lifted their strange heads, took notice of us, and whickered their strange whickers. They did not run, but they watched us warily, and I began to feel that we had walked into an illustration for an apocryphal bestiary.

I tried not to breathe.

The animals were chalicotheres. They vindicated my dreams. Dry dirt powdered their equine muzzles, and their legs looked inordinately thick and ponderous. Their lively ears and stunning pelts, however, invited admiration. The chalicotheres had been digging with their claws at the base of a tree, digging furiously, and our arrival had interrupted their search for tubers. Despite having seen such creatures in some of my earliest spirit-traveling, today I was an adventurer just stumbled into an enchanted kingdom of dragons and unicorns. Was this meeting really happening? Extinction confers on the has-been the same mythological status that imagination confers on the never-was.

The Minids, unfortunately, had an entirely different perspective on the matter. Alfie approached me, put his hand to my holster, and signaled that I should draw and fire. We had had very little meat since our hut-roast pork, and the Minids saw these chalicotheres as fair game. I did not. Their scarcity suggested that they were already well on the road to Fairy Land, and I wanted no part of hastening their journey, even in the simulacrum past to which White Sphinx had posted me. For all I knew these two chalicotheres could be the last two in the world. My world, and theirs.

"No," I told Alfie. "Hell, no."

Hearing this, the beasts whickered again, bumped into each other, and cantered off to the east, moving like graceless ballerinas on the tips of their incongruous talons. Once, not so very long ago, I had told Blair before a good-sized audience in Pensacola that I had seen chalicotheres eating flesh. I had lied not principally to embarrass the Great Man but to shake his faith in his own preconceptions and to insure that he remembered me. Also, by first deflating orthodoxy in the matter of chalicothere vegetarianism I had hoped to establish my impartiality in attacking Blair's mistaken view of human evolution. If I was a firebrand and an iconoclast, I wanted him to understand that at least I was open-minded about whose altars I burned and whose idols I smashed . . .

Now, watching the chalicotheres retreat, I was ashamed of having lied about them. Like unicorns and dragons, they were lies embodying a lopsided verity. It would have been a dream come true to lasso, bridle, and ride one of those lovely falsehoods. In fact, seeing them pause and glance back at us, as if reluctant to abandon their little bower, I was stricken with a powerful sense of loss. If only I were a wizard or a virgin, it seemed to me, I could have tamed and communicated with those chalicotheres.

Helen entered the cluster of trees deserted by the chalicotheres. Strolling about almost casually, she surveyed the ground. Then, not far from the holes that the animals had been digging, she knelt and picked speculatively at what looked to me like a clump of loose soil. Every few seconds or so, however, she withdrew her fingers as if a thorn had pricked them. Our curiosity aroused, the rest of us pressed into the bower to see what was going on.

My dream beasts, I discovered, had bellies and bowels. Because they had inhabited this copse long enough to litter its floor with excrement, the droppings had attracted a species of coprid beetle dedicated to dismantling each and every pad. The beetles separated the grass-shot dung, shaped it into brood balls, and rolled the balls away for burial. Considering the scarcity of my fossil beasts, this variety of coprid was probably not exclusively adapted to chalicothere dung. No. These beetles were opportunists. They had moved into the bower with such speed and determination because pickings were slim elsewhere, and they had happened to be close by.

The reason for Helen's herky-jerky finger movements had finally revealed themselves. She was trying to snatch a beetle out of a pad already broken down into fragments, but, rearing back on its four hind legs, the little demolitionist refused to cooperate in its own capture. It looked like a miniature triceratops with an additional pair of legs, and it used its horns, mandibles, and forelimbs to fight off Helen's fingers. Between engagements it returned its full attention to the dung pad, as if my bride's persistence annoyed rather than frightened it. At last, though, Helen got the beetle by its chitinous thorax and lifted it high into the air.

As I watched, the other Minids spread out through the bower to find dung beetles of their own. The young habilines—Jocelyn, Groucho, Bonzo, and Pebbles—sought to daze the insects by rapping them with their knuckles, the way I had once stunned and captured a scorpion, but everyone else tried to grab the beetles by the horny plates behind their heads. The competition for the biggest specimen was fierce, and the point of it all seemed to be to acquire the prestige of ownership rather than to satisfy a between-meals hunger. No one hurried to devour the coprids they found. Instead, the Minids pushed their captives along the ground, held them aloft, or flipped them over onto their carapaces to watch their struggles to get right again.

Eventually I overcame my scruples about digging in a dung pad—I had overcome nearly every other, after all—and sat down to fish for a beetle. I caught one a little smaller than Helen's, one with blue-black armor and rakishly plumed legs. It swaggered in my palm, prising my fingers apart every time I tried to make a fist. If we ever got going again, the beetle would not be easy to carry, and I wondered if the habilines would give up their pets when we had to decamp.

Pets. Interesting word, and one that seems entirely appropriate in context. In fact, I think a case could be made that our ancestors' first nonprimate companions were not bung-sniffing dogs but dung-sifting beetles.

Subsequent activity in the bower told me that few of the Minids were going to relinquish their captives. Many of the adults and almost all of the children had beetles stashed in weaverbird baskets, clutched uncertainly in hand, or dangling from pieces of thread unraveled from the tops of my socks.

For Helen I took even greater pains. I cut a piece of tangled fish line from my survival kit and tied it about the thorax of her beetle. Scarabs, you see, were a habiline's best friend, pets that could also be animate, iridescent jewelry. Helen wore her coprid from her left ear. Pendant from not quite two inches of doubled fish line, it twirled and grappled. Each time it caught her hair she shook the beetle loose again, glancing sidelong to watch its perturbations. I hooked my pet over the snap of my holster, but the other Minids were far more envious of Helen than of me. As we resumed our march, the intensity of their admiration apparently made up for the inconvenience occasioned by the beetle's wiggling. Helen was the belle of our lackadaisical anabasis.

Although vanity of this sort has led to scarification, foot binding, bustles, and tuxedos, that afternoon I could not begrudge Helen her small triumph. Three or four hours later, however, when she yanked the beetle off its thread and popped it into her mouth like a bonbon, I was flabbergasted.

The habilines—Helen not least among them—never lost their disconcerting knack of turning my preconceptions upside-down.

Later that day I cut my beetle loose and tossed it out into the savannah. If it were industrious, it would survive. Those who derive their sustenance from others' shit rarely perish. Ecologically speaking, they are the universe's chosen creatures—there is generally available so *much* of what they need to perpetuate their life styles.

CHAPTER NINETEEN

New York City, The Bronx

April 1979

HE AWOKE TO the faint, uncertain cadences of a child's voice—his own voice, as he had sounded at ten or eleven.

". . . *a set of eyes,*" he heard his younger self saying. "*All I am is a set of eyes, and the people I'm watching—they're almost like people, but different, too—they can't see me. They're very hairy, but naked just under their hair. The women-ones have . . .*"

In the three years since Hugo's death Johnny had not wholly accustomed himself to waking up in his mother's eighth-floor apartment in a building overlooking the Hudson River. This building reminded him of a huge tombstone riddled with termite cells. One morning he had cracked the Venetian blinds and caught sight of a bloated human corpse bobbing along in the river. It was worse waking in the apartment at night.

Especially if he had been dreaming of giraffes and gazelles, habilines and prototypical hartebeest. Then it hurt to realize that the beaches of Florida did not lie just beyond the wall—not beaches nor Kansas wheatfields nor the desolate prairies of Wyoming. Nothing familiar to give reality ballast. Of course, he had never been able to hang on to Pleistocene East Africa, but lately his return from each spirit-traveling episode had begun to seem like abandonment on the doorstep of an infernal orphanage. The apartment's heating vents hissed a herpetologist's white noise, and the sounds of sirens in the streets soared above every other noise like coloratura advertisements for the current opera season. In Johnny's imagination, respectable Riverdale was a landscape more saurian than urban.

"... eating meat out of their hands. I don't know what kind of meat because they were already eating it when I began to watch. Baby-ones, and ones older than babies, children I guess, try to make the men-ones pay attention to them. They want ..."

What was going on? Clad only in his Fruit of the Loom briefs, Johnny threw back the covers, put his bare feet on the floor, and cocked his head. He was listening to a portion of his recorded dream diary, the chronicle of his spirit-traveling. This was a segment he had recorded not long after forsaking the complex symbology of his notebooks for the convenience of oral transcription. Since his tenth birthday, when he received the portable recorder, he had logged every one of his spirit-traveling episodes on tape. The cassettes, nearly a dozen, he kept filed in a shoebox, the way some kids stored their baseball cards.

It was 2:27 in the morning. His watch, another gift from Hugo, gave him this reading digitally.

He turned on the tensor lamp hooked over his headboard and padded silently to the closet. He found the shoebox, one hiking boot and a pair of tennis shoes nearly concealing it, and in the box, as neatly aligned as if by the Dewey Decimal System, eleven cassettes. The symbols with which he had cryptically decorated each little talking book told him that these were the originals, not clever substitutions meant to throw him off the track.

"... with their arms around them. Some of them pass meat to the children when the men-ones give it to them to do that. There are, well, families, sort of. They eat together, but usually ..."

His own childish voice was inexpertly recapitulating one of

his spirit-travels, a particularly vivid one, but the cassette on which he had chronicled this dream reposed under his hand in its usual place, undisturbed. He set the box back on the closet floor and reeled out of his room toward the sound of his own prepubescent voice. At the entrance to Jeannette's bedroom-study he halted and stared at his mother. Because she was sitting at her tilted desktop, a kind of drafting board, making notations in ink on a long sheet of type-covered paper, she did not see her son come up behind her.

Galley proofs you called the kinds of pages on which she was working. You got them when a manuscript you had submitted to a publisher was just about to become an honest-to-God book. This, then, was a project that Jeannette had almost brought to completion. For the last three or four months, however, she had been complaining about how badly her work was going.

On a shelf above the drafting board hummed a portable tape player much like the one Hugo had given John-John. Jeannette suddenly punched a key, rewound the machine, and punched a second key to activate her son's youthful voice again.

"... give it to them to do that. There are, well, families, sort of. They eat together, but usually the babies, the children, move around to get what they can from whoever's handing it out. Later ..."

"What are you doing?" Johnny interrupted John-John's voice, his sixteen-year-old tenor overriding his ten-year-old boy soprano.

Jeannette started, gasped, dropped her ballpoint pen. She was wearing a white dressing gown embroidered about the collar and hem with an Egyptian motif (King Tut's treasure had come through town during the nation's Bicentennial celebration, inflicting jackal hieroglyphs and golden cobra rings on the devotees of haute couture), and her hair was clasped at her nape in a way that made her look like a girl. Recovering slightly, she gave a mighty sigh and stabbed the cassette recorder to a standstill.

"What are you doing?" Johnny demanded again.

"Having the huckleberries scared out of me. What are *you* doing, Master Monegal?"

"You've taken my tapes out of their shoebox and copied them, haven't you? You've made your own cassettes. Why?"

Instead of answering Jeannette shuffled the long galley sheets together. Johnny glided across the room and took them from her hands.

EDEN IN HIS DREAMS

The Past Through Oneiromancy, A True Story

Jeannette R. Monegal

A VIREO PRESS BOOK   * *   New York

This book was about him, and Jeannette had neither informed nor consulted him. She had put his skin on a typewriter platen, rolled it into place, and, if he knew anything about her literary inclinations, banged out one of those "inspirational" tomes that lay waste subject and author alike. The lares of candor and the penates of depth analysis were the tutelary deities of such writers, and Jeannette had sacrificed him to these gods.

Angrily riffling the galley proofs, Johnny picked out words like *allopatric, endocranial, speciation,* and *collective unconscious*. His own name was on nearly every page, with passing or extended references to Seville, Spain; Van Luna, Kansas; Cheyenne, Wyoming; Fort Walton Beach, Florida; and New York City. At last he let the pages go and watched them sideslip to the carpet in a random scatter.

"It's scheduled to appear this fall, isn't it?"

"I was going to tell you."

"When?"

"As soon as everything was set. I'd intended it as a surprise, a tribute to what you've suffered, John-John."

"Oh, I'm surprised. Yes, ma'am, one thing I am is surprised. God *damn!* am I surprised."

"Johnny—"

"I was going to see it when it came out. I'd be strolling along Sixth Avenue past the goddamn Vireo Press bookstore, and *pow!*—like a karate chop to the windpipe—I'd see *Eden in His Dreams* by my very own mamma. *That's* when I was going to see it, *that* would've been the surprise. Lord, Mamma, I feel like throwing you out the window without even opening it. How'd that be for a surprise?"

"Johnny, please."

"I like your title, though. It's a helluva lot classier than your last one. It's a rip-off, too, of course—but a *subtle* rip-off."

Jeannette had called last year's book for the Vireo Press *I Couldn't Put It Down, and I Was Sorry When It Ended.* It had been a collection of whimsically philosophical essays about American reading habits since the advent of commercial television in the late 1940s. At least three different reviewers, working on three different urban newspapers in three different cities, had independently arrived at the same five-word notice for Jeannette's book ("I could, and I wasn't"), but it had sold nearly forty thousand copies in hardcover and ten times that in paperback. The success of this book, her second, had enabled Jeannette to pioneer a totally independent life without taking Anna out of college or putting John-John to work evenings as a bus boy or carhop. She undoubtedly believed that a little gratitude was in order.

"Listen," she began, calmly enough. "Listen, Johnny—"

"If you go ahead and publish this, Mamma, I'm going to . . . I can't *believe* you've done this, I really really can't—"

"Johnny, two-thirds of my advance money is spent. I've missed my deadline twice."

"You said you were doing a book on Dust Bowl days in de heart ob de heart ob de country."

"Stop it. I was. I am. But this took me over, John-John, it took precedence, I intended it as a—"

"Yeah, I know. A tribute."

It was a "tribute" that marked a rupture in their relationship as vast and unbridgeable as the Great Rift Valley itself. Jeannette, he told himself, was not really his mother; she had never viewed him as anything other than a social experiment, as some people might gingerly indulge a proclivity for pedophilia or peach-flavored soda pop. For sixteen years he had been her personal experimental subject. It was past time to end his mother's experiment and to discover who he was without her aid or intervention.

"Do whatever you want," he told the woman at the drafting-board desk. "Publish it, don't publish it. You're never going to see me again, anyway. Not ever, *mujer.*"

"You're sixteen, Johnny. You've got another year of school. Do you think you're ever going to—"

As if constrained by weight limits other than those dictated by his own size and strength, he packed light. His mother—the woman named Jeannette Monegal—watched him, but he had nothing more to say to her and got out of the apartment as quickly as he could.

Dressed for the mid-morning chill of April, he caught a taxi across the George Washington Bridge into Jersey. This trip cost him dearly, so he hitchhiked into Paterson, riding high in the cab of a West Point Pepperel semi. The driver, a burly man with a soft southern accent, had a rattlesnake skin stretched across the dashboard. The skin resembled a dingy cellophane scabbard, and the hitchhiker put his hands between his legs to keep from accidentally touching the discarded sheath.

The driver grinned a great deal but talked only intermittently. In Paterson he agreed to carry the hitchhiker right down the turnpike into Dixie, if only his passenger would sing to keep him awake. The driver preferred songs that were either sprightly or obscene. Or both. "La Cucaracha" proved to be one of his particular favorites, and the hitchhiker sang it virtually without letup for the first sixty miles on the turnpike.

"That's pretty," the driver told him. "What's your name?"

"Kampa," said the hitchhiker. "Joshua Kampa."

"Right," the driver responded, wringing the steering wheel as if it were a dishrag. "Only a Mexican could sing 'La Cucaracha' the way you do . . ."

CHAPTER TWENTY
A Disappearance

HELEN WAS THE one who finally made a clear sighting of the creatures that had been following us for the past two days, and she informed the rest of us by throwing back her head and emitting a single ear-splitting bark. To the east, not more than two hundred yards away, I saw three small figures looking at us from the lip of a wedge-shaped kopje. They scrambled out of view as soon as Helen's cry reached them, but I no longer had any serious doubts about the identity of our pursuers.

A large band of gracile australopithecines—*A. africanus*—had been moving almost parallel to our own line of march, using the high patches of savannah grass and the oasislike islands of thorn trees and acacias as blinds. Since my arrival in the Pleistocene I had seen only a few representatives of this supposedly well-distributed hominid species, always at a great distance. Although I had seen members of the allegedly rarer *A. robustus* at closer range, circumstantial evidence suggested that both species were rapidly dying out.

Alfie and the other Minids wasted no pity on the australopithecines. Now that they understood how close our tag-tails had drawn, they seemed to be considering the wisdom of a sally against them. A nervous alertness informed everyone's behavior; the men kept exchanging glances and making noisy feints in the direction of the graciles, who, after skeedaddling to deeper cover, remained altogether out of sight for the next hour or so. As I had not wanted to shoot a chalicothere, neither did I wish to join a war party against our hobbity shadows to the east.

Helen came to me and peered into my eyes as if trying to communicate a profound or frustratingly complex notion. We had paused for a moment on the edge of an arroyo, and I stared down into the cracked stream bed trying to arrange my intuitions into a sensible pattern. What did Helen want to convey? I had no idea. She, as if to prompt me to comprehension, patted one lean, hairy breast and made a mewling sound. Again, shrugging my shoulders and opening my hands to demonstrate my bewilderment, I wished fervently that she could speak. Charades have never been my forte.

"Helen—Helen, I don't know what you want."

Helen retreated from me, leapt down into the stream bed, and began following it northward, back the way we had come.

"Helen, what are you doing?" I cried. "Where are you going?"

The other Minids seemed unperturbed. I jumped down into the gully and trotted after her, but she waved me back without ceasing to retreat from us. When she clambered up the eastern bank, plunged into a thicket some thirty or forty yards farther on, and completely disappeared from my vision, my heart sank. I was astonished and hurt. Later, with more facts at my disposal, her departure made sense, but at the moment it struck me as arbitrary, erratic, and maybe even suicidal. The last glimpse I had of her was a flash of vivid red from the bandanna about her neck, and that red seemed frighteningly portentous.

Reluctantly I followed the others.

Afternoon sloped into evening. What was going on? How

had I offended Helen? By failing to understand her? By refusing to make bellicose gestures at the band of *A. africanus* shadowing us? Had Helen's disillusionment with me sent her off across the savannah in search of another husband? Pathetically egocentric, these questions pinched at my forebrain and hung on like angry crayfish. Reason would not shake them loose. I began to wonder if I could survive without Helen.

Toward twilight we approached a water hole on whose opposite bank stood a female black rhino and her hairy calf. They snorted at the water, nuzzling it with vaguely prehensile lips. The evidence of their hides—splotched, mud-caked, rubbery-looking—suggested that they had already enjoyed a good wallow and were now just fooling around, keeping other thirsty animals at bay by refusing to depart. Swarms of bot flies danced about their impervious bodies, looking for dry places to alight.

Ham led us down to the water hole to drink, and the rhinoceroses' piggy eyes strained after our outlines while their big purse-shaped ears absent-mindedly tracked our chatter. Much to my relief, they did not attempt to chase us off.

When the Minids and I had finished drinking, Malcolm took up watch in a tree.

The darkness had a tincture-of-iodine quality about it, and my anxiety over Helen's desertion had begun to take on a hysterical edge. Unable to sit still, I paced the western shore of the water hole. Alfie and the others divided their attention between me and the rhinos, which finally lumbered up the opposite bank and out onto the evening grasslands.

Suddenly Malcolm hooted a warning from his tree, an urgent warning, and I hurried to join him aloft. All the other Minids took cover, too. Soon I was installed in a pale, polished tree fork higher than Malcolm's lookout, and I saw that a pack of giant hyenas was approaching the two departing rhinos. Above Mount Tharaka the full moon—a huge, luminous brood ball—heaved into view, spotlighting the confrontation on the veldt.

The hyenas' joint purpose was to induce Junior to charge, thereby separating him from Mamma and making it possible to gang-tackle him. To this end, two of the hunger-crazed hyenas danced in, swatted the calf on his fuzzy fanny, and darted away. Mamma blustered from place to place, trying to disperse the hyenas, but because they saw far better than she or Junior did, they could easily skitter out of her path. In fact, her huffy offensive maneuvers seemed to be wearing Mamma down. Junior jostled along in her lee whenever he could, but his mother's increasing frustration and bad temper kept deflecting her into stupid games of tag with their tormentors.

Most of the hyenas, I noticed, were sitting some distance away, watching. Their eyes were yellow agates in the moonlight. The dog work of harassment they left to a pair of agile bullies who stood nearly four feet high at their shoulders. The noise from this scrimmage—the lunges, snorts, and foot feints—seemed somehow remote. Abstractedly I wondered if a kill on either side would take my mind off Helen, and if the Minids could get in on the spoils. So far the contest had engendered only sound and surliness, most of it from Mamma.

This changed. When the female thundered to her left to rout one lean hyena, Junior rashly attacked the renegade nipping at his flank on the right. His charge took him forty or fifty feet toward the hyenas lounging in the low grass east of the water hole. Several of these creatures sprang up to capitalize on his folly. Almost before I could blink, the calf was down, thrashing and squealing as a pair of his assailants dragged him along by his skinny tail and one hind leg. The remaining hyenas rushed in to rip open Junior's belly.

The calf's high-pitched protests turned Mamma around. Stampeding to his rescue, she bayonetted one monstrous hyena with a dip of her snout. With a resounding crack that probably signaled a broken spine, the wounded animal flipped brains over butt to its back. As the other hyenas scurried for safety, Junior was able to regain his feet. He trotted to Mamma for consolation.

The set-to was over, for the hyenas had lost the will to test the huge female again. Secure in their triumph, Mamma and Junior angled off into the bush. Their departure was dignified, even lordly.

Once they had gone, the hyenas moved in to tear the guts out of their fallen mate. Jockeying for position, they nudged the carcass, quarreled viciously with one another, and fed.

Alfie, in the tree next to mine, periodically hurled a piece of debris at the hyenas—a fruit husk, a scab of bark—but with more symbolic than real effect. The hyenas went on gorging themselves. As they were finishing up, several of them broke away and crept down to the water hole to drink. Stranded aloft, we intensified our efforts to drive them off, hurling whatever came to hand: rotten limbs, nuts, berries, old birds' nests, the works. We also assaulted the hyenas vocally, carrying on like banshee divas at an operatic wake.

This aggressive strategy boomeranged. The hyenas—the entire pack, at least a dozen—withdrew from the roiling water hole without really surrendering it to us. They either prowled the edges of the thicket or lay in the grass out of missile range. Our dissonant abuse did not greatly upset them. They were prepared to wait us out.

Vultures settled out of the air, as if from the mother-of-pearl uterus of the moon, and the night kindled with insect song and lethargic wing beats.

We were under siege, the Minids and I, and it occurred to me that in times of trial a resourceful people nearly always finds a means of allaying its fears and bolstering its courage. Usually either an acknowledged leader (F.D.R., say) or a person with a special attention-focusing talent (Betty Grable, for instance) steps in to nerve, comfort, and cheer the demoralized multitudes, by oration or tap dance.

None of us was in a position to tap dance. But because the Minids required this kind of psychological boost, I decided that I must speak to them in the forceful and reassuring tones of a story-telling patriot. Or maybe I simply needed to reassure myself. In any case, I told them a tale, a spur-of-the-moment tale, that probably ought to be called "How the Reem Got Her Horns."

"Once upon a time," I declaimed, furiously free associating, "the rhinoceros had no horns at all. Further, in those distant days she was known by her Creator, Ngai, as the reem rather than as the rhinoceros. This later word, O habilines, implies the possession of a horn that the reem did not yet have.

"I want to tell you how she got it.

"Yes, in those days the reem was a miserable, defenseless creature whose great size was her only seeming asset. In truth, she could seldom use her size to good advantage because she was slow, hard of hearing, and near-sighted to boot. All the other animals, including even the hares and the hyraxes, taunted her with impunity. It had not taken them long to discover that her armo plating was something of a sham, for her skin was thick only a the underlayer. Provided one knew just where to strike, the reem could be made to bleed like a hemophiliac.

"One day the dog, an ill-bred jackanapes, amused himself for several hours at the reem's expense. He nipped her flanks, chewed her toes, and, every time he took a turn beneath her belly, tickled her teats. By late afternoon several more animals—the behemoth and a retinue of lesser bullies—had joined this game, and the poor reem was soon a rucksack of tears and shapeless fatigues. Slumped on the ground, she waited for darkness to drive her tormentors to their beds.

"Later, when they had departed, the reem resolved to petition Ngai for aid. He had overlooked her when distributing such self-protective necessities as speed, cunning, ferocity, and camouflage, and she was determined to upbraid him for his carelessness, to shame him into playing her fair. Despite her weariness, then, she set off before dawn to visit the Creator in his dwelling on the slope of Mount Tharaka.

"Many days elapsed between her departure and her arrival, and the Creator, disguised as a highlands blue monkey, saw her coming even before she had reached the foot of the great mountain. He remembered how he had inadvertently slighted her on the Sixth Day of Creation, and his irritation at being reminded of this negligence prompted him to climb into a tree. From this vantage he hurled a fusillade of fruit at the ugly creature lumbering up the wooded draw toward his dwelling.

"The reem endured the Creator's fit of pique. Eventually he stopped flinging missiles and asked her in an aggrieved tone what she wanted of him. The reem was glad to be asked. She explained her predicament—the shame of her defenselessness—and demanded a boon to offset the handicaps with which he had so pitilessly encumbered her life.

" 'Very well,' said Ngai. 'Go back down to the plain and practice your running.'

"The reem did so. She discovered that the Creator had given her speed of a kind. In short bursts she could run as fast as the antelope. However, she tired easily, and it struck her that animals with more endurance would still be able to trifle with her, to treat her as meanly as they liked. She returned to Mount Tharaka and bearded Ngai in a garden of fragrant succulents.

" 'It is a help,' she said, 'but it is not enough.'

" 'Not enough?' the Creator demanded, scandalized. 'Not enough?'

" 'No, Your Godship. And I do not intend to leave until you have made it possible for me to do so without fearing for my safety among the other animals of your creation.'

"Scowling, the arrogant little blue monkey picked a pair of nearby palm leaves, shaped them into funnels, daubed them with silt from his sacred stream, and stuck them into the reem's open ear holes. What a difference! Full of wonder, the reem listened to the wind, the lyric babbling of the water, and the plangent cries of tiny, cloistered birds. She rotated her ears to catch every quiver and frequency of sound. Her augmented hearing pleased her greatly. Nevertheless, another objection took shape in her mind, and she hurried to intercept Ngai, who was busy climbing to a nest of woven twigs and colobus fur.

" 'Wait!' she cried. 'Wait! Some of those who torment me are as silent as the stars. The leopard and the dog still have power over me. Please, O Mighty One, have pity on my helplessness.'

"The Creator was so angered that he took his own name in vain, but his exasperation did not alter the fact that the reem had spoken truthfully. Ngai calmed himself down by degrees.

"Night had fallen by this time, and a horned moon floated above Mount Tharaka like a weapon. Seeing it, the Creator gathered so much air into his monkey lungs that the reem was left gasping for breath. He thereupon grew into his primordial incarnation as Big Gorilla Ngai. In this awe-inspiring form he strode to the top of Mount Tharaka and ripped the gleaming moon from the sky.

"This was not easy, however. The moon did not want to come down from the sky and so put up a struggle. Gorilla Ngai nearly had to herniate himself to achieve his goal. When the moon finally came unstuck from the heavens, his anger was such that he snapped the horned moon across his hairy thigh and carried the halves down the mountain in heavy-footed disgust. As he descended Mount Tharaka, he grew smaller and smaller. By the time he reached the astonished reem, he was no bigger than an adult baboon and still shrinking.

" 'Here,' he said peremptorily, and he fixed the halves of the moon to her snout, one behind the other. 'Now, my impertinent bicorn, I beg you to leave me—so that I may sleep and, sleeping, recover my godly strength.'

"He had dwindled to the size of a tree mouse.

"This display, besides literally taking her breath away, thoroughly and chastened the reem. Indeed, she forgot to petition the Creator for better eyesight. Considering his current disposition, though, that was probably just as well.

"Down the mountainside she galloped, scything her head

this way and that. Her heart, like a gemsbok melon, was brimming with sweetness, and the world seemed altogether lovely, one glorious, balmy wallow.

"Alas, several hours from home the reem found herself face to face with the pestilent dog. After circumnavigating her great bulk and gazing scornfully at her snout, he began to snigger.

" 'Horny toad will be envious,' he declared. Then, disdainfully, he trotted past the reem. Once behind her, however, he whirled and nipped at her backside. The reem also whirled, so quickly that the dog was dumfounded. His snout was inches from her warty face.

" 'Have a care for my feelings,' the reem admonished him. 'If you do not, I will be forced to deal harshly with you.'

"This warning, from such a notorious weakling and blunderer, infuriated the dog. Determined to put her in her place, he leapt for her throat. He did not come down alive. The reem impaled him on both her horns, shook him loose, and kicked him into a gully like a pancake pile of steaming dung. So much for the dog.

"Upon learning of his death, the other animals fell into a lengthy round of debate and recrimination. How had the reem become so powerful? All were outraged that the butt of their merciless merrymaking had suddenly acquired strengths comparable to or greater than their own. Who could be behind this heinous betrayal? Why, only the Creator, of course, and he must be made to pay.

" 'We must annihilate Ngai,' the tusk-bearer told the behemoth and the other animals. 'We must kill the Creator.'

"Soon everyone on the plain had taken up the cry 'Kill the Creator!' And so aroused, they shambled off in unruly ranks toward his dwelling on the mountain.

"The reem, alerted to their intentions by their cry, hurried to warn her unsuspecting benefactor of the mischief afoot. In his dwelling on the slope the reem found Ngai febrile and shrunken, no bigger than a dung beetle. Quickly apprised of his subjects' intentions, he begged the reem to take him aboard (he would sit between her horns) and give him passage to the safety of an uninhabited southern desert. The reem readily acceded to this request.

"When the tusk-bearer, the behemoth, and the others found the gardens on Mount Tharaka bereft of Ngai and saw the dust clouds billowing from the southern plains, they deduced that the reem was assisting the fugitive. Still, a vigorous pursuit would accomplish their capture, for she had insufficient stamina to maintain her pace and the Creator himself could hardly be at his best if he had chosen this unorthodox method of escape.

"Indeed, the reem soon began to tire. She halted in the broad vacancy of the savannah to recover her wind. Instead she lost a little—for at that moment she felt the necessity of relieving herself and let fall several droppings. Almost at once a coprid beetle that had been sleeping nearby awakened and scurried over to make use of this unexpected windfall.

" 'Hurry,' the Creator squeaked, peering over the reem's brow at their pursuers. 'They're nearly upon us.'

" 'Yes, oh yes,' the reem acknowledged, holding back tears. 'And the next time I stop they will certainly overtake us. Even though I am willing to die *with* you, Ngai, I would far rather die *for* you—but I'm exhausted, almost at my limit, and whatever befalls us, befalls us.' She tactfully did not mention that Ngai might have solved this problem by granting her stamina along with his other tardy favors, but she *was* sensible of the irony of their plight.

"The dung beetle, who was not blessed with a sense of the ironic, had overheard this exchange between Ngai and the reem. He forsook the reem's droppings to circle the beast and address her from a point just below her drooping snout.

" 'I love the Creator well,' he piped, 'for he has provided for me abundantly. The world is full of manure. Tell the Sacred One to come down from your horns. I will then enclose him in a concealing brood ball.'

" '*A brood ball!*' exclaimed Ngai and the reem together.

" 'At your service, O Mighty One,' replied the coprid. 'By

this expedient the reem may run ahead as decoy while you husband your strength and purchase enough time to reestablish your rightful rule.'

"The Creator, won over by the beetle's sincerity, agreed. It was not pleasant being plastered up inside a dung ball, but it was preferable to being murdered.

"The reem, meanwhile, trotted off to the south, drawing the Creator's enemies after. When next she stopped, they surrounded her—rather warily, she noted—and vilified her as both a traitor and a trollop. Surely, they implied, she had done beastly things to entice Ngai to bestow such lethal armament upon her. Where was he, anyway?

" 'I have no idea why he equipped me with these horrors,' the reem asserted, craftily scything her snout this way and that. 'I asked him only for the birthright withheld from me on the Sixth Day of Creation—better eyesight or more gracefully turned ankles. After killing the dog with these horns—accidentally, you understand—I realized what a cruel trick the Creator had played on me, depriving me of my peaceful nature and equipping me with these abominations. I determined to use his evil gifts to wreak my vengeance upon him, for in that, I felt, there would be a great deal of justice. However, Ngai saw me coming and fled Mount Tharaka toward the south. If you, my friends and fellows, will join me in this crusade, I am certain that very soon we will run the rapscallion to ground.'

"This speech much impressed the animals, most of whom followed her southward for three more days. I should add, however, that many of the dogs' relatives demurred. Grumbling without much conviction about their comrades' guillibility, they began the long trek home. On their way they chanced upon the brood balls of the beetle who had confined the Creator in some of the reem's aromatic waste.

" 'Look,' said one of the dogs. 'See how large this ball grows. And the beetle does absolutely nothing to help increase its size. This demands our undivided and most reflective attention.'

"The dog's many kith, kin, and kind sat down to observe

the strange brood ball, while the coprid, who had begun to regret his involvement in the entire affair, stayed out of sight.

"Ngai was sweating in his little prison. He knew that, outside, the dog's family sat in a suspicious ring, waiting for a fateful revelation. Although his strength and size were slowly returning, he was still no match for a pack of dogs. Therefore, making the best of a bad situation, he nourished himself on the surrounding dung (just as would the larva of a coprid) and mixed his sweat with the remaining material to provide the ball with an ever thinner and more transparent rind. This labor cost him much effort, and its sacred heat imparted to the brood ball's surface a silver-gold glow.

" 'Ah ha!' cried the dog's family. 'Here is the culprit, here is the Dastardly One responsible for our brother's death.' And they immediately came forward and began nosing the brood ball, which had by now attained the size of, say, a tsama melon.

"As it happened, all the other animals were returning from their unprofitable Wily God Chase when they saw the dog's relatives playing ball with a luminous sphere. To winkle out the secret of the ball's remarkable contents took them only a moment—that glow was a dead giveaway—whereupon they joined in the game.

"The Creator was kicked and pushed from one end of the bushveldt to the other, and in a short while his head ached fiercely. It had been all he could do to keep the expanding brood ball from splitting open and spilling him out on the ground—to be trampled, bitten, pecked, and gored. Probably to death. Undoubtedly to death.

"And then the reem appeared. She narrowed her piggish eyes in an attempt to follow the action, but twilight had come and all she could really tell was that the animals were scurrying about in pursuit of an incandescent ball. My god, she thought, my God! Those animals have rooted out the truth.

"Shaking off her weariness, the reem charged. What she could see best, of course, was the glowing brood ball, and she rushed toward the shapes shoving it about.

"Ah, what a collision!

"The reem lifted the Creator into the sky with her horns. Upward and away he whirled, there to replace the moon he had broken.

"So that is how the reem acquired her horns, and likewise how the moon was restored to glory after a brief dethronement. Much is taken, but much abides."

And, surrounded by hyenas, we continued to abide in the trees beside the water hole. Ah, but Helen had taken herself from me, I remembered, and my story had not really helped me to disguise this unsettling fact from myself.

CHAPTER TWENTY-ONE
Blackwater Springs, Florida
July 1985

LATE IN THE afternoon of the day following Alistair Patrick Blair's lecture in Pensacola, Joshua was in a small community several mile north of the vast ordnance ranges of Eglin Air Force Base painting a water tower. He was suspended beneath the hemispherical belly of the tank in a set of rope falls, stretched out almost horizontal to the ground, when he saw a dark blue vehicle enter Blackwater Springs from the southeast. Lackadaisically rolling paint onto the underside of a thick steel supporting girder, he watched the automobile out of the corner of his eye. Its movement along the highway was in decided contrast to the little town's stubborn lack of animation. So far, the most entertaining groundside event of the day had involved a pack of dogs. Heatedly quarreling among themselves, the dogs had followed a lame mongrel bitch into the alley behind the Okaloosa Café. You could see a lot from a hundred feet up, but in Blackwater Springs not very much of it was edifying.

Joshua was an employee of Gulf Coast Coating, Inc., a Fort Walton company specializing in sandblasting, painting, and sometimes epoxying a variety of large metal structures. Water tanks. Bridges. Mining equipment. Towers. Joshua had been nearly six years on the job—ever since running away from home and arriving back in Florida from New York. Although he routinely checked his safety belt before changing altitudes beneath the tank, he had long since lost his fear of falling. The cardinal rule of the steeplejack, or water-tank mechanic, was to keep his brain in gear. Joshua usually did, for which reason, along with experience, he was probably the best man in a set of falls then employed by Gulf Coast Coating, Inc.

As talented aloft as Tarzan.

That was what Tom Hubbard, the president of the company, said about him. Hubbard knew Joshua's worth, and Joshua knew that he knew it, and the result was that Joshua sometimes took liberties with his work schedule or made disparaging remarks about Hubbard's business acumen. If the boss got his back up and canned him, Joshua could count on being rehired within a week or two, so long as he appeared repentant and asked for his job back. In six years Hubbard had canned and rehired him a grand total of fourteen times. This game united the two men in a resentful dependency on each other.

Of late, though, Joshua's discontent had begun to outpace his boss's. He had finally realized that he was never going to own his own tank-painting company. Or any other sort of business, either. What the future held for him, if he continued to jockey up and down in harness, was thirty more years as a blue-collar trapeze artist, right up to the day his brain clicked off and he tumbled ninety feet to the concrete or touched his spray gun to a power line and electrocuted himself. In time, both his luck and his skill would run out.

If he survived, he would look like a Jim Crow version of poor old R. K. Cofield. Cofield was a sixty-year-old peckerwood from east Alabama, who, at the moment, was operating a blasting hose in the tank directly over Joshua's head, doggedly stumbling about in a sandstorm of his own creation. Out from under his blasting hood the old man was a toothless zombie; he had once broken his back in a fall, and his eyes absolutely refused to focus on another human being's face. His whole life had been devoted to tank work, and although Joshua had once heard him mutter that every other sort of employment, viewed from a steeplejack's vantage, "looked like pitiful," Cofield was himself a doddering object lesson in the curriculum of the woebegone. Hubbard found him wonderfully dependable, but the only reason Cofield reported to work each day, Joshua felt, was that the alternative—calling in sick or quitting, then confronting at every turn the ruins of his own personality—terrified him. That was also why he stayed drunk every weekend.

Joshua did not want to end up even a slightly less dissipated version of R. K. Cofield. Nevertheless, the demands of self-sufficiency and the narrow compass of his marketable skills were channeling him, inexorably, in that very direction. Also to blame were pride and inertia. He could not get off center. Yesterday, though, the pressure of his dreams and the threat implicit in Cofield's vanquished eyes had set him zipping down Highway 98 to Pensacola.

On the greensward just beneath Joshua, Tom Hubbard was monitoring the operation of a sand pot and a yellow air compressor. A tall man whose eclectic tonsorial style included a William Powell mustache and jet-black Elvis Presley ducktails, he was shouting over the noise of the compressor and beckoning Joshua to descend. His arm movements were urgent, typically uncoordinated and brusque.

What the hell's going on? Joshua wondered.

Then he saw the Air Force limousine parked at the curb behind the equipment truck, well within the restricted area where falling paint could lightly polka-dot its dark-blue finish. Near the snaky tangle of hoses lifting sand and fresh air to Cofield stood Alistair Patrick Blair and the colonel who had attended last night's lecture with him. They were gawking at Joshua, their heads thrown back.

"Damn," Joshua muttered. "The bastard came."

He let go of the extension pole on his paint roller, which fell until the thong securing it to his seat caught it up and held it tick-tocking beneath him like a pendulum. The paleoanthropologist, clad today in a conventional business suit, smiled and waved.

"Get down here, Kampa!" Hubbard shouted after he had turned off the air compressor. "These gentlemen want to talk to you!"

Joshua maneuvered his ropes toward a fixed ladder on one of the tower's colossal legs. It would have been easier to descend on his falls, but for reasons he could not quite articulate—to annoy Hubbard, to astonish Blair, to please himself—he wanted to make a spectacular dismount, even if it entailed a stupid as well as an illegal risk.

Undoing his safety harness, he swung clear of the falls. Then, gripping both hand rails, he pistoned backward down the ladder until he had reached one of the resilient support rods tying the legs of the tower together in a webwork of diamond-shaped diagonals. Here he leapt out, caught the support rod, and plummeted along it in a breathtaking glide. Sixty feet from the ground, at an intersection of diagonals, he reversed directions and came careering back toward the ladder.

"Goddamn it, Kampa!" shouted Hubbard. "Stop right there! Use the fuckin' ladder! Whaddaya think you're doin'?"

Joshua, like a paratrooper on a practice line, launched himself out along another support rod. Feet dangling, arms above his head, he rocked and swooped. He was so in control of his descent that he was able to enjoy the full range of expressions on the faces of the men below him. Then, about twenty feet up, he was back at the leg ladder again. Here he paused.

"You're in violation of the Occupational Safety and Health Act," Hubbard told Joshua, primarily for the others' benefit. "Do that one more time, Kampa, and you're gone. I'll can your ass, I swear to God I will."

Triumphant in his contemplation of Blair and the colonel, Joshua hitched a ride on another support rod. About six feet from the ground, he released his grip and landed in a crouch directly under the tank. Even before he could straighten up, Hubbard was stalking circles around him, rebuking him for his carelessness and insubordination, telling him not to report for work on Monday. This was it, Joshua's swan song, he was gone for good. Still in control, Joshua picked his way over the air and sand hoses to his visitors.

"If he'd cut his hand on a burr doing that," Hubbard appealed to Blair and the colonel, tagging along, "his natural instinct would've been to let go of the rod. He'd be gone. My insurance rates are outrageous already, God knows. A dead man in my debit column sure as hell wouldn't lower 'em none, either."

The owner, president, and on-the-job foreman of Gulf Coast Coating, Inc., waved his hand about in exasperation, then turned the air compressor back on and sat down dejectedly on a stack of silicate-sand bags near the blast-cleaning machine.

Because of the noise Blair suggested that Joshua return with him and the colonel to Fort Walton Beach in the limousine. Joshua told the two men that he had transportation of his own. Besides, he wasn't going anywhere with them until he had had a Coke with a double handful of crushed ice. His thirst was enormous.

As a consequence, Joshua and his visitors wound up in a corner booth at the Okaloosa Café, about a block and a half from the water tower. The only other customer in the place was a local policeman. A heavy-hipped waitress with a beehive hairdo and a dramatic streak of peroxide over one ear brought them their menus. Joshua felt that had not Blair and the colonel been with him, she would have used his paint-spattered boots and coveralls as an excuse to deny him service. Or maybe the fact that he was bleeding from his right palm.

"Are you all right?" Blair asked Joshua.

Exhilarated by the Great Man's solicitude, Joshua said, "Sure. Sliced it on a burr skating that first rod, eighty feet up. Didn't let go, though, did I? Just lipped my fingers over the bad spot and kept on comin'."

Blair belatedly introduced the colonel, a full bird by the name of Crawford, the base commander at Eglin. He was a compact, round-faced man only slightly taller than Joshua, with a haircut that made him seem a refugee from Eisenhower's 1950s. The light coming through the flyspecked front window of the Okaloosa Café glinted off his insignia and danced in his violet eyes.

"How did you find me?" Joshua asked.

"Telephoned the number on the slip of paper you gave Dr. Blair last night," Colonel Crawford explained. "Got the manager of your motor court, Mrs.—"

"Mrs. Gelb."

"Right, Mrs. Gelb. She, in turn, told us where you were working, and we drove up here."

Nodding meaningfully at the cut in Joshua's palm, Blair put the message slip on the table and smoothed it out with his fingers. "The name, address, and telephone number are self-explanatory, young man, but, pray, what is the significance of this tiny black hand with the eye in the middle?"

"I kept a diary when I was small. I kept it in code. That was one of the symbols I used."

Colonel Crawford asked, "What did it stand for?"

"Homo habilis, I think."

"Homo habilis!" Blair exclaimed. *"Australopithecus habilis,* you mean. The former was a term badly in need of overhaul even when you were a child. Nobody could ever quite agree which fossil specimens belonged in the category. As I tried to explain last night, *habilis* was decidedly more ape than man."

"If the terminology's screwed up," Joshua said, "what better way to solve the problem than by a symbol? This hand with the eye in the middle means a certain kind of hominid, and only that kind."

"But what criteria did you use to establish the category?"

"Observation."

While Blair was trying to digest this claim, and perhaps to collate it with Joshua's remarks about chalicotheres at last night's lecture, Colonel Crawford asked, "What kind of diary was this, anyway?"

"A diary of my travels."

The two men stared at Joshua.

"A dream diary," he said in qualification. "When I was nine, my mother—my adoptive mother, I mean—suggested that I begin recording my dreams. So I did, in code. All my dreams were a kind of . . . well, I called it spirit-traveling. My spirit-traveling always took me to the same goddamn place. I'd had these special sorts of dream ever since I was a baby, but it wasn't until I was seven or eight that I began to realize not only *where* I was going but *when.*"

Joshua chewed some of the ice from the Coke that the disapproving waitress had just brought him.

"It scared me shitless. It scared my mother shitless, too, to see me in one of these trances. Usually, you know, my eyelids skinned back and my eyeballs rolled in my head. Jeannette—my adoptive mother—she must have wondered if I was dying. But I wasn't dying. I was only—spirit-traveling."

"To Pleistocene Africa?" Blair asked.

Joshua nodded.

"What makes you so bloody positive that the"—Blair groped for a word "—that the *testimony* of your dreams isn't rife with nonsense and false colors? Nightmares don't often correlate with the substance of objective reality. Yours may not, either."

"No, mine do. They almost always do. Except when they're mixed up with real nightmares. I can almost always tell when my genuine spirit-traveling is being muddled by regular dreaming." Joshua told the two men of the time he had cross-wired a flight of B-52s into the world of prehistoric East Africa. The airplanes had pocked the landscape with bomb craters and sent all sorts of extinct creatures scurrying for cover. Of course, these images had filtered into his dreaming mind only a few days after Jeannette had read to the children a letter from their father, who was stationed on Guam and working as the chief of a B-52 ground crew during the saturation bombing of North Vietnam and Cambodia. On an earlier occasion, right after the first U.S. moon landing, Joshua had even contrived—or, rather, his subconscious had—to introduce space-suited astronauts into the terrain of his dreams.

The colonel rocked back on the rear legs of his chair. "Did that—*does* that—happen often?"

"No, sir, it's rare. I can think of only a few intrusions like that. Once, though, I watched a band of quasi-people scavenging a mastodont that had fallen off a ledge into a gully and—"

"A mastodont?" Blair interrupted.

"Well, some sort of elephanty critter. I was maybe eight or nine. I hadn't yet started checking books to see what kinds of animals were popping up in my spirit travels. Besides, I didn't need names for my dream diary—I just made up a symbol for each different animal and used that."

"What about this 'mastodont'?"

Joshua closed his eyes and snorted in bemused self-contempt. "I didn't need a name for it. It was an intrusion, and it never came back after that first time. You know what that animal was?"

Blair and the colonel shook their heads.

"Snuffle-uppagus." Joshua grimaced and flashed hot with embarrassment. "Yeah. Weird. I know."

Zarakal's Minister of Interior, uncomprehending, looked to Colonel Crawford for an explanation.

Joshua hurriedly said, "Snuffle-uppagus was this big, furry, elephanty creature on a PBS children's program, *Sesame Street.* I don't know whether it's still on or not. Anyway, Snuffle-uppagus had silly cartoon eyes with long, flirty lashes and a voice like a bassoon's, slow and deep and sad. His best friend was Big Bird, a seven-foot-tall featherbrain who could never convince any of the adults on the program that Snuffle-uppagus really existed. Every time Bird tried to introduce Snuf to Maria or Mr. Hooper or somebody, Snuf would go wandering off somewhere, swaying from side to side, and Bird ended up looking like the bozo who cried wolf."

Joshua took a sip of Coke, put his glass back down on the wet circle it had made. Neither Blair nor Crawford took their eyes off him.

"That gave me the willies, that betrayal. It was the same goddamn thing that happened to me when I slipped and let somebody know about my spirit-traveling. Disbelief. Disbelief, indignation, sometimes even outrage. I couldn't produce any evidence of what I was laying claim to, only some awkward drawings of the things I saw. Since the proof wouldn't come, and since nobody knew what to make of my witness, I got labeled a liar. A liar and a freak. That's why—before I was seven—I finally just shut up about it all." Joshua grinned. "And that's why I *hated* that goddamn, two-timin' Snuffle-uppagus."

The policeman at the counter had swiveled about on his stool, and Colonel Crawford bumped his chair back down and put a hand on Joshua's wrist to warn him about speaking too loudly. His touch made Joshua start.

"Go ahead," the colonel urged. "Finish about Snuffle-uppagus."

Joshua drank off the remainder of his Coke and lowered his voice: "A group of hominids—black-hands-with-eyes, that's the kind they were—scurried around in the watercourse where old Snuf had fallen. They were getting ready to cut him up with tiny stone knives flaked from larger core tools. 'Oh, nooo-ooo-ooh,' moaned Snuf, who wasn't quite dead yet. 'What's going to become of me, Bird?' The quasi-people set to work. They scored his shaggy belly with their flake tools and let the blood run. 'Oh, dear me, Bird,' Snuffle-uppagus said, 'I'm afraid I'm going to die.' Just like that. In that sappy, mournful voice of his. He wasn't even struggling."

"And then what happened?"

"Well, I guess he died, Colonel. And then the quasi-people probably ate him. I don't know. My mother woke me up. I was sitting in the middle of my bed wrapped in a blanket—this was in our house, our basement apartment, in Cheyenne—and my eyes had probably rolled up in my head. My mother couldn't stand to see that. She shook me out of it and held me, just held and rocked me." Blair, Joshua saw, was fiddling with a paper napkin. "That was a tainted instance of spirit-traveling. A little of the here-and-now had leaked down and contaminated my long-ago soul. I knew it. I knew it even before Jeannette woke me up."

Blair folded the napkin and patted it into the breast pocket of his suit jacket. "What kinds of hominids do you ordinarily see when . . . well, when you go back?"

"Three sorts, just like the Leakeys claim. When I kept my dream diary I used a black-hand pictogram for each of them. I put an eye in the palm of the symbol for the most human-seeming group. They have tools, crude shelters, the beginnings of a family system."

"Habilis," Blair said. "Go on."

"Then there's a more brutish bunch, bigger and less bright. I identified them in my dream diary by putting a mouth with thick, square teeth in the center of my black-hand symbol."

"Australopithecus boisei or *robustus,* the robust 'southern ape.' "

"Yes, sir, but I didn't know the terms then. And, finally, the remaining species—little jokers like furry elves or hobbits. They're about three and a half feet tall. For them I used a simple black-hand pictogram with nothing in the palm. That's simply how they struck me when I was a kid."

"Australopithecus africanicus, the gracile 'southern ape.' Your symbolism may be completely appropriate, Mr. Kampa. It's possible that *habilus* and *robustus* both derived from *africanus.* Even though it survived to be their contemporary, it antedates them in the fossil record."

The waitress arrived at their table with the check, which she placed face down in a water spill. The policeman creaked about on his stool, saluted them sardonically, and banged out the front door into the withering July sunshine. When they were alone again, Colonel Crawford put his elbows on the table and leaned forward.

"Listen, Mr. Kampa, Dr. Blair interrupted an incredibly

busy schedule to seek you out. We're going to have to have answers to two more questions to know if the interruption was really worthwhile."

The Great Man said, "Of course it's been worthwhile, Hank."

"What questions?"

"First, do you ever dream *yourself* back into the Pleistocene? By that I mean, Are you yourself ever one of the identifiable figures in that ancient landscape?"

"Not really. I dolly in and out like a movie camera. I'm nothing but a pair of free-floating eyes. That's why I call it spirit-traveling."

"Good," Colonel Crawford said.

Creasing his forehead, Blair asked, "Why is that good?"

"Woody could explain this much better than I can. It's because he hasn't contaminated the period with . . . well, with the anomaly of his own physical presence. His real body may be able to go back because his psyche has never permitted a dream image of himself to do so. You'll have to sit down with Woody if you want a more cogent explanation."

Joshua looked hard at the colonel. Up to this moment he had seemed to Joshua like a third wheel on a bicycle, an onlooker at a two-handed card game. Base commander or no base commander, he had accompanied Blair to Blackwater Springs in the capacity of chauffeur. Or had he? Joshua was beginning to reassess the terms and degree of the colonel's real involvement. And who was Woody?

"What's the second question?" he asked.

Tom Hubbard threw open the door of the Okaloosa Café, then eased it shut behind him. "Glass o' water and a ham sandwich," he told the waitress, crossing to Joshua's table. Before Colonel Crawford could jockey aside to give him room, Hubbard had turned a chair around and straddled it backwards. "Goddamn it, Kampa, listen. You can't leave me up here on this job with old R. K. Cofield and that new kid who thinks tank epoxy is some kind o' disease."

"You canned my ass."

"Yeah, well, if you promise to quit pullin' that rod-skatin' crap, I'll take you back on."

Colonel Crawford said, "We've been trying to interest Mr. Kampa in a new line of employment."

Joshua caught the colonel's eye. "The hell you have."

"That was my second question. I was just about to ask it."

"You fellas recruiters?" Hubbard wanted to know.

"In a manner of speaking." Colonel Crawford looked at Alistair Patrick Blair, then back at Joshua. "Mr. Kampa, how would you like to join the Air Force?"

"I'm too short."

"Not for the assignment we have in mind."

"Yeah," Hubbard put in, "Uncle Sam can always use cannon fodder in Central America and the Persian Gulf. Africa, too. Sam likes to send darkies to jungle hot spots. Each side can tote up the other's kills when it's making out a body count."

"This time, Tom, I intend to stay fired."

Hubbard shook his head. "Suit yourself. Leave me in the lurch. Strand me with R. K. Cofield and the Help-me-I'm-fallin' kid."

In the end, a napkin clenched in his bleeding hand, Joshua embraced Hubbard in the middle of the Okaloosa Café, then followed Dr. Blair and Colonel Crawford out the door.

Ten minutes later, astride his Kawasaki, he was trailing the Air Force limousine down State Highway 85 through the desolate ordnance ranges of Hugo Monegal's last base. Mouth wide open, his voice lost in a backwash of humid wind, he sang, at the top of his lungs, a sprightly old Beatles tune . . .

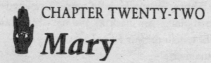

CHAPTER TWENTY-TWO
Mary

WHEN MALCOLM TOUCHED my shoulder, I nearly leapt from the acacia into the water hole. During my recitation he had climbed up beside me without my noticing. His goatee wobbled back and forth on his receding chin, for, altogether pointedly, he was "talking," silently speechifying.

"Just trying to get us through a difficult night," I told him. "What story are *you* trying to tell?"

The habiline nodded succinctly at the .45 on my hip. I had nearly forgotten it and did not wish to remember it now. My hope had been that the hyenas, either bored or insulted by my tale, would trot off haughtily into the night. No such luck. They were still out there, waiting.

"This is *not* the ultimate answer to every question, you know. Do you remember what happened to Genly?"

Malcolm pointed his forefinger at a hyena whose agate eyes glittered greedily from a nearby clump of grass. He clicked his tongue. Like a ruminating goat, he waggled his chin whiskers.

In light of our predicament, my scruples about using the pistol again at last struck me as misplaced.

"All right," I said grudgingly.

And drew my pistol from my holster. And, as Pete Grier had once used a spotlight to murder a defenseless deer, took full advantage of the moon to shoot that offal-eating brigand between the eyes. The report, echoing away, had an orgasmic quality. I felt drained and unaccountably saddened by the hyena's death.

The other hyenas, along with a pair of scruffy vultures that belatedly managed to get airborne, had already hightailed it, but I fired off the remainder of my clip, anyway.

Malcolm clung almost cravenly to the tree during this fusillade, but afterward, our besiegers dispersed, swung to the ground and ran along the water's edge like a man emancipated from bondage. I slid the hot machine back into its holster and watched the other Minids descend from the surrounding trees. Soon they were all on the ground. Some of them—mostly males— ventured out onto the prairie to examine the corpse of the hyena I had shot. I, however, stayed upstairs, determined to keep the watch that Malcolm had abandoned.

"Look, I'm not going to do this all the time," I informed the Minids. "But it does work when we need it, doesn't it?"

The women and children turned dubious, moonlit faces upward, while Roosevelt, Fred, and Malcolm squatted beside the hyena with lava cobbles and pieces of chert, flaking these into tools with which to butcher the carcass. Morning was still many hours off, but they seemed disinclined to surrender my kill to the vultures by coming back to the thicket for a little well-earned shuteye. I watched them working without envy or appetite.

More than likely I dozed. When I awoke, Fred was standing sentinel in another tree, and the remainder of our band had found sleeping spots on the ground. So many bodies lay about that the scene triggered thoughts of massacre or holocaust.

Fred made a cooing sound and pointed into the underbrush. Rousing myself, I saw nothing, only thorn trees and desolation under a falling moon. Fred continued to coo, and a moment later a shadow emerged from a thicket to the northeast. At the sight of this figure my heart began *ker-chunking* like an engine block whose bolts have shaken loose.

It was Helen.

I repressed the urge to halloo, to scramble down to meet her. The Minids deserved to sleep, and my rushing to Helen would inevitably rouse and perplex more than a few of them. My heart laboring noisily, I waited for her to pick her way across the intervening territory to our water hole. Fred, having alerted her to our position, stopped cooing, but Helen did not seem to make good progress toward us. Ordinarily she was lightfooted and quick. What was taking her so long? Had she sustained some terrible injury?

No, she had not. Helen was carrying something, clutching it in front of her like an idol. It was a baby. I remembered the baboon infant that, some time ago, she had brought back from a foraging expedition. That infant had not long survived its abduction, and if this was another stolen child, as it certainly appeared to be, the inarguable result of Helen's frustrated maternal longings would be the poor creature's death. Sweet Jesus, I thought, not again.

As quietly as I could, I went down to Helen and met her at the far side of the water hole. She handed me her darling, which was not a baboon but an australopithecine baby—from the *africanus* troop that had shadowed us all the way from New Helensburgh. The baby came willingly into my arms, and my first thought was that she resembled a human child in furry long johns. Her feet were more or less bare, and her knees—as if she had worn holes in her pajamas—were naked, calloused knots very like my own. She refused to look at me, glancing instead at Helen before staring wistfully out into the darkness of the bush. She was slightly larger and slightly hairier than Fred and Nicole's A.P.B., probably more than a year old.

"At least you had the sense to steal one that's old enough to eat solid foods," I told Helen.

Helen took the australopithecine child out of my arms and

set her on the ground between us. Then, embracing me, she patted my back with both hands, all the while gibbering a series of syllables that had little relation to any I had taught her. Their unintelligibility did not obscure their binding import. As surely as if we had conceived this child ourselves, Helen and I were the australopithecine's mother and father. It was our responsibility to see that she grew into a healthy adult.

"This is crazy," I protested. "Helen, she's not a habiline. She's a kidnaped southern ape. Even if we manage to shepherd her past adolescence, what kind of life do you suppose she'll have?"

Still patting my back, Helen mumbled a string of incoherent sweet nothings. With foolish fond eyes she looked down at our daughter, who appeared to be lapsing into an autistic trance.

"Who's going to mate with her?" I continued. "She'll be lucky if the Minids tolerate her presence, much less accept her as one of their own. Nor are her own folks going to want to take her back. She'll be despised by *habilis* and *africanus* alike, Helen, just as if she were a half-breed. Can't you see what folly this is, what potential disaster?"

Helen was having no part of my faintheartedness. She hunkered beside the tiny girl-child and tenderly groomed her head. Now I saw that on her raid against the australopithecines Helen had not totally escaped injury. Blood from a series of claw marks striated her inner arm. And yet she had stolen this child with no worse hurt than that, a feat of such competent derring-do that I could only shake my head. The look on Helen's face said that I should tend to the child while she took a few moments to see to her wounds. Awkwardly I knelt beside the little hominid and went nit-picking through her scalp, a courtesy that her trance did not permit her to acknowledge.

On the other side of the water hole Emily awoke, sat up, and looked at us. After yawning sleepily, she rose and ambled around the pond to satisfy her curiosity. Were we real or only a midnight apparition? Squatting as Helen had, she touched the kidnap victim on the chin. Then, fascinated by the australopithecine's passivity, she pulled her finger back and stared. Helen and I scarcely dared to breathe—as if Emily's next decision would spell either life or death for the abducted child.

At last I said, "Her name is Mary." I looked at Helen. "Is that all right with you? Mary?"

"Mai mwah," Helen said. "My mirror," I thought, was a reasonable approximation of "Mary." Let it stand. Let it stand.

"Good. That's settled."

Satisfied that Emily intended Mary no harm, Helen left me in charge of the child and disappeared into the night again. When, ten or fifteen minutes later, she returned, she was carrying a good supply of *ol dwai,* wild sisal, with whose sticky balm she treated the claw marks on her arm. Emily helped her, smoothing Helen's sparse forearm hairs aside and squeezing the natural anodyne of the wild sisal into her cuts. Why such solicitude? I wondered. Maybe it was the late hour, the presence of the child whose head I was still desultorily searching for lice, or the all-pervasive quiet. Whatever the reason, I too was at peace, my misgivings about adopting the australopithecine routed by an army of fatuous hopes.

Alfie roused us from sleep by banging his stave repeatedly against the bole of a tree. It was almost dawn. In clusters on the plain, like cowlless monks at matins, sat the vultures that had settled on the corpse of the hyena impaled by the female rhino and gutted by its own fellows. The other hyena—the one I had shot—had been dragged down to the water's edge, out of the birds' reach. Even so, the vultures kept their eyes peeled for an opportunity to move in.

Any troop of self-respecting baboons would have breakfasted before departing, but Alfie, along with Ham and Jomo, moved us out into the veldt with nothing in our stomachs but muddy water and the fluttery sensation that accompanies either doubt or encroaching illness. The idea was to get us going before the arrival of a lion or the return of the hyenas pinned us up for the better part of the morning.

Today Helen marched at the center of our procession, taking Mary with her. Now that she had a child she was indisputably entitled to give up her roles as outrider, sentry, and bodyguard in favor of those as veldtwife, mother, and ward. Dragging her acacia stave behind her like a broken rudder, she carried little Mary on her hip. A weapon in one hand, a baby in the other. If she was confused by the disparate allegiances embodied by these symbols, her heart—at least for now—was with the women. Nor did the women harass or cold-shoulder her for joining them.

Once the Minids had all become aware of her, Mary focused their occasional attention without provoking their hostility. I had expected angry faces, angry gestures, maybe even an assault. Instead, the habilines took turns examining the child, whom they seemed to delight in sniffing and gently poking. Helen allowed the Minids their inspections. If Mary were to survive, they must satisfy their curiosity about the kidnaped child and accept her as one of their own. Without once whimpering or struggling to get away, Mary clung to Helen with wide, terrified eyes, fatalistically enduring her ordeal.

During our march the child overcame some of her fear of the Minids, and on one occasion, when we stopped to rest, she toddled away to join Bonzo, Duchess, and Pebbles, who appeared to be experimentally tormenting a pair of coprid beetles left over from yesterday's encounter with the chalicotheres. The children did not prevent Mary from taking up with them. In fact, they allowed her to participate in the dismemberment of one of the insects, and both Helen and I looked on dotingly. After that, Mary, for all intents and purposes, was a habiline.

By noon we were in more or less open country, full-fledged savannah, but the mountain—still, I decided, about fifteen miles away—sometimes appeared to retreat from our approach.

A brake on our progress, the children continued to tumble about like puppies and to lolligag over any bit of desiccated matter in the grass. Mary was one of them now, and Helen sometimes edged out of the center of our column as if to renounce mother-hood for sentry duty. She hurried back to Mary, though, each time the child showed signs of fatigue or crankiness. Her dedica-tion to our daughter made me pensive and a little resentful. I had liked Helen as a comrade as well as a lover.

Late that afternoon Ham separated from the group and ran gimpily ahead of us to a depression in the grass. He circled this small concavity (which, but for Ham's strange behavior, I would not have looked at twice), then halted and cautiously cir-cled it in the other direction. He hooted for reinforcements. When the other habiline men arrived, me among them, he lurched for-ward and yanked a large wedge of sod from the hollowed-out place in the savannah.

A high, perilous hissing sound ensued. I supposed that Ham had uncovered a snake, maybe one of those egg snakes whose ceaselessly coiling bodies and cobralike hoods make your blood turn to ice. But their behavior is all empty bluff, and Babington had taught me not to fear them.

What Ham had found, though, was not an egg snake or a bona fide cobra. Not at all. He had uncovered a litter of cheetah kittens. I counted four of them, elegant little felines with masks for faces and jewels for eyes. In their immature, silver-blue coats, they pressed against one another spitting out their fear and indig-nation. Their outrage was humorous. Mother was off hunting somewhere, but she would be back soon and we had better scram before she caught us poking around in their crib. Who did we think we were, anyway?

Even after several months in the Pleistocene I was sur-prised when I found out.

Roosevelt and Fred clubbed three of the kittens to death, showering blood and gray matter all over the grass. The fourth kitten tried to run, but Alfie booted it in the butt and fell upon it with his knee, cracking its ribs and pinning it to the ground. He killed it by biting through its neck. When he next looked up at me, blood was running from his mouth and there was a tuft of beautiful, wintry fur caught in his beard.

I retreated with Mary to the edge of the Minid gathering. As if the child were a magic shield or an inflatable life jacket, I clutched her to me for the comfort she afforded. Together, neither of us quite comprehending the other's dismay, we watched the eaters eat.

As soon as every gut had taken on a load of kitten loin, torpor descended. No one wanted to leave. Although we could have traveled several more miles that afternoon, the satiated habilines had decided to make camp where we were.

A more vulnerable spot it would have been hard to find. There was not a tree or kopje within two or three hundred yards. Setting up housekeeping in that open place was a little like pitching a tent on an interstate highway. You were asking to be run over. But, gorged and insouciant, the Minids either did not recognize or blithely dismissed the possibility of peril. Fortunately, we were able to while away the late afternoon without having to defend ourselves against roving predators.

The sun went down like a Day-Glo bob in the mouth of the Primal Perch. There, then gone.

A logy habiline is a bad insurance risk. Because I did not trust any of the men to keep their eyeballs peeled past moonrise, I decided to build a fire. Helen kept Mary beside her while I roamed the plain gathering the brittle, prickly limbs of gall acacias and the whorly, friable Frisbees of dried elephant dung. I soon had a homy blaze crackling in our midst.

My spirits began to improve. Maybe I had been suffering from hesperian depression or evening melancholy. Watching the ants on the thorn branches curl up into weightless clinkers revived my sense of camaraderie with the habilines. Insects, unlike cheetah kittens, were not mammals. You could consign them to perdition with lighthearted hallelujahs, then stand back from the roaring hellfires and gleefully watch them burn.

Fred—feckless, reckless Fred—returned not with kindling but with a weaverbird basket full of fuzzy little fruits. Where he had found them I had no idea. They were lavender-yellow ellipsoids with a sour-sweet musk. I did not eat one until Dilsey, who had taken charge of Fred's basket, consumed six or seven with steadily increasing gusto and no conspicuous ill effects—when, by rights, she should have been stuffed to the jowls with cheetah flesh. Fruits, I told myself, watching Dilsey, were even farther down the evolutionary ladder of sentience than ants, and by now I was hungry enough to demand my share. Helen brought me a handful.

My first taste of one of these fuzzy ellipsoids inspired me to name them. I called them puckerplums.

Puckerplums inebriate.

Indeed, I got drunk on puckerplums. I was not the only one, but I was by far the most maudlin of all the maudlin Minids reeling about our fire in ambulatory contemplation of the nastiness, brutality, and brevity of life. Why, in only umpteen hundred thousand years, I reflected aloud, all my habiline acquaintances—never, oh never purged from mind!—would be as Phoenician sea wrack on the condominium sands of Miami Beach. No one would ever know—*really* know—the living details of how they had steered their course toward the serendipitous disaster of our survival. How much we owed them, I thought, and how little most folks cared about what they had suffered for us. It was a goddamn shame, I told the Minids, that latter-day ignorance of their courage and sacrifice had pretty much denied them a place in the Annals of Great Human Heroes. They deserved better, much better, and maybe, when White Sphinx retrieved me, I would rectify this ignoble oversight.

And then, striking one of my waterproof matches and lifting its impudent head against the travertine streaks of the horizon, I searched my memory for a haunting snippet from Yeats:

"Dear shadows, now you know it all,
All the folly of a fight
With a common wrong or right.
The innocent and the beautiful
Have no enemy but time;
Arise and bid me strike a match
And strike another till time catch . . ."

"In the days of the chalicothere," I said, "there came unto you a chiromancer—that is, a diviner of palms—and I am he who will riddle the life lines in your secretive hands."

I went first to Dilsey, only a yard or so from the fire. Taking her scarred old hand into my own—the habiline hand with the abbreviated, crooked thumb—I tried to tell her who she was in order to predict what she would become and what would befall her.

"Dilsey, long ago you met a small, dark man who swept you off your calloused feet and rose to a position of influence among the Minids. His name was Ham. Upon you, with your complicity, he begot the son whom we know today as Alfie. Alfie is the gemsbok melon of your eye, but your daughters Miss Jane and Odetta are also well beloved of you and your consort. In this savage place, Dilsey, you have lived a good and useful life. Though your body crawls with vermin and your mouth .frequently vents the stench of rotting meat, in dignity and honor you are immaculate. Your life is as lengthy as the Nile, but you are already near the fathomless ocean into which it and all other lives inevitably pour . . ."

I dropped Dilsey's hand and stared around at the shadows staring back at me. Not quite spellbound, the old woman pushed another puckerplum into my mouth. I ate it, realizing that I had prophesied Dilsey's death. What everyone wanted from me now was the details. Taking up her hand again, I tenderly rotated its palm into view. My saliva, I noticed, was ropy, ropy and bitter.

"Dilsey, my dear Dilsey, you will be decapitated when the Toyota in which you are riding slips beneath the tailgate of a logging truck. Ham, your driver, will suffer the same grisly fate, but the sheriff's report will absolve him of culpability because of local weather conditions and the failure of the logging vehicle to display a flag on the end of its projecting cargo.

"Odetta will enter a multimillion-dollar suit against the implicated pulpwood company on your family's behalf, but the litigation will drag on for years, in part because the coroner's inquest has revealed an unacceptable percentage of alcohol in Ham's bloodstream at the time of his demise. Puckerplum intoxication, apparently.

"As for your and Ham's funeral, Dilsey, it will be a grand event, with many hyenas and vultures in formal attire gathered together at graveside. Oh, yes, a grand event. The talk of the savannah for weeks. None of this posthumous notoriety will matter to you, however, because in addition to being dead you are a deferential and unassuming lady who does not permit such silly flapdoodle to set her head spinning."

After kissing Dilsey on her bony brow ridge, I reeled away into the darkness beyond the fire, which the children were continuing to feed with twigs and dung pats. Jomo caught me and led me back into the semicircle of adults. Insistent, he shoved the fingers of his open palm into my chest.

"What do you want me to tell you?" I demanded. "Dead of cancer, of gunshot wounds, of radiation poisoning? No, sir. No, ma'am. To hell with that. Gone with a bang or a whimper, I don't want to prophesy our end, and I *won't*. Tonight I'm not going to think any more about it."

Helen approached me out of the windy desolation of the veldt, Mary in her arms. Our fire whipped about madly, and my tattered bush shorts popped like a string of fire crackers. Helen wanted a reading. She adjusted Mary on one hip and held her palm out to me.

"Mai mwah."

"This is the last one," I told the Minids. "This is the last habiline palm I'm ever going to read. Do you understand?"

They said nothing. Helen waited.

Clasping her arthritic-looking hand, I declared, "Helen, you're going to fall in love with a water-tank painter and live happily ever after. You'll have a few so-so days, of course, blah times when you're depressed by the international situation or the gloomy wood paneling in your mobile home. You'll like Florida, though, and your husband's the sort who'll try to let you, you know, *actualize your creative potential as an autonomous person.* Every anniversary he'll, uh, take you sandblasting inside some little community's elevated water tank, where you'll pretend you're pioneers exploring the hollow core of another planet. This is one of the ways you'll continually renew your romance. All things considered, it'll be a decent, serene, unassuming life. You could do a helluva lot worse. You really could."

Helen put Mary's tiny hand into mine, the hand of a hirsute alien. I abruptly let it go.

"Mai mwah."

"No, I said I wouldn't, Helen, and I won't."

Helen shifted Mary from one hip to the other and wandered aimlessly away. The Minids—dear shadows all—watched me stagger several steps after her. They wanted something more of me, the Minids did, an epilogue or an exegesis. I halted and held up my palm so they could see its lines.

"This says I'll never betray you. I'm here to stay. I'm going to time-travel only one more time—by dying and leaving my bones for Alistair Patrick Blair to discover. Maybe he'll give me my own taxonomic designation."

I was openly weeping, caught between two contradictory impulses, my affection for the habilines and a sudden powerful homesickness.

"I've come back to you from a tomorrow you're not yet capable of visualizing, but you must never assume that I'm the be-all and end-all of your development as a people. You must try to look beyond what you cannot yet visualize toward that which is absolutely inconceivable. Even if it's misplaced, you must have faith in your destiny. My .45's not solely what you're striving for, nor is my first-aid kit. The culmination of what you have begun, O my Minidae, will be a triumph that I am altogether incapable of imagining."

The next day we straggled without incident across the grasslands to the gentle hills at the foot of Mount Tharaka. Helen, who obviously did not feel well, permitted me to tote Mary much of this distance and spent her time foraging vegetable foods for the australopithecine child.

Our arrival near the mountain was highlighted by the appearance on the scrub-covered ridge above us of three or four hunters from another habiline "nation." We had trespassed into their territory, and in a season of drought, when dispersal spells survival, our advent must have seemed a challenge to their dominion. Holding Mary and gazing up into the glitter of snow frosting Mount Tharaka's peak, I heard . . . well, I heard ancestral voices prophesying war.

Actually, Alfie, Jomo, and Ham were hallooing to the sentinels on the ridge, and the sentinels were hallooing back. These eerie how-d'ye-dos diddled the high dells of the mountain and loop-de-looped across the grasslands. They frightened Mary. She dug her toenails into my thighs and tried to climb me like a tree. She was strong, too, strong and persistent; I virtually had to squeeze the wind from her lungs to dampen her hankering for a howdah perch on my head. At last Helen noticed our struggle and relieved me of the imp. In her adoptive mother's arms, even as the hooting on the ridge modulated from threat into invitation, Mary quieted.

As we labored slantwise up the incline, I realized that Mary was not the only naturalized Minid who dreaded the impending encounter. I was as out of place among the habilines as she, a bran flake in a box of Cheerios. What kind of reception could we expect from the strangers on the ridge? Their faces took on specific identities as we climbed, but I still found it hard to think they were people in the sense that the Minids were people.

They were attired no differently (a hairy sort of nakedness being the uniform of the epoch), and their weapons had a familiar look (cudgel, bludgeon, stave, and femur), but they reminded me of Yahoos rather than human beings. This was a visceral prejudice that I would have to uproot or sublimate. It was, I told myself, unworthy of Joshua Kampa.

Ham and Jomo seemed to have had prior dealings with the hunchbacked honcho of this other band. (Attila Gorilla, I mentally dubbed him, for his habilines were Huns.) They presented their credentials, laying their weapons at Attila's feet to demonstrate our peaceable aims and our willingness to beg the Huns' indulgence while passing through their stomping grounds. Alfie, hanging back with the womenfolk, clutched the burnished thighbone of a wildebeest like a gigantic swizzle stick. If our reception proved less than hospitable, he looked altogether capable of mixing our adversaries into a habiline cocktail. Fortunately, this did not prove necessary.

Although I could not decode the guttural gibberish in which negotiations proceeded, in a matter of moments our uneasy truce had become a friendship treaty. Following Attila's lead, our entire band scurried down the backside of the ridge into a briary dale. On Mount Tharaka's elevated skirts there were trees and stands of bamboo, while the snow on the overleaning peak sparkled like the slush in a frozen banana daiquiri. We threaded our way through the briar patch, debouched into a naked ravine, and climbed through the ravine toward the delicious ices of the summit. A quarter of the way up, we maneuvered clockwise along a forested shelf to the Huns' tiny mountain resort.

The habilines here regarded Mary and me with frank suspicion. I was the more disconcerting anomaly, a buffoon with boxy feet and blowzy britches. They had never seen anything like me before. They had no words—indeed, no mental concepts—for many of my accouterments. My shorts did not completely befuddle them, but only because some of the female Huns wore crude, animal-skin cloaks, a concession to the cooler temperatures at this altitude.

In spite of their antipathy toward me, these people left me alone. The Minids, after all, had me in tow, and I was several inches taller than Attila, their own acknowledged boss man.

Mary the Huns ogled with less self-consciousness. She was an idiot child who caricatured them simply by being who and what she was. They could not seem to decide if they wanted to cuddle or cudgel her, for which reason Helen was careful about accompanying Mary on all her little jaunts about the village, an odd assortment of lean-tos and huts. I was protective of Mary, too, and found myself holding her a great deal of the time.

We stayed with these habilines for six days, and I never did develop any affection for them. They interacted well enough with the Minids, I suppose, to the extent that Mister Pibb began laying the groundwork for a liaison with a dainty Hunnish ingénue—but I did not care for our hosts' tastes in animal flesh, which ran heavily to bushbabies, colobus, vervet, and blue monkeys.

At intervals throughout this week Helen was fiercely sick, victim to a recurring malady that I attributed to our sudden change in habitat and diet. By the end of our sixth day on the mountain these bouts of vomiting had so enfeebled her that she spent the night prostrate but wakeful under my care. After patting Mary to sleep, I fetched back moist compresses of moss from the trickle-out of a nearby stream and applied these to Helen's throat and forehead. Eventually I curled up beside her to sleep.

When I awoke, the highland forest was emphatically swaying. The impetus for this motion was not the wind. Instead, the flank of the mountain had begun to convulse beneath us in just the way that cowhide convulses to dislodge a persnickety fly. Both Helen and Mary were gone. I staggered outside. Through the swaying foliage I saw them on the bank of the spring from which I had filched my compresses. Helen was holding Mary, but a lurch of Mount Tharaka knocked her legs out from under her. The child tumbled from her arms to the ground.

"*Helen!*" I shouted. "*Mary!*"

Mine was just one more voice in a chorus of confused voices. A crew of Hunnish habilines had spread out through the woods above the spring, chastising the mountain for its bad behavior and celebrating their own fearlessness. Their whoops and catcalls piped a puny counterpoint to Mount Tharaka's rumblings, but none of the Huns seemed to believe that their lives were at hazard. In fact, they grew angrier. The louder the mountain rumbled, the more vehement their protests. Like pinballs, the Huns caromed about among the trees caroling their courage and their outrage.

Mary leapt to her feet, and Helen hurried to catch her. Before she could, one of Attila's henchmen swept down on the australopithecine child with a club. One swing nearly severed Mary's head from her neck, and the next narrowly missed Helen. I wanted to scream, but could not get any sound out. Instead, my pistol jumped into my hand. With hate in my heart and a trembling grip I pointed it at Mary's murderer.

Whereupon Mount Tharaka shrugged again, tumbling all of us.

When, a minute or two after this convulsion, I again lifted my head, Helen was presenting her posterior to the Hun who had killed our daughter. He touched her gently on the rump, then walked past her into the leafmold where Mary's corpse lay. To each of the other habilines who arrived at the spring Helen also presented her buttocks. When none of them either accepted this invitation or kicked her down the slope, she went groveling to the feet of the premier culprit. In the extremity of her terror and grief she was seeking reassurance from an unconscionable barbarian. The barbarian gave it. As his comrades-in-arms dismembered our daughter's headless corpse, he patted Helen on the shoulders, stroked her consolingly, and murmured Hunnish commiseration.

I fired my pistol in the air, one shot for each habiline. Although they had not scurried for the mountain's rumblings, they scurried for my gunshots. The quake, by now, had run its course, and the reports were as clean and hard as the sound of an icepick chipping ice. A few moments later Helen stumbled down the debris-cluttered slope into my arms. Much more tenderly than Mount Tharaka had just rocked all of us, I rocked her, rocked her and rocked her.

Later, as Helen lay glassy-eyed and immobile in our hut, I gathered up what was left of Mary and buried these remnants in the soft earth near the spring. Then I took a walk.

In the twilight, preserved in a bed of volcanic tuff high on the mountain's side, a cyclopean skull caught my eye. It was the skull of either a mastodon or a dinothere, a rope-nosed beast that had ventured up the slopes of Mount Tharaka in search of shoots and leaves, only to die before being able to rumba back down to bush country. What seemed to be an immense eye socket in the animal's skull was in fact its nasal cavity, but the early Greeks would later mistake such skulls for those of one-eyed giants and would stand in glorious awe of the visions conjured by their imaginations from this error. I, too, stood in awe of the skull.

Polyphemus was a pachyderm.

After prising the enormous skull from the tuff in which it was partially embedded, I let it steer me back down the mountain.

At Mary's grave I erected it as a headstone, a memorial to our daughter.

CHAPTER TWENTY-THREE

Panama City, Florida

Summer 1981

THE MUSIC FROM the pavilion on the beach was stale disco stuff, jukebox leftovers from another summer. Lots of activity, though, and the activity drew him.

Clad in huarache sandals and cut-off jeans, Joshua ambled down from the Miracle Strip to see what was happening. Hubbard had just paid him, and with Hubbard's intervention at a local bank he had recently obtained a loan to buy a motor bike. The bike was padlocked in a rack next to the public showers near the highway, and as he angled over the yielding white sand to the pavilion, he revolved to admire it. A red Kawasaki, just beautiful. Money was independence.

Old music, new wheels.

Down at the pavilion Joshua propped one foot on a wooden rail and watched the dancers. Continually eclipsed by half-naked, spasming bodies, the jukebox on the floor seemed to expand and contract like a huge, opalescent lung. The sun had just set. A lingering red stain lay on the waters of the Gulf, and this same color was reflected in the concrete floor of the pavilion. Joshua was hypnotized. The rhythms pounding out of the jukebox held him, as did the flamboyant, robotic movements of the dancers. They were mostly white college kids or giggling teenyboppers, but the predominant impression was of damned souls undergoing the torments of hell and perversely enjoying them. Joshua did not see much hope of his fitting into either group.

If you want company, he told himself, scoot back over to Eglin and look up some of your old Air Force buddy-buddies.

Of course that was not possible. Nobody he knew from the days before Hugo's death lived in base housing anymore. Military families were professional refugees. They came and went like gypsies. Last October he had hitched a ride onto base with a young airman and then strolled past the old Capehart unit in which the Monegals had lived for nearly three years. Out front, one of those headache-green plastic tricycles for preschoolers . . . You can't go home again, particularly if you never had one.

The number on the jukebox ended, not by resolving itself but by fading away into wounded silence. The next tune was a ballad with a lovely flute solo lifting above the repetitive thud of the bass. Sunburned bodies clutched each other and swayed together like amorous drunks. Refusing to acknowledge his disfranchisement, Joshua continued to watch.

Then a small miracle occurred.

A frail, brown-skinned girl with hair like liquid graphite was staring at him from the other side of the pavilion. Dragon Lady's kid sister, he thought; an Oriental innocent. When she saw that he had seen her watching him, she closed her eyes and let her hair gust from side to side with the melancholy piping of the flute.

Alas, she was not alone. Beside her, gazing glassily at the dancers, slumped a skinheaded young man in a pair of polyester slacks and a pale yellow T-shirt commemorating the Freedom Flotilla of 1980. A trainee from one of the bases in the area, he had probably overdosed on potato chips and light beer, sunshine and Seconal. His date wanted to dance, but he was doing well to stay upright. Finally, his scalp shining obscenely pink, his chin fell to his breast and he began sliding slowly toward the floor. The girl tried to rescue him, but he was clearly too heavy for her to support alone. Struggling with his weight, she appealed to Joshua with her eyes, and the unequivocal message in that look was, "You see the trouble I'm having. Come on, turkey, give me a hand." Joshua circled the crowd at the rail to do just that.

After some initial fumbling for handholds, Joshua and the girl walked her dehydrated beau back up the beach to the Miracle Strip, where they thrust his head beneath a shower spray and tried to revive him to at least zombie status. No go. The trainee regarded them with the bulging, transparent eyes of a whitefish. Dragon Lady's kid sister wiped his face with a silk scarf and signaled her helplessness to Joshua by shrugging. They had exchanged no more than ten words since leaving the pavilion.

"Where's he from?"

"Hurlbutt Field," said the girl with no trace of accent, in spite of which Joshua had decided that she was of Thai or Vietnamese extraction. "He tells me he's going to be a Ranger."

"Hockey, baseball, or forest?"

"I don't know what you mean."

"Never mind. We'd better put him someplace where he can sleep off his zonk. If he goes back to Hurlbutt like this, he'll spend the next few days bayonetting potatoes instead of make-believe Iranians."

"He rented a car. It's over there."

They laid the would-be Ranger in the back seat of the rental car, a blue Plymouth Fury, rolled up his pants legs, and placed the girl's dampened scarf on his head for a compress.

The girl drove west along the highway to a deserted section of the dunes. Joshua followed on his Kawasaki. In the lee of a mimosa tree they discussed what else they should do for the fellow. By now, stars were guttering in a fabric of blowing clouds.

"He doesn't have to be back until five o'clock Sunday evening. His pass is for the entire weekend."

248 || **Michael Bishop**

"Let's crack a couple of windows, lock the keys up in the car with him, and let him sleep. He's not going to convulse or suffocate, and nobody'll bother him out here."

In khaki-colored shorts and a T-shirt like her companion's, the girl resembled a rather coltish Brownie Scout. She was almost exactly Joshua's height, but slender, ethereal-looking. She was noticeably hesitant about accepting his suggestions, not so much out of loyalty to her date, Joshua thought, as from a cagy distrust of his own motives. No dummy, this one.

"I'll let you drive," he said, pointing at his motorbike. "If I misbehave, you can steer us into oncoming traffic and put the fear of God back into me."

"If you drive, maybe you'll be too busy to misbehave."

"But you'd have no control over where I was taking you."

"Would you go someplace besides where I asked you to?" She cocked her head and studied him critically. "If it comes to it, I can hitchhike home." She set off through the dunes toward the highway.

Flustered, Joshua walked along beside her. How was he supposed to address this sensuous Asian waif with magical hair and eyes like a pair of melting chocolate kisses? Not even his residence in New York—his exile, as he sometimes thought of it— had taught him how to proceed. He was a novice in these matters, an aspirant.

"How old are you?" he blurted.

"Seventeen."

"I'm nineteen this November." Even though November seemed at least as far away as Ho Chi Minh City, that put him back up. "I meant it when I said you could drive. I've just been paid. Take me back to the Strip and I'll buy you something to eat."

The girl halted. "A foot-long and a Coke?"

"Anything you want. I've just been paid."

"Yeah, you told me." She glanced back at the rental car beneath the mimosa tree. "All Rudy wanted was uppers, downers, and onion rings. He washed 'em down with white wine and Pabst

Blue Ribbon, back and forth—just like this." Rustling her hair like a veil of chain, she demonstrated Rudy's unmannerly technique.

"Jesus."

The girl smiled. Her smile was the fulcrum upon which his hopes precariously teetered. "I've never ridden a motorcycle," she said. "I think I'd like to try."

Her name, once upon a time, had been Tru Tran Quan, but now she was known as Jacqueline Tru. Her father, who had emigrated to the United States long before anyone had ever heard of Boat People or suspected that Saigon was ripe for the picking, ran a small ethnic restaurant where foot-longs and onion rings were not even on the menu. Although Joshua and Jackie did not eat in the old man's establishment that first night, before the summer was over they had devoured rice, diced chicken, and fried vegetable sprouts in so many different combinations that Joshua began to regard mayonnaise as an exotic condiment and hamburger soup as a consommé devoutly to be wished.

Kha, the old man, had been a colonel in the Army of the Republic of Vietnam until early in the first administration of Richard Nixon, at which time he had come to Lackland Air Force Base in Texas with his wife and three children on a mission of mercy approved by the U.S. State Department. Madame Tru was suffering from a rare blood disorder for which she had been promised treatment at either the base hospital or the facility in Houston where Dr. Denton Cooley had made heart transplants as commonplace as tonsillectomies. A wealthy man, Kha had reputedly reimbursed the American government for the privilege of bringing his entire family into the country during a time of private as well as public anguish.

Unfortunately, Madame Tru collapsed and died upon first setting foot in an examination room at Lackland, a victim of the combined effects of her disease, her wearisome trip, and her own apprehensions. Reacting swiftly, Kha told the authorities that he was resigning his commission in the ARVN and requesting political asylum in the United States. He did not want to go back to the institutionalized chaos of a disintegrating war effort and a corrupt South Vietnamese regime. Besides, his only son was thirteen, fast approaching draft age.

"But you can't seek political asylum in the country of your government's foremost ally," a bespectacled official from the State Department told Tru. "It doesn't make sense."

"It does not make sense to ask a favor of a friend?" asked Tru Quan Kha.

"Of course not. You ask political asylum of a foe of the government you are seeking to flee."

"My friend and my foe have the same face."

"Then surely you can see your way clear to return to Saigon without resigning your commission and provoking an embarrassing incident."

"The Republic of Canada honors your northern border," Tru Quan Kha reflected aloud. "It is safer here."

The government sought to return Colonel Tru against his will, but his son—a boy well-versed in both the English language and the many uses of the public media—went to the San Antonio newspapers with his father's story and the startling disclosure that Tru would pay a handsome sum to any unattached native-born American woman who would marry him. By this stratagem, the boy admitted, Tru hoped to secure for his children and himself the same inalienable blessings of liberty enjoyed by the American people. Owing to quick government reaction, only a few of the newspapers containing this story made it to the streets. Nevertheless, ten or twelve patriotic bachelorettes responded favorably to Tru's offer, and the publicity attending this local uproar threatened to leak out of San Antonio into other parts of the country. Gun-shy, the government relented. Tru was permitted to marry a fiftyish lady named Brenda Lu Bruno and so to acquire his citizenship.

Tru promptly moved to Florida, for he wanted to see grapefruit trees, Disneyworld, and Ritki's Gift & Souvenir Emporium. He and Brenda Lu Tru did not live together, but corresponded regularly and filed a joint tax return each year to keep Uncle Sam off their backs. For over a decade, then, his son and daughters an ever-present solace, Tru Quan Kha had been a happy man.

Joshua did not initially increase his happiness. The old Vietnamese looked upon blacks as walking burn victims, who, if he touched them, would scream or slough off a pink-backed rind of charred flesh. Nor did he like being so much taller than Joshua. Even the age-induced curvature of his spine did not lower him to the young man's eye level. Was his daughter—a good Catholic girl rechristened Jacqueline after the slain president's widow—was Jacqueline going to marry a bruised toe of a man instead of a Robert Redford clone with a bankbook as thick as the Gutenberg Bible? Perhaps. No one could fathom Jackie's intentions. And if Joshua was in her plans, how could Joshua increase Kha's happiness?

First, by increasing Jackie's happiness, a task at which he seemed to excel; and second, by amusing her father. The boy—the *young man*, rather—could tell marvelous stories. Stories in which vaguely human creatures, in order to sustain themselves, dug tubers out of the ground, captured small birds, and scavenged the leftovers of predators larger than they. Many unlikely animals shared the ancient grasslands with these fascinating near-men, whose expulsion from Eden was a fall from savagery into the continuing benediction of the Agricultural Revolution and Joint Checking Accounts. Because Kha was no longer a wealthy man—first the Thieu regime and then the North Vietnamese Communists had seized his former properties—the material poverty of Joshua's prehistoric hominids struck him as idyllic rather than distressing. He enjoyed listening to Joshua talk about what no living person could know firsthand, and he lavished food on his daughter's suitor to keep him on the premises, contentedly reeling off such stories.

Jackie, meantime, would sit at table with the two men, tolerant of their interplay. Owing to her father's belief that her intellectual capacity and her independent frame of mind destined her for a calling higher than waiting tables, she had few duties at the Mekong Restaurant. (It had once been a Texaco service station.) Kha's elder daughter, Cosette, therefore worked for him as hostess, waitress, cashier, and assistant cook. Despite a cavalcade of tourists up and down the Strip, the Mekong seldom had many customers, and Kha, until a patron arrived, could usually abandon the kitchen with impunity. Joshua supposed that the lack of traffic through the dining room (it had once been a double garage) prevented Cosette from indulging too active a resentment of her younger sister. Jackie, after all, would one day be a history teacher in the Florida public schools or a simultaneous translator at the United Nations in New York.

As for Dzu, the boy who had taken Kha's story to the San Antonio papers, he was now employed by the State Department as an expert in the processing of foreign refugees, whether from Southeast Asia or the Caribbean. Joshua had never met Dzu, but tonight Joshua was wearing another of the Freedom Flotilla 1980 T-shirts that Dzu had sent to his sisters as mementos. Jackie and Cosette had spent the last year passing them out to friends, acquaintances, and even blind dates. In the Mekong's kitchen was a pantry shelf stacked with these shirts.

"Father, he's had enough to eat, and you've heard enough of his talk for one evening."

Kha shrugged unrepentantly, mumbled in Vietnamese.

"He says you should write down the stories you tell," Jackie translated.

"I don't have to. If I wait long enough, I'll see the replays in my dreams." But he stood up, bowed to Kha, and told the old man that he had promised to take Jackie to a movie. He kept his billfold in his pocket because Kha regarded any effort to press payment upon him as a gaudy sort of insult.

"An ill-remembered dream is a lost opportunity," Kha said in English. "You should write them down."

Jackie kissed her father on his splotched forehead, waved cheerily to Cosette, and led Joshua out the plate-glass door into the hubbub of surf and engine noises that characterized the Strip.

"No movie," she said pointedly. "You."

"Where?"

"What's wrong with your trailer?"

"Gene's just come back from a job in Louisiana. More than likely he's reclaimed his kingdom. Beer cans on the toilet tank, clothes down the hallway, a butter tub of guacamole on the TV. Not my idea of the perfect trysting place."

Big Gene Curtiss was Joshua's trailer mate, the foreman of Gulf Coast Coating's out-of-state tank-painting crew. He was twice Joshua's age and half again as heavy. Three times the victim of heartbreaking, wholly unexpected divorce suits, he went to church every Sunday, but truly worshiped only Dizzy Gillespie, the memory of Billie Holliday, and the Tampa Bay Buccaneers, no matter their record. He did not consider Negro an unacceptable term for People of Color and had never heard of Jomo Kenyatta, Steve Biko, Robert Mugabe, or Eldridge Cleaver.

"I've got enough money for a motel room."

"Nix on that."

"Where, then?" Joshua could hear a note of exasperation in his voice. He had been thinking movie, the new Brian de Palma.

"Why don't you surprise me?"

"Christ."

"Don't be profane, Joshua. I'll give you a better review than you'll probably give the flick."

Her whim—which, if he were honest, he could easily make his own—required preparation and a little thought. At first these requirements had short-circuited his enthusiasm, but now that he and Jackie were aboard his motor bike, weaving in and out of traffic past cinderblock motels awash with neon, stucco beach-goods shops, and the fiberglass fauna of various miniature golf courses, he was excited again. He would surprise her; overwhelm her, in fact. Together they would attain to the same fabulous estate of passion previously occupied by Caesar and Cleopatra, Lancelot and Guinevere, Bonnie and Clyde. It was a long way to Joshua's motor court, a distance complicated by campers, pickup trucks, and boat trailers, but, breezily negotiating this strung-out slalom, he got them there in less than an hour.

"Wait here," he told Jackie. "I'll be right out."

Big Gene lay sprawled on the living room's sofa bed watching a television program. He lifted a beer can in salute. Joshua nodded at him, hurried down the skivvy-littered hall, and returned a moment later carrying a heavy-duty flashlight and a quilt.

"What's that?" the big man asked.

"Flashlight. Quilt."

"What for?"

"Clambake," Joshua improvised, pushing open the door and nearly missing the first step. "Don't wait up."

"Fuckin' fool kid," said Gene amiably.

Joshua made a saddle of the quilt. Jackie, clutching the flashlight, climbed on behind him, and they traveled northeast along a desolate stretch of highway bordering the military reservation.

Palm trees surrendered to scrub, which in turn surrendered to kudzu, pine trees, and curtains of Spanish moss. In the shoals of summer darkness Alabama loomed up like a barnacled boat bottom. This was territory where, as late as fifteen years ago, backwoods entrepreneurs had erected billboards atop their filling stations and feed stores declaring, "We Want White Peoples Business." Joshua had never seen such a sign, but Tom Hubbard and Big Gene Curtiss had vouched for their reality. A finger of apprehension drew its nail through the maze of his lower intestines. He wrung the right handlebar to increase their speed and shouted over his shoulder the news that they were almost there. Jackie squeezed his collarbones in acknowledgment.

A line of brick buildings opened out of the countryside like a stage set revolving into view. Joshua backed his hand off the accelerator and let the bike drift into a town with a solitary traffic light. For the past week a crew from Gulf Coast Coating, Inc., had been at work on the little town's water tower, sandblasting its tank interior down to white metal and applying to every other surface a rugged primer. The belly of the water tank glistened above them like the turret of a Martian war machine.

A fence surrounded the base of the tower, isolating it from the sleeping business district by a good fifty or sixty yards. Every ancient storefront was shuttered, and the traffic light rocked back and forth in a gentle, midnight breeze. Green, amber, red. Green, amber, red. The intersection was empty.

"You think this is better than your trailer?"

"More private."

She put her chin on his shoulder. "You might as well have taken me to a tennis court or a football field."

"Not down here. Up there, Jackie. Inside the tank."

Her expression, softly starlit, did not change. She tilted her head to estimate the height of the tank and the difficulty of the climb. Joshua was pleased that she did not angrily veto his idea, disappointed that she did not seem more surprised. They had come a long way together, both tonight and over the course of the summer. He, she had admitted, was her fourth lover, whereas he had nervously forfeited his virginity to her amid a small range of sand dunes not far from Santa Rosa Beach. Jackie's readiness to fornicate inside a metal globe one hundred feet above *terra firma* was probably far less miraculous than her willingness to fornicate at all. A Vietnamese by birth, a dutiful daughter, and "a good Catholic girl," she ought to have been as chaste as a nun, but Florida had transformed her without really negating these attributes and now she considered herself an enlightened woman of the world. She insisted on embracing diversity.

"Very imaginative, Joshua."

"Not for me. For me it was an obvious notion."

They left his Kawasaki capsized in the grass, vaulted the low fence, and climbed the ladder to the catwalk about the tank's middle. Joshua carried the flashlight in his belt and the quilt over his shoulder like a serape. As insurance against Jackie's slipping, he brought up the rear, while she protested that because of the crap he was carrying he was the more likely to fall. Neither of them fell, but the climb made even Joshua dizzy, and they rested on the catwalk before proceeding up the hemisphere-hugging ladder to the hatch in the top of the tank. This time Joshua went first.

Perched on the hatch lip, he played the flashlight beam about the inside of the tank. Scale shone dully on the surfaces that had not yet been sandblasted, and the smell of chlorine, rust, and scoured metal made him hang fire. Maybe this wasn't such a brilliant idea, after all.

"Go on," Jackie urged him. "What are you waiting for?"

He descended into the tank. Nimbly, Jackie followed. Against one of the lower slopes, near the abyss of the tower's riser pipe, they found an island of migrating sand from the blasting. Here, in a conspiracy of whispers and useless hand gestures, they spread the quilt. The butt of the flashlight struck the side of the tank as Joshua was working, and the resultant clangor was deafening.

"People *drink* the water from these tanks?"

"It's sampled every month for impurities."

Her face rendered gargoylish by shadows, Jackie glanced about at the slime and scale. "Ugh."

It occurred to Joshua that if she could differentiate his face from the encompassing darkness, he must look even more alien than she—but, touching his chin, she leaned forward to kiss him. They melted like candles to their knees. They collapsed into each other on the floating surface of the quilt. Their flesh was warm paraffin, and in the blindness of their melting they were transparent to each other.

When Joshua was next aware of himself as a separate person, they lay side by side, naked and sweat-lathered. The Garden of Eden on stilts, that's what the stinking water tank had become. The scale corroding the tank emitted not a stench but a perfume. Their bodies were relaxed, purged of lust, and no serpent had yet appeared.

"Nice."

"Four stars," Jackie said. "Highly recommended."

"Let's get married."

She let these words echo a moment before saying, "Oh, no, Mr. Kampa. You are a bitter young man who's not yet totally happy with himself. I don't want to be the live-in private secretary who records your dreams."

"I asked you to marry me. You didn't even think about it."

"I've thought about it many times. I just didn't think you would ever ask me—Joshua, I've got other things to do."

"Like what?"

"Have you ever heard of Mother Teresa of Calcutta? She's a role model not many people have tried to follow. I think a lot about trying to do work comparable to hers."

Joshua yipped like a chihuahua.

"I'm not kidding. It sounds ridiculous to you because you can't imagine me undertaking a spiritual mission. A mission of mercy. That's your problem."

"I asked you to marry me."

"I told you no, and I told you why. You don't want to get married either. Think about these dreams you have, Joshua. The apemen in them—the apemen trying to become human—they're the key. You want what they want, but you don't know how to get there any better than they do. You're perplexed and conflicted."

"I love you, Jackie."

"That's your glands talking. Glands and gratitude. You don't get married for those kinds of reasons. You shouldn't, anyway."

"Jackie, I've had these goddamn dreams since before I could speak. I've been 'perplexed and conflicted' since infancy."

"That's because you've got a mission, and you don't know what it is yet."

"You."

"Fuck that nonsense."

"How the hell do you know you're *not* my mission?"

"Because I have a mission of my own. Otherwise, you know, I would not have been spared when so many others were taken."

Jackie's quasi-mysticism was unanswerable. It reminded him that at the center of his own life lay a mystery which he had come to regard as both commonplace and disreputable, like a touch of the clap. He had revealed this mystery to the Tru family because their foreignness—that is, their assumed distance from the prejudices and thought patterns of *real* people—had made them seem safe confessors. Besides, telling his dreams had helped to win Kha over and demonstrably heightened Jackie's interest in him. At least at first. Now she was blithely dropping depth charges into the fragile fishbowl of his hopes.

"Anyone who's alive has been 'spared,' Jackie. Trouble is, nobody knows for how long or for what."

"Some do, and some should."

"Listen to you, you're gloating."

"You're at odds with yourself, Joshua, not with me. So stop it. You're also at odds with your own family, and there's no longer any reason to be."

"What are you talking about?"

"Eden in His Dreams."

Ah, yes. His mother's—rather, Jeannette Monegal's—proposed book about his uncanny chronic affliction. So far as Joshua knew, the book had never appeared, under either that title or another. He had walked out on her, and she had apparently dropped the project. Jeannette still had no idea to what sanctuary he had fled, however, for he had not tried to get in touch with her since his defection from the West Bronx. Nor was he ready to repair the breach with a telephone call. No, ma'am. No long-distance orgy of apology and forgiveness for him. Who would apologize, who forgive? Joshua closed his eyes and tried to center himself in the impenetrable dark.

"You don't want to talk about that, do you?"

"No," he said. "Not really."

After a while Jackie said, "What about your job, then? Are you willing to talk about that?"

"You don't like my job? You don't want a steeplejack for a husband? A tank painter's wages don't thrill you?"

"None of that has anything to do with what I'm talking about, Joshua. Your job is a detour, a stopgap. You go into some little town and set about sprucing up its most conspicuous phallic landmark. It's hard, honest work, but for you it's also a kind of masturbation. Mindless and lonely."

"Holy shit. I can't believe this."

"Can't believe what?"

"You sound like Lucy in a 'Peanuts' cartoon. Spouting off jargon under a sign that says 'Psychiatric Care—Five Cents.'"

"You quit your job occasionally, don't you? And then Mr. Hubbard rehires you when you come back. That's true, isn't it?"

Joshua said nothing.

"You're just preparing yourself for the final break. One day you'll feel good about quitting forever. You'll get your mission, and you'll do what you're supposed to. So maybe your mission is *supposed* to be delayed for a while. I'm not telling you to quit your job. I'm not trying to tell you how to run your life."

"You're not?"

"You know I'm not. But if we were married I might. And you'd do the same to me, not even meaning to." She laid her hand on his chest. "Don't fret, Joshua. It's not a tragedy that I've already got my mission and you're still waiting for yours. It'll happen."

Chuckling ruefully, Joshua covered her hand with his own.

"What're you laughing at?"

"Getting my mission. You talk about it the way some girls

I knew in New York used to talk about getting their periods. You make it sound biological. Inevitable. Foreordained. I don't think I believe that, Jackie. It doesn't compute—as an analogy, I mean." He twisted aside and began feeling about for his clothes. He had struck right through her peculiar variety of psychobabble. For her a "mission" was a kind of psychic menarche, and she was being so understanding about his tardiness in achieving this condition for the same reason that she would avoid ridiculing a girl in a training bra. People develop at different paces. Joshua could feel his gorge rising, a prickle of anger erupting like a rash. "I'm ready to go," he said. He found the flashlight and fumbled it on.

"Me too," Jackie acknowledged, her voice as straightforward and bright as the flashlight beam.

That fall Jackie began to attend a local junior college. Joshua saw less and less of her, and his ambiguous passion for the girl with the magic hair modulated into friendship. Later she transferred to George Washington University in the nation's capital, and their relationship gradually dwindled away to letters, postcards, memories, and silence.

Joshua continued to work for Gulf Coast Coating, Inc., and he continued to dream . . .

CHAPTER TWENTY-FOUR
Dream Seed

Soon after Mary's murder we separated from the Huns and made an encampment for ourselves on the northeastern flank of Mount Tharaka, eight or nine miles from our former hosts and at a considerably lower elevation. The mountain appeared to approve of our arrangements, for it refrained from bellyaching about them, and we could lie down at night without fearing that an outbreak of burps and belches would jolt us all awake. I may have been the only Minid who worried at all about the stability of Mount Tharaka's gastrointestinal tract. These worries I suppressed by a very simple expedient: I shut down most conscious mental activity and drifted from one day to the next as if *dreaming* the successive episodes of my outward life.

I became, as in my spirit-traveling episodes before White Sphinx, a disembodied observer, a camera on a mobile boom—with the telling exception that among the Minids I retained my body as a camera housing. For the next several weeks, then, my life was a picaresque narrative without a protagonist, a runaway

Ferrari from which the driver has leapt, not out of panic but from a ripening indifference to its destination. The wind still scoured my flesh, and the night might kindle my vision with the fagot tips of stars—but now I drank in these phenomena without consciously remarking them.

Helen eventually recovered from the bouts of nausea that had plagued her in the highland kingdom of the Huns. She continued to mourn our loss of Mary, however. Picking a fruit from a galol tree or digging a tuber out of the ground, she would suddenly pause and cast a pitiable glance on Zippy or A.P.B. To distract her I would usually put one of my own grimy discoveries into her hand and gesture her on to the next likely foraging site. When we separated from the others, such descents into funk were rare, for we were away from the stimulus to melancholy that the children represented.

Our new camp—twig and brush hovels through which the wind played sonatinas—lay in a bamboo thicket near a spring not far from the savannah. Temperatures here sometimes dropped alarmingly, and Helen and I would lie entwined in each other's arms against the cold. My teeth made typewriter racket, and my body often quivered like a clapper-struck bell, but I did not suffer unduly. The running sore at the corner of my mouth, the insect bites damasking my flesh, the bruises and abrasions incising their steel-blue intaglios on my shins . . . none of these annoyances truly annoyed me. Helen and I held each other, and the nights ricocheted away around us like the fragments of primeval chaos. I had become a habiline. So far as I could tell this transformation did not mark a devolution but a detour. I was dreaming myself into being out of the forgotten materials of preconsciousness, and Helen was my guide through the dark.

I dreamed that my chukkas were wearing out, and they were. I had already broken and replaced several shoelaces, but now the rubber soles were fissuring, the scuffed Maple Cuddy leather cracking open to reveal the aromatic little piggies penned up inside. Babington would have been ashamed of me for not discarding my boots and going barefoot, but I patched them with bark, bound them with moistened strips of bamboo, and pretended that my repairs were successful. They were not. One day I tripped on a binding, tore out the side of my right chukka, and, in disgust, hurled both my beloved boots into the canebrake below me. Thenceforeward, until my feet had developed a new set of calluses, I lurched about like a gimpy middle guard. Surprisingly, maybe because I was dreaming, the calluses were quick to form.

My shorts also went. First the crotch seam split. Although I mended it with a fish-hook needle and a remnant of fishing line (which, for want of an opportunity, I had never used in Lake Kiboko or anywhere else), the resewn seam promptly ripped out too. In any event, thorn bushes, briars, and hard wear had opened numerous tiny windows in the fabric. My flanks were exposed, and I was fighting a doomed rear-guard action against nakedness. Because a couple of my pockets had long since worn through, I had already transferred their contents to my knapsack. It was no hardship to displace my remaining belongings to it as well, and to surrender my shorts to Helen for a kaross.

More and more frequently I left my .45 in its holster in our hut. I covered the weapon, my bandolier, and my backpack with dried grass and walked upon Africa's good earth as naked as any Minid. The minor surgery Babington had performed on my masculine member in Lolitabu distinguished me from the other males in our band, but it was hardly a conspicuous addition to my several points of departure from the anatomical standard. In fact, naked, I was finally in uniform. Giving up the security of the .45 and the bullet-laden bandolier was easier than giving up the security of my bush shorts. Dreaming, still dreaming, I had almost totally divested myself of my twentieth-century identity.

For the first time in my life (I can see, in retrospect) I *fit*. My dreaming consciousness did not invalidate my desire to belong to both the Minid community and the larger Pleistocene community encompassing it. None of Helen's people made any attempt to tell the dreamer from the dream . . .

. . .

One day, parched by my dream of interminable drought, I dreamed that it rained. And it did.

The following morning the valley below our camp and a significant sward of savannah looked as if they had been decorated for the senior-class prom. Flowers boogalooed in the breeze, flipping scarlet petticoats and saffron capes. To walk through those dancing flowers would have been akin to shuffling through a post-party spill of perfumed crepe paper. I drank the scene in. It intoxicated me, but not in the way that puckerplums could do. I still had my basic motor skills, and with these intact I led Helen down the ridge from our camp into the holiday ground cover—into, it seemed, a garden.

We were not alone in this celebration, for the other Minids also came cavorting down the slope. Experimentally uprooting handfuls of scarlet or lavender, the children went sniffing from blossom to blossom, much in the way that kids in Florida frolic in the virgin white graupel of a rare February sleetfall. Groucho, Bonzo, Jocelyn, and Pebbles stayed the longest of all the habiline youngsters, but Helen and I outlasted even them, and when they had finally departed, we collapsed panting amid the luxuriant vegetable filagree of our narrow mountain valley.

Below, on the revivified pasturage of the plain, elephants, zebras, gazelles, and lanky giraffids grazed, but Helen and I ignored them in beatific contemplation of each other's navels.

Literally.

I saw that Helen's abdomen had taken on the contour, if not the coloring, of a cantaloupe. Astonished, I touched her taut tumescent tummy and searched her eyes for some sign that she understood the significance of this alteration in her figure. In the land of the lean of loin, the pot-bellied person is . . . well, pregnant.

"Helen, you're going to be a mamma. A mamma, do you understand? Hell, *I* don't understand—but it's terrific, it's great!"

"Mai mwah," she replied, plucking a violet blossom between forefinger and crippled-looking thumb.

. . .

Pregnant? My Helen, pregnant? Once over my initial lethargic surprise I accepted Helen's pregnancy as natural, foreordained, and welcome. But surely a human-habiline union could not be fruitful because of a basic chromosomal incompatibility between our two species. Even with males of her own kind Helen had heretofore been barren.

How, then, had I overcome these formidable obstacles to *getting her with child?*

I do not really know. Much of what occurred during this period had the lazy inevitability of events in a vision or a fugue. Today, though, I can emphasize that *barren* does not necessarily mean *sterile;* it first implies the absence of offspring and only secondarily the inability to conceive them. Until she actually delivers a child, therefore, it is by no means incorrect to call a woman barren. Misleading, perhaps, but not incorrect.

Why did Helen not conceive a child by Alfie or one of the other male habilines, then?

Not being a gynecologist, a fertility researcher, or a certified expert in habiline insemination techniques, I must again confess ignorance. The most ingenious explanation I can hazard suggests that, genotypically, Helen was a forerunner of a hominid species closely resembling *H. sapiens.* Because her reproductive organs reposed farther forward than was usual among the females of her kind, she may have appeared too early to exploit this latent genetic potential—except, of course, by accident. I was Helen's accident, an unforeseeable throwback from the future already encoded in her DNA. For which reason she conceived my child rather than Alfie's, Malcolm's, Roosevelt's, or anyone else's.

But members of distinct species—even within the same genus—are seldom interfertile.

Well, how often do they get a chance to be?

Still, it is said that apes and humans cannot profitably mate.

Profit is not *always* the primary motive in such encounters. Does this epigram constitute a statement of empirical fact, a pending piece of Natural Law, or an ethical imperative? None of the above, I'm afraid. Moreover, the expression "cannot profitably mate" runs headlong into the highly suggestive fact that a siamang and a gibbon of another species confined together several years ago at Atlanta's Yerkes Primate Center surprised their keepers with a cuddly wee one. Admittedly, neither a siamang nor its gibbony lover is a human being, but by the same token the lady I called Helen Habiline was *not an ape*. That simple truth bears reiteration.

Now, years later, I have the words of the following unimpeachable scientific authorities, whom I cite to intimidate the untutored:

Eugene Marais, South African naturalist and primatologist: "I am strongly inclined to believe that the offspring of no two sub-races of the same anthropoid will be found to be sterile." (Some of the terminology may be dated, but the sentiment is unequivocal.)

Carl Sagan, American astronomer and poet laureate of scientific syncretism: "For all we know, occasional viable crosses between humans and chimpanzees are possible. The natural experiment must have been tried very infrequently, at least recently." (One can only speculate about the biological consequences of the liaison so discreetly chronicled in John Collier's *His Monkey Wife.*)

Donald Johanson, American paleoanthropologist and discoverer of the fossil remains of the Australopithecus afarensis *specimen known as Lucy:* "It would be interesting to know if a modern man and a million-year-old *Homo erectus* woman could together produce a fertile child. The strong hunch is that they could; such evolution as has taken place is probably not of the kind that would prevent a successful mating." (However, one might reasonably suppose that a million-year-old woman had long since passed through menopause.)

Of late it has been fashionable for critics to dismiss my claim as a contemptible form of sexual braggadocio. I refute this mean-spirited charge by confessing my inadequacies as a lover.

First, a quotation from the pens of Richard Leakey (Blair's

Kenyan nemesis) and Roger Lewin (erstwhile editor of *New Scientist*): "As a biological response to female sexuality, human males have evolved a penis that is larger than any other primate, including the gorilla whose body bulk is almost three times that of a man's."

Sic, sic, sic.

(A connoisseur of others' slip-ups and solecisms, Blair once hung a sampler bearing this remarkable assertion on the wall of his private office in the National Museum in Marakoi.)

Despite an indefatigable popular belief in the sexual prowess of males of my pigmentation, my penis is not as large as a gorilla. It is not even as large as an Airedale. It may be as large as a lesser mouse lemur, but I do not propose to put this supposition to the acid test of direct comparison. And although I might pay for a quick glimpse of someone whose masculine member reminds Messrs. Leakey and Lewin of a mountain gorilla, I do not believe I would envy this person. He would probably have to purchase two fares each time he contrived to board a bus.

Second, neither do I possess exceptional staying power. Alfie was more than a match for me in this regard, as his exploits with Emily, Guinevere, and Nicole clearly demonstrated. Fortunately, even in her periods of utmost receptivity, Helen's sexual appetite was modest, and I did not have to overextend myself to give her her fill. The fact that I remain single today may be a function of my quiescent libido. Since Helen, I have not been drawn to any other woman, and my political obligations have exercised most of my energies.

Very well, then, setting aside chromosome counts, anatomy lessons, appeals to authority, and ritual self-abasement, how *do* I account for Helen's unlikely pregnancy?

Well, it may have been a miracle.

CHAPTER TWENTY-FIVE

Fort Walton Beach, Florida To Van Luna, Kansas

September to December 1985

WOODY KAPROW was an enigma. He did not consider Florida home, but he paid so little heed to his physical surroundings that no other place in the world (with the possible exception of a marshy area in Poland from which his family hailed but upon which he had never laid eyes) could claim that distinction, either. He was truly at home only in his own mind. A civilian, he let his mind to the Air Force under the terms of a complicated military research-and-development contract. A bachelor, he was married to this work. A loner, he was surrounded by assistants. A genius (if you could trust the judgment of these often fuddled minions), when it came to literature, music, art, or the likely contenders in this year's Super Bowl game, he had the attention span of a third-grader. Time—its properties, paradoxes, metaphysics, measurement, and maddening theoretical possibilities—was Woody Kaprow's passion. It was his career. A vocation that did not prevent him from misgauging the number of minutes it required to heat a frozen TV dinner. A passion that he could indulge while rinsing out a pair of socks, picking his nose, or attending committee meetings.

Kaprow, in person, was unprepossessing. A slender, middle-aged man with dark hair and eyes like bloated cocktail onions, he seemed younger than his years. (Joshua felt that this was because his ruling passion gave him a distracted, adolescent air, like a teen-ager in love with opera or astrology.) His clothes were always minimum-maintenance: dungarees, drip-dry shirts, chinos, turtleneck pullovers, jean jackets, sweatshirts, deck pants, and, occasionally, an orange, multizippered flight suit that he had purchased from a retiring fighter pilot. Even in the flight suit, however, he looked less like a military man than like one of the surviving members of the Flying Wallendas. Indeed, with his head cocked just so, his eyes afloat in the martini-bright waters of Abstract Speculation, he sometimes seemed to be walking a high wire invisible to mortal ken. At such times the jaunty, orange flight suit merely accentuated the incongruity of his metaphysical derring-do. A cough, a word, the slamming of a door would only infrequently shatter his concentration, but when they did, you could see him slipping from the wire and plummeting earthward like any other workaday Joe of average ambition, intelligence, and inspiration. Unprepossessing. Off the wire, almost —but not quite—a dullard.

Joshua had first met Kaprow in the mammoth Quonset hut given over to his workshop and laboratory. The physicist had been lying flat on his back on a grease-monkey's sled, apparently examining the chassis of an ugly, buslike vehicle that took up most of the floor space at the north end of the Quonset. Only Kaprow's Converse tennis shoes were visible, their scuffed rubber toes pointing toward the skylight. Not the most awe-inspiring of the man's attributes, these sneaker-clad feet, but Colonel Crawford knelt beside the bus and announced in a clear voice that White Sphinx's newest recruit was awaiting Kaprow's pleasure. Whereupon the physicist scooted out from under the bus, jumped up like a calisthenics instructor, and warmly, albeit distractedly, took Joshua's hand. He looked back and forth between the colonel and Joshua as if trying to connect them to the work he had just been doing. Satisfied that neither visitor was a ghost or an imposter, he smiled and slapped Joshua on the shoulder.

"Here you are," he said. "My dreamfarer."

"Alistair Patrick Blair thinks I'm his."

"Actually," Colonel Crawford put in, "you belong brain, belly, and balls to the U.S. Air Force."

"Yes, massa."

Kaprow slapped him on the shoulder again and smiled a sweet, lopsided smile. "A dreamfarer's principal bondage is to his dreamfaring. All the others are secondary. Isn't that so, Mr. Kampa?"

"Anything you say, sir."

In September Blair was concluding his American Geographic Foundation lectures, which he had interrupted for two weeks in August to hold a series of meetings with officials of the departments of Defense and State in Washington, D.C. These meetings had produced—very quickly—an important agreement between the governments of Zarakal and the United States, a codicil to the recent treaties establishing American military bases in Blair's homeland. Now, having fulfilled both his diplomatic and his paleontological obligations in the United States, he was returning to Marakoi. He stopped at Eglin to confer with Woody Kaprow and Joshua Kampa.

Hands thrust deep in the pockets of his boiler suit, the Great Man stood as if hypnotized before the cut-away body of the vehicle that would eventually translate Joshua to an earlier geologic epoch. Physics and engineering, not being his specialties, intimidated him in the same way they intimidated Joshua. But Blair did not enjoy being intimidated, and he was out of sorts. Kaprow interrupted the paleoanthropologist's sullen reverie to thrust a small, flat instrument rather like a pocket computer into his hands, then crossed the workshop and bestowed the instrument's mate on Joshua, who had spent most of the morning session sitting at the physicist's metal desk feeling like a tiny third wheel on a high-rolling bicycle that never let him touch ground. Blair and Kaprow had scarcely spoken to him. He might as well have spent the day on the beach.

"What's this?" Blair asked, looking across the workshop at Kaprow.

"An intertemporal communicator," the physicist replied. "I call it a transcordion, though, because that's catchier."

Joshua lowered his feet from the desk and studied the instrument. It appeared quite simple. It had a keyboard something like a typewriter's and a display area where messages could appear.

"All right. I give up. What are we supposed to *do* with them?" Blair asked Kaprow.

"Communicate, of course. Go ahead and exchange a few messages. It'll make you both feel better."

"Oh, I daresay."

"You know how to type, don't you?"

"Two-finger hunt-and-peck. In the early days of the National Museum I was my own bloody secretary—reports to the government, requests for funds, all that sort of rot. I vowed to give up typing forever. Now, for God's sake, *this.*"

"Send Joshua a message."

"What do I want to say?" He pondered the problem.

As he pondered, Joshua decided to plunge. *"Now is the time,"* he typed, *"for all old men to fade from the dreams of their dotage."*

Blair received the message and pointed his chin at Joshua. "Are you referring to me?"

"Touch the key marked *Clear* and send him a reply," Kaprow urged the Great Man.

His naked forehead furrowed nearly to his crown, Blair complied: *"Old dreamers never fade, they just fossilize."*

"Fossil lies are the stock and trade of fading paleontologists."

"The hell you say." Blair played the transcordion to this

effect: *"Desist and decamp, Joshua Kampa. Josh me no more, I pray."*

Joshua responded, *"A prayer from Blair is hardly fair. It's not the Darwinian Way."*

Aloud the Great Man said, "Rotten doggerel. And what does it prove, Dr. Kaprow? That fifteen feet apart we can send and receive like genuine radio men?"

Kaprow sat down on the edge of his desk and folded his arms across his belly. "It proves they're operating, Dr. Blair. They'll do just as well when you're separated by time as well as space. Every set of transcordions shares a crystallographic harmony that's independent of temporal considerations. They'd interresonate even if we sent Joshua to, God forbid, the Precambrian—so long as we didn't displace him spatially, too. Then we'd have to put up with a radio delay like those familiar to astronauts. Between a Now and a Then that are spatially congruent, though, the transcordions provide virtually instantaneous communication."

"Does 'instantaneous' mean anything under such circumstances?" Joshua asked.

"Call it a metaphor, then. The transcordions operate on a principle of physical correspondences rather than on the doubtful proposition of simultaneity. Simultaneity's an assumption of no real usefulness when you're dealing with persons sundered from each other by time. By definition, the past and the present do not, and cannot, coincide."

Joshua said, "Or they'd be the same thing."

Kaprow accepted Joshua's remark with a distracted nod. "However, in another sense, perhaps they are."

"Oh, God," Blair interjected. "One hand clapping."

"No, don't worry. I'm not going to go Zen on you just yet. The instantaneousness I'm talking about derives from a metaphorical simultaneity based on the concord between the time-displaced receiver and its mate. In a physical dimension about which we are pathetically ignorant, the past does indeed run parallel to the present."

Joshua slid his transcordion across the desk to Kaprow,

who picked it up and fondled it absent-mindedly. If the past and the present ran parallel to each other, why, damn it all, they *were* simultaneous. At least insofar as Joshua could get a grip on the matter. What good was a metaphor that muddled your metaphysics past all rational recourse? In comparison, one hand clapping was altogether comprehensible . . .

"Wait a minute," Joshua cried. "Time travel involves movement in space, too, doesn't it?"

"Of course it does. Every particle of matter travels along a world line consisting of three dimensions in space and one in time. Once we've transferred the physical components of White Sphinx to the Lake Kiboko Protectorate, Joshua, and once you've harnessed yourself to the Backstep Scaffold, we'll reverse the equations of motion for the finite region of space enclosing you. Then we'll transport that region backward along its various world lines to the destination dictated by your dreamfaring."

"My spirit-traveling, you mean."

"The terminology's of no consequence. The dreamfarer is himself the key to the journey, because time, like our universe, is an attribute of consciousness. In fact, it's possible that it has no significant meaning apart from consciousness. White Sphinx cannot shift inanimate objects—these transcordions, for instance—into the past without the intervention of a living psyche."

The workshop, with its corrugated walls and cold concrete floor, its high fluorescent tubes and hanging pulleys, its snakelike electrical cables and blocky machine presses, seemed more than an ocean away from the grasslands, rhino wallows, and wattle huts of East Africa. Indeed, it was. It was a little cathedral to human progress, a memorial to the evolution of insight and ingenuity. It was a starting place. Joshua was not sure, however, that he liked it very much.

"Listen," he said. "I've been thinking about this, about my . . . my *physical* displacement into the past."

"That's natural enough," Kaprow said. "And?"

"I'll be going back to the general vicinity of Lake Kiboko's eastern shore almost two million years ago."

"The site of our most productive digs," Blair put in.

"Okay. But I'm going to end up in an ancient Africa that occupies the same space-time coordinates as present-day Africa. Have I got that right, Dr. Kaprow?"

"Pretty much. I won't quibble with your construction of the matter."

"How?" Joshua demanded. "How does that happen? Our sun, the solar system, the whole damn galaxy—they're *moving*, aren't they?"

"Right. At a speed of approximately six hundred million miles a year, foot to the floorboard."

"Then to what goddamn East African Pleistocene will I really be going? It won't be the same one that existed two million years ago. The Earth supporting that geological epoch no longer exists. That Earth is a ghost-Earth a giga-zillion miles behind us somewhere, and there's no way to set me down on it without some sort of zippy, faster-than-light contraption. Right?"

"Right," Kaprow acknowledged.

"Well, I don't think that"—he nodded at the buslike vehicle beside Blair "—qualifies. In fact, I'm sure it doesn't. So where the hell exactly am I going to end up?"

Blair's expression betrayed surprise, dismay, chagrin. Joshua's objections, as Joshua himself could see, were ones that he had never considered. The idea that time travel has a spatial dimension was a novelty to him, a revelation. It gave the paleontologist pause. If Joshua did not emerge from Kaprow's machine into a primeval world of hominids, dinotheres, and antlered giraffes, but instead into a formless void like the clock tick before Creation, Blair had no hope of obtaining any concrete proof of his theories about human origins. Further (no small consideration), Joshua might gasp for breath, draw none, and die. Was it possible that Blair had delivered his developing third-world country into the arms of the Americans for a trade-off of dubious long-term benefit? Had he been duped?

"Listen," said Kaprow, addressing both men. "My previous work—some of it in West Germany, so that I know I'm not dealing solely with a local phenomenon—has demonstrated that common to every Earthbound site all along its distribution across the time axis, there's a kind of persistent . . . well, call it a geographic memory. That memory, Dr. Blair, is objectifiable. In other words, it's *visitable*."

"A pseudoscientific rationale for ghosts?"

"For ghosts, hauntings, and a few other supposedly paranormal phenomena. If calling that rationale 'pseudoscientific' pleases you, be my guest." He crossed the workshop and removed the transcordion from Blair's hands. "The point is that Joshua is already psychically geared to a specific set of these geographic memories. When we drop him back to the Pleistocene—with his active cooperation—he'll find himself in a physical dimension congruent with that epoch as it actually occurred. Joshua's name for what he does in his dreams—spirit-traveling—is a good name for what White Sphinx is all about, too. Like my term dreamfaring, though, it *does* ignore the important aspect of bodily displacement. But there's really no reason to—"

"We'll be installing him in a bloody *diorama* of the Pleistocene! A simulacrum of East Africa two million years ago! That's not time travel, Kaprow—that's a contemptible fraud!"

Kaprow's eyes seemed to bob in their almost transparent whites. "That's what my government thought, too. To begin with."

"Until they discovered they could sell Zarakal a worthless bill of goods for a couple of military bases. That's what you're trying to say, isn't it?"

"You're also receiving several hundred million dollars of direct American aid. That played a rather substantial role in President Tharaka's decision to permit the bases, wouldn't you say? Besides, he'd made up his mind on that point a month or two before White Sphinx was part of your working vocabulary. We're gravy, Joshua and I. Why are you making ugly accusations?"

"Gravy or no gravy, Kaprow, it doesn't forgive the duplicity of this diorama business."

"Please listen to me, Dr. Blair. Joshua may be going back

to a 'diorama' of the Pleistocene, or a 'simulacrum,' to use another of your words, but it's going to be a *living* diorama, a *perfect* simulacrum."

The Great Man's forehead wrinkled skeptically.

"Time travel as H. G. Wells envisioned it is an utter impossibility. The future is forever inaccessible because it hasn't happened yet. It has no pursuable resonances. The past is accessible only because of adepts like Joshua here, a person whose collective unconscious—whose *psyche,* if you prefer—establishes an attunement to a particular place at a particular time. This is an extremely rare talent."

"Curse," Joshua said.

"All right, curse. I'm afraid I agree with you. But it permits time travel of a vivid secondary sort, and it's *not* to be spurned as either worthless or trivial."

"A dream fossil is a worthless fossil, Kaprow."

"Dr. Blair, you should count yourself lucky that one of the people afflicted with this curse—I know of only three others, although worldwide there may be a few hundred—happens to be a young man with an attunement to the time and place of your own researches. Had his spirit-traveling taken him to the Trojan War, say, I'd probably be talking to a high-ranking classicist from Asia Minor. And you could have kissed this entire project goodbye."

"Name another," Joshua said.

"Another what?"

"Another person afflicted with the curse."

"Well, I'm one, I'm afraid." Kaprow pulled a folding chair away from the desk and sat down in it with his face in profile to the other men. "The first I ever knew to exist. That's why I've made a career of trying to harness the energy of my dreams." He chuckled glumly. "Even convinced the Pentagon there was a valuable military application for my work. Believed it myself."

"Oh? And what was that?"

"Well, Dr. Blair, the introduction of agents—call them saboteurs, if you want—into the time flow downriver from the present. To warn of the attack on Pearl Harbor, say, or to prevent the assassination of Archduke Franz Ferdinand in 1914. Or, somewhat closer to home, to dispatch murderers like Idi Amin and Pol Pot even before they come to power."

"That's rather grandiose, isn't it? Not to mention irresponsible. Those 'cures' would invariably trigger events impossible to anticipate. The results might prove worse than the original diseases."

"You're correct in theory, of course."

"And in fact?"

"Time travel of that effective sort is out of the question. We can go back to a past exactly like our real past, but because it's a projection, or a resonance, of an inaccessible reality, we're powerless to bring about changes in our consensus present. It's a vantage without teeth."

"I'll be damned if I care for it, Kaprow. We'll be sending young Joshua here into a landscape of phantoms."

"They'll have teeth, though. He'll perceive them to be every bit as real as himself."

The paleontologist shook his massive head, shifted his feet among the cables on the concrete floor.

"In one sense, Dr. Blair, what we must accept is better than the alternative you seem to desire. It would be folly to send a contemporary human being to a crucial juncture in the evolution of our species—the old story of the time traveler shooting one of his ancestors. Joshua could conceivably disrupt the course of evolution, bequeathing to our conjectural present a world in which humanity never quite arose from its hominid forebears."

"I'll be careful. Word of honor."

"But by sending him to a perfect simulacrum of the Pleistocene," the physicist continued, "we sidestep the Grandfather Paradox without sacrificing the *concept* of time travel. In my opinion, Dr. Blair, what White Sphinx has accomplished is a small miracle. Not only do we have our cake, we eat it too. We can visit our ancestors with impunity."

Joshua said, "The only danger is to the time traveler himself. He might be eaten by ghosts."

"True enough," Kaprow admitted.

Kaprow never talked about his own attunement. He never talked about previous experiments with the apparatus designed to translate a dreamfarer bodily into the past. He never bragged that already there had been several successful trial runs of his equipment—not at Eglin, because Kaprow had never located a dreamfarer afflicted with a Gulf Coast attunement, but in both Western Europe and the Black Hills of South Dakota. He never mentioned that the Oglala Lakota tribesman who had gone dreamfaring aboard his equipment the previous winter had returned unharmed and promptly refused any further jaunts to the nineteenth century. In fact, Kaprow never talked about either his successes or his failures, and Joshua learned about them—a few of them, at any rate—by discreetly pumping the man's assistants.

One evening in late September, however, Kaprow invited Joshua home with him for TV dinners and drinks. The physicist had a tiny cottage on the beach, and the first thing Joshua noticed about it when he stepped through the door was that every wall was lined with books. Most of them appeared to be math or science texts, but the glass-fronted cabinet near the kitchen was devoted entirely to tomes about Germany's Third Reich: memoirs, biographies, historical studies, photographs, psychological monographs, and even a healthy smattering of novels, although until this moment Joshua had supposed Kaprow completely indifferent to fiction. Fiction with a specific historical basis was apparently another matter.

The fried chicken in the frozen TV dinners seemed to have been basted with orange marmalade, and the mashed potatoes were like warm lumps of moist flour, but neither Joshua nor Kaprow was a dedicated gourmet, and they ate without complaining. Afterward Kaprow broke out a bottle of Napoleon brandy that made up handsomely for the minor indignity of the dinner. They sat in the living room, in the gathering dusk, and drank. The books on the shelves grew darker and darker, and Joshua found himself sinking by twilight degrees into a state of mellow grogginess.

"Am I going to survive this business?"

"The brandy?"

"No, sir. The dreamfaring."

"Well, soon enough you'll be undergoing survival training in Zarakal. That ought to help."

"I'm talking about the psychological aspect, I think. The way it's going to hit me when I come face to face with the substance of my dreams and I'm no longer exactly dreaming. That's what I want to know if I'm going to survive. The trauma. What do you think?"

"You're probably a better judge of that than I am, Joshua. I'm not you, after all. And vice versa."

For several minutes Joshua watched the light dance across the surface of the brandy in his snifter. "What happened to the Indian who spirit-traveled back to Seventh Cavalry days?"

"Who told you about that?"

"Stallworth. I stayed after him, though. It wasn't exactly voluntary."

"Nothing happened to the Indian."

"He quit, didn't he?"

"Yes, he quit. Not because of any emotional trauma, however. He didn't like being surrounded by machinery—technological artifacts, he called the components that helped get him back. He decided the dreamfaring process violated his heritage. And so he went his way, sadder but wiser. I suppose."

"What about you?"

Kaprow looked across the darkening room at his visitor.

"What about you?" Joshua persisted. "Where do you go, when you go? Which when do you visit? What's your attunement?"

Kaprow leaned back in his chair and put his feet on a hassock. A moment later he said, "Hitler's Germany. Dachau. In clever Aryan disguise, Joshua, I visit the ovens."

They talked for a long time.

That December the elf-sized effigies in the display window of the record shop looked to Joshua less like angels than embryonic bats. Each little figure was outfitted with cottony wings, a gown sprinkled with glitter, and a halo that appeared to be a Frisbee spray-painted an ugly gold. Worse, nearly every "angel" was holding in its malformed hands an album jacket featuring a full-color close-up of either a syphilitic or a coke-disfigured recording artist. (The simulation of disease- or drug-induced lesions was a minor showbiz trend this holiday season.) The effect was sublimely tacky. On the other hand, in its calculated contempt for every Christmas bromide, the display was perfect, the sort of flamboyant decadence that gave Big Gene Curtiss fits.

Past other gussied-up windows and shop fronts, Joshua moved aimlessly through the mall. He had money in his pockets and a full month of leave before the Air Force sent him PCS (Permanent Change of Station) to East Africa. Before he left Eglin, he had presents to buy—for Big Gene Curtiss, Cosette Tru and her father at the Mekong Restaurant, and Woody Kaprow and a few of the other personnel working on the White Sphinx Project. None of them expected gifts, of course, but they were the only family he had these days and he wanted to do a little something for them.

As for Jacqueline, well, she was still in school in Washington, D.C., newly engaged to a friend and colleague of her brother Dzu's in the State Department. She had eased herself out of Joshua's mind as painlessly as a pickpocket lifts a wallet, in part because he had come to agree with her objections to his suit, in part because the last year and a half had revealed to him the mission foreordained for him at birth. Jacqueline, for her part, appeared to have given up her hope of being canonized a second

Our Lady of the Slums in favor of marriage and a civil-service career. Maybe these last goals were not, finally, incompatible with the first . . .

Almost against his will, Joshua thought of the family he had abandoned. It had been nearly seven years since he had seen his mother, Jeannette Monegal, and even longer than that since he had talked to Anna, his sister.

Adoptive mother, he mentally corrected himself. *Foster* sister.

But the qualifiers did not sanitize the guilt that suddenly came seeping up through him like a tide of untreated sewage. Anna he had always loved. His mother he had repudiated because she had betrayed him for the sake of a spurious tribute consisting, in fact, of a sizable advance for a book that he had kept her from publishing. After all this time, that betrayal, coupled with her treatment of Hugo, still rankled, still made him see red.

Et tu, brute.

Dante had consigned those treacherous to their own kin to the first round of the ninth, and final, circle of hell. These contemptible folks were imprisoned up to their necks in a vast lake of ice. Why feel guilty, then, about simply removing oneself from a betrayer's sphere of influence? In comparison to Dante's vindictiveness, Joshua was the saint that Jackie Tru had always wanted to be . . .

"Jesus, runt, watch where you're going!"

Startled, Joshua rebounded from a clean-cut young serviceman who, but for the passage of four years, could have been the identical twin of the would-be Ranger in whose company Joshua had first encountered Jackie. The serviceman angrily shook his head and escorted his companion—a blue-jeaned ingénue with a simulated lip lesion—around Joshua, who mumbled an apology and backed away. More than likely he would be going overseas soon, this strapping GI. Everyone seemed to be going overseas. The United States had more foreign outposts than the Roman legions.

Whether by chance or unacknowledged design, Joshua

edged along the wall of plate glass behind him into a bookstore.

This Christmas the most prominently displayed paperbacks in the open storefront were a series of photo-novels devoted to the exploits of Count Stanislaw Stodt, a vampire in the employ of the CIA. A boxed set of five of these adventures was being touted as this year's most popular stocking stuffer. Joshua sidled past these displays to the hardcover tables, where management had laid out its inventory of serious fiction: hauntings, space operas, espionage thrillers, movie tie-ins, political biographies, and the complete works of Wilkie Collins, now enjoying a renascence in updated abridgments by Stephen King.

"Can I help you?"

Glancing up, Joshua beheld a slender young man with watery blue eyes and the mustache of a Central American revolutionary. The standard response to this standard query, Joshua knew, was "No, thank you, I'm just looking," but Joshua invariably employed another—to engage, if only briefly, the clerk's professional expertise and to dispel the impression that he was merely one more itinerant airman killing time. To wit:

"Do you have Jeannette R. Monegal's *I Couldn't Put It Down, and I Was Sorry When It Ended?*"

The young man laughed. "Boy, *that's* an old one. I'm afraid it's out of print, even in paper."

Now, of course, the clerk was supposed to apologize and wander off, leaving Joshua free to browse as he liked.

Instead the clerk said, "She's written a new book, though. Maybe you'd like to take a look at it. Our copies came in just last week."

"A new book?"

"Yes. I forget the title. Right over here."

Joshua's heart began to hammer his chest the way a fetus sometimes pummels its mother's stomach. But he followed the young man to a shelf from which he withdrew a thick book in a glossy dark-green jacket. Frightened, Joshua could feel the warmth draining from his hands, almost as if his fingers were spigots. He closed his eyes.

"Eden in His Dreams."

"I beg your pardon," the clerk said.

"That's the title—*Eden in His Dreams.*"

"No, sir. Not by this author. Here, why don't you thumb through it? It's not selling all that well yet, but we expect it to."

Joshua blurted, "But this is a novel."

"Yeah. Her first foray into fiction. *Publishers Weekly* liked it, for whatever that's worth. Give it a gander."

The clerk left Joshua alone with the book, which, as hefty as a Hebraic tablet, he clutched in trembling hands.

It was entitled *The Outcast.* The cover showed a tatterdemalion child crouching in the shadow thrown by an immense barred door. Yes indeed. A novel.

Joshua let the book fall open and began to read. His mother's narrative style seemed to be a cross between perfervid Mary Shelley and early Joyce Carol Oates. He tried to pick up at least a strand of the story line from this perusal, but so intense was his relief that the book was not *Eden in His Dreams,* he could think of little else. Gratitude welled up, and another fetid hint of guilt.

Jeannette had spared him. In fact, she had spared him for nearly seven years. That, insofar as he understood the law, marked the statute of limitations for a great many criminal offenses. If old movies and numerous detective novels did not err, a person who had not been heard from in seven years could be declared legally dead . . . Maybe it was time he began to forgive his mother, demonstrated to her by word and deed the fact of his continuing existence. In less than three weeks he would be descending the ramp of a commercial airliner at Marakoi International Airport in Zarakal. He would not return to the States until the end of the decade, assuming, of course, that he did not perish in the iffy ghost-past to which White Sphinx would eventually post him.

Joshua carried the book forward to the cashier's island and placed it on the counter. A dark young woman in a red velour jumpsuit turned the book around, studied the jacket painting, and then keyed the book's price into the cash computer: $21.95.

"You like Jeannette Monegal's stuff, huh?"

"I don't know. I've never read a novel by her before." He put three ten-dollar bills on the counter and waited for his change.

"You're some gambler, then. You wait long enough and you could probably pick this up on a discount table for less than the paperback. Four and a quarter or so."

"With me it's now or never. I've never been able to delay the gratification of my impulses."

"I know a bunch o' fellas like you." The cashier raised her eyebrows, slid *The Outcast* into a brown paper sack, and counted out his change.

Joshua winked a conspiratorial goodbye and left.

On the shuttle bus back to Eglin—he had sold his Kawasaki to an airman in recreational services—he took the novel out of its grainy, biodegradable sack and opened it on his knees like a dictionary or a Bible. Then he thumbed forward from the end papers to the table of contents. While he was riffling these leaves, an inscription at the top of an otherwise virgin page caught his eye, and he turned back to see what he had missed.

It was the dedication:

In memory of
Encarnación Consuela Ocampo
and
Lucky James Bledsoe

—

for all that they gave me

That evening Joshua telephoned his mother's Riverdale apartment from the day room in his barracks. No one answered. He dialed the number every half-hour. Shortly after eleven he reached a thin masculine voice that told him, peevishly, Jeannette Monegal had not had this particular telephone number for at least five years. Joshua called information and learned that although his mother no longer had a listing for Riverdale, the directory did show a few other Monegals whose first initials corresponded to his mother's. He tried three such numbers with no success and a sense of mounting frustration. At midnight he hauled himself upstairs and fell into bed.

In the morning his first thought was *Ah ha, I'll call Anna.*

But Anna had left Agnes Scott in Atlanta at least five years ago, and when he finally reached a hired official in the school's alumnae society and tried to talk her into divulging the present whereabouts of Miss Anna Rivenbark Monegal, class of 1980, he was met with a distant, scrupulously polite, "Sorry—not a chance," the implication being that he sounded like a rapist, a salesman, or some other unsavory blight on the stately live oak of civilization.

Then, like being sideswiped by a Greyhound bus, it hit him: *Van Luna, Kansas!* Where but Van Luna, Kansas, would his mother and his sister retreat for the Christmas holidays? Nowhere else but!

Excitedly Joshua put through a long-distance call to the residence of Mrs. William C. Rivenbark of Van Luna, Kansas. In 1972, at precisely this time of year, Old Bill had died of a heart attack in Cheyenne. He and Peggy had come to Wyoming—their second such trip—to visit their daughter and grandchildren for Christmas while Hugo was supervising the loading of B-52 bomb bays at Anderson Air Force Base on Guam. Under decidedly peculiar circumstances, in the bedroom of Pete and Lily Grier, the Monegals' former landlords, Bill Rivenbark had collapsed and nearly lost consciousness. Pete Grier had been out of state at the time, attending a bowl game in New Orleans with a cousin from Texas, and Lily, in an exemplary dither, had telephoned Jeannette to come and rescue her father before Peggy, asleep in the Monegals' old apartment downstairs, discovered that her husband was upstairs with Lily rather than stretched out beside her in connubial repose.

Angry and distraught, Jeannette had answered Lily's plea, taking ten-year-old John-John with her to the Griers' house since Anna was spending the night at a friend's. Upstairs his grandfather had lain supine on another man's bed, his dentures clamped together like a strip of yellow whalebone. The old man's eyes had been as elusive as welding sparks, seeming to go everywhere without settling on anything. Bill had suffered a second heart attack in the hospital's emergency room and that one had finished him off . . . Joshua's recollection of this incident took on embarrassing vividness as the widow's telephone rang. Maybe this was a mistake. He held the receiver away from his head and considered hanging up.

"Hello?" A cautious female voice, girlish rather than elderly.

"Anna?"

"Who is this, anyway?"

Joshua told her. There intervened a silence like the silence a bowler experiences after lofting a gutter ball. You couldn't hear a pin drop.

"Come on, Anna, talk to me."

"What do you want?"

"Is Mom there? I saw Mom's book, the novel."

"She's not here, Johnny. She may get here for Christmas, she may not. Everything's up in the air. Where are you?"

He wanted to tell her about meeting Alistair Patrick Blair a year and a half ago, but realized that every aspect of the White Sphinx Project, especially the involvement of the Zarakali paleontologist, was classified. Besides, Anna and he were using an unprotected public line. Besides, she probably didn't give a damn.

"Can't talk long. I've been finger-feeding this squawk-box quarters for hours, just trying to run you folks down. 'Bout out o' change. Anna, I've got to know if Mom—"

"Are you coming?"

Joshua Kampa, alias John-John (Johnny) Monegal, studied the receiver as if it were the single bone of contention separating him from his family. Deliberately he asked, "You inviting me?"

"Get out here, you goddamn little defector. Of course I'm

inviting you. Of course I'm—" Anna stuck, exasperated or overcome. "Just get on out here, all right?"

It took two days to catch a MAC transport aircraft from Eglin to
Lackland Air Force Base in Texas, but only six hours to claim a
seat on a giant, pelicanesque C-141 departing Lackland for Mc-
Connell. He rode in the belly of this prodigious bird with twenty
other space-available bindlestiffs, a convoy of six haunted-looking
blue buses, and several canvas-draped cylinders.

One young airman claimed that the cylinders were un-
armed nuclear warheads, while a paunchy officer in wire-rim
glasses pooh poohed this notion, declaring them experimental
plastic cisterns for catching and storing water in certain hypothetical combat situations. Their ultimate destination was Fort
Carson in Colorado. Joshua did not wait to see who emerged
victorious in the warhead/cistern controversy. He disembarked
the C-141 as soon after it had set down as the pilot would permit.
It was cold in Wichita, and he pulled his Air Force horse-blanket
coat tight about his neck and chest.

Once off base, Joshua walked the right-hand side of the
highway to Van Luna waiting for a ride. Finally a captain in a
1956 Nash Metropolitan picked him up and carried him the remainder of the way.

Van Luna, once a farming village as well as a modest
bedroom community for people employed in Wichita, had spilled
over the countryside like the markers in a vast Monopoly game.
Tract houses, convenience stores, and motels were everywhere.
The highway between McConnell and Van Luna afforded only
an occasional glimpse into the pastureland or the cottonwood
copses beyond the roadside clutter; and Joshua, despite a long-
term familiarity with the mercantile sprawl of Florida's Miracle
Strip, felt betrayed. Even if he had lived here only five years, Van
Luna was the Eden of his dreams of childhood. Its streets and
fields had represented, at least in memory, the landscape of his

choppy evolution toward self-knowledge, a process he still did not regard as complete. This ongoing complication of the simple geometries—the *innocent* geometries—of the original town was demoralizing.

"Damn."

"You're welcome," said the captain, letting him out not far from the building that had once housed Rivenbark's Grocery.

The old business district, the cobblestone heart of Van Luna, did not look greatly different from Joshua's memory of it. Although under the proprietorship of a stranger, the grocery was still a grocery. Even better, the façade of the old Pix Theatre had been restored. Joshua walked through an older neighborhood to his mother's mother's house, aware of the townspeople's tentative curiosity and the chilly tingle of the December air.

At the front door of an old-fashioned red-brick house with Tudor trim and ranks of gorgeous evergreen shrubs around the porch and walls, Joshua knocked. No one came. He pressed the buzzer and heard a thin, protracted raspberry deep inside the house. Whereupon the door swung open and there stood Anna, simultaneously smiling a welcome and trying to shush him to absolute silence. She was pregnant, quite far along, and their enthusiastic hug had to accommodate itself to the salience of her belly.

"Come in," she whispered. "Don't stand out there in the cold—come in, Johnny, come in."

He did not budge. "What's the deal, Anna? You married?"

There in the doorway she explained that, yes, she was married; her husband was a man named Dennis Whitcomb, but Anna had not taken his last name. An ensign in the Navy, Whitcomb was stationed aboard the nuclear carrier *Eisenhower*, which was presently at rest in the harbor of the new naval facility at Bravanumbi, Zarakal.

"Zarakal!" Joshua exclaimed in a high-pitched whisper.

"Mutesa Tharaka's country, Johnny. You know, the place where all those people starved to death a few years ago. On special occasions he wears some sort of early human skull on his head."

"Your husband?"

"You know what I mean."

"Right, I do. It's a habiline skull, Anna. President Tharaka wears it to celebrate the origin of humanity in his own backyard. It's also a sign of his own preeminence in Zarakal."

"Good for him. Do you mind if we go inside?"

"Lead the way."

Anna, wo had not yet spoken above a whisper, led him to a sofa upholstered in a satiny floral print. She made him sit down, but did not herself take a seat. Instead, one hand in the small of her back, she paced a threadbare Oriental rug whose faded pattern reminded Joshua of a paisley shirt he had owned in Cheyenne. The room smelled of camphor, cedarwood, and, strangely, peppermint. It was shuttered, curtained, and wallpapered. The miasma of Peggy Rivenbark's widowhood drifted from room to room like nerve gas, and Anna, suddenly, appeared to be suffering a convulsion of memory.

"Do you still have those dreams, Johnny?"

"Sometimes, yeah, I do. But I'm undergoing a treatment that's supposed to help me control them."

"I was afraid the damn things would kill you."

"They might yet."

"But if you're learning to control them—"

"Scratch 'They might yet,' Sis. Melodramatic license. I'm fine."

"You've joined the Air Force. Following in Dad's footsteps?"

"Not too far, I hope." Anna took his meaning, and he said, "The President ordered the Joint Chiefs of Staff to waive the height limitations for me. A blow for the civil rights of short people."

"Now you have a reason to live."

"Amen, Sister."

"Are you being sent overseas, too?"

"Right after New Year's."

"Where?"

He decided, unilaterally, that this much, at least, he could divulge to his own sister. "Russell-Tharaka Air Force Base in—"

"*Zarakal!*"

"I thought we were supposed to be whispering."

Halted in front of Joshua, Anna lowered her voice again: "Maybe you'll be able to meet Dennis. —No, probably not. They're set for a long cruise in the Arabian Sea and the Persian Gulf. I don't know exactly when. Soon, though. The *Midway* and the frigate *T. C. Hart* were strafed recently by American-made jets flown by—well, they think they may have been PLO sympathizers in the Saudi Arabian Air Force. No one knows for sure. They're keeping it out of the news, Dennis says. It's weird. Weird and scary."

"Yes."

"I met Dennis in Athens."

"Greece?"

"Georgia, you turkey. He was going to the Navy School there. Did you know that Roger Staubach went there in the sixties?"

"No, I never did."

"Anyway, I'd gone over to Athens for one of the University of Georgia's drama productions. *Buried Child* by Sam Shepard. During the second intermission I bumped into Dennis."

"Which intermission resulted in *that* bump?" He nodded at her belly.

"You mean 'intromission,' don't you? Well, we've never kept count. And I don't remember you being such a wise guy." Anna eased herself onto the sofa beside Joshua and kissed him daintily on the temple. "Welcome home, short stuff."

Under a gingham canopy in an antique four-poster in the master bedroom, Peggy Rivenbark lay. She had been sickly ever since Bill's death thirteen years ago, but only over the Christmas holidays, in perverse commemoration of the betrayal that had made her a widow, did she surrender to the elegant purdah of her bed. Who would have thought that, taking advantage of Pete Grier's absence, Bill would have crept upstairs from his daughter's former apartment to the boudoir of frumpy, frozen-pie-faced Lily, there to commit a cardiac-arresting instance of extramarital hanky-panky?

"Should I go in to see her?" Joshua asked.

"I don't think we even need to let her know you're here."

"She still associates me with that night, doesn't she? I let it slip where Mom and I had found Bill, and I'm still the evil messenger of the Rivenbark household."

"It's been a damn long time, honey. Peggy's convinced herself that you're dead. This probably isn't the best time to show her you're still kicking."

"Okay, I'll play. No ghosts for Grandma."

"Good."

Before he could ask Anna about their mother, she rose by pushing off against his shoulder and beckoned him into the sunny kitchen on the house's southwest side.

Green glass canisters for sugar, flour, and tea. Knotty-pine cabinets. A bay window overlooking a margin of neat, winter-brown lawn, the kind of lawn that cries out for touch-football players and blithely romping dogs. Van Luna's suburban sprawl was nowhere in evidence here.

Joshua sat at a wrought-iron table with a Formica top while Anna served him coffee and leftover biscuits. When the heater kicked on, she spoke without whispering for the first time since he had entered the house.

"You just about killed Mom, you little twerp. For two years she was strung out like an elastic clothesline, almost ready to snap. She tore up *Eden in His Dreams* and couldn't get anything else going. The third year, well, she spent that right here in Van Luna, as if this house were a sanatorium for terminally bereaved females."

"Where is she now, Anna?"

"Maybe I'm not ready to tell you."

Alarmed, Joshua ate crumbs off his fingertips. More than likely he deserved to be taunted in this tender, hair-trigger fashion. If Anna really squeezed, though, he would go off like his grandfather's heart, in either apoplectic anger or tearful remorse. The latter if they were lucky. He remembered how Hugo had used to ascend from a grumbling snit into one of his infrequent but terrifying Panamanian eruptions . . .

"You got any Fritos, Anna?"

She turned and faced him, her arms folded on the ledge of her pregnancy. "Jesus, you've got the recall of an elephant."

"Dumbo the Dinothere at your service."

"I remember almost everything about that little expedition—but, of course, I was twelve. I *ought* to remember."

"What about Mom? Where is she?"

Anna crossed the little kitchen, walking on her heels, and patted him on the head. "Neat diversion, John-John. I got a cable from her yesterday. You won't be seeing her this year."

"Why not, for Christ's sake?"

"She's got a contract from Vireo to do a book on the Spanish monarchy—the impact of its restoration on the people and on European politics in general. She's in Madrid. She plans to be in Spain for at least six months. She wanted to beat a possible moratorium on air travel—that's why she took off so suddenly. It was my year to babysit Peggy, anyway."

"Shit."

"I'll write and tell her you're in Zarakal."

"You can't. I shouldn't have told you. You can tell her when you see her in person. Then swear her to secrecy. Cross your hearts and hope to die."

"Are you a commando or something, Johnny?"

"Or something, I guess. It's a kind of grandiose depth-psychology therapy for my lifelong affliction."

"The one you're learning to control?"

"Right. At government expense. You won't see my eyeballs roll up into my head this trip, Sis."

"Unless I shoot you." She sat down at the table with a cup of coffee. "That's why you're going to Zarakal, isn't it? A correlation between that country and the landscapes of your dreams."

"My lips are sealed."

Conscientiously concealing his presence from his grandmother, Joshua stayed through Christmas. Peggy Rivenbark lay abed like a superannuated angel, decaying into the expensive linen mulch of paradise and dreaming for the unborn great-grandchild in Anna's womb a future of crash-proof spaceliners and pristine colony planets. Well, maybe not. She was an old woman who had been born five years after Kitty Hawk, and it was more likely that she hallucinated not the future but the past. Meanwhile, she henpecked heaven with her prayers.

What was it that Woody Kaprow had said? *The future is forever inaccessible . . . It has no pursuable resonances.* Joshua was not sure he believed that. The past, after all, was the friable medium in which the future germinated. And the present was an illusion, another aspect of the great material lie known among Hindus as *maya . . .*

So much for metaphysics.

For fear that the sight of him would kill her, Joshua purposely did not reveal himself to Peggy Rivenbark.

Anna and he spent most of the holidays talking. When it came time for him to leave, they had exhausted hundreds of topics without depleting their stores of mutual affection. The name tag on his uniform jacket might say *Kampa,* but he was also a Monegal, and maybe when he got back from his tour of duty in the Horn, they would finally be reunited as a family. Anna and he affirmed this hope aloud over and over again, but on the transport aircraft flying back to Eglin, Joshua had his doubts. His past was a dream, and the future was inaccessible.

CHAPTER TWENTY-SIX
Life in Shangri-la

In many ways the period after the unexpected rainfall—the five or six months after I discovered Helen's pregnancy—comprised an Edenic idyll of the kind Jacqueline Tru's father had conjured from the dream stories I told him in the Mekong Restaurant. Our little village became Shangri-la.

Suddenly we had plenty to eat. No one had to bust a gut either foraging or hunting. Occasional hominid killers like leopards and hyenas ignored us to concentrate on the gazelles, zebras, and antelope that had filtered back into our area from the vast grasslands south of Mount Tharaka. I was dreaming this idyll. Submerged in my experience without benefit of continuous rational consciousness, I may have been more alive, alert, and accepting than at any other time in either of my pasts. Bearded and sinewy, I glided among the Minids like a dispossessed spirit from their own uncertain future.

Helen glowed. Her face shone the way licorice shines, her belly the way a jawbreaker sucked down to streaky indigo glistens

against the palate. Her several bouts of nausea before and after
Mary's death had of course signaled the habiline equivalent of
morning sickness. Her metabolism had finally adjusted to the
changes wrought by conception, though, and now she was a candidate for the "after" photograph in a health spa ad, sleek and
vivacious in spite of that abdominal bulge. Half my mind began
to wonder when she would bear our child, the other half to formulate lullabies of haunting prehistoric sweetness.

We were people of leisure.

During this same period I began to rise before dawn to lift
my own wordless aubades to savannah and sky. These songs came
out of me from sources unidentifiable then and altogether untap-
pable now. Although during my adolescence and young manhood
I had written poetry prompted by some of my spirit-traveling
episodes, my new songs were almost entirely spontaneous. I awoke
them from preconsciousness and released them to the light as
crude melodies.

Other habilines—not only Minids, but Huns in their high
fastnesses southwest of us—answered my songs. The melancholy
baying of wolves and the uncanny arias of humpback whales reso-
nated alike in our voices, and the timbre of our singing seemed to
impart outline and solidity to that quasi-prehistoric landscape.
To put it another way, our morning songs made my dream world
real.

My total absorption into both the Minid band and their
curious simulacrum of the Pleistocene altered even the texture of
my subconscious mind. I ceased to dream about my twentieth-
century past and began to experience night visions full of ancient
East African imagery. By becoming a habiline and accepting the
reality of their world I had purified my dreams. Seville, Van
Luna, Cheyenne, Fort Walton Beach, Riverdale, and all the other
hot spots of my childhood no longer figured prominently in these
visions. Now I was far more likely to dream about the fauna
around Lake Kiboko, the wildflowers along the rivercourses, or
my relationship with Helen.

This change embodied a kind of paradox. Whereas during

my life in the twentieth century such dreams would have been spirit-traveling episodes, now they were merely dreams. My physical displacement into the past had cured me of the principal affliction of my life. At last I was "normal." My dreams proved as much. And I hoped that I would never again have to suffer the disorienting indignity of spirit-traveling . : .

One day was like another. Each began with sunrise and limped through the heat of noon toward the exit signs of twilight. Between these clear-cut demarcations we took care to consume at least the recommended minimum daily requirements of nutrients sufficient for survival. The savannah was our supermarket, Mount Tharaka our after-hours convenience store. When not playing habiline games or furiously loafing, we shopped. Our purchases were paid for in the coin of cunning, persistence, luck, or various combinations of all three. If we ever encountered inferior merchandise or empty shelves, there was no manager to complain to and no way of getting our money back. Stumbling across an extraordinary bargain was one of the few unfailing means of burning a noteworthy brand into the otherwise bald backside of the day.

About two-thirds of the way through Helen's pregnancy, when her belly was ripening like a huge Concord grape, she and I tripped over an extraordinary bargain. The jolt of this discovery bumped me out of dream consciousness into the predicament of rational awareness. Because what we had found was too big for us to dismantle alone, I left Helen on the edge of a small rivercourse and returned to Shangri-la for Alfie and the others. By eye movements and clumsy vocalizations I made them understand my welcome news and led them down the mountain to the stream bed on the steppe.

Helen was sitting on the bank of the little gully jabbering insults at the carrion birds swooping on our find. It lay capsized in the water, trapped by the submerged stones into which it had apparently lumbered while alive. The vultures could get at it only by alighting on its shiny flank or wading determinedly through the muddy stream, their outspread pinion feathers dripping and their neck ruffs comically frazzled. When Alfie, the rest of the Minids, and I burst onto the scene, the vultures scattered, but settled near enough at hand to glut themselves with envy if not with flesh.

Helen and I had found a hippopotamus, a representative of *H. gorgops*, that rare species with bulging, periscopic eyes. Moreover, we had found it quite soon after its death, in a section of rivercourse partly concealed from the eyes of carrion eaters by the surrounding shrubbery. Sheer serendipity. Had we been a day earlier, we might have supposed the hippo contentedly wallowing and so passed it by. On the other hand, had we been a day later, the vultures would have reduced our supermarket special to an immense naked rib cage. Ecologically speaking, we had come in the niche of time, and the hippo was ours, all ours.

The beast disturbed me, though. It was an albino hippopotamus, with skin the color and seemingly the consistency of blancmange. Finger-long freckles of pink and pinkish-brown dappled its back, and its eyes, which arose from the massive head like elongated burn blisters, appeared to track my movements—as if the hippo and I had an affinity of which I was ignorant. I was alert to the dead animal's scrutiny, its implied criticism of my status as a scavenger. My consciousness had engaged, and suddenly, frighteningly, I felt that not even Helen's love could legitimately bind me to these savage doings. The white hippopotamus was an omen, probably an evil one.

It occurred to me that recently I had dreamed a dream in which Helen and I, astride a pair of docile chalicotheres, had ridden down from Shangri-la onto the moonlit savannah. During this ride we had seen an albino riverhorse run across our path from one half-hidden stream bed to another. Other disconcerting events had followed, including my own painful transformation into a state that I could no longer recall. In fact, I probably would not have remembered dreaming about a white hippopotamus if Helen and I had not, quite by accident, found this one. What a strange concatenation of circumstances.

Wading into the water to butcher and cheerfully apportion our find, the Minids fell to. My sense of estrangement heightened. Once, as a boy, I had relished a gone-awry dream in which a band of hominids mutilated and devoured a creature from a children's television program. Today, though, the Minids were scavenging an image from one of my recent Pleistocene dreams. How could I abet them in the complete destruction of that image? This was a world in which even the projections of the dreaming mind were converted into food.

I sat apart and watched the habilines carve the hippo into strips with craftily ad-libbed flake tools. Alfie and Malcolm worked over the carcass in the water, while Ham and Jomo passed chunks of flesh to the women and children on the bank. Fred and Roosevelt cooperated in gutting the beast and washing its luminous internal organs in the muddy water. I had dreamed a very substantial, very meaty behemoth; its flensing required concentration and time. I concealed my distaste and tried hard to recall what Babington had taught me about hippos.

"It might interest you to know," I informed the Minids, "that you're butchering a first-rate source of protein. As much as four ounces out of every pound of hippo flesh is solid protein, about twice what you'd get in a comparable amount of mutton, beef, or pork."

Irritated, Alfie gestured for me to join him and the others in the water.

"Forgot my pocketknife," I begged off. "Stay at it, though. Nearly three quarters of a hippo carcass may be usable, whereas even with a blue-ribbon Four-H steer you're sometimes lucky if *half* the carcass will render. You know, if only President Tharaka had had the foresight to encourage hippo ranching, Zarakal might have been able to avert famine in its frontier districts."

Alfie, shaking his head, grumbled over the curl of his bottom lip, and I relapse into silence. When I looked up again, I saw that Helen had taken notice of my change of mood. She waded through the ankle-deep water to join me beneath the trees on the sandy bank. Her manner was quietly reassuring.

"I'm all right," I said. "Go ahead—eat with the others. It's not every day we run into something like this."

Helen would not budge from my side. She sat with one arm draped over my shoulder. Upon occasion she would wave off an encroaching vulture or fling a handful of sand, but otherwise she was motionless. She seemed to be willing to share my lack of appetite. I looked down at the swollen ball of her abdomen. Its surface bulged once, then surrendered to a run of elastic waves. The fetus—our child—was fisting out feisty rhythms in the bistro of Helen's womb.

"You're eating for two, Helen. Go on now, get down there, take your share."

She would not budge. She was adamant. If I would not eat, neither would she. I wanted to make a sacrifice for her, to give her an excuse to eat—but I could not face the prospect of forcing down a single bite of blancmange, not even one, and so kept Helen from feeding with the others. I was ashamed of myself and half in awe of Helen. She was a saint, a genuine habiline saint.

Jomo fell ill. Unable to eat, hunt, or tolerate the japeries of the children, he tried to remove himself as a burden to the Minids by wandering off alone into a distant thicket on the plain. That same afternoon, missing him, Guinevere conferred anxiously with Helen. Tottering wide-eyed about Shangri-la, singing her distress in eerie bass notes, the old woman raised a small expedition to search for her husband.

Ham and Roosevelt accompanied Guinevere, Helen, and me down the mountain, tracking Jomo by scent and virtually imperceptible trail signs. Within an hour we had found the old man. He was sitting in a beautiful Kaffir boom tree, staring out over the savannah with glassy eyes. He would not come down. His languid intractability on this point so discouraged Roosevelt and Ham that they began foraging their way back across the grasslands. If a crazy old habiline wanted to sit by himself in a tree, who were they to interfere?

Guinevere, Helen, and I waited out the long starry night in the clearing beneath the Kaffir boom. In the absence of any leaves, the tree's coral-colored flowers waved petals like tiny tentacles. The trunk of the tree bristled with blunt spikes, but Jomo had climbed to his perch without any regard for the hurt they were inflicting upon him.

Once, foolhardily braving these spikes, I tried to climb up to Jomo, but he placed the sole of his foot on my head and levered me to earth with a single forceful thrust. That dampened my enthusiasm for trying to rescue him. Scratches tattooed my belly and thighs, and all that night my right buttock throbbed incessantly. If a crazy old habiline wanted to sit by himself in a tree, who was I to interfere?

Then I remembered Genly's death and its ritual aftermath, events that seemed as long ago and far away as my childhood in Van Luna, Kansas. Jomo, I realized, had taken his own funeral arrangements in hand. If the penultimate resting place of a Minid was the fork of a tree (the ultimate, of course, being a leopard's maw or the gullets of a gang of carrion birds), why, then, he would install himself in the tree of his choice. He had picked a beauty, too. His vertical coffin was a truly awesome coral tree, with wood of resilient softness and durability.

With the three of us alternating watches beneath the old man, he lasted two days in the tree. Vultures began circling overhead on the second day, however, for the odor of Jomo's mortality hung heavier in the air than did the fragrance of the tree's scarlet flowers. Finally, his spirit—his *soul,* if the species known as *Homo habilis* possessed that intangible commodity—left him, and he toppled out of the Kaffir boom in a heap.

You could not leave a patriarch like Jomo—who had perhaps once occupied the Minids' chieftaincy—lying crumpled on the ground. We must get him back up his prickly tree. Helen, after indicating by mumbles and signs her intentions, set off to Shangri-la to retrieve another prospective corpse-booster or two. During her absence I used a lava cobble to grind off as many of the Kaffir boom's spines as I could reach. Guinevere, meanwhile, lay across Jomo's body, daintily picking vermin from his grizzled beard and mane.

The vultures kept circling.

Ham and Alfie came back with Helen. They touched their dead comrade with the tips of their clubs, wiped the death smell into the dirt, and made threatening noises at the birds. Back and forth beneath the coral tree they strode, as if Jomo's death were a great personal affront to every Minid, an ill-advised practical joke by a Landlord who did not deserve such forbearing tenants.

Helen was exhausted. I had no idea what due date an Air Force physician would have assigned her, but her time could not be too far off. She did not join Ham and Alfie in their protest, but crouched stiffly beside Guinevere and beckoned me forward to assist her. I saw then that she had brought my Swiss Army knife from our hut. She passed the knife to me, and Guinevere sat up to see what was happening.

Doubtful about the wisdom of humoring Helen, I pulled the knife's large pen blade free and stropped it several times on my lava cobble. Helen retrieved the knife from me and put its point to Jomo's right temple.

"Whoa," I said, thinking of the *Homo erectus* skulls found once upon a time in a limestone cave at Choukoutien, China. The spinal cords of several of the skulls had been painstakingly enlarged, presumably to permit the removal of the brains. Did Helen wish to dine on Jomo's gray matter? Did she think such a meal would impart to the old man's unborn grandchild some of his knowledge, cunning, or wisdom?

My speculations were misplaced. Helen wanted to cut off the old man's right ear. Hindered by her belly, she leaned over the mop of his hair and tentatively set to work. She was no more adept at this task than she had been at pulling the blade from the handle. Frustrated, she returned the knife to me and held the rubbery brown cauliflower of Jomo's ear away from his head so that I could slice it off.

Swallowing my objections, I quickly did her bidding. Helen packed a bit of dried grass on the old man's head to absorb the oozing blood and took possession of the ear. She then extended it on her palm to Guinevere, who looked back and forth between this offering and her daughter's solemn face.

"It's a keepsake," I whispered. "Something to cherish."

Guinevere finally accepted the melancholy gift.

A moment later Alfie, Ham, Helen, and I were boosting Jomo's corpse back into the Kaffir boom. That accomplished, we consigned the old boy to the immemorial obsequies of the vultures.

In its own way, it was a lovely funeral.

Several days later Helen awakened me early, if only in my dream. Stick-pin stars held the darkness in place, and Mister Pibb was still on sentry duty in the flame tree beneath whose crepe-hung branches we slept. In an uneasy trance, for I was dreaming, I followed Helen down the mountainside to the moonlit chessboard of the savannah.

Friendly beyond all expectation, a pair of chalicotheres approached. Like camels, they knelt on their forelimbs and lowered their sloping hind quarters to the ground. Helen mounted the female, gripping its silken mane for purchase. With a curt nod she indicated that I should mount the other chalicothere, the male. Although I feared they would not be easy creatures to ride, I obeyed. A moment later both animals were back on their feet, and, swaying from side to side, our fossil steeds trotted out into the grasslands on their enormous talons.

This was the grand tour. We passed herds of dozing zebras, fitfully dreaming dinotheres, asleep-on-their-feet gazelles. Giraffes teetered through the distant thornveldt like antlered sea serpents; and, strangest of all, an albino hippopotamus ran across our path in painful slow motion, its thick neck extended and its legs languidly treading air. It was the color of blancmange, this hippo, with boiled-looking freckles on its broad back, and I remembered that I had seen one like it not very long ago, perhaps in a waking dream.

When it disappeared into the rivercourse toward which it had been loping, our chalicotheres turned aside, carried us past a gang of thuggish hyenas, and stampeded through the low grass toward a destination unknown to Helen and me. Desperately we clutched their manes and dug our knees into their shedding flanks.

A leopard appeared ahead of us. It had flattened its body against the ground, but not quickly enough to go unremarked.

Helen's mount leapt like an impala, tossing her to the ground. I too was thrown, and as we struggled to our feet, rubbing our bruised buttocks and exchanging glances of wounded commiseration, the chalicotheres fled. I was so afraid that Helen's heavy fall might result in the miscarriage of our child that the nearness of the crouching leopard did not greatly trouble me. I began running toward Helen, intent on embracing and comforting her.

The leopard sprang from nowhere, swatted me across the chest, and immobilized me by sinking its canines into my skull. Helen screeched and scrambled away. I was glad to see her saving herself. She could hardly hope to rescue me, and, Ngai be praised, my own discomfort was minimal. A helpful mechanism of my preconsciousness had switched on, shunting both hurt and fear into a sensory limbo beneath my dreams. My neck snapped, but I had already relaxed so completely that the noise seemed like a burst of light rather than a crack of pain.

Dragging me between its legs, the leopard struggled across the savannah to a tree.

The landscape turned upside down. The leopard, setting and resetting its claws in the tree trunk, hoisted me to a convenient fork about nine feet from the ground. Here it wedged me into place and, holding one rough paw on my lower spine, began to feed. Its teeth tore inward through my kidneys, pancreas, bowels; and its tongue lapped speculatively at my warm, rich blood.

Neither terrified nor pain-racked, I died into the night.

Hunger awakened me. It was still too early for the habilines' aubades, and the two-legged corpse under my paws was good for another meal only if I ate daintily and paced myself. That was not my style. I shifted the body and devoured as much of the stringy, acrid flesh as I could stomach. As I was eating, an upright figure appeared on the plain about forty feet away. This was the female companion of the nearly hairless biped I had stunned and dragged aloft. Except for the low-slung tumor of her pregnancy, her profile had a graceful slenderness. I lifted my head from the ravaged carcass to see what the female intended to do. She came stalking on a leisurely diagonal. Her progress toward me was hypnotic. I considered the desirability of making another kill and found the notion attractive. The fetal sweetmeat in the woman's womb would make a fine dessert.

Suddenly she made a sweeping motion with her arm.

A rock or a hard-shelled nut ricocheted off the tree trunk past my head. I flattened my ears and roared, but the roaring did not daunt her. In fact, it may have provoked her, for she let loose a barrage of invisible missiles. I could not see them, but I could feel them. One struck me in the upper lip, cracking a tooth.

I sprang headlong to the carpet of grass and furiously rushed my tormentor.

She did not quail away, but passed her club from one hand to the other and braced her feet to accept my charge.

I hesitated. The carcass on which I had been feeding slithered from my tree, a pudding of torn flesh and splintered bones. This female habiline, I realized, was avenging a loss, not merely ordering up dessert, and her steadfastness arose from the urgency of her purpose. I had to be equally firm to triumph over her. Ignoring her mate's fallen body, I resumed my charge. At the last instant, however, she danced aside and thwacked me on the hind quarters with her club, shattering a vertebra and so pitching me sidelong to the ground.

Although I bucked over to my belly, the woman was astride me before I could regain my feet. Her gnarled legs clutched my flanks like calipers, and her fingernails raked through the astonished vermin in the matted fur behind my head. I howled, but my dinner had settled in me heavily and I could not get off the grass. What ignominy. I had never suffered such humiliation before. I was terrified that she would kill me where I lay. The pain from my shattered vertebra was almost unbearable.

And then the female began to sing. Wrenching my ears and directing my gaze toward the moon, she divested herself of a canticle of harrowing purity. My fear evaporated, and the pain in my hindquarters surrendered to the hallucinatory loveliness of her song. Without dislodging the female habiline I got to my feet. Then, under her strong, forgiving hands, I lumbered off toward Mount Tharaka.

The lady and the leopard.

Entering the Minid village without alerting its sentry, we skulked through the shadows to the windbreak shelter that the woman had shared with my latest victim. Here we lay down side by side, nuzzling each other like rootling cubs. Then we fed our passions beyond the limits of her former lover's appetite. Thus did we cuckold the dead. Afterward we curled together into a ball and jointly dreamed this dream.

Eventually Helen awakened me. Upright among my fellow habilines, I lifted my voice in the fearsome tabernacle of the dawn.

Our numbers were diminishing. The deaths of Genly and Jomo had left only six adult males, myself included, among the Minids. Mister Pibb, the sole adolescent male in our band, had recently taken up with a sweet young thing of the Hunnish persuasion, and we could no longer expect to compensate for our losses from within our own ranks. Ham was visibly aging, growing increasingly more decrepit as the days passed, and I felt sure that one day soon he would emulate Jomo's voluntary walk to oblivion.

The Minids, of course, were in no danger of either disbanding or dying out. Our population was twenty-one, down only three since my arrival, and of the eight remaining children, three were girls, two of whom would soon be passing through the fires of adolescence. They were the salvation of the Minids, for when they began to attract suitors, our band would open its constricted throat and swallow these young males like fingerlings. The franchise would not fold. It would begin a rebuilding program with its nubile females' first-round draft choices. Indeed, I was one of these choices.

A brief digression:

Never during my sojourn with the Minids, in this region a few hundred miles north of the equator, did I have a clear sense of seasonality. I had dropped into the Pleistocene during a drought-stricken July in 1987, but since my arrival I had been unable to distinguish any significant gradations between hot and not quite so hot. Often, owing to the elevation of the areas around Mount Tharaka and even Lake Kiboko, the nights were cool—but the relative coolness of the nights did not translate into any significant variation in the daytime temperatures of the savannah. I could not have said that this hot day occurred in August, this one in September, and this other in April. Months had no meaning.

Of course, the true measure of seasonality in equatorial regions is not temperature but rainfall. The Somalis call the rainy period from March through May *gu*, and that from September to late November *dayr*, but if you believe that the precipitation during these periods never slackens, your brain has absorbed a crucial portion of the rainfall intended for the Somalis. Drought traditionally parches the area, even in the "rainy" seasons. Although Blair had assured me that the Lower Pleistocene was a wetter period than our own, and the vegetation accordingly more lush, I must have stepped into an unusually protracted dry spell. Lake

Kiboko, just as Blair had predicted, rode higher then, but to obtain relief from the anomalous drought afflicting the grasslands, the Minids had left their traditional territory for a highland haven on the skirts of Mount Tharaka. There we had finally seen rain.

And rain brings me back to Helen's pregnancy.

In the aftermath of a rainfall, I had discovered that Helen was carrying our child.

Well, some considerable while after Jomo's funeral, rain seemed to be in the air again. The wind blew in warm gusts from the east, screaming over the countryside from the Indian Ocean, then whispering away into muggy, nerve-racking stillnesses. At night we could hear the sepulchral grumbling of thunder, and sheet lightning lit up the horizons. Spooked by the weirdness of the sky, the herds on the grasslands ricocheted from place to place. Sometimes lions roared rebuttals at the thunder, and sometimes the gazelles and wildebeest settled down to watch the horizon-wide lightshows. Up on Mount Tharaka where the lightning flashed its bridgework, we were apprehensive, too.

This kind of weather—maybe you could call it a season— lasted for several days. Every evening was a siege. I saw theater scrims of rain over Lake Kiboko, but in our balcony seats in Shangri-la these storms never touched us.

Helen's time came upon her suddenly, on a night of cannonading thunderheads. In spite of the noise I had been sleeping—until Helen rose from our pallet of grasses and, one hand in the small of her back, ducked outside into the artillery din of the storm. I waited for her to return. She did not. At last, then, I blundered outside after her.

Far out on the northwestern horizon a carrier task force of clouds had just received several torpedoes amidships. Directly overhead, though, was a webwork of gauzy stars. The wind was beginning to blow spiritedly. An inauspicious night for the birth of a half-breed kid who was probably going to have plenty of troubles anyway. I called to Helen, but received no answer.

"Hunnnh!"

This was from Malcolm, who seemed to spend nine-tenths of his waking hours in trees. From his lookout in the Nandi flame, he pointed me to the clumsy windbreak in which Guinevere usually slept. That made sense. During the delivery of her first child Helen would naturally go to her mother for help. I climbed through a rocky section of Shangri-la to Guinevere's shelter.

Neither Helen nor her mother tried to keep me out, but they did practically ignore my arrival. The hovel had no roof, and starlight and torpedo bursts of sheet lightning served to illuminate its small interior. Helen was in pain, and Guinevere had shoved a great quantity of dry grass against a section of the windbreak to support her back. By the time Helen's water burst, I reasoned, it was entirely possible that the gathering clouds would also split their containing membranes and inundate us.

Don't let it rain, I supplicated Ngai, or whatever deity had tutelage over this ghostly dimension. *Please don't let it rain.*

Helen did not have it easy. Intense, painful contractions came upon her. At every cramp her eyes disappeared behind her brow ridge (giving me to understand the horror that this sort of eyeball rolling had held for my adoptive mother) and her hand squeezed mine tightly. This repetitive ritual went on for at least an hour, Guinevere and I occasionally shifting places to allow the other a chance to shake the kinks out of our knuckles. While I was at Helen's side, I kept up a steady, asinine murmur that was meant to be heartening and supportive.

"It's gonna be okay, Helen, gonna be oh-so-fine. The monkey spit tobacco on the streetcar line. The streetcar it broke, and the monkey got choke', and they all went to heaven in a little red boat," et cetera and so forth, the more sinister implications of this refrain going completely over my head and fortunately over Helen's and Guinevere's too.

Although I am certain that Helen never understood the significance of the nausea early in her pregnancy, she knew what was happening to her now. She had seen others give birth; twice, at least, she had kidnaped the infants of vaguely collateral species to hold them in her arms; and she had felt her own baby kick. Motherhood was the reward for all this pain, the land-rush territory beckoning the battered buckboard of her body onward to a permanent homestead, and she knew what her pain signified.

Although the rain held off, over Lake Kiboko the lightning show was heating up, and admonitory rumbles made the horizon tremble. Everything was happening northwest of us, out where Zarakal, Ethiopia, and Somalia would one day put their troops in a deranged effort to establish borders where no one had ever observed any.

Helen paid no attention to the noise. She was trying to bear her child, but her body would not cooperate. The baby's head, which had descended through the uterus as far as it could go unaided, was too big for Helen's narrow pelvic structure. She was taller than any other female habiline, but her tallness was of the sylphid kind, loose and willowy. Because my endocranial volume outpointed hers by at least seven hundred centimeters, her baby had inherited from me a genetic template for a brain case perilously larger than the habiline norm.

In pain shalt thou bring forth children.

The price for the development of a mind capable of making abstract moral judgments is pain in childbirth, while the penalty for paying the price is expulsion from the Garden. Looking at Helen's strobe-lit face, I knew that her expulsion would come not at the hands of dutiful cherubim but instead through the cold instrumentality of Death. She was not going to make it. Her eyes trembled in their sockets. Her naked forehead ran with sweat. The flashes of sheet lightning over the distant lake seemed to drain the indigo sheen of health from her face. Her skin was slack and gray.

I went back to our shelter and found my pocketknife. It had proved useful in separating Jomo from his ear, but now it must perform a more urgent task, saving Helen's life. I gathered together all the dry grass in our hut, carried it outside, and set it afire with one of the last of my matches. Then, as Malcolm gazed down skeptically, I piled brushwood on the fire and sterilized my large pen blade in the unruly flames. Snatching the knife out again, I blistered my fingers, but the pain was of no consequence, and I ignored it to get back to Helen.

Emily, Dilsey, and Alfie had also entered Guinevere's semicircular windbreak. Their eyes turned toward me, going almost immediately to the knife. I gestured with it, eased my way inward, and knelt by Helen with a premonition of disaster settling in my belly. My entire body seemed to be held together by gummy resins and tangled strings.

Helen cried out, an inhuman cry of warning and pain. Everyone looked at her, then at me. I raised the knife and told the habilines in clear, calm, rational tones that it might be necessary to make an incision in the outer edge of Helen's vagina to facilitate delivery. My fear was that this cut, even if I could make it cleanly, would prove an inadequate remedy for her troubles. In fact, I had brought the knife thinking that if she died in labor, I might be able to rescue the infant with a crude Caesarean section.

The clinical clarity of this plan broke down under the weight of Helen's suffering. The idea of even touching her with the knife sickened me, and I dropped it into the dirt. In deepening perplexity four silent habilines looked on, consoling one another with embraces and absent-minded pats. I do not think that even Dilsey had ever witnessed so taxing a labor.

As the storm drifted southwest from the Horn—sheet lightning giving way to zigzag slashes of almost unendurable brilliance, thunder whip-cracking after every bolt—Helen somehow managed to evict the tiny torturer in her womb. Guinevere, not I, received the child. In the oppressive glow of the storm its body shone neither blue-black nor gray but a startlingly phosphorescent white.

The baby's skin was blancmange, the color of milk pudding. How could this unappetizing little grub be the issue of my lovemaking with Helen? The mired hippopotamus that the Minids had eaten had been a lovelier hue, a more comprehensible variety of mutant. I had refused to eat of it for fear of violating the integrity of one of my dreams—but this creature, my daughter, how was I ever going to be able to love her? Her head was too large for her gaunt body; her pallor suggested not merely albinism but illness.

"*Mai mwah,*" said Helen feebly from where she lay.

I placed the grub at full length between my wife's breasts. Helen enfolded the child in her hairy arms, lifting her head to peer downward at the little creature. Her lips parted. "*Mai mwah,*" she said again. No one moved. The grub found one of Helen's breasts and began to suckle: a small ivory incubus drinking the heart's blood of the woman who had borne her.

CHAPTER TWENTY-SEVEN

Northwest Frontier District, Zarakal

July 1987

HAZY IN THE harsh light of dawn, emptiness. Once, long ago, this part of Zarakal had been fertile grasslands; today it looked like a petrified sea, broken here and there with combers of thorn scrub, grit kicking up in spray at the unpredictable bidding of the wind. A lone hyena stood on the salt flat watching a caravan of three vehicles moving northwestward along the highway connecting Russell-Tharaka Air Force Base in the country's heartland with the Lake Kiboko Protectorate in the Great Rift Valley. The highway had been built over the past two years with American money, machinery, and supervision, although the Zarakali Minister of Interior, Alistair Patrick Blair, had insisted on a large management role for himself and a coolie work force of indigenes. One part of the highway linked Marakoi, the capital, with the air base thirty miles northeast, but the remaining three hundred miles of macadam struck many observers, both native and American, as Blair's private expressway to nowhere. The Great Man had grown weary of replenishing the supplies of his field workers at the Lake

Kiboko digs by helicopter or light aircraft. Hence this ribbon of asphalt through the awesome emptiness of the Zarakali desert.

Joshua murmured, "Not a used-car dealership in sight."

"Our military still hasn't been here all that long," replied Woody Kaprow, who was driving the second vehicle in the car avan. "Give it time, Joshua. Give it time."

"God forbid there should ever be that much time."

Alistair Patrick Blair, riding between Kaprow and Joshua in the cab of the big vehicle, laughed. "God and Woody Kaprow, physicist supreme. They jointly hold the patent on all temporal properties."

"Not so," Kaprow replied. "Not so."

Ahead of them, the lead vehicle in their caravan, cruised a Land Rover that had been modified to accommodate not only a swivel-mounted machine gun but also a hundred-gallon drum of drinking water. An American air policeman was driving this escort, a uniformed Zarakali security agent riding shotgun. Behind Joshua, Blair, and Kaprow, the caravan's caboose was a huge truck with a covered flatbed pulling a generator more suggestive of a collapsible camper than a caisson. Both the Land Rover and the truck were a dusty olive-drab, chevroned with the doubtful camouflage of zebra striping.

Of the three vehicles in the caravan, the one in which Joshua and his companions rode had the strangest design and the most mysterious purpose. Half again as long as the truck, it resembled an Airstream trailer coated with a layer of protective plastic; its almost aerodynamic-looking hull was as sleek as the skin of a porpoise, while its cab protruded like the nose of an immense electric iron with a wraparound windshield set into it. Six monstrous tires bore the weight of this vehicle, which Kaprow had recently taken to calling, with subtle bravado, The Machine. Only a month before this expedition to Lake Kiboko, it had arrived in Bravanumbi, Zarakal's principal port city, aboard an American aircraft carrier; and Kaprow, who had accompanied t on that voyage, would let no one else drive it. Blair had offered to spell him at the wheel during their night-long trip from the air base, but Kaprow had firmly declined the offer. Although its development had been funded with U.S. tax monies, he regarded The Machine—if not Time itself—as his personal property.

"But I'm an excellent driver," Blair had sweet-talked the physicist, "and you've done yeoman duty these last two hours."

"It would be immoral for me to let anyone else sit here."

"Immoral?"

"Absolutely. If you wrecked The Machine, Dr. Blair, I'd despise you forever. That wouldn't be fair to either of us."

"But if *you* wreck it . . . ?"

"Well, if I wreck it, I'll be damned pissed off, of course, but eventually I'll forgive myself. To err is human, especially if it's you who's done the erring. Otherwise it's intolerable."

"Dr. Blair's transcended the merely human," Joshua had put in. "Everyone in Zarakal knows that. Maybe you could trust him for thirty minutes or so."

"Demigods are always chauffeured. You can look it up. Try *The Iliad,* for instance."

They had laughed at that, but Kaprow had not relinquished the wheel, and they had been traveling since midnight, a departure time settled upon to protect the caravan from midday temperatures and the possibility of aerial surveillance—although everyone understood that a sophisticated spy satellite would find mere darkness no impediment at all. On the other hand, a paleoanthropological expedition was hardly a prime target for the espionage operations of Zarakal's Marxist enemies.

The sun had just risen. Joshua watched the hyena ahead of them on the salt flat turn sideways and break into a frightened lope. Hunting had apparently been none too good of late; the ugly creature was all bones and mangy to boot. Joshua leaned his head against the side window and closed his eyes.

Blair said, "You're not having second thoughts, are you, Joshua?"

"Lately all my thoughts are second thoughts."

"There's still time to go back, of course."

Joshua opened his eyes. "All right. Let's go back."

Blair shifted his pipe in his teeth, a meerschaum like the one Hugo had lost to the rhesus monkey at Ritki's Animal Ranch. Kaprow shot him a swift sidelong glance. Both scientists, their pet projects in the balance, were visibly alarmed.

"Joke," Joshua comforted them, patting Blair on the knee. "Didn't mean to scare you shitless. I'm as obsessed as you two are. It's just that I didn't ask for my obsession."

"Neither did I," Kaprow countered.

"My saying we could take you back wasn't an insincere formality, Joshua. If you want us to, we can."

"It's okay. Really. I've got a bad case of preflight jitters, that's all." A model of innocence, he lifted his eyebrows. "Only human, you know."

"I wouldn't blame you if you wanted to—"

"Renege, Dr. Blair?"

"Pull out, I was going to say."

"Of course you wouldn't." Joshua closed his eyes again, in spite of which he was hungry rather than sleepy. Mentally he superimposed a segment of Florida's Miracle Strip on the desolate African landscape sliding past him outside. "What Zarakal needs out here, I think, is a good International House of Pancakes."

"Come now, Joshua. A moment ago you were applauding the absence of used-car lots."

"Or a Burger King."

Blair chuckled appreciatively. "In a place where many of the people, not omitting the local police, poach elephants for a living?"

"Burger King would fry 'em, Dr. Blair."

"Jesus," said Kaprow. "At a time like this."

The Great Man mumbled something about the delicious banality of Joshua's wit, and their conversation concluded. The Machine hummed along the highway until the highway itself ran out, and the Land Rover ahead of them eased down into the thornveldt, its wheels negotiating the bumpy track to Lake Kiboko like four pallbearers on uneven ground. Then Kaprow committed The Machine to this same formidable course, and the truck with the generator came rattling and clanging after. The caravan was now deep within the two hundred square miles of eastern lakeshore territory that Blair had persuaded President Tharaka to designate a "paleontological protectorate."

During his training at Russell-Tharaka Air Force Base, Joshua had heard conflicting stories about the prevailing Zarakali attitude toward the Lake Kiboko Protectorate. People in Marakoi and Bravanumbi regarded the area as a national treasure, the site of the discovery of *Homo zarakalensis,* and they supported Blair's work there as a means of thrusting their country into the world spotlight. These folks never set foot within the protectorate, however, and probably had no wish to. Let the interior minister dig to his heart's content, until the camels came home from Ethiopia and the sand flea went extinct.

The pastoralists and seminomadic tribespeople who had once driven their camels and cattle through the area had another view, but it did not apear to count for much because their life styles disfranchised them from the politics of a nation struggling desperately to modernize. Industrialization and agricultural recovery were far more pressing concerns than the doubtful proprietary rights of either the Moslem nomads or the Sambusai pastoralists who often used this land. Only those whose trespass Blair specifically approved were supposed to set foot within the protectorate, and the Great Man seldom made concessions to either group.

After all, fossils lay exposed on the arid surface here, and the danger was that the Sambusai warriors, or their stupid cattle, would kick the skullcap of one of Adam's ancestors to uninformative smithereens. The importance of paleoanthropological research was beyond their understanding. Because they wanted to *use* the land, rather than simply stalk and sift it, they actively resented the government's decision to set aside two hundred square miles for Blair's researches. That this decision was unenforceable did not appease the Great Man, however, when he saw several Sambusai herding their livestock through the protectorate in haughty disdain for the legislation prohibiting their access.

"Damn! Look there! Those beggars've blocked us!"

Three Sambusai drovers had prodded their herd across the unpaved track approaching the lake. The air policeman in the Land Rover got out and began waving his pistol around. Neither the cattle nor their masters found this performance a compelling reason to move.

"Let me out, Joshua. Your compatriot needs my help."

Joshua unlatched his door and climbed down into the withering morning heat; Blair followed. Outside The Machine, Joshua felt as vulnerable as a turtle that has ill-advisedly wriggled out of its shell. Blair marched toward the confrontation.

One of the Sambusai warriors, contemptuous of the angry air policeman, suddenly leapt high into the air. He did not move his iron spear from its steady vertical, and at the summit of his leap he trembled his shoulders rakishly and smiled a faraway smile. As soon as he had touched down, a second Sambusai performed the same sort of leap. The red ocher on his plaited hair dusted up visibly when he landed, a halo of crimson grit.

Seeing Blair and Joshua approach, the air policeman holstered his pistol and returned sheepishly to the Land Rover.

His withdrawal seemed to trigger the leap of the last Sambusai warrior on the path. Because this herdsman was naked under his scanty, ill-secured toga, his penis performed a tardy recapitulation of his leap. Joshua, intimidated by these prepossessing men, hung back several feet. In comparison to them, he was a pygmy or a child. He could see the first two warriors nodding at him, appraising him, consigning him to some unflattering category reserved for runts, outsiders, cowards, or crazy persons.

Blair barked a greeting at the Sambusai. Having ceased their gymnastics, they inclined their heads just perceptibly in response. They seemed surprised to hear their own language coming out of the mouth of a paunchy white man with drooping mustachios and a bald brown pate. Nevertheless, they palavered amiably with Blair, nodded more than once at Joshua and The

Machine, and stalwartly held their ground. Wiping his brow with a handkerchief and humorously pursing his lips, the Great Man returned to Joshua.

"They're a decent enough crew, I think. Ignorant about human prehistory, of course. We'd probably do well to indulge them in a couple of their whims."

"What were they saying about me?"

"Why, nothing. Nothing more than what they were saying about the lot of us, that is."

"And what was that?"

"Referred to us, jocularly, as *iloridaa enjekat,* I'm afraid. Sounds lovely if you don't know what it means."

"Iloridaa what?"

"Enjekat, Joshua. Means 'those who confine their farts.' Has to do with the kinds of breeches we wear."

"Jocularly?"

"Well, I would say so. On the whole, they were quite pleasant."

"What do they want? Did you tell them to move?"

"I *asked* them to move, Joshua. However, they're not going to pack off without a concession or two from the man who had this traditional grazing area proclaimed a state protectorate."

"They've got your number, then."

"Well, they know who I am, of course. Figured that out readily enough. It tickles them to have run up against the High Mucky-muck of the interior ministry, so to speak. I'm the chap who displaces living people to dig up the bones of dead ones."

"They *look* tickled."

Kaprow stepped down from The Machine. He stood with one hand on the door, waiting for Blair and Joshua to come abreast. "What's the matter?" he asked. "If Joshua's going to get off by tomorrow morning, we need to get set up."

Blair said, "Dr. Kaprow, a great many things in Africa are on permanent hold. I'm afraid you're going to have to—"

"We have a schedule. If we don't—"

"We will, Dr. Kaprow, we will. I should have had a police unit from one of the frontier outposts sweep the area. Unfortunately, the protectorate's a little too big to fence."

"Unfortunately," Joshua echoed the Great Man. He pulled the moist material of his shirt away from his rib cage and wiped his forehead with his wrist. Out here, stickiness was a chronic affliction.

"What do they want?"

"They each want an item in trade, Dr. Kaprow. In addition, two of them would like a special favor."

"Trade? What do we get?"

"Their cattle out of the road, I would imagine."

"And the special favor?"

"Let's meet their specific demands first, shall we? The special favor is going to require a little of our time."

"That's exactly what I had hoped to save, sir."

"Nevertheless," said Alistair Patrick Blair.

The warriors' specific requests were simple, either poignant or grasping depending on your relationship to the item forefeited. Joshua yielded a leather belt with a brass buckle on which the jaunty figure of Mickey Mouse had been embossed. Kaprow, bewildered, forked over several American coins, while Blair made a lavishly eloquent presentation of his meerschaum pipe. The air policeman in the Land Rover, despite protesting that its sacrifice would put him in violation of the Air Force dress code, gave up his silver helmet, along with its camouflage net.

Finding that the helmet fit perfectly, the Sambusai warrior who had acquired it began chanting softly and doing gentle leaps, a Mona Lisa beatitude veiling his features. His tribesmen staggered about laughing, unable to puncture his composure with their jibes and catcalls. Then, controlling their mirth, they approached Blair with another request.

"What now?" Kaprow asked warily.

"They're envious of the helmet, but don't see any others to choose from. They'll settle for cardboard sun visors."

"Oh, good."

Joshua saw that a group of technicians (Americans) and field workers (Zarakalis) had climbed out of the covered flatbed of the truck behind them. Several were wearing sun visors, which they readily doffed and handed over to Blair to give to the importunate herders. As soon as the Sambusai had put these on, they began leaping with their helmeted comrade. The support personnel from the truck came forward to watch. One or two of them joined the dance, pogo-sticking with good-natured incompetence. The activity reminded Joshua of fuzzy kinescopes of *American Bandstand* segments on which Philadelphia teen-agers had surrendered to a form of rhythmic seizure called the Watusi. It had not looked *exactly* like this, but then the Sambusai were not the Watusi.

Kaprow said, "All we need now is a punch bowl and some helium balloons."

The sun visors, Joshua noted, were red and white. They were emblazoned with the trademark of an American soft drink.

"My goodness, Dr. Kaprow," said Blair. "You're awfully young for a curmudgeon."

"What's the special favor they want? We need to grant it, if possible, and get on into camp."

"They want to look inside The Machine."

"Look inside The Machine!"

"They've never seen so fat a motor car before, and it arouses their curiosity."

Kaprow turned the angry russet of a baked apple. "They can't. It's impossible. You know it's impossible."

"How badly do you want their cattle out of the road?" Blair put his hand on the physicist's shoulder. "You don't think they're going to steal your Nobel Prize poking around in there, do you? I've never been able to make brain or bunion of the whole untidy scramble."

"It's not your specialty, Dr. Blair."

"Oh, I see. You believe these Sambusai herders are secret graduates of MIT, *magna cum laude?*"

"No, of course I don't. It's just that White Sphinx—"

"I'll show them around inside," Joshua interrupted. "A tour guide who doesn't speak their lingo isn't going to spill much, is he?"

Because he had to, Kaprow acquiesced. Blair politely intervened in the Sambusai's dancing, and a moment later Joshua was leading two of the warriors to The Machine, where he pulled himself into a control space behind the cab. In this cramped chamber the Sambusai towered over him like professional basketball players. Their bodies gave off a unique commingling of scents: dung and cowhide, ocher and tallow, dust and sweat. To Joshua's surprise they seemed even more nervous than he.

"This way, gentlemen."

Joshua turned a key and a door panel slid back into the insulated six inches of interior bulkhead. The Sambusai were delighted. They grinned, exchanged unintelligible commentary, and sauntered into the bizarre cargo section of The Machine. A metal rail outlined a rectangular catwalk around the inside of the vehicle. Opposite the three men was a small bell-shaped booth of smoky glass, and beside the booth stood an air policeman with a submachine gun.

"It's all right, Rick. We've got Dr. Kaprow's permission."

"They don't plan to use those spears, do they?"

"Not that I know of. We'll take a quick look around and get out of your hair."

"What's going on?"

"Intercultural collision. Fill you in later."

The air policeman—Rick, a blond Iowa farm kid—lowered his weapon but maintained the alert feet-apart posture of a sentinel. He had, Joshua knew, only a distorted inkling of the purpose of the arcane machinery inside Dr. Kaprow's vehicle, believing it a variety of mobile intelligence-gathering equipment meant to bolster Zarakal's military position in the Horn. Why Dr. Kaprow had driven The Machine inland to Lake Kiboko he had no clear idea, however. He was a GI who kept his nose clean by obeying orders.

Sometimes, though, he wondered. Several months back, in the barracks at Russell-Tharaka, Rick had told Joshua that he could not imagine why anyone would go to war over such godforsaken territory. Step outside Marakoi and the ritzier sections of Bravanumbi (Rick had found two ritzy sections there), and Zarakal was your typical desert hellhole. Its world-famous big-game animals were being hunted to extinction or dying off naturally, and in another hundred years the Sahara would have crept so far south that half of Africa would consist of nothing but sand dunes. By then, according to Rick, Zarakal would be a sort of subsilicate Atlantis, submerged if not forgotten, and Uncle Sam's initial investment would be utterly lost.

Joshua gestured the Sambusai herdsmen to the left. He tried to see the apparatus hanging at the heart of The Machine through their eyes. This was not impossible because he himself did not fully understand either the placement of the various parts or the rationale behind their design. The Sambusai could scarcely be more baffled than he. Nor had the act of plugging himself into the components of this equipment—as the only living element in the assembly—revealed to him the mystery powering its weird gestalt. His dreams may have led him to this place—to this jumped-up dynamo of Woody Kaprow's fevered invention—but his dreams had not yet enabled him to fathom the technology. He, Joshua Kampa, was not only a part of that technology but also its essential payload.

How did you explain these notions to a pair of spear-carrying herdsmen who had astutely pointed out that Western-style clothes were fart-confining? Yes, how?

"H. G. Wells revisited," Joshua said. "It's a time machine. Only trouble is, you have to be me to use it."

At present most of the machinery arranged in the vehicle's cargo section was deployed at eye level or higher. A pair of heavy metal rotors mounted in movable boxes on opposite walls met in the middle of the van; their interlocking blades half enclosed a platform suspended from the ceiling by a pair of extensible aluminum tubes. In operation the platform rose and fell inside the toroidal fields of the rotors, which themselves moved in synchrony with the platform.

"Kaprow calls those rotors Egg Beaters, at least when he's talking to me. The platform he calls The Swing, even though it doesn't. It just goes up and down. He also calls it the Backstep Scaffold, though, and that pretty accurately describes its function."

One of the Sambusai put a hand on Joshua's shoulder, whether to silence him or to offer comradely reassurance he could not tell. Then the warrior dropped his hand and muttered at his companion. They were bored with the tour. The Egg Beaters, the Backstep Scaffold, and all the attendant paraphernalia—coils, tubing, insulation, motors, and whatnot—were complex all right, but you could take them in visually with a couple of sweeps of the eyes. In the absence of comprehensible explanations, the machinery had no magic for the Sambusai tourists.

But what had they expected? A wet bar with Coca Cola, 7-Up, and seltzer water? A picture gallery of Walt Disney characters? A display of modern weapons?

Who could possibly guess?

"I'm afraid that's all there is to it," Joshua said. "Sorry we can't give you a demonstration."

Nodding farewell to Rick, he pointed the herders to the exit. They emerged smiling, pleased with themselves for having explored The Machine, even if it had not altogether thrilled them. Joshua noticed that before returning to their comrade in the silver helmet they conferred briefly with Blair, who was sitting on the running board in the shade of Kaprow's open door. Soon all three warriors, reunited, were shooing their cattle out of the roadway, herding the animals out of the Lake Kiboko Protectorate toward the southwest.

"At last," said Kaprow, starting the omnibus.

Later, in the cab, Joshua asked Blair what the drivers had said to him before allowing their caravans to proceed.

"They wanted to know the purpose of the machinery."

"What did you tell them?" Kaprow asked.

"That it's a very expensive means of making contact with our ancestors."

"And?" Joshua wondered aloud.

"I'm afraid they laughed. You heard them, didn't you? The entire idea is ridiculous to them because they get in touch with their ancestors through ritual incantations and dreams. To require the assistance of so much metal and glass and plastic, well, that indicates to them that we must be painfully backward."

"Not 'we,' sir. 'You.' All I've ever needed is my dreams, and that's why I'm here."

"He's right," Kaprow said.

"Of course," Blair responded. "Of course."

Surprised by his own bitter querulousness, Joshua watched a jumbled ridge fall away to the left and the lake appear before their caravan like a huge spill of mercury. The western wall of the Great Rift Valley seemed far, far away, an arid lunar battlement.

Lunar battlement . . .

This image reminded Joshua of the day, nearly eighteen months ago, when Blair had first escorted him to a meeting with President Tharaka. The morning had begun with the pale-oanthropologist and his baffled American protégé blinking in the ferocious sunlight parching the parade ground outside the cin-derblock building in which Joshua had been living since his ar-rival, five weeks before, in Zarakal. The heat was unlike the heat of the Gulf Coast, and he did not know if he would ever get used to it. Although he was pigmented like a native, that accident of birth did not seem to help very much. Maybe later, when he was acclimated.

"Ah. Here come the WaBenzi," Blair had said.

"The WaBenzi? What are the WaBenzi?"

"My colleagues in the ministries, Joshua. Minor local offi-cials. Jackals highly enough placed to demand a little dash."

"Dash, sir? What's that?"

Sliding his thumb and forefinger together silkily, Alistair

Patrick Blair nodded at the motorcade of sleek black vehicles coming through the main gate of Russell-Tharaka Air Force Base. Beyond the gate, the bare candelabra of sisal plants lined one side of the melting asphalt strip to Marakoi, while on the other side the salt flat stretched away toward an unconfirmed rumor of the Indian Ocean. Joshua noted that the automobiles in the motorcade were all Mercedes-Benzes.

"Dash is bribery?"

Blair affirmed this deduction with a grunt.

"President Tharaka is susceptible to bribery?"

"Only on a large scale. How else do you suppose the United States managed to place its bases here?"

"You're not immune to a little dash dealing either, are you?"

The Great Man bridled, slipped voodoo needles into Joshua's body with his eyes. "I was referring to the bounders in the motorcade, Kampa. The provincial commissioner, the district officer, the minister of science, and the other pettifogging mucky-mucks who've come up here from Marakoi for the day."

"You sound like a closet Klansman."

"Rubbish, Joshua! The WaBenzi are a persistent scourge on the backs of our citizenry. I'd despise their venality even if it came cloaked in Anglo-Saxon pinkness. You can stop that adolescent smirking. It's a measure of your ignorance."

"My ignorance? About what?"

"Africa. I'm a white man, granted, but this is my bloody country, and these are my people. You're a black man, but you're still a cultural dilettante and an outsider when it comes to comprehending what you see here."

Joshua said, "That'll put me in my place."

Blair expressed his contempt for this comeback by snorting like a bush pig. Meanwhile, the President's cavalcade—eight automobiles and a pair of khaki-clad outriders on motorcycles—passed behind a row of whitewashed administration buildings and turned onto an access road leading to the testing ranges in the salt flats. Two American air policemen on motorcycles and a navy-blue staff car belonging to the base commander had joined the procession at the main gate, and they were dutifully bringing up the rear, maintaining a discreet distance between themselves and the WaBenzi. This was a low-key reception for the leader of the air base's host country, but Mzee Tharaka, the fabled Zarakali freedom fighter, vacillated between pomp and austerity in matters of governance, and you could never be sure what occasions would provoke which response. Today, apparently, it was a little of both, a motorcade but no fanfare.

"Let's go," Blair said. "The President wants to meet you."

"Yes, sir. I know."

Joshua followed the Great Man to a Land Rover parked on the edge of the parade ground and abashedly climbed in on the passenger's side. Blair was put out with him. He had offended his mentor with that Klansman slur, then compounded the insult by smarting off. What a clumsy comedy. This was Africa, all right, but he was a long way from home. The Land Rover accelerated to overtake Mzee Tharaka and his obsequious WaBenzi retinue. The Great Man played the gear-shift knob as if it were the handle on an unforthcoming slot machine.

"At least there's youth to excuse *my* petulant behavior."

Blair glanced sidelong at Joshua. "Ha," he said, grudgingly amused. "He got here earlier than I expected. We should have been out there waiting for him. Delays annoy him."

"Uh-oh."

"Do you know why Mzee Tharaka values your presence here?"

"No, sir. Not really."

"You're part of his modernization program. You'll be visiting the realm of yesterday for the greater glory of Zarakal's tomorrow. Integrating the technological with the spiritual is a passion of his, even if he is sometimes unsure how to accomplish that goal."

The Land Rover sprinted up the access road until it was cruising three or four car lengths behind the base commander's vehicle. One of the American air policemen dropped back on his motorcycle to see who they were, then saluted and waved them on.

Ten minutes later the procession slowed. Ahead of them Joshua saw a barricade of chain-link fence and another boxlike sentry post. On duty here was a young African soldier wearing pinks, rose-colored khakis, and a helmet like a deep-dish silver hubcap. He held his awkward, palm-outward salute until even the Land Rover had passed through the gate, upon which hung a large sign stenciled in Day-Glo red letters:

Authorized Personnel Only—
By Order of ZAPPA

"ZAPPA?" Joshua said.

"It's an acronym for Zarakali Administration for Peace and Prosperity through Astronautics."

"Astronautics?"

"Surely that doesn't boggle your bourgeois brain, Joshua. After all, you're a Zarakali chrononaut."

"Yes, but—"

"Astro-, chrono-, what matters the prefix? President Tharaka is visiting all his nauts today. That's why you've been summoned."

"Yes, sir. But I'm a special case, aren't I? It's a little hard to believe that Zarakal has a *space* program, too."

"What Mzee Tharaka wants, Mzee Tharaka gets."

A wooden reviewing stand with a high oblong hutch resembling a press box appeared in the hazy middle distance, bleacher-green against the dirty beige of the desert. A pair of revolving sprinklers watered the narrow travesty of lawn in front of these bleachers, and six spiky palm trees in tubs lined the walkway that bisected the reviewing stand. Not an especially auspicious site for a football or soccer stadium. As it turned out, however, the reviewing stand overlooked not a well-kept playing field but a barren depression, or cut, in the landscape.

The enameled WaBenzi limousines slotted by ministerial

rank into crudely marked spaces on the lip of the gorge, but an armed African soldier in pinks deflected the Land Rover into an unpaved parking area and told Blair that he and Joshua would not be able to dismount until the President had climbed to his place in the hutch at the top of the bleachers. The battered Land Rover did not qualify as an official vehicle, nor Blair himself as a bona fide WaBenzi.

"Suits me," the Great Man said. "I'm delighted he doesn't know we're late."

"Very good, sir."

Finally, clicking his heels and opening Blair's door, the soldier announced that the President would receive them, and Blair and Joshua marched across the parking area to the bleachers. All you could see between the two halves of the reviewing stand was a vast, pitted plain. And in front of the plain a huge, alkaline crater. There was a terrible charnel beauty to this landscape.

At the beginning of the decade several million people—refugees from the civil conflicts in Ethiopia, nomadic pastoralists fleeing drought and tribal warfare—had straggled into this region to die of starvation and disease. A portion of what was now Russell-Tharaka AFB had once been a receiving area for the refugees, the focus of an international relief effort run jointly by the Zarakali government and the United Nations Development Program. Skirmishes with Somali irregulars along a disputed border and battles with Ethiopian Army units in the Djilbabo Plain had eventually cut off the southward flow of the dispossessed, a rather mixed blessing, if a blessing at all. Meantime, graft in Marakoi had undone the relief effort by diverting food and medical supplies to Zarakali soldiers in the frontier regions. The WaBenzi had played a telling role in this fiasco, but, magnificently irate, Mutesa David Christian Ghazali Tharaka had purged the most blatant offenders. Now he had a new batch of WaBenzi, and the dead . . . well, the dead were dead. The vultures and hyenas had obliterated nearly every trace of them. For having briefly suffered the dazed tread and shuffle of a hapless multitude, the land looked little if any different.

A sign on the metal rail designed to prevent a visitor from slipping and falling into the depression below the bleachers caught Joshua's attention:

Weightlessness Simulation Incline
ZAPPA

"Up," Blair said. "The sign's meaning will become clear only when you witness the use to which we put the incline."

They climbed a set of switchbacking metal stairs to the hutch nearly sixty feet above the ground. The climb seemed altogether familiar to Joshua, a dream numbly repeating itself. Blair wheezed in the heat, wiped his sweaty brow, and nodded curtly at three black officials—WaBenzi all—seated under an immense vinyl umbrella in the center of the reviewing stand. Plainly the President had not granted them permission to sit with him above.

In the carpeted, air-conditioned hutch, Mzee Tharaka received Blair and Joshua as if he had planned this entire outing around their presence and participation. Standing before a rectangle of delicately tinted plate glass, Joshua found his right hand imprisoned between the strong, plump hands of the President, like a mug from which the old man was about to quaff a potent and exotic brew.

"Welcome, Mr. Kampa. Welcome."

The voice was hoarse, the English impeccable, but what disconcerted Joshua about the old freedom fighter was his attire. A man of medium height, with no single compelling feature other than his eyes, which were penetrating and mournfully red-rimmed, Mzee Tharaka today shunned the Western-style business suits of his retainers in favor of a Sambusai toga, a gorget of monkey's teeth, a red silk cloak featuring a pattern of alternating fleur-de-lis and (of all things) golden appliqué pineapples, and a set of silver anklets, from which depended tiny effigies of the country's vanishing wildlife, an ornamental touch that reminded Joshua of the grade-school name bracelet to which his sister, Anna Monegal, had once added charms depicting a puppy, a broken heart, a pair of saddle oxfords, a football, and so on.

The President's feet were bare. His head was not. Atop his grizzled sponge of hair he wore a felt crown to which had been affixed an enameled hominid skull discovered by Blair at Lake Kiboko in the early 1970s. Joshua was able to get a good look at the skull, which usually gawped upward at sky or ceiling, only when the President bowed ritually to the paleontologist and warmly clasped his hands. This skull, Joshua knew, was genuine, not a plaster cast or a clever facsimile. Blair had yielded it to the President, under stern and probably injudicious protest, only after his staff at the National Museum had obtained a plaster duplicate from an American physical anthropologist and had catalogued for posterity every known fact about the valuable fossil.

This episode in recent Zarakali history had provoked worldwide interest and comment. The *Times* of London had run an article predicting Blair's expulsion from the native government and his possible arraignment for criticism deterimental to the country's best interests, but the affair had blown over in a fortnight, the President privately placating Blair by promising to restore the hominid crown to the National Museum at his death, and Blair appeasing Mzee Tharaka by agreeing to refuse public comment on the issue and to reaffirm his loyalty pledge to the old man at an open session of the National Assembly. The paleontologist had kept his promises. What Mzee Tharaka would do no one could say. He might choose to be buried wearing the crown. In the meantime, however, he was by universal acknowledgment the only head of state who periodically proclaimed his sovereignty by donning the skull of a human ancestor nearly three million years old.

"Sit," said the President, indicating the padded swivel chairs in front of the window. "Sit, sit. Mr. Kampa is our guest. He must see that Zarakal is pursuing its future as actively as any other great nation."

"His especial interest is the past," Blair said.

"But not for its own sake, surely. Very few people are interested in the past for its own sake. Where we have been, gentlemen, shapes what we are. Further, it implies where we may be going." The President patted Joshua on the hand. "Zarakal is humanity's birth place, young man, and it will not be a negligible factor in determining our species' ultimate destiny." He gestured at the merciless blue sky, at the rugged yawn of the gorge. "Here you behold the primitive but fateful beginnings of Project Umuntu, the diaspora of our evolving intelligence to the stars."

Joshua looked out the window at the Weightlessness Simulation Incline. Three of Zarakal's astronauts-in-training stood on the opposite ridge, paying homage to their Commander in Chief with the stiff, palm-outward salute that was a relic of the days of British colonialism. They were dwindled by distance, these trainees, but their white uniforms and tight-fitting headgear reminded Joshua of hospital workers in rubber bathing caps. Each man was standing by a large, upright barrel, and each barrel was balanced on the edge of the incline by wires connected to cables strung across the gorge like an unfinished suspension bridge. Red, yellow, and blue, the barrels appeared to be made of a hard, dent-resistant plastic. They were perforated with air holes, and at the moment their hatch covers were up, quite like toilet seats.

Looking down the counter to an official hunched over a microphone, Mzee Tharaka said, "It's time to begin."

"Prepare for drop-off," said the man at the microphone. *"One minute and counting."*

The official's amplified voice echoed over the bleak desert landscape like the voice of God. The astronauts climbed into their capsules and closed the hatch covers.

Mzee Tharaka said, "It's ridiculous that of all the nations of the earth only the United States of America and the Union of Soviet Socialist Republics, and perhaps the People's Republic of China, should be trying to conquer the frontiers of space."

"Isn't it equally ridiculous for a nation with insufficient resources and personnel to be making the attempt?" Joshua asked. "Zarakal has more pressing business to attend to, hasn't it?"

The President's flinty eyes flashed, but with delight rather than disapproval. "One need not be a giant to have great dreams, Mr. Kampa. As you well know."

"Yes, Mzee." The shrewd old bastard.

"For just that reason, and for the reason that although Zarakal may be no giant, Africa is a colossus stirring with a new-found sense of its strength, I am the champion of African astronautics, Mr. Kampa. It was I, incidentally, who initially convinced President Kaunda of Zambia that we must put an African on the moon without the assistance of the so-called super-powers. Zambia's fledgling space program collapsed under the weight of a staggering economy, but our program is taking wing."

"We've recently replaced our obsolescent beer kegs," said Blair, wryly, "with expertly engineered 'descent cylinders.' "

"True, very true." The President laughed, not at all offended. "But now we have direct American aid—not for space technologies, mind you, but for military and economic programs that will permit us to develop such. The prospect of bartering coffee, sisal, and refined petroleum products for computer technology and educational opportunities is a major step forward."

"Thirty seconds and counting."

"That's aid from a superpower, isn't it?" Joshua remarked. "I think you're splitting hairs on this point."

"Well, certainly, we intend to take advantage of what others have learned through trial and error. It would be stupid to insist that we *ignore* existing technologies, put blinders on ourselves, and create an unadulterated Zarakali space program in the desert of our national purity. And we are *not* stupid, Mr. Kampa."

To change the subject, Joshua said, "Are those barrels padded?"

"Most assuredly. Finest quality American foam rubber."

The wires connecting the barrels to the suspension-bridge cables began slackening. The barrels themselves began rocking from side to side as their pilots prepared for launch. Through the larger holes in the capsules Joshua could see the men's immaculate white uniforms, like bits of tissue paper in punctured cookie tins.

"Ten, nine, eight, seven—"

"Pay attention, Mr. Kampa. The first trial run is often the most exhilarating, for the observer as well as the trainee."

"—three, two, one: DROP-OFF!"

The wires on the capsules yanked free, and the Zarakali astronauts came barreling down the Weightlessness Simulation Incline at a dizzying clip. The barrels bounced like balloons from some surfaces, skidded like rolling pins along others, occasionally caromed off one another like billiard balls. In a matter of seconds, it was over. The hatches on two of the barrels popped open, and their pilots wriggled out into the bottom of the gorge. The man in the remaining barrel, however, required assistance, and he was carefully extracted and led into the shade by his comrades.

"Brave men," said Mzee Tharaka. "Very brave men."

"Much braver than I, Mr. President." Joshua believed it, too. All he had to do on Woody Kaprow's Backstep Scaffold was close his eyes and dream. The time-displacement equipment and his own dreaming consciousness did the rest. It was as easy as falling downstairs.

"Not necessarily, Mr. Kampa, but perhaps you would be interested to know that many of our astronauts-in-training must overcome a powerful psychological reluctance to take part in these experiments. Tribal ways and allegiances sometimes militate against their willingness to test pilot our WSI vehicles."

"I don't understand."

"These trainees are members of the Kikembu tribe. In their society, Mr. Kampa, one of the punishments reserved for sorcerers—evil persons who inflict illness or misfortune on their neighbors—quite resembles an exercise on the Weightlessness Simulation Incline."

Joshua waited, knowing that the President intended to detail the similarity whether he replied or not.

"When the sorcerer is apprehended, you see, usually by a

contingent of men who have lain in wait for him, they find an immense beehive, put the sorcerer inside it alive, seal the hive, and send it tumbling down a slope. At the bottom, Mr. Kampa, the sorcerer is invariably discovered to have given up the ghost. One of our first trainees, interestingly enough, died of fright during his maiden descent of the WSI. He must have assumed that his selection to our program constituted a formal accusation of sorcery. On the other hand, he may actually have been guilty of poisoning someone or practicing witchcraft. As a result, his guilt combined with the trauma of weightlessness simulation to punish him for his crimes. Not only are our trainees brave, they are virtuous."

"I reckon so," Joshua said.

"What about you, Mr. Kampa? You modestly downplay your own bravery, wich must be considerable—but are you virtuous?"

"Virtuous?"

Everyone in the hutch, including Alistair Patrick Blair, was looking at him. Was he virtuous?

"Pardon me, Mzee. I'm not sure how to answer. I voted Democratic in the last two presidential elections."

Mutesa David Christian Ghazali Tharaka patted Joshua's hand; whether in tribute or consolation was not clear. They watched four more barrel races before the President wearied of the show and returned with his retinue to Marakoi.

"You made a good impression," Blair had told Joshua on the way back to his barracks.

"How?"

"Perhaps by preserving your sang-froid when you caught sight of his ceremonial attire. Besides, he's always been partial to Americans."

Yes, sang-froid. That was what he would require now, for Kaprow's omnibus was prowling the lake margin (the lunar battlement of the Rift's western wall like a mirage on their left), and tomorrow morning he would be playing chrononaut for keeps. Joshua's stomach knotted, and the jumbled slide show of his past clicked away inside his mind with every jolt of The Machine's balloonlike tires. This was his mission. He had finally got it, or it had got him, and his entire life had been pointing toward this place and this time. A time that encompassed an infinity of moments. An infinity of possibilities.

"You all right?" Kaprow asked, wrestling with the steering wheel. "You've been mighty quiet."

"He's anticipating the morrow," Blair put in.

"More than that," Joshua confessed. "Lots more than that."

CHAPTER TWENTY-EIGHT

A Gift from the Ashes

THE STORM BROKE over Shangri-la and soon enveloped the entire mountain in its shroud. I squatted beside my wife and daughter in Guinevere's hovel, in the sting of the astringent rain, and tried to sort out my fragmented emotions. News of the birth had spread through our encampment, even to those who had been sleeping, and while I watched my Helen struggle futilely against the stealthy machinations of death, every Minid in our band passed by her resting place—her makeshift bier—to see the baby. I could not pinpoint the moment of her dying, for she went without a wince or a murmur, the victim of lacerations and internal hemorrhaging, having exerted the last reserves of her strength to force our daughter into the impersonal slaughterhouse of the world; and the rain, the cleansing and astringent rain, had distanced me from the full intensity of her suffering.

"She's dead!" I shouted at Alfie, Guinevere, and the others. "God damn it, I think she's dead!"

I did not look to see what their reaction was. I turned my

attention to the issue of Helen's womb. Despite our daughter's pale skin and greedy suckling at her mother's breast, I began to feel a powerful affection for her, a desire to comfort and protect. I took her into my arms and sheltered her from the pounding rain.

The storm passed over us, moving seaward. Dawn broke bright and cool. Several of the Minids greeted it with song.

But I could not understand the persistence of thunder on so fine a morning. The habilines were quicker than I to deduce the answer, to identify the source of this noise, and their gathering panic finally opened my eyes to what was happening.

The thunder was not overhead but underfoot.

Like a boiler full of clabbered tapioca, Mount Tharaka was churning inside, its sticky contents threatening to burst, brim, and overflow. The thunderstorm, along with the confusion attending the birth of the Grub, had disguised from us the mountain's premonitory rumblings—but now, all too plainly, we could hear and feel them. The higher the sun mounted the more pronounced and emphatic these warnings.

We began to make preparations to leave Shangri-la, and our preparations included the manufacture of a travois on which to place my wife's body. I was hurriedly trying to tie together the frame for this sledge when Mount Tharaka's highest peak flew apart like a gigantic tooth dealt a shattering hammer blow.

I pitched to the ground. Foliage blocked my view of the summit, but above this line of foliage a billow of smoke and ash climbed into the sky, twisted in the air, and drifted downwind like the fallout from Death's powder puff.

Another explosion wracked the mountain.

Below our encampment Alfie and Malcolm were hooting frantically. Quite clearly from where I lay, only a few feet from Helen and the Grub, I could hear other habilines calling back and forth across the ridge. I turned on my side and saw Guinevere hurrying out of her windbreak and down a worn footpath toward the men.

Emily, Fred, and Nicole next came scurrying past me, and Nicole was carrying A.P.B., whose eyes were fixed over his mother's shoulder on the prodigious bonnet of ash cowling Mount Tharaka's truncated peak. The ground was tilting and heaving even as they fled, and it occurred to me that I had only two possible courses of action: I could die with Helen or I could bid her farewell and perhaps save my life. And the Grub's.

Kicking aside the struts of the unfinished travois, I threw myself into Guinevere's shelter. There lay Helen. The Grub squirmed against her breasts, where I had placed the infant to free my hands for work. About her neck my dead wife still wore the red bandanna that my sister Anna had given me in Cheyenne. I unknotted it, wiped Helen's forehead, and, after closing her lackluster eyes, tied the bandanna around my own neck. Another powerful explosion shook the mountain. Time was tightening like a noose.

"Come here, baby. Come to Poppa."

I picked my daughter off Helen's chest again and, cradling her in the crook of one arm, mouthed an incoherent goodbye to my lady. Then I darted out of the windbreak in desperate pursuit of the other Minids. The ridge sluiced with yellow mud, but I kept my balance and overtook the habilines in the very meadow where I had first learned that Helen was going to have a child.

Hot ash was showering down. From the vantage of the meadow it was evident that Mount Tharaka had blown away a good four to five hundred feet of its summit. Most of the smoke and soot—or at least the darkest plumes—trailed off to the east, while the sky directly above the mountain had the benighted look of a mirror draped with a black mantilla. Rivers of mud—of scorched tapioca—were oozing down the northwestern flank from the fractured summit, and several of these had already breached the timber line.

Chance and the mountain's peculiar topography had diverted these floods away from Shangri-la, toward the citadel of Attila Gorilla and his unfortunate people. Unless they had been far more prescient than we, it was hard to imagine that they had escaped their lofty fastness.

Numb, the Minids and I walked away from Mount

Tharaka. The men had clubs of one sort or another, but otherwise we had fled the volcano without any worldly goods. The Grub and Helen's red bandanna were all I had salvaged from the catastrophe still unfolding behind us.

On the savannah elephants trumpeted and guinea fowl paced. The foremost concern of every creature was not to kill a fellow refugee for lunch but to put a healthy distance between itself and the angry mountain. Therefore our evacuation proceeded almost like a parade. We saw baboons abreast of us, unruffled ostriches sprinting into thornbrakes, and giraffes moseying along in self-possessed pairs. As for us, we seemed to be heading toward our old capital cities in the gentle hills east of Lake Kiboko.

The Grub soiled me and began to cry. Her high-pitched mewling alarmed the Minids. I held my daughter at arm's length, scrutinizing her pallid body and monkeyish features. Her head, too heavy for her scrawny neck, lolled. Her face was a jigsaw puzzle of splotches and lines. Most surprising, her eyes were not the white-rabbit pink of pure albinism but a pair of obsidian dots, hard and penetrating. These dots disappeared when she howled, as she now recommenced to do, and I brought the child back into the cradle of my embrace.

Prolonged exposure to the sun would probably blister an infant so bereft of pigmentation. I tried to shade her with my chest, but the Grub did not stop crying. Shade was not all she wanted.

She was hungry. I was not equipped to satisfy that need and began to fear that I had rescued her from Mount Tharaka only to condemn her to starvation on the veldt. I might just as easily have left her writhing on Helen's corpse. Milk was what she required.

Guinevere drew alongside me, gesturing for her granddaughter. I handed the Grub to her and watched the baby nudge the depleted reservoirs of her dugs. The futility of this struggle was dismaying—but Guinevere carried her forward to Nicole, who was striding along with A.P.B. sitting jockey-style on her upper back. The child's dark, downy legs encircled his mother's waist like sooty pipe cleaners; and when Guinevere tried to transfer the Grub into Nicole's arms, A.P.B. poked at my daughter with jealous fingers. I hurried forward to deal him a hearty slap.

Nicole beat me to it, knocking A.P.B.'s hand aside. Then Guinevere removed the toddler from his mother's back and put him on the ground. The Grub—as soon as she was in Nicole's grasp—began to nurse, and this charity saved her life.

For much of that day Nicole treated the Grub as her foster child. She even took pains to keep my daughter's body in the shadows cast by her own.

When the Grub was not nursing, I occasionally carried her. The men now seemed to regard me as a kind of habiline transvestite, for if you put on a child in this society, you were automatically dressed as a woman. They stayed clear of me. The Grub, meanwhile, was frustrated by the uselessness of my nipples, which she eventually learned to ignore in order to concentrate on sleeping.

In sleep her translucent eyelids flickered. Sometimes they fell back to reveal the jaundiced whites of her eyes, and I would carefully shut them again, remembering the way Helen had stared at me in death, as if seeing into a future realm of reversed chiaroscuro. The Grub was of Helen's flesh, but what could the Grub know of either Helen's suffering or mine? Watching her trembling eyelids, I feared she knew too much.

Late in the afternoon Mount Tharaka boomed so mightily that the aftershocks ran out across the savannah in waves. Debris spewed upward in billows, and several strata of ash layered the southern horizon. Dust quilted the air overhead and drifted down like snow. Our bodies collected the cindery flakes.

Clad in lightweight surcoats of ash, looking like the Clay People in an old Flash Gordon serial I had seen on television in Van Luna, Kansas, we trudged on. The drifting ashfall, I told myself, was a natural sun shield for the Grub. I gave her back to Nicole believing that some power, maybe even my own will, was guaranteeing her survival. I would not lose her. She was Helen's legacy to me, my wife's final bequeathment from a past I had dreamed and dreamed again.

Although it thundered that night, it did not rain.

The next day found us still pushing northwestward, through thorn thickets and open grasslands. The gazelles and wildebeest seemed to be grazing on carpets of dusty gray wool, the zebras to be melting into the very air. Our entire world was a negative steeping in the chemicals of a photographer's developing solution. Nicole fed the Grub, while the rest of us ate whatever we could find, whether ash-dusted fruits or an occasional dull-witted guinea fowl. Everything tasted gray, and the grit in our eyes made every hour the hour before dusk

Night brought more clouds from the northeast, immense black dreadnoughts, and the air crackled with electricity. Although we rested for a time before plunging on again, we did not pause to sleep. Everyone appeared to be fueled by adrenalin and nervous energy. Hyenas and leopards were nocturnal hunters, after all, and our knowledge that we were attempting a migration during their biological uptime kept us alert. Five male habilines with clubs might be able to hold a pack of overgrown Pleistocene hyenas at bay, but the battle would be unpleasant.

Fortunately, cloud-spanning bolts of lightning unraveled often enough that we could monitor the transfigured landscape for predators, most of which were cowed by the incessant booming and crackling. The storm discomfited us, too, but we triumphed over our fear with the idiot, inbred bravado of our species. In fact, I put these dreadful flashes and bombinations out of my mind by thinking about Helen.

Not too far ahead of us, maybe two hundred yards, lightning struck a solitary baobab, exploding the tree's fibrous trunk and setting its branches ablaze like a Christmas candelabrum. To burn so splendidly it must have been rotten to the heart. It stopped us dead. The equatorial heat had dried the ground and grasses so thoroughly after the rains that fire ran down the torch of the baobab into the savannah. The breeze fanned these fires toward us from the northeast. The lightning leaping overhead had an earthly counterpart in the crimson and amber flames dancing across our line of march.

In spite of the wind, these fires burned wherever they wished. They consumed the shrubbery and tussocks slanting toward the lake and the patchy ground cover carpeting the steppe in front of us. Equatorial East Africa was instantly an inferno.

The Minids' bravado deserted them. Their masquerade of defiance collapsed. Alfie came pushing back through the women and children to organize a retreat. Flakes of ash clung to his beard and body hair, and his eyes coruscated like garnets. The barricades of fire radiating from the baobab had lengthened with such speed that no one resisted his command to fall back toward the danger we had escaped.

Certainly he meant for us to fall back only until we could outflank the prairie fires and so discover another route to our destination, but his panic—and that of the other Minids—suddenly alienated me from their aims. With Helen dead, I no longer wanted to subject myself to the stark imperatives directing their lives. I did not want to go back to Shangri-la or either of the two Helensburghs. My present—even my present in this prehistoric dream territory—had antecedents outside of habiline experience, and I wanted my daughter to grow up with all the twentieth-century advantages. I had to get her out.

Nicole had the Grub. She was fleeing with the others. I caught Nicole's arm and took the child away. The fires partitioning the savannah continued to subdivide, extruding wall after wall of madly flailing light. I was crazy not to flee with the Minids, but a different notion had taken possession of me. Dreaming of another kind of deliverance and holding my daughter against my chest, I trotted through a flame-etched corridor of darkness toward the ancient Rift Valley lake.

My plan was to find a safe passage through the burning grasslands to the southeastern shore of Lake Kiboko. In fact, I wanted to return to the very spot from which I had leapt into the Pleistocene.

Was it possible that after nearly two years Kaprow's omnibus could still be parked beside the lake, awaiting my return? Possible maybe, but not very likely. After losing transcordion contact with me, Blair and Kaprow might have reluctantly concluded that I was dead. Further, for all I knew, Somali irregulars could have overrun the lakeside protectorate or a cataclysmic world war put period to the persistent human hope for a global utopia. Either of these events, or any number of less traumatic ones, could have made White Sphinx a historical irrelevancy and me the anonymous victim of the project's demise.

The walls of fire crisscrossing the savannah tantalized and fretted the Grub. She arched her back, waved her tiny hands, kicked her legs. It was all I could do to keep from fumbling her to the ground like a wet football.

Holding her, I trotted along in the imbecile conviction that my fate really did matter to my century, that my colleagues were faithfully waiting for me. They had to be. Otherwise the Grub and I would die, and the Grub, I felt confident, had not been born to waste her sweetness on the desert air. Even struggling in my arms, she did not cry.

Ahead of us, hypnotized by the crackling barricades of fire, three giant hyenas stood in a kraal of darkness, panting like dogs. They were directly in our path. Kneeling beside a gall acacia, I exerted my strength and uprooted the bush with one hand. Then, in a blazing tussock not far from a massive bank of flames, I ignited this bush and advanced on the hyenas. For want of any alternative route away from the lake, they had begun jogging toward the Grub and me, shambling like three emaciated bears in motley. We were on a collision course.

One of the hyenas leapt through a break in the wall of fire and disappeared into the darkness beyond. The other two creatures halted. In the triangular lanterns of their skulls their eyes shone eerily. The smaller of these two hyenas suddenly turned tail and loped back through the corridor of flames toward the lake. Undeterred by these defections, the third animal vented a hysterical laugh and resumed its swaying trot. I shook my outstretched brand at it to no avail.

Even though the burning bush had begun to broil my fingers, I did not let go. I was immune to both pain and fear. After all, I had once survived the onslaught of an entire pack of these animals. On another occasion I had helped the Minids outlast a siege of giant hyenas by reciting a story and obediently shooting one of the besiegers with my .45. I had survived many other dangers to boot, ranging from puckerplum besottedness to wholesale ingestion by a leopard. Why, then, should I fear this frenzied, stinking hulk of a hyena?

Running past me—away from the brand that I tried to plunge into its face—the hyena twisted its body about and took my leg into its jaws. By bracing its feet and forcibly tugging, it upended me. This, I remembered, was virtually the same tactic the hyenas at the water hole had used to drag down the rhino calf. As I fell, I tossed aside my torch and tried to shift my weight so that the Grub would receive none of the inevitable impact.

My butt struck the ground, then my head. Despite my preparations, these sudden jolts sent the Grub tumbling through a powdery coverlet of ash. Stunned, I lay where I had fallen, unable to go after my daughter or to resist the hateful savagery of the hyena.

What then occurred will strike many as an improbable *deus ex machina* solution to our dilemma. I cannot effectively counter this complaint. To argue that I dreamed this solution is to cast into doubt everything else that happened during my sojourn in Pleistocene East Africa. (However, it is entirely possible that I foresaw this solution in a childhood spirit-traveling episode, one that, at the time, I had believed a tainted or impure dream.) On the other hand, to insist on the absolute reality of this occurrence is to violate the self-consistent world to which the director of the White Sphinx Project posted me. Let me, therefore, justify the following strange events in the only way possible, by declaring that they conform to the reality of my subjective experience immediately after falling to the hyena's attack. If they have any other justification, I do not intend to record it here.

After the thunder, an explosion. I believe that Mount Tharaka was erupting again. Doomed in any case, we were too far away to fear destruction from the volcano. The hyena pricked its ears and scanned the southeastern horizon.

Then, out of a matte-black sky, there fell toward the Grub, the hyena, and me a small constellation of flaring stars. A shadow appeared among these flames, and this shadow was the spidery frame on which the vehicle's vernier jets were mounted.

At which point I realized that this was no constellation, but a wingless space module dropping out of the heavens to our rescue. With a whoosh it swept by overhead and touched down about fifty yards away, right in the middle of the fire-flanked corridor through which the hyena had attacked us. A flurry of volcanic dust eddied like snow about the module's legs, and firelight reflected from the angular surfaces of the craft, which bore upon one high plane a vivid decal of the Zarakali flag: a hominid skull on a golden ground.

Jolly Roger, I thought, trying to rise. I could not get up.

After the hyena had fled, I crawled to my daughter, rolled to a sitting position, and lifted her out of the ashes. Her limbs were flailing, and her features were screwed up into a moue of utter outrage. She was not pretty. I had to dig a paste of dust from her nostrils with the nail of my little finger. Her phosphorescent whiteness made me fear that she was either radioactive or afflicted with the high luminosity of an unknown prehistoric illness. I rocked her, wiped her face with my saliva, and sang her a soothing song:

"I remember the time
That the goose she drank wine,
And the monkey spit tobacco
On the streetcar line.

Well, the streetcar it broke,
And the monkey got choke',
And they all went to heaven
In a little red boat."

A hatch on the Zarakali space module opened, and two tall, gaunt astronauts in tight-fitting suits with oxygen packs and helmets clambered down. Behind them they unreeled thick lengths of hose. These hoses the men turned on the grass fires raging to the right and left of their craft. They also directed streams of water toward the Grub and me, extinguishing flames, settling the ash cover, and filling the night with the distinctive stench of wet char.

When they had finished, and the only fires still visible were several bright fuses running eastward against the wind, they stashed their hoses in the module and came bounding over the landscape to see what they could do for us. Two or three bounds were all they required to close fifty yards, so proficient were they at maneuvering in the giddy weightlessness of their country's distant past.

Inside those streamlined helmets, black faces.

The astronauts bent solicitously over the Grub and me, murmured inaudible words of consolation, and scrutinized my writhing daughter from head to toe. One of the men tapped her chest with a gloved finger, tested her reflexes, gently pinched her naked limbs. To my questioning look he returned a broad, unequivocal smile. Undoubtedly the medical expert in the crew, this same man heightened my gratitude by examining my leg and flashing another reassuring grin. We were going to be okay.

A moment later the medical officer was supporting me as we limped through the dark to the brightly illuminated module. The captain of the mission was carrying the Grub, who had stopped squirming.

Once inside the cramped vehicle, I glanced about at the ranks of switches and dials, immensely relieved that I did not have to try to make sense of them. I could shunt to these brave astronauts all the responsibility for our deliverance.

We lifted and flew. The flight was smooth, exhilarating, and brief. When we landed again, the module balanced astride a peculiar flat outcropping of tuff on the southeastern shore of Lake Kiboko. In the dark the lake looked like a vast oil slick, but I could smell the fertile fishiness of the shallows and knew that I was almost home.

One of the astronauts helped me down the ladder to the ground. The other, waiting below, put the Grub into my arms as if presenting me a trophy for surviving my ordeal. Then they returned to their vehicle, closed the hatch, and ascended again into the sky on delicate streamers of fire. Two gods in a machine.

After their departure, the Grub and I were on our own again. I scrambled over the outcropping of tuff searching for the spot where Kaprow had parked the omnibus.

There. There it was.

Suspended in the air as if by Hindu legerdemain, the Backstep Scaffold. I knelt beneath it and stared up into the interior of the bus, an equipment-crowded chapel of stinging white light. There were Kaprow's Egg Beaters, huge coppery rotors, and enclosing them were the padded interior walls and ceiling of the omnibus. Deliverance.

"We're going home, baby. Going home."

I pushed the Grub up and over the edge of the Backstep Scaffold, which was about a foot above eye level, then chinned my way onto the platform and settled into its contours with my daughter in my left arm. It took me a moment to locate the toggle for retracting the platform, but when I found and activated it, the rotors inside the omnibus began to spin and the past to drop away beneath us like an ill-remembered dream. My baby and I were going home. Home.

CHAPTER TWENTY-NINE

Russell-Tharaka Air Force Base, Zarakal

September 1987

"WELCOME BACK, JOHNNY. I was beginning to think you were going to sleep the rest of your life away."

At first he did not recognize the face outlined above him against a window of robin's-egg blue. The face was a gentle caricature of one he remembered from another time. Most disconcerting, its skin was pale, with hints of applied color in the cheeks and lavender crescents on the eyelids. His tongue would not move.

"Don't try to talk yet, Johnny. You've been sedated for several days. I've . . . well, I've watched you sleep for the last three. Off and on, that is. They've given me a room in the Visiting Officers' Quarters. First time I've ever had officers' quarters in my life. Hugo would have scoffed at me for even accepting them—but noncoms' widows don't rate an on-base hostelry all their own and it's better than trying to commute out here every morning from Marakoi.

"God, Johnny, they did everything they could to keep me out of this country, everything but charge me with a federal crime and lock me up in Leavenworth. Suddenly, though, just a few days ago, their resistance collapsed, and here I am . . . I don't think I've ever watched you sleep so many straight hours without your eyeballs disappearing up into your forehead. Maybe you're over that now. Maybe that justifies what they've done to you. Maybe that absolves them of using you for a guinea pig in some sort of temporal I-don't-know-what . . . Woody Kaprow tried to explain it. He was the one who insisted on their letting me into the country once you got back from wherever the hell you supposedly were. I owe him for that, I know I do, but the rest of it— the secrecy, the deceptions, the bullyings, the run-arounds—God knows when I'll be able to forgive them for *that*. God knows."

The face was coming into focus, taking on a recognizable human aspect. It was an older face than he remembered, but he had not seen it for—well, for what?—eight years? ten years? more than two million? It belonged to the woman who had raised him, an aging woman against whom he had perpetrated a terrible wrong, believing himself, at her hands, the victim of an unforgivable treachery. He had forestalled any future treachery by cutting all ties with her.

Now—whenever Now was—here she was again. He did not resent this torrent of words from her or even the implicit assumption underlying them, that they could resume their lives without agonizing over or even referring to the cause of their break. That was a false assumption, however. He had a good deal to answer for. He knew it, and he tried unsuccessfully to make his tongue work.

"No, really. You don't have to say anything, Johnny. They said you might have trouble. Apparently you've awakened briefly twice before. Kaprow and a couple of Air Force doctors were with you, but you couldn't talk. Not a word. They wanted a kind of deposition from you, I think. A debriefing document. You weren't ready to give it. Flustered Kaprow lots, I'm afraid, even if at bottom he's a reasonably decent fellow, one of the few people I've met who won't duck the implications of his own responsibility for a fiasco like this one. He acknowledges his part in involving you, for instance. Blames himself for losing contact with you while you were gone, for the injuries you've sustained. Everyone else—Air Force brass, the local interior ministry, Defense Department officials back home—everyone else seems to be working on a C.Y.A. basis. They wanted a deposition attesting to the complete success and worthiness of this project . . . You don't even remember Kaprow and the others coming in here, do you? You ought to see your face—it's an acting-class paradigm of Total Bewilderment."

His mother gave a nervous laugh, wiped his forehead with a wet cloth, and leaned aside so that the African sky in the window overwhelmed him with its raw immensity. A jet fighter flashed by from left to right, as if it had just taken off from a nearby runway, but the sound of its engines was muted by the hum of the air-conditioning and the thickness of the walls in the cavelike hospital room.

C.Y.A. meant "cover your ass," an old and deservedly hallowed Air Force abbreviation. He had not smiled at his mother's use of the term because what she was telling him was vaguely troubling. The last image in his mind, prior to the appearance of her face, was of the coppery blur of the rotors in the omnibus. That blur had seemed to enfold and annihilate him. When could Kaprow, or anyone else, have tried to talk to him since the dream of his deliverance?

"Lie back, Johnny, just lie back. They lost you for a month, were afraid they wouldn't be able to retrieve you at all. I think Kaprow finally brought pressure to bear on the authorities to let me come see you when you failed to respond to either the doctors or him. You were like a zombie, he said. Thought the sight of a familiar face might jolt you back to reality. Here I am, then. A shot of Old Jolt, Johnny. Am I working? I think I am, I can tell by your eyes . . . This reminds me of when you were little. Didn't speak a word until you were almost two. Said 'cao' in Richardson's pasture on the outskirts of that new housing area in Van Luna. You had the most expressive eyes, though. You could talk with them as well as some people can with words. You haven't lost any of that ability, either. I can see by your eyes that this shot of Old Jolt has gone right to your head."

"Right," he echoed her, smiling.

"And that's the prettiest word I've heard you say since your first really emphatic 'cao,' I swear to God it is, John-John." She turned her head away, refused to look at him. "Yesterday was my birthday. I told them you'd wake up for my birthday. You're only a day late, and it's a fine, fine present." She looked at him again. "I'm fifty, can you believe that? Half a goddamn century. I feel like Methuselah's mother."

He worked to get the words out: "I'm Methuselah, then."

"You all right?"

"Think so."

"Don't talk. Don't try to get up. You're going to have a raft of visitors once they know you're conscious and able to talk."

He lay back in the stiff sheets and found that he was clad in a hospital gown, a gray sheath like a wraparound bib. His leg ached dully, and the antiseptic tang of the room offended his nostrils, worked its way into his throat like a hook. When he was very small, Jeannette had once let him take a whiff from an ammonia bottle and he had screamed as if she had gassed him. The smell in this room, he realized, was equally offensive. Water came to his eyes, flushed from his tear ducts by the stinging smell of disinfectants, rubbing alcohol, arcane medicines.

"Helen," he said. "Helen."

The woman beside his bed looked at him peculiarly but did not question him. He felt a tremendous surge of affection for her simply because she had the good sense to keep her mouth shut.

"I can't wear this. It hurts."

Before she could summon help, he swung his feet to the opposite side of the bed, tore the hospital gown off his back, and tottered a few steps toward the corridor. The linoleum under his feet was exactly the color of bleu cheese dressing, with chives. This comparison came to his mind unbidden as he struggled toward the door, outside which stood a sentinel with a weapon. Rick, looked like. The air policeman who had been assigned to White

Sphinx not long after his own arrival in Zarakal. The kid should have rotated home by now. Why was he still playing soldier for Kaprow? He had always pooh-poohed the idea of reenlisting.

"Johnny!" his mother called.

The bleu-cheese floor was treacherous. His legs were not going to negotiate the crossing.

"Where's my daughter?" he cried. "Where's the Grub?"

When he fell, his mother and the air policeman helped him from the floor. He was scarcely conscious of being assisted. The sting in his nostrils, the weakness of his legs, the salty film in his eyes—these things bespoke a deeper discomfort, a more compelling hurt.

"What the hell have you people done with my baby?"

He was virtually a prisoner in the hospital, the only patient in an otherwise deserted ward on the third floor. After they had sedated him again, and his mother had returned to the VOQ, and he had slept another six to eight hours, Woody Kaprow visited him. The blue African sky in his window had been displaced by sunset, a conflagration of interthreading pastels. Stars were also visible, high and sparse. Although he was shivering in the chilly room, he liked the starched hospital gown no more than he would have a straitjacket.

As his mother had done earlier, Kaprow engaged in a lengthy monologue. He stared across the bed at the door, scrupulously avoiding Joshua's eyes. Even though he never moved his head, his pale eyes flickered excitedly as he explained that they had almost given Joshua up for dead; that the entire White Sphinx Project was under a cloud because of their inability to monitor his activities in the past; that Blair expected and ought to receive a series of extensive reports on the mission as soon as Joshua felt well enough to face the Great Man; and that he, Kaprow, had approved Jeannette Monegal's visit to help Joshua ease himself back into the turbid waters of the late twentieth century.

"In a sense, Joshua, you've been reborn. You're going to have to take a little time to grow back into your old world. I'll do whatever I can to help you."

"I want to see my daughter."

"Joshua, that isn't your daughter."

"I want to see the child I brought back with me." Joshua pulled himself to a sitting position and looked piercingly at the physicist, who shifted his gaze to a photograph of President Tharaka that some wag had hung on the door to the water closet. The old man was wearing his hominid skull and a plush leopard-skin cloak. "Just tell me if I brought a child back with me, Dr. Kaprow. Was that a dream or did it really happen?"

"There's an infant in the maternity ward downstairs, Joshua, an infant you were clutching in your arms when we retrieved you from the Backstep Scaffold. She's a strange little creature but perfectly healthy. They treated her for jaundice right after we brought the two of you in. Put her under sun lamps with cotton batting over her eyes. She's well now, though."

"I *fathered* her, Dr. Kaprow."

"Joshua, you were away from us only a little over a month. It's natural you should be disoriented, though. There's no need to worry. Things'll straighten out for you soon enough."

"A little over a month?"

"Thirty-three days. I insisted that we drop the scaffold at least four times a day, for two hours each go—but our transcordions were apparently out of synch, and if you hadn't returned when you did, well, pretty soon I would've had to buckle under to an order to depressurize The Machine and cut our losses."

"Namely, me."

"You and a sizable amount of time and money."

"I was gone at least two years. I fell in love with a habiline, I fathered a child, I watched my wife die in childbirth. What you're telling me doesn't correspond to what *I* know about what happened, and *I* was the one who was there. *I know what happened to me, Dr. Kaprow!*"

"Look, here's a calendar on your bedside table—"

"I don't give a damn about any goddamn calendars," Joshua said levelly. "I brought a child back with me, and I'm her father."

Kaprow finally looked directly at Joshua. As colorless as glass, his irises danced in their whites. "All right. Maybe because of the *distance* you went into the past you experienced a kind of time dilation—the opposite of what a passenger aboard a faster-than-light vessel would experience subjectively, when those remaining at home age dozens of years to the spacefarer's one or two. A time dilation would—"

"I want to see the Grub!"

"The Grub?"

"My baby."

Kaprow's eyes cut away to the door again. "Okay, Joshua. I'll go with you. Maybe you'd appreciate a pair of pajama bottoms."

"Suit yourself."

The physicist smiled. "I'm suited. You're not." But he sent an orderly after both the pajama pants and a pair of slippers, with which the man quickly returned. Although Joshua had to turn up six or seven inches of the pajama legs into lumpy cuffs, the slippers fit almost perfectly.

Not speaking, he and the physicist rode an elevator to the carpeted maternity ward on the first floor, where they paused outside the bright little aquarium given over to the showcasing of newborns. A nurse was pushing one of the movable bassinets into a farther room, but the bassinet contained no baby. Joshua searched for the Grub.

There she was. Her head was the same—disproportionately large, a kaleidoscope of grimaces—but the color of her skin had deepened from blancmange to beige, probably as a result of the sun-lamp treatments that Kaprow had mentioned.

"At least you didn't hand her over to a veterinary clinic."

"She's human, Joshua. Nobody doubts that."

"Then how do you explain my bringing her back from a

period when human beings weren't supposed to look like she does?"

Kaprow said, "Why don't *you* explain that, Joshua?"

"I want to hold her."

"Hold her?" The question conveyed the physicist's helpless distaste for this idea; also the hint that, even if he wanted to, he could not persuade the nurses to honor Joshua's request.

"I'm her father. I want to hold her."

Joshua did not wait for permission. He trotted around the corner of the display room, skipped down a narrow corridor immediately behind it, and pushed his way through a swinging door into the off-limits inner sanctum. The nurse who had just removed a bassinet from the aquarium looked up from an instrument counter as if Joshua had surprised her filching penicillin suppositories. No words came out of her open mouth. Before she could sputter even a semi-intelligible objection, Joshua was cradling the Grub in his arms. Then Woody Kaprow burst into the display room's antechamber, and he and the nurse collided trying to get to Joshua.

"She's developing," he said, smiling at his daughter as they confronted him amid a small fleet of bassinets.

"Of course she's developing," the nurse angrily responded. "That's what they do at this age, and for a good many years after." She adjusted her uniform. "What do you think you're doing in here, anyway?"

"Not *developing,* damn it! *Developing!*"

Nonplused by the small figure in rolled pajama bottoms, the nurse merely gaped. What kind of madness did the little man represent?

Kaprow said, "As in photography, I think he means."

"Right. She's getting darker. All it took was bringing her out of the film pack and into the dark room."

Joshua rocked the Grub. She grinned prettily at him, and he marveled at the way her skin was ripening toward a delicate duskiness. His daughter, developing . . .

CHAPTER THIRTY
Marakoi, Zarakal
September 1987

THEY WERE SEATED beneath the fringed awning of Bahadur Karsanji's on Tharaka Boulevard in the blindingly bright heart of the capital, Marakoi. Karsanji's, a café, was one of the few businesses in the city still under Indian ownership after the wholesale "Africanization" of Asian-run establishments in 1972. It had escaped because it had a cosmopolitan clientele, a reputation for excellence antedating by three decades Zarakal's political independence, and an owner of discreet Machiavellian canniness in matters of mercantile survival.

Nearly every table under the red-and-white awning was occupied, and the crowd inside the restaurant was creating a din twice as nerve-racking as that of the traffic in the streets. Joshua and his mother, three days after his awakening in the base hospital, were eating spinach-filled crêpes (Jeannette's idea) and drinking a good California Chablis (his). At two o'clock that afternoon she would be departing the country from Marakoi International Airport, and they did not know when they would see each other again. The enlistment time remaining to Joshua complicated his situation, and so did his paternal claim on the infant in the hospital. Neither Kaprow nor Blair had welcomed this claim, for the paleoanthropologist viewed the Grub as the spoils of Joshua's mission while the physicist regarded her as a vexatious temporal anomaly. Jeannette had no idea the infant even existed, for Joshua had refrained from mentioning her after collapsing in front of his mother and Jeannette had supposed his ravings about a daughter the products of disorientation and delirium. At present the child was the ward of the United States Air Force, with a room of her own on the hospital's third floor and a round-the-clock guard. Though Joshua had begged and ranted, the small special staff assigned to his daughter would not permit him to feed, bathe, or hold her. In fact, he had seen her only once during the past three days. An awkward swallow of Chablis choked him, blurring his vision.

"There you go," said Jeannette Monegal, thumping his back. "You just haven't readjusted to the pleasures of fine food and drink yet. What have they been feeding you at the hospital?"

"Rice."

"What else?" she asked rhetorically. "I wrote you a letter, Johnny,"

"A letter? Why?"

"In case they wouldn't let me see you."

"They did, though."

"Amazingly. Through Dr. Kaprow's good offices. Neither the Air Force nor Alistair Blair nor the Zarakali government wanted to let me in. My book on Spain—it's just come out—has already given me a reputation as a caustic international muckraker. I had to sign a document declaring that I was coming to Zarakal solely as a tourist. Supposedly, having signed the damn thing, I can't even publish a travel article without first clearing it with the American Embassy and two or three local ministries."

"You agreed to that?"

"To see you, yes—I certainly did." She withdrew an envelope from her large straw purse. "Here's the letter. Please don't read it till I go. If you have any questions, you can write me in care of Anna in Newport News, Virginia. She and Dennis Junior are visiting in-laws. Here's the address. I've got your APO number. We'll stay in touch, okay? If you remove yourself from my life for another eight years, John-John, I'll be an *old* woman when next we meet. So stay in touch, okay?"

"Yes, ma'am."

She slid a bill of large denomination across the table and stood up. He rose, too, but she would not permit him to accompany her to the airport, insisting that an airport farewell would "demolish me utterly," phraseology he had never before heard on her lips. They had both changed in eight years, eroded or subtly augmented by the sweep of time's river. The rattle of wine glasses and silverware, the background babble of English and Swahili—Joshua suddenly felt isolated and bereft. He wanted his mother to go quickly because he did not want her to go at all. She kissed him on the forehead, the blessing of a matriarch on one of her smallest and most beloved.

"*Ciao,* Johnny."

"*Cao,*" he responded automatically.

Jeannette laughed. "I hope I'm not supposed to construe that as a slur. Even if I deserve it. 'Bye, honey. Be good." She threw him a kiss and, carrying her own bag, stooped into the rear seat of a minicab parked about a quarter of a block from Karsanji's. When the cab came cruising past the restaurant, she gave him a faint smile before stoically averting her gaze.

He ate the remainder of his crêpe, drank the last few sips of his wine, and, buoyed by the money she had left, ordered a custard and another bottle of Chablis. He was already high, and many of the people around him undoubtedly attributed his furtive glances at the street, his maniacal alertness, to the quantity of wine he was putting away. Or maybe he was involved in an illicit affair and both his drinking and his nervous watchfulness were inspired by guilt. The predator for which he kept watch might be his paramour's cuckolded husband.

Actually, he was thinking of Helen and wondering what

she would have made of this bizarre scene. The primeval savannah underlay nearly thirty square blocks of concrete, stucco, and glass. Males in cutaway jackets and leather sandals brought food to you at a table. The streets were full of unimaginable noise, and the women walking upright past the shop windows wore plumage as bright as, or even brighter than, that which the males wore . . . Joshua was glad Helen had not survived to witness the benign horror of civilization, equally glad he had survived to reexperience it. To dislodge Helen from his mind, he opened his mother's letter—which, over a year and a half ago, she had composed in longhand in Madrid.

Apologies and a quiet plea for reconciliation dominated the first page or so, shading away into news about Anna and her handsome new son. Johnny was an uncle; she, Jeannette, a grandmother. They would be a real family again when he and Dennis Whitcomb returned from East Africa—for Anna had ignored Johnny's advice and spilled the beans about his assignment to Russell-Tharaka Air Force Base.

Well, of course she had. Joshua had belatedly realized that she would, driven by her sense of family and her respect for family hierarchies. It was all right. Joshua forgave Anna her trespass, which was less against him than against the Air Force and the sovereign state of Zarakal.

At which point the letter shifted gears again, moving from the topic of family bonds to that of blood relationships. A subtle, even disturbing shift. Joshua's hands began to tremble—not merely from the heat and the wine—as he continued reading what his mother had written:

> After doing my one and only novel (which did not of me an Agatha Christie or a Barbara Cartland make—so quickly back to nonfiction), I contracted with Vireo to do *The Reign in Spain: Life and Politics in Post-Franco Iberia*. Then I came here to research and write my book. Or, at least, the book was my ostensible reason for coming. The truth is that I thought you might be here, too, searching for a part of your own past you never had the opportunity to verify on your own.

Do you remember, when you were in your early teens you sometimes used to flaunt the *nom de guerre* Juan Ocampo? Usually you were pretending to be a Latin American shortstop on some major-league baseball team, but you also liked to sign that name to poems, to secret pacts with your boyhood friends, and to confidential Declarations of Independence from the tyranny of Mother and Father Monegal. These last documents you often managed to leak to the tyrants themselves by "caching" them in such out-of-the-way places as my American Heritage Dictionary or the catch-all drawer in Hugo's work bench in the utility room.

Anyway, this behavior led me to suppose that you cherished the idea of an identity separate from the bourgeois one with which we had saddled you, and that one day you might try to inherit this alternative life. Maybe, in fact, this submerged identity would free you from the dreams that so frequently estranged you not only from us but from yourself. *If he thinks that being Juan Ocampo will free him* (I reasoned), *he is very likely to go to Spain in search of the latent Juan Ocampo in his heart.* The idea for the book I am now working on came to me as a pretext—a *literal* pretext—for following you to Spain.

And then Anna wrote to say you were going to Zarakal, shattering my hopes of finding you here and sentencing me to six months at hard labor on this brilliant book of mine.

The Reign in Spain (by Eliza Doolittle).

Anyway, I decided to find your mother. If she still happened to be alive. My researches were going to take me to Andalucía and Sevilla, in any case, and I might as well combine book business and my quasi-maternal curiosity to see what I could see.

Does the name Carl Hollis mean anything to you? Undoubtedly not. He was the intelligence agent who declared—during our interview in Colonel Unger's office at Morón AFB almost a quarter of a century ago—that Encarnación Ocampo had disappeared, probably forever. I never knew if by that he meant that she was dead or that she had simply vanished into the concealing vastness of the countryside like a guerrilla fighter. Because the former assumption pretty much preempted hope, I decided to proceed on the latter.

A good thing, too, for, John-John, I found your mother.

Sam Spade and Phillip Marlowe have nothing on me, son— not, at least, when it comes to tracking Missing Mothers. (Missing Sons I am not so good at, even when they take up residence within spitting distance of their fathers' last duty assignment. In a couple of other senses, though, I am *damned* adept at Missing You.) I won't go into the details here. Suffice it to say that I returned to the tenement where Encarnación lived with you in 1962-63. Because I was obviously not a policewoman or a pusher of some vampirish sort, a surprising number of people talked to me. In many ways, after all, Encarnación was—*is*—a memorable figure, menacing or plucky depending on your point of view. I had always leaned to plucky—because, when she might have surrendered you to her despair, she saw you to the safety of Santa Clara.

Anyway, my informants—three of them, John-John—remembered your mother very well and gave me some profitable leads.

I traced Encarnación to an Andalusian village called Espejo. Here she is living today, Johnny, no longer either a prostitute or a black marketeer. She has redeemed her life in an extremely old-fashioned way, at least for the female of our species, and I will not presume any sort of political comment about this fact. Not, at least, in this letter. You see, she is married to a robust, red-haired barkeep and bodega owner named Antonio Montaraz, who appears in his boisterous way to dote on her. She *must* be approaching the change of life, but she has had at least nine children by this man, the youngest a babe-in-arms whom she suckles between stints as a barmaid in Señor Montaraz's dingy but prosperous hole-in-the-wall tavern. The children also help their father, and although there is a lot of public bickering and noise, the barkeep's regime seems to be popular even among the older siblings. This is a tight-knit family, with both Antonio and Encarnación in stolidly traditional roles. It looks suffocating to me—pardon me, my slip is showing—but your mother seems to be *more* than content with her lot.

The principal question now in your mind is probably this: Did I talk to her? Tell her about you? Trot out my own maternal experiences as a counterweight to your mother's? The answer to this question—these questions—is *No, of course not.* You see, Johnny, to the cheerfully busy Montarazes I was a dowdy/doughty Englishwoman, with a phrase-book command of Spanish, who had stumbled off a tour bus disastrously misrouted out of Córdoba. I did not try to correct this false impression.

Suppose that I had blurted out my story to Encarnación. Would she have recoiled from me as an evil messenger intent on destroying her present life with lurid tales of her past? It's quite possible. Or suppose that my mentioning you, out of the hearing of her husband, had afflicted her with a terrible anxiety about your whereabouts, your safety, your happiness. Because I still cannot completely reassure *myself* on these points, I could not have reassured her, either. So I pretended to a tourist's illiteracy and spoke only a little.

Do you, there in exotic Zarakal, remember your Spanish? Even a little? Well, the surname Montaraz means "wild, primitive, uncivilized," and to some extent this is a perfect characterization of your little half-brothers and half-sisters. None is as dark as you, John-John, and I doubt seriously that any of them ever suffers cripplingly vivid dreams about prehistoric East Africa, but, in many respects, they are nevertheless a feral crew. Their mother signals them with rapid-fire hand gestures, which, even though they can all speak, they relay to one another with remarkable deftness, cutting their eyes for emphasis. They communicate as effectively without words as with them, but they are noisy for Antonio's sake. He is a raconteur and yowler who cannot keep his mouth shut.

I don't think this is a milieu you would find especially compatible, but one day you may want to visit the Montarazes and decide for yourself. The address in Espejo is 17 Avenida de Franco. I caution you, however, to think about the likely impact of such a visit. The ramifications go far beyond the mere satisfaction of your filial curiosity.

That Encarnación is alive and happy in a world such as ours strikes me as a miracle, and miracles are their own justification. Although hope, faith, optimism, and the formidable power of what the late Dr. Peale liked to call "positive thinking" are clearly essential to the progress of our species—toward what? toward what?—only a fool ignores the potential *wartiness* of both circumstance and the human heart. As a matter of fact, I approached my search for your biological mother as something of a fool's errand, expecting from the outset to learn that she had hanged herself in an abandoned building, or suffered a fatal beating at the hands of a psychotic client, or surrendered to the ravages of venereal disease, or maybe even walked beneath a construction platform from which a scuttle of bricks had just fallen. I did not like to believe any of these possibilities, of course, but until my search ended, each seemed as likely as what has actually occurred. More likely, in fact, given your mother's unpromising background and the prejudice against her as a *bruja morisca*. So cherish this miracle, Johnny, and think very carefully about your biological mother's present happiness.

I also know what happened to your biological father, Lucky James Bledsoe. No miracle here. The bad news is that as a member of the Army's First Cavalry Division he was killed twenty-one years ago in the Ia Drang Valley in South Vietnam. He had just turned eighteen. I discovered his fate by tracing his parents' whereabouts through the Air Force locator service at Lackland.

The Bledsoes live in Little Rock, Arkansas. You would probably be a welcome visitor to their home, should you decide to approach them. Photographs of their son in his Seville Dependent High School Basketball uniform, his letter jacket, and his senior cap and gown—from a segregated civilian school in Montgomery, Alabama—decorate the walls of the Bledsoes' paneled living room. I visited them five years ago, when I still had no inkling where you were, on the chance that you had somehow contrived to find them before I did.

Because LaVoy, Lucky James's father, remembered Hugo from the days of their professional relationship on the flight line at Morón, the Bledsoes accepted me into their home. Neither LaVoy nor his wife Pauline believed that I had sought them out solely to renew an acquaintance that had never been very close to begin with. When I told them of Hugo's death, they commiserated in a touchingly heartfelt way—but, while Pauline plied me with whiskey-and-7-Up cocktails, LaVoy asked harder and harder questions about the trouble I had gone to to find them, and I finally confessed that their dead son had a living heir.

This news did not shock or upset them. I think they were almost grateful for it. Which is why I believe you could step into their lives without wounding or discomfiting the Bledsoes. They are your grandparents, Johnny, and that night, when they asked me where you were, I had to confess my ignorance, my guilt, my sorrow. I wept unabashedly for ten to fifteen minutes, and Pauline—bless her—wept with me. We have written each other or exchanged telephone calls at least once a month ever since my visit, but I have not yet told them you are alive and presumably safe in another country. (Anna, after all, was not supposed to tell me.) That remains for you to do, if you believe they deserve this small consideration. To my mind, they do.

Lord, look how long this letter has grown. I've been working on it for three straight hours—while the streets of Madrid seem to be washing away under a heavy April rain. *Después de Juan Carlos, el diluvio.* The reign in Spain, I fain would claim, is not mainly on the wane. Nor the rain, either. But I am growing giddily weary of writing, as my prose shows, and I had better close. Scratch this entire paragraph, Johnny.

—*Eden in His Dreams.*

See how stubbornly I resisted writing those words, how tenaciously I delayed the inevitable. Between writing "Scratch this entire paragraph, Johnny" and the next four words, nearly an hour passed. The sky is perceptibly lightening, the rain slackening. And I have finally written the phrase upon which this entire epistle teeters, even if that four-word fulcrum seems more than a tad off-center.

Johnny, forgive me. You will never fully understand how much I regret what I did, nor how dearly you have made me pay for that error. I am sorry for the pain I caused you, sorry for the pain I have reaped myself. If we should ever see each other again, I will probably not be able to speak of some of these things. This is why I have written about them at such stupid, even stupefying, length. You have an immense extended family, but though I have hurt you with one ill-considered act, and bewildered you by evolving from one sort of person into another (as I had to do), I hope that you will not exclude me forever from a place in this family. I belong there, too. In spite of everything, Johnny, I belong there, too.

All my love,
Mom

Joshua reread the letter twice, slid it back into its envelope, and put the envelope in an inside jacket pocket. He was wearing civilian clothes because off-duty American personnel, by treaty stipulation, were not permitted to wear their uniforms in either Marakoi or Bravanumbi. No one on either side wished to foster the impression that the Americans comprised an occupation force. Joshua therefore resembled an ambitious young native politician, a newcomer to the WaBenzi tribe. Although his nervousness distinguished him from most of the other smart go-getters drinking their lunches at Karsanji's, he had not yet drawn undue attention to himself.

His mind turning like a merry-go-round past all the items in his mother's letter, he drank, ordered more wine, and drank again. The last shuttle back to base left the embassy grounds at midnight; he could spend the next ten hours right here. For dinner, a kidney pie and a mug of thick Irish stout; then back to wine again. If he could not decide which long-range goal to pursue now that White Sphinx had ended and a thousand conflicting options vied for his approval, at least he could kill the remainder of the day. Effortlessly. Painlessly.

"May I join you?"

Joshua looked up to see Alistair Patrick Blair standing beside the chair his mother had deserted. Unenthusiastically he nodded the Great Man into the empty place.

"Where is Mrs. Monegal?"

"Leaving the country."

"So soon?"

"She's supposed to begin a promotional tour for her new book. Her visit here required her to drop four stops from her schedule, and her publisher did not exactly smile on the deletion."

"She should tell her publisher to go to blazes," Blair said amiably. "I never tour for my books."

"Only to raise money for your digs."

"That's true enough."

"My mother makes her living from her writing. My father made no arrangements to provide his family with survivors' benefits, and he died before he got his Air Force pension."

"I'm sorry to hear that, Joshua."

The two men stared at each other. Yesterday Joshua had unburdened himself of two years of his subjective experience in the distant past. Alternating questions about paleonanthropological and temporal matters, Blair and Kaprow had grilled him for ten solid hours—for the benefit of their own insatiable curiosity and two silently grinding tape machines. Joshua had *told all*, not omitting the details of his long and intimate relationship with the habiline woman he had named Helen.

That relationship explained the Grub, and Joshua did not intend to yield his daughter to anyone for the purpose of illegal, unethical, and immoral biological experiments. She was, as Kaprow had already conceded, a human being. Any viable offspring of a human parent was by definition—yes, by definition: *his*—a human being, and by denying him custody of the child, the United States Air Force and the Zarakali government were in violation of one of his most basic human rights. At the end of the ten-hour session Joshua had broken down and cursed both men, surrendering wholeheartedly to rage if not to tears.

"You've been drinking quite a lot, I think. Do you mind if I try to overtake you?"

"What for?"

"Well, Joshua, a celebration."

"Of the fact that I've blown your *Homo zarakalensis* theory right out of the water?"

"If you like. However, I'm not convinced that you have, you know."

"Or of your scuzzy treatment of my daughter and me?"

"Joshua, the child is a native Zarakali, with all the rights and privileges accruing to citizens of our republic. It's possible that we could find excuses to limit *your* freedom, but never hers."

"What, then, are we celebrating?"

"I thought Americans passed out cigars. I've not yet got mine. I suppose this excellent vintage must suffice."

Joshua stared at the Great Man.

"Your first embarkation on the ocean of fatherhood." Blair lifted the glass that one of Karasanji's wine stewards had just provided him. "To Joshua Kampa, the New Adam, Futurity's Sire."

"Bullshit."

"Very pretty, very aromatic bullshit."

"But bullshit nonetheless."

"Mzee Tharaka told me this morning that no matter what either I or the American authorities wish, your daughter must be remanded to your custody immediately. Should we balk on this point, he will expel me from my cabinet position and the Americans from their expensive new military facilities."

"You told him about the Grub?"

"He already knew, Joshua."

"How?"

"It seems that two of our nation's would-be astronauts are also intelligence agents. They ran a fishing launch up and down Lake Kiboko during the White Sphinx Project and recorded your return to us through the telephoto lens of a hand-held movie camera. It was impossible to get you and the child from the omnibus to the medical station without bringing you briefly into the open."

Joshua dimly remembered having seen a boat on the lake—a small boat, always at a distance.

"There's more. Some of those bothersome Sambusai who occasionally come foraging over the protectorate—well, it appears that one or two of those fellows are also in Mzee Tharaka's employ, for our President-for-Life has many eyes and ears. He was quite impressed with you the day you visited the Weightlessness Simulation Incline. He considers you a brave man. Before you return to the United States, you will be made an honorary citizen of Zarakal in a private ceremony at the President's Mansion. Do you begin to understand what you have to celebrate, Joshua?"

"The Grub is mine!"

"I would think you might wish to give her a more dignified name. Mzee Tharaka is sure to demand that much."

"How do you think President Tharaka would like Monicah?"

"Monicah?"

"It's a nice monicker, don't you think? It's the name I've

had in mind, a decent English/Zarakali name." When Blair did not reply, Joshua added, "What else does the President intend to demand?"

Nonchalantly sipping, Blair beaded his mustachios with tiny rubies of Chablis. He patted his mouth with a napkin and eyed the passing traffic. "I fear that I've misspoken, Joshua. The President *hopes* you will always consider this country a second homeland; that once you have left the American military you will agree to reside in Zarakal with your daughter for at least a portion of each year. To this end, he has determined that you should receive a small annual stipend for your part in solidifying relations between our two countries. Also, a high-rise apartment here in Marakoi. It would be a shame, he believes, for, ah, Monicah to grow up solely as an American, nourished on hamburgers and banana splits, educated by television programs and cassette recorders, uprooted from the soil, the people, and the culture of her homeland. The idea of such total deracination appalls the President, and he is sure that you, as an intelligent black man, will see the matter pretty much as he does."

"A high-rise apartment in Marakoi takes care of the problem?"

"Not entirely, no. Mzee Tharaka wishes you to regard yourself as a bridge between two worlds. Marakoi is merely one of the anchors for the span. The other anchor could be Pensacola, Florida, or Cheyenne, Wyoming, or Wichita, Kansas. Wherever you like. But if you reject the high-rise apartment here in Marakoi, the bridge collapses for want of support, and commerce between your daughter's native land and her adoptive one must necessarily cease, at least for you and your daughter. President Tharaka's watchword has always been *Let there be commerce.*"

The wine he had drunk in the heat of the day had not made Joshua receptive to syllogistic argument. He felt that he had fallen into an intricate web. Now he was creeping along a filament leading deeper inward rather than out. What multi-eyed predator awaited him at the heart of this pattern?

Distracted, he muttered, "Persephone."

"I beg your pardon."

"He wants Monicah to spend a portion of each year in the underworld and a portion on earth with the living—like Persephone."

Blair laughed. "Ah, yes. But which is which?"

"I've brought her out of the land of the dead, Dr. Blair." He gestured at the crowd in the restaurant, at a strip of sky visible through a gap in the awning. "Everything up here is both. Not just in Marakoi. All over. Everywhere. There, too; even in the underworld."

"You're a trifle tipsy, aren't you?"

"You've influenced President Tharaka in this. You want Monicah in Zarakal a part of each year so that you can prod and poke and measure and compare. Am I right?"

"That would be helpful. And no more harmful to the Grub, I would think, than a yearly physical examination."

"She's not one of your goddamn fossils!" Joshua was conscious of heads turning to track this outburst. He lowered his voice: "Not one of your goddamn fossils. A human being. Helen's daughter."

Blair put his glass aside, scraped his chair back, and stood. "Of course. And *your* daughter, too. The medical people at the base have confirmed as much. So she's yours, and Mzee Tharaka has interceded to insure that no one disputes your claim to her. His intercession warrants a little gratitude, don't you think? Please consider this, Joshua, when the time comes to make a real decision." After paying for his share of the wine with several notes engraved with portraits of the President in his hominid-skull crown and leopard-skin cloak, the Great Man gave Joshua an affectionate pat on the shoulder and headed off down Tharaka Boulevard toward the National Museum, from which he had apparently come for his midday break.

Joshua gave the African wine steward and the Indian waiter extravagant tips. Then he toddled uncertainly into the sunlight. The brightness of the buildings and the paving squares stunned him. Peacocks strutted in a small emerald plaza beyond the nearest intersection. He walked about aimlessly for nearly an hour. Engine noise made him look up. Over the city a jet arrowed north-northwest into a wilderness of achingly empty sky. It was his mother's flight to Rome, the first stop on her journey back to the States.

"*Ciao*," he told the aircraft, saluting. "*Ciao*." The other word he left unspoken, reverberating in his memory.

A chapter in his life—an era, rather—had come to a close. The slide show had finally ended. The early Pleistocene was no longer accessible to him in dreams, and the White Sphinx program was over, probably for good. Here he was, not quite twenty-five years old, and he was going to have to make a new life for himself. A host of options lay before him, but, tipsy with Chablis and sunshine, at the moment all he could truly feel was a powerful sense of loss and uncertainty. All the routes to his previous self—the self that had tried to survive as a loner in Fort Walton Beach—were blocked, and he did not know which new path to choose.

"*Ciao*," he said again, and this time he was not talking to his mother.

CODA

Daughter of Time

August 2002

WITH MY MOTHER'S blessing I entitled my book about my adventures in prehistoric East Africa *Eden in My Dreams*. It was not published in the United States until 1994, seven years after my return from the distant past, when the American government grudgingly lifted the lid on the White Sphinx Project and acknowledged officially that my cockamamie stories about visiting the Pleistocene as an Air Force chrononaut were not cockamamie after all. In the interval, however, I had become a Zarakali citizen and cabinet minister. Indeed *Eden in My Dreams* had first been published in 1993 in English and Swahili editions by Gatheru & Sons Publishing Company of Marakoi. The American press had been quick to report the appearance of my book and to accuse both the administration and the Pentagon of sullying my name and appropriating millions upon millions of tax dollars without Congressional approval, an eerie recapitulation of the flap that had attended my departure from the States in 1990. By this time, though, I was too busy taking care of my daughter and serving as

Zarakal's Minister of Tourism and Intercultural Affairs to worry about the fuss and flutter in Washington, D.C.

Time, as it always does, passed.

On the fifteenth anniversary of my return from my stay among the habilines (the very date in August that Monicah, a.k.a. the Grub, had at the ripe old age of six chosen as her "official birthday"), I took my daughter to the spanking-new Sambusai Sands Convention and Recreational Centre on the shores of scenic Lake Kiboko. This was my birthday gift to her. She would soon be off to the States to resume her education at a private school in Kent, Connecticut, and I was hoping that a few days of paddle-boating, Ping-Pong, shuffleboard, swimming, crocodile watching, and casino games would erase her melancholy mood.

Although White Sphinx had long ago purged me of my spirit-traveling episodes, I knew what Monicah was suffering. She dreamed as I had once dreamed. Not of her mother's cat-eat-chalicothere grasslands, however, but of a vivid utopian tomorrow whose inaccessibility sometimes frustrated her beyond bearing. I, the past; she, the future. By nature Monicah was a cheerful child, whom both Jeannette and Anna had come to know and like, but in the wake of recent sociopolitical catastrophes (from which Zarakal, by means of a friendship treaty with the Pan-Arabian League and a strong leadership role in the East African Confederation Movement, had partly insulated itself) her dreams had increased in number, duration, and intensity. She was a tormented young woman, my Monicah. If this holiday did not rub the rust from the rose, I could not in good conscience send her off to school in Connecticut.

I had then served in Zarakal's cabinet for nearly a decade. At thirty-nine I was still the youngest member of the National Assembly with an appointment to the President's cabinet, and it was one of my duties to be on hand for the gala Grand Opening of the Sambusai Sands Hotel and Cabaret. Not merely by chance, this event coincided with the anniversary of my deliverance from the Pleistocene and with Monicah's birthday.

My position had its perks. When Monicah and I arrived at

the newly completed Alistair Patrick Blair Airport, a group of Sambusai *ilmoran,* or warriors, met our private jet and escorted us into the terminal—where two of their number, apparently the winners of a lot drawing, attached themselves to us as additional bodyguards. Imposing in their ceremonial cloaks and ornate beaded headbands, they were soft-spoken fellows who had attended a Catholic mission school at a nearby frontier outpost. They towered over my daughter and me.

Monicah, despite my protests in Marakoi, had shaved her head and donned elegant African garb as (her own words, I swear) "prophylactics against the corrupting influence of the resort." Now she would have to wear a wig to her classes at Kent School. Our Sambusai bodyguards did not mind. They turned their deep brown eyes on Monicah with respectful admiration. Good. I had begun to fear that all my plans on her behalf were going to be thwarted by her own intransigent attitude. Maybe the casual closeness of a pair of innocently virile males would improve her disposition. I sent her down to the paddle-boat marina with the Sambusai warriors and one well-armed security agent while my aide and I checked in at the hotel's main desk and rode upstairs to scrutinize our V.I.P. suite.

"Very WaBenzi."

"Yes, sir," agreed Timothy Njeri, a fiftyish Kikembu assigned to me not long after I had won my seat in the National Assembly. Timothy's briefcase contained sophisticated electronic gear, which he immediately deployed to scan the room for listening devices. "It seems to be quite clean," he said at last, carefully packing his equipment away.

I told Tim to fix himself a drink from the suite's well-stocked bar. Then I eased myself into an Agosto Caizzi fishnet pullover and a pair of designer bush shorts and descended to the Sands lobby to fulfill another of my obligations on this multipurpose mission.

One-armed bandits whirred and rang in the gaming room to my right, while in the left-hand casino a dozen roulette wheels ratcheted through their fateful orbits. There were more Americans than ever in Zarakal, and the Air Force, in response to our treaty-extension stipulations, had just inaugurated free shuttles from Russell-Tharaka and the naval facility at Bravanumbi for all eligible military personnel. Further, an American coffee concern had built a company town in the central highlands, and there was a Ford suncar plant on the outskirts of the capital, where Zarakali laborers pocketed four times the average hourly wage of other native workers but only a third of what their American counterparts in Dearborn and Detroit were making. In spite of the continuing drought in the Northwest Frontier District, our economy was booming. Marakoi's *East African Ledger* made occasional mention of my contribution to the boom.

A black man in Western clothes wearing a distinctive scarab tie pin caught my eye and pushed through the smoky revolving doors to the terrace overlooking the lake. The tie pin identified the man as my contact, a liaison between the custodians of the moribund White Sphinx Project and the Zarakali government. For obvious reasons Matthew Gicoru, our Vice President, had selected me to represent our interests in this meeting, but I still did not understand either the need for such a get-together or the liaison's insistence on these embarrassing James Bond tactics. After ten minutes in the arid lacustrine heat his enameled scarab would melt right down the front of his tie.

I followed the man outside. My contact, after checking to see that *I* was not being tailed, led me along a palm-lined parapet away from the hotel. It was three o'clock in the afternoon and much too hot for such foolishness. Bookended between her Sambusai galley slaves beneath a big polka-dot parasol, my Monicah was a passenger in the only paddle-boat plying the turquoise waters of the lake. A small rescue vessel stood offshore to rescue any boater who fell victim to the heat.

To the north of the hotel we were building a nine-hole golf course, with Astro-turf fairways and greens, but it was difficult to imagine anyone but a rich Bedouin ever using it. In addition to dehydration and sunstroke, there were other hazards. My contact, jumping down from the retaining-wall promenade, ignored a tall stone obelisk warning of these:

GUESTS PROCEED AT OWN RISK
BEYOND THIS POINT.

* * *
* * *

Beware of lions and other potentially dangerous wildlife.
Automatic one-year prison term
for any unauthorized person bearing firearms
into restricted area.

This message, repeated in Swahili, French, and Arabic, bore a replica of my own signature:

Minister of Tourism and Intercultural Affairs. It was counter-signed by the Interior Minister.

Several dozen yards beyond the obelisk my contact halted on a ridge overlooking the fossil beds where Alistair Patrick Blair had made his reputation as a paleoanthropologist. The heydays of the seventies and eighties were no more. A chain-link fence enclosed the area where the Great Man's successors labored to keep his work alive in the mocking shadow of the Sambusai Sands Hotel.

I did not like to come out this far because memories nagged at me here. One of them was commemorated by a bronze sculpture of a hominid skull that turned on a stainless-steel pivot above a cairn of mortared stones. This monument stood in front of the wattle shack that had been Blair's headquarters at Lake Kiboko. Tourists could enter the protectorate, shrunk from two hundred square miles to a few hundred square yards since the

Great Man's death, only on Sundays, and they were always accompanied by armed guards who did not permit them to wander from a preordained route. The guards' pistols were to intimidate the tourists as well as to defend against lions. The plaque on the cairn read:

ALISTAIR PATRICK BLAIR
STATESMAN AND SCIENTIST
1914–1991

Blair's ashes were buried under the pedestal.

"Dirk Akuj," the man on the ridge greeted me as I drew near. He was thin, coal-black in color, and ascetic-looking. "A pleasure to meet you, Mr. Kampa."

"It would have been more pleasant in the air-conditioned hotel."

"But less private. And from here, sir, we can monitor your daughter's leisurely progress across the lake."

"What does my daughter have to do with this?" I demanded, angry.

"A lovely young woman. It surprises me, sir, that a famous person like you allows a famous person like her such free rein. The world is full of unscrupulous people."

"Am I talking to one of them?"

"Don't think ill of me, sir. There is no other like Monicah. Her safety should be a matter of great concern to all of us."

"The year she was born, President Tharaka declared her a national resource, a national treasure. Those Sambusai warriors know that, and so does my man at the marina. Should anything happen to her on this outing, they will suffer the consequences."

"Yes, sir—but would their punishments, including even their death, repay you for your daughter's loss?"

"Nothing repays a parent the death of a child." I took a freshly laundered, pale-pink kerchief from my pocket and wiped my brow. "What's all this to you, Mr. Akuj? I don't much like your questions."

"I'm from White Sphinx."

"I know *that*, Mr. Akuj. But you're Zarakali, I think, and White Sphinx died fifteen years ago today."

"Actually, Mr. Kampa, I'm a Karamojong from Uganda. That's not terribly far from here, though, and I look upon this as my country too." His eyes swept the lake, the desert, the eastern horizon. Then he nodded at another barren ridge inside the chain-link fence. "The Great Man died there, didn't he?"

"Yes. A horrified American Geographic Foundation cameraman got it all on film. Blair stumbled while prospecting that embankment, toppled down and broke his neck."

"Striving for the impossible."

I shot Dirk Akuj an annoyed glance.

"He *was* striving for the impossible, don't you think? He died on his very own Weightlessness Simulation Incline."

"Who's to say what's impossible?" I asked testily.

"Who indeed? Not I, Mr. Kampa. White Sphinx, you should know, has been born again from Woody Kaprow's ashes."

This news stunned me because I had not known that Kaprow was dead. I had not heard from the physicist in eight or nine years, and had last seen him at Blair's funeral in Marakoi, but I had always supposed he was incommunicado for security reasons. The U.S. government had shifted him into other lines of temporal research, and, happy as a ram in rut, he was rigorously pursuing these. So I had supposed.

"His ashes? He's dead?"

"I was speaking metaphorically, Mr. Kampa, but we do feel certain Dr. Kaprow is dead. Eight years ago he failed to return from a mission undertaken at Dachau in West Germany. The mission was supposedly a test for certain improvements to the temporal-transfer machinery, but it now seems that Dr. Kaprow insisted upon this dropback out of . . . call it 'racial guilt.' He went to join the martyrs."

"And never came back?"

"No, sir. We think he purposely rejected that option."

I scrutinized the young man's face. " 'We'? "

"Like you, Mr. Kampa, I have dual citizenship. I am the assistant project director for the new incarnation of White Sphinx. My association with Dr. Kaprow began three years after yours ended."

"You dream," I said under my breath. "You spirit-travel."

"I hallucinate, sir. It began when I was a seven-year-old child in a relief center in Karamoja, slowly starving to death." He paused. "Does my story interest you? I would be happy to tell it."

"Let's get out of the sun."

I led Dirk Akuj down from the ridge and along the lakeshore to the fence surrounding the protectorate. Here I fumbled with my keys, unlocked the gate, and found a second key to admit us to Blair's mud-and-wattle shack, now a sort of makeshift museum. Inside, we sat down at a rickety wooden table before a large cabinet containing mastodon tusks, suid teeth, and the skull and horn cores of a medium-sized buffalo, *Homioceras nilssoni.* Each item was tagged, but a visitor would search in vain for any hominid fossil other than a few jigsaw-puzzle skull fragments. At the cash register postcards featuring the bottomless grin of *"Homo zarakalensis"* were on sale. I moved to turn on the air-conditioning, for the hut was oppressive with heat and dust motes, but the Ugandan held up his hand.

"I will make my story brief, Mr. Kampa."

Dirk Akuj explained that in the crowded relief center, after better than a month of watching skeletal children die of malnutrition, disease, and, sometimes, lovelessness, the night turned to plastic for him—here, illustratively, he tapped his scarab tie pin—and out of the melting indigo of his vision a delicate, almond-eyed savior took shape. This unlikely being swallowed Dirk Akuj with a laugh. The boy's essence flowed into the blue tubing of the stranger's esophagus, belly, and intestines. Then these organs turned themselves inside-out and unraveled a vast membrane of sky above the desert. Like a cloud, the boy was pulsed across this luminous membrane to a place where he dissolved into rain. "Endless torrents of nonexistence," to use my contact's own words. He did not extract himself from this state—nor did he want to, ever again—until a merciless dawn in Karamoja awakened him to the clamor, dirt, and pathos of the relief center.

Three days later a slender Oriental male closely resembling the "savior" in Dirk Akuj's dream, or hallucination, arrived in camp. This unusual-looking man, an anomaly among the bearded European photographers, whey-faced nuns, and unsympathetic black soldiers from Kampala, selected five children, seemingly at random, and spirited them out of the camp, out of Uganda, out of Africa.

"To the United States," the man concluded.

"How?"

"It's difficult to recall. With many official-looking papers and a persuasive manner. He was soft-spoken but very insistent and direct. He did not permit himself to be hassled, you see."

"But what was his motive?"

Despite a *Do Not Touch* placard, Dirk Akuj lifted the tooth of an ancient warthog from the display cabinet and turned it between his fingers like a jewel. His only response to my question was a half-mocking, half-saintly smile.

"Only five?" I asked the Ugandan.

"He did what he could. I was raised in the family of a wealthy real-estate broker in Southern California. I continued to hallucinate my future. One such hallucination prophesied my meeting with Dr. Kaprow on a high school R.O.T.C. trip from San Bernadino, where we lived, to Edwards Air Force Base And . . ." He let his voice trail off.

"And what?"

"And it came to pass." He returned the suid tooth to the cabinet. "It *is* hot in here, isn't it?"

"Why did you want to talk to me, Mr. Akuj?"

"Why don't we resume our discussion in a more comfortable setting? This, sir, was just a get-acquainted session. I am also Uganda's representative to the official opening of the Sambusai Sands. We'll see each other this evening in the cabaret." Before I could raise a protest, he glided to the door and out into the glare of late afternoon. "Wait a few minutes before following me back to the hotel, Mr. Kampa. I can let myself out."

Annoyed, suspicious, perplexed, I stood on the porch watching my pantherine visitor retrace his path to the metal gate. Here he pivoted and waved, his plastic scarab glowing almost incandescently.

"I can scarcely wait to meet your daughter," he called. He pushed through the gate and strode nimbly toward the butt end of the retaining-wall walkway back to the hotel. I wished that a lion would fall upon him, a crocodile leap from the water to seize him.

Monicah and her regal galley slaves were no longer on the lake. Why had Dirk Akuj brought her into our little talk so frequently? This question frightened me because I thought I knew the answer.

In the cabaret—more accurately, the grand entertainment hall of the Sambusai Sands, a multitiered dining floor with an orchestra pit and an immense stage hung with zebra-striped foil curtains—a thousand or more people had gathered for the official grand opening of our billion-dollar Convention and Recreational Centre. Portions of the complex had been operating for nearly three months, but tonight marked the culmination of our labors, a new beginning on the road to economic independence. At tables scattered like islands in the electric dark sat many African dignitaries, residually wealthy Arabs, American service personnel, and casino-hopping European playpeople. On each side of the hall, at balcony level, leopards stalked back and forth in lifelike dioramas of the Pleistocene.

Nearest the orchestra pit (from which the strains of "Born Free" had been emanating for twenty minutes) were the tables reserved for Zarakali cabinet ministers, the commanding officers of the bases at Bravanumbi and Russell-Tharaka, and the representatives of every country in the East African Confederation.

Monicah and I shared our table with Vice Admiral Cuomo and the Tanzanian representative, a handsome Arusha woman who clearly disapproved of the festivities.

A table away sat Dirk Akuj, vaguely sinister in a phosphorescent lime-green tuxedo jacket. His name, I had discovered after returning to my suite, did indeed appear on the official guest list, but I had never supposed that any African invited to our grand opening would also be a shill for White Sphinx. I tried to avoid the man's glance, but he kept ogling Monicah and giving me enigmatic smiles, and I was hard pressed to ignore him.

Admiral Cuomo was something of a help because he had engaged the Arusha woman and me in animated small talk about his favorite subject, ice hockey, about which he supposed us intensely curious because of our lack of exposure to the sport. Monicah sat silent, encouraged in her moroseness by the chilly attitude of Rochelle Mutasingwa, the Tanzanian. She was unaware of Dick Akuj's interest in her, and I was grateful for her failure to notice the man. As Admiral Cuomo faithfully recounted the high points of last year's Stanley Cup finals, the evening seemed to stretch out before us like a deathwatch.

The dying strains of "Born Free" at last fell captive to silence, and the Marakoi Pops struck up a fanfare. The expectant nattering of the crowd faded away, the stage was brilliantly spotlighted, and the American singer-composer Manny Barrelo emerged from the wings beside the self-propelled wheelchair of President Mutesa Tharaka.

As one person, everyone in the hall rose to accord our aged President a standing ovation. Without whistling, foot stamping, or unseemly cries of praise or thanksgiving, it was nevertheless thunderous. Even Monicah was moved, for this was the first time in nearly three years that Mzee Tharaka had made a public appearance. On most state and ceremonial occasions Vice President Gicoru acted in his stead, and no one had anticipated a change of these arrangements even for the long-awaited grand opening of the Sands. Our applause lasted nearly five full minutes.

Nodding and smiling, Barrelo quieted us by raising his

hands and addressing us to the effect that we were all "eyewitnesses to history." The President, meanwhile, sat slumped in his chair like a well-heeled scarecrow, the gilded skull on his crown staring out into the dark with a threat that everyone implicitly understood but nervously disregarded. The roar of the leopard stalking the left-hand balcony was audible even through the bullet-proof plastic of its diorama, and Barrelo saluted the creature without interrupting his remarks.

". . . lots of fine live entertainment for you this evening, folks, and continuous gaming in the casinos just off the lobby." Whereupon he squinted down into the footlights at the tables just beyond the orchestra. "Is Joshua Kampa here this evening? Of course he is, what a ridiculous question. Josh, c'mon, Josh, stand up, please. President Tharaka wants you to take a bow for making Zarakal's beautiful Lake Kiboko resort genuinely competitive with Vegas and Monte Carlo. Stand up, stand up. Ladies and gentlemen, this is the man whose mind conceived the Sambusai Sands Convention and Recreational Centre!"

Numbly I got to my feet, stood blinking in a white-hot spot, and sat back down to the dovetailing applause of hundreds of fellow *Homo sapiens*. The Centre, I wanted to tell them, was not entirely my fault.

"President Tharaka wants everyone here tonight to know that the revenues generated by this complex will fund schools, agricultural programs, cultural exchanges, and technological progress for everyone in East Africa. Already ZAPPA—the Zarakali Administration for Peace and Prosperity through Astronautics—has been revived, and you can bet your ostrich feathers that an African will walk on the moon before this decade is out. That's what President Tharaka and Minister Kampa had in mind when they made construction of this complex a top national priority only six or seven years ago. Why, Mr. Kampa gave up a place on the lucrative American lecture circuit just to return to Zarakal and run for a seat in the National Assembly. He's a credit to his country—*both* his countries—and I think he deserves another round of applause."

We got it, Manny Barrelo and I, a bigger round than we had received before (even though Barrelo had grossly muddled the facts about my desertion of the "lucrative American lecture circuit"), and Admiral Cuomo patted me on the back. At the adjacent table Dirk Akuj smiled at me cryptically.

"But enough talk. It's time for these festivities to begin, and our opening act, our overture, is a tribute to Mr. Kampa, his beautiful daughter Monicah, and the emergence of Zarakal as a potential space-age power . . . Ladies and gentlemen, for your pleasure, *Lisa Chagula and the Gombe Stream Chimps!*"

Manny Barrelo gestured toward the right-hand wing, then spun the President's chair around so that they could exit stage-left. The Marakoi Pops broke into an up-tempo version of *Thus Spake Zarathustra*, and applause again filled the hall.

The zebra-striped curtains parted to reveal a back-lighted scrim upon which a convincing, two-dimensional replica of a volcano was erupting over a muted pastel landscape. A many-pronged bolt of lightning flashed against this scrim, and about the trunk of a papier-mâché baobab streamers of red and orange crepe paper danced like flames. Wearing African garb from the Lake Tanganyika region, Lisa Chagula entered and positioned herself on the outer apron of the stage. Then she whistled.

Five champanzees swaggered in from stage-right, one of them having been shaved to simulate a quasi-human nakedness. I saw through the chimp's imposture immediately, and so did everyone else who knew the details of my legendary trip into the distant past, i.e., everyone in attendance. The ape was supposed to be me. A further clue to its assumed identity was the pink plastic doll cradled in its arms, a surrogate for Monicah in her original incarnation as the Grub. The chimps quailed from the "flames" surrounding them.

"Oh, God," murmured Monicah, and my heart misgave me.

For two years after the trauma of my involvement with White Sphinx, I had made a good living in the States recounting my adventures for college students, television talk-show hosts, and the readers of Sunday magazine supplements. Because the Air Force and the U.S. government routinely ridiculed my claims, and because I would allow no one with a degree in physical anthropology to examine Monicah, I had been widely regarded as an amusing crackpot. For a time my notoriety grew, bringing me more money, an unwanted retinue of hangers-on, and the curse of instant recognition on any street or side road in my readopted homeland. Then the bottom had fallen out, and I had gone the way of yesterday's superstar, straight down the lonely cul de sac of media neglect to the crumbling brick wall of oblivion.

My mother and my sister's testimony dismissed as worthless, my amusement value squandered, my livelihood compromised, I had dropped from the semireputable status of a psychic or a newspaper astrologer to the pathetic one of a palmist or a flying-saucer nut. Too proud to accept my mother's charity, I had briefly, and altogether seriously, considered going back to work for Gulf Coast Coating in the Florida panhandle—whereupon, through a consular official in Washington, D.C., President Tharaka had publicly confirmed my story, chastised the United States Air Force for making me out a liar, and invited me to return to Zarakal. *"I have important work for you to do,"* read the portion of the communiqué addressed directly to me; *"please come home."* Grateful for aid from this unexpected quarter (President Tharaka and Alistair Patrick Blair had maintained an impregnable silence for two years), I made haste to emigrate, leaving behind a thoroughly bewildered American public and a rancorous congressional debate about abuses of power in the Pentagon and the executive branch.

In Marakoi I was served with a subpoena haling me before a Senate investigative committee, but with Mutesa Tharaka's blessing I ignored it and began laying the groundwork for my campaign for a seat in Zarakal's National Assembly. After a parade through the capital and a hero's build-up in the East African press, I ran unopposed. Only two weeks after my election I received an appointment to the cabinet. Since that time, by hard work and a scrupulous avoidance of the WaBenzi image, I had won the complete respect of my constituents and had reestablished my credibility with American officials in Zarakal.

Although I had long since concluded that President Tharaka had played his Kampa card to win American concessions of which I was still unaware, this suspicion did not compromise my gratitude to him. Monicah and I had finally found our place in the sun. I was the man who had traveled in time, she was a diminutive African Eve, and, as Dirk Akuj had noted that afternoon, we were celebrities whose story had inspired international controversy. Indeed, upon his death, the flamboyant mantle of Alistair Patrick Blair had passed to my daughter and me.

Now, in the dinner theater of the Sambusai Sands, the Gombe Stream Chimps were reenacting one of the final episodes of the Joshua Kampa legend. This "tribute" having been kept a secret from Monicah and me, I had had no chance to approve it beforehand. That was bad. The champagne we had been drinking, along with my own embarrassment, made the mimicry of Lisa Chagula's chimpanzees seem especially intrusive, a violation of something sacred. I gripped the edge of the table and said nothing. The reenactment would be over soon, and quickly forgotten as other performers and divertissements succeeded it. No point in disrupting the evening with an indignant outburst.

Only the ape impersonating me remained in view, sheltering its baby doll from the myriad swirling tatters of crepe paper. The other chimps had hurried off stage-left when projectors mounted all about the hall threw holographic images of several spotted hyenas into their midst. To the oohing and ahing of the audience these hallucinatory creatures advanced on my pongid counterpart, their eyes scintillating like topazes. Lisa Chagula, on the apron of the stage, pantomimed her sympathetic horror, covering her eyes with her forearm and crouching away to one side. At which point a gaudy mock-up of a lunar module descended from on high—on wires—to rescue Monicah and me. This contraption contained a pair of chimpanzees in show-business spacesuits, who jumped from their craft and began pulling bright yellow fire hoses out its hatch.

"I can't stand this!" Monicah exclaimed, loud enough to be heard over the clamorous music.

"Do you feel your dignity is being assailed?" asked Rochelle Mutasingwa, as if it were rather late to worry about the matter.

"Not mine, the chimpanzees'."

"Lisa Chagula and the Gombe Stream Chimps have been Tanzania's good-will ambassadors for years. Their dignity has never been questioned."

"Maybe not," Monicah replied. "But this is a vulgar exploitation of the little chaps."

"Exploitation!"

"You heard me. Those chimps are your niggers, Miss Mutasingwa, and the late President Nyerere would never have approved anything so mean and disgusting."

"Ladies," said Admiral Cuomo. "Ladies."

"Your daughter's remarks go beyond the bounds of adolescent irresponsibility," Rochelle Mutasingwa told me angrily. "I wonder if they have your approval."

"No, of course not. Monicah hasn't been—"

"For God's sake, Daddy!"

On stage, the Grub and I were climbing into the lunar module with the chimps in the sequin-covered pressure suits. Doused, the crepe-paper streamers lay flat on the floor, while ancient Mount Tharaka, delicately backlit, continued to mutter and spew. Monicah did likewise, using vivid American expressions that I would have thought alien to the vocabularies of her affluent classmates. The lunar module, meantime, ascended on paper flames—and wires—into a canvas empyrean.

When Lisa Chagula and all seven chimps returned from the wings to exult in their triumph, Monicah abruptly stood up and swept her champagne glass to the floor. More monkey business appeared to be in the works, and she was going to have none of it. Fortunately, the darkness cloaking the hall concealed her distress from everyone but those in our immediate vicinity.

"Daddy, I don't feel well. I've got to get out of here."

I was torn. To desert my guests would be inhospitable, almost a breach of diplomatic etiquette. However, if Monicah were genuinely ill, I owed it to her to escort her back to our suite. During the entertainment to follow, my absence would be of small consequence to these people.

As the Gombe Stream Chimps initiated a tumbling exhibition, Dirk Akuj pushed back his chair and made a tactful half bow. "At your service, Mr. Kampa. Allow me the honor."

Alarmed, I tried to protest.

"He'll do fine, Daddy. Spiffy jacket, polished shoes, a credit to his tribe, whatever it may be."

"Karamojong, Miss Kampa."

"Right. A survivor. He's got to be okay, Daddy. Ta ta. We'll see you whenever you can tear yourself away."

Arm in arm, they disappeared together into the multi-tiered dark. Tim Njeri and another security man would intercept them at the door and accompany them upstairs, but I still did not appreciate the turn that events had taken. Dirk Akuj was a stranger with admitted ulterior motives, and his interest in my daughter, just fifteen today, struck me as ominous, something other than the tardy fibrillations of a young man's fancy. After all, the Ugandan was not *that* much younger than I.

Carrying congratulatory birthday telegrams from Jeannette Monegal and the Whitcombs, I stumbled off the elevator onto the fourteenth floor. It was two-thirty in the morning, and Tim Njeri and Daniel Eunoto were standing sentinel at the door to my suite. Actually, Daniel was in a kind of upright trance while Timothy crouched doggo behind a potted eucalyptus. They might have been *ilmoran* in the bushveldt rather than security agents in the corridor of a resort hotel.

"She's feeling better, I think," Timothy told me.

"What about Mr. Akuj from Uganda?"

Tim nodded at the door.

"He's still with her?" I was incredulous.

"Unless he jumped from the balcony, sir. There's no place else for him to go." Tim correctly read my disapproving look. "Miss Monicah insisted, Mr. Kampa, and today is certainly her birthday."

"Yesterday was certainly her birthday."

I went inside and found to my relief that Dirk Akuj was boiling water in a small ceramic kettle on my hotplate, a pair of piddling WaBenzi luxuries about which I never suffered any guilt pangs, not even in establishments prohibiting their use. He had shed his phosphorescent tuxedo jacket but was otherwise fully attired. Although that meant nothing five hours after my last sight of him, I pretended that it did.

Lying on the colorful cloak she had worn around her shoulders that evening, Monicah was snoozing in her Sambusai maiden's outfit. Her tiny breasts were exposed, and her shaven skull gleamed like an obsidian egg. A twenty-year-old photograph of President Tharaka kept watch over her from the wall above the bedstead. I put my daughter's telegrams down next to her outstretched hand and turned to face the intruder.

Dirk Akuj toasted me with a demitasse cup of tea and asked me if I would care to join him. I declined.

"Why are you still here?" An astringent medicinal scent pervaded the room, probably from his tea.

"I wanted to talk to you in a more hospitable setting than the protectorate, sir."

I took off my coat and shoes and slumped into a chair. I hoped that my posture would convey my weariness.

Dirk Akuj said, "You never spirit-travel anymore, do you?"

"The flesh is willing, but the spirit's weak."

"Have you ever wondered why, sir?"

"Why the spirit's weak?"

"Why you've been 'cured' of the dreams that set you apart from your fellows as a child."

"Because Woody Kaprow and White Sphinx used my attunement to make me *live* those dreams, that's why. I got them out of my system, and for the past fourteen years I've been an ordinary person."

"Ordinary celebrity, sir."

I conceded this stickling emendation with a grimace.

"Have you ever considered that your spirit-traveling, your dreamfaring, was *predictive?*"

"Of what?"

"Of what happened to you during one long month in the late summer of 1987. Your dreams were premonitions of the time-travel experience that finally took place through the agency of White Sphinx. You had been seeing the future as well as the past. Do you understand?"

"It's too late for this, Mr. Akuj."

"Has none of this ever occurred to you, sir?"

"No, none of it ever has. My spirit-traveling episodes didn't correspond to what happened to me once I'd been physically displaced into the past. So they *weren't* predictive, you see."

Dirk Akuj sipped whatever was in his cup and strolled past the wall-sized window overlooking the lake. My annoyance did not discomfit him. His manner suggested that the satisfaction of his curiosity was more important than the satisfaction of mine. What did he want? What was he driving at? I wanted to shout these questions at him but did not like to disclose so nakedly my eagerness for answers. Monicah stirred in her sleep.

"How do you feel about what happened to you back there?" he asked, gesturing at the window with his cup. "I mean, how do you feel *today* about the strange interruption of your life?"

"I try not to think about it, Mr. Akuj."

"Why, sir?"

"Because it's grown more and more remote with each passing year, and I'm half afraid none of it ever really happened."

"Paradise Lost?"

I raised my eyebrows. What was that supposed to mean?

"But there's your daughter, Mr. Kampa." Dirk Akuj nodded at the bed. "To doubt her reality would be akin to doubting the world's."

"I'd doubt the world's first, let me assure you."

"It's interesting you should feel so. Dr. Kaprow often used to displace himself into the past for brief stays. He kept them brief to prevent using up his ability to make the transition. But upon coming back, Mr. Kampa, he would sometimes say that he had returned to a 'simulacrum' of the present. His very word, *simulacrum.*"

Pensive, Dirk Akuj touched his lips to the rim of his cup, then drew them back.

"Even continuous transcordion contact did not reassure Dr. Kaprow. When he reemerged from our displacement vehicle, he feared that he had given himself into the society of ghosts and *Doppelgängers*. Each trip, he once informed me, put him at a further remove from the real. Eventually the horrifying past of the martyrs became his prime reality, and he chose to stay there."

This little narrative frightened me. If I lay down to sleep beside Monicah, might I awaken to find that the Sambusai Sands had disappeared into mist, that the world itself had evaporated? Where would I be then? A limbo in which the terms of my ghostliness prohibited any further contact with the people who had played a part in my life? The lateness of the hour, the champagne I had drunk, and the disorienting presence of Dirk Akuj set me trembling.

"Do you believe yourself to be a ghost?" I asked my nemesis.

"Certainly, most certainly, Mr. Kampa, but not perhaps in the way that Dr. Kaprow meant to imply. Each one of us is a ghost of every other, I think. Each one of us is possessed by the spirits of our ancestors, living and dead. Otherwise, how could we dream? Not to believe ourselves ghosts in this sense would be to cut ourselves adrift from our beginnings."

It's too late for this, I thought, not understanding.

Aloud I said, "What do you want, Mr. Akuj? What is this all about?"

On the carven sideboard fronting the window he set his demitasse cup. A highlight twinkling on its handle mocked the glittering of the stars above the mountains on the western side of the Rift.

"White Sphinx has been revived, Mr. Kampa, but with a different emphasis. Now we choose to go forward instead of back."

"No pursuable resonances," I murmured.

"Despite what Dr. Kaprow may once have told you, it's possible, sir. The chief requirement is a chrononaut whose spirit-traveling episodes propagate along *advancing* world lines."

Dismayed by this intelligence, I looked at my daughter.

"I've discussed this matter with Monicah, Mr. Kampa. She's eager to participate. The rewards are many."

"WaBenzi rewards!" I exclaimed, rising and going to the bed. "I won't let her." I sat down beside Monicah and took her hand, which was warm and poignantly soft. How could I commend her into the custody of Dirk Akuj, whose interest in her was probably carnal as well as mentorly? Monicah's eyes opened, and for a moment they were transparent, luminescent, bottomless, like the Grub's before our return.

"Spiritual rewards," countered Dirk Akuj, hoisting himself onto the sideboard and crossing his feet at the ankles. "Not only for herself, but for all those who survive to make the future their present."

Monicah drew up her knees and scooted away from my touch. Her face wore a startling expression. Although her appearance had always been more human than habiline, as if my blood had overwhelmed her mother's, tonight she looked like Helen. The strange glint in her eye bewitched as well as terrified me.

"You need parental permission for this," I told Dirk Akuj. "Monicah's still a minor, and you need my consent for her participation."

"You'll give it to us, sir."

"The hell I will."

After a brief pause the Ugandan said, "I've been fasting for two weeks. A little sisal tea is the only nourishment I take during fasts, and when I fast, I hallucinate. I hallucinate the future, you understand, and earlier this evening, in Monicah's presence, I saw you agreeing to let her participate."

"Why would I do a crazy thing like that?" There was a quaver in my voice.

"To regain her good opinion. You've lost it, I think, for the same reason your mother, the writer, once lost yours. She tried to take advantage of your relationship for certain unworthy, short-term ends."

"Monicah, is that what you think I've done?"

My daughter stared at me, virtually unseeing.

"She's possessed, Mr. Kampa. You woke her before she could sleep off the effects of her trance."

"You've drugged her!"

"With her full complicity, sir. In this state she communes across the years with her mother's spirit. You never speak of her mother, Monicah says. For a while, then, I helped her *become* her mother."

"Bring her back," I commanded the Ugandan.

"Far better that we should go to her, Mr. Kampa. Surely you'll take this opportunity to touch the spirit of your habiline wife?"

I glared at the man. The winter I had returned from the States to Zarakal, Thomas Babington Mubia had taken me to the world of *ngoma* by way of a Wanderobo incantation. There he had formally married my spirit to that of his dead Kikembu wife, Helen Mithaga, whom he believed a twentieth-century avatar of my Pleistocene bride. Later that winter Babington had died, but as far as I was concerned, Helen and I were linked forever, legally as well as emotionally, and my former mentor's impromptu rite had formalized our bond even in the Here and Now.

"Did you truly love Helen, Mr. Kampa, or was your dalliance with her a matter of rut and propinquity?"

"Bring my daughter back and then get out of here!"

"Forgive me," Dirk Akuj said. "Of course you truly loved Helen, and you would like to commune with her again."

"Listen!" I barked. "Listen, you miserable—"

"But you do, sir. You do wish to commune with your long-dead wife, and I can help you do that."

My resolve weakened and, intuitively recognizing that he had beaten me, he headed for the door: Dirk Akuj, a Karamojong physicist with ingrained animist sympathies. He invited Timothy Njeri and Daniel Eunoto into the suite, arguing that the participation of one of these two men would help me achieve a harmonious relationship with the ghost in Monicah's body. The other security agent would stand aloof from the ceremony as an observer, a control. This arrangement would free us from the worry that I was utterly in Dirk Akuj's power. However, neither Timothy nor Daniel looked eager to take part in this scheme. They awaited some word from me, but all I could do was stare bewilderedly at the girl on the bed.

Dirk Akuj crossed to his tuxedo jacket and removed from an inside pocket a pair of plastic bags containing what appeared to be leaf cuttings and roots. He opened the bags, shook their contents into the tea kettle on the hotplate, replenished the water in the kettle from a bathroom faucet, turned on the hotplate, and decocted this potion for a good five minutes, all the while humming a tuneless melody. A pungent odor rose into the air with the steam from the kettle's spout, a smell like minty ammonia.

Timothy and Daniel flipped a coin to see who would act as observer. The coin came up heads (President Tharaka's), and Daniel retreated to the door to watch.

After stripping to his T-shirt and briefs and urging Timothy and me to do likewise, Dirk Akuj showed us how we should empty our lungs and inhale deeply of the fumes from the kettle. We followed his advice. Then the three of us sat down in a triangle in the center of the room and began drumming our knees with our knuckles. The steam in the open kettle on the floor focused our attention, and soon the hotel was blinking in and out of existence in time with our drumming. Monicah gazed down on our ceremony as if from a great height. She seemed to blink in and out of existence on the off-beats.

I closed my eyes and time ceased to have any conventional meaning. History had been repealed, the future indefinitely postponed.

Then I opened my eyes and beheld around me a grayness pulsing with the promise of light. I was alone, but in a place with neither substance nor dimension. My hands had no body, my body no hands. Then a door swung inward, and my long-lost Helen was standing in this doorway, radiant in an immaculate white dress and apron. She was even wearing shoes. Her feet looked enormous in shoes, like monument pedestals. Tears freshened my cheeks, and I hurried to draw her out of the pale rectangle of the doorway.

"You shouldn't be wearing these," I told Helen, kneeling in front of her. "It's demeaning for you."

Her shoes were cheap blue sneakers with heavy rubber soles. I began unlacing them. My tears made it difficult to see what I was doing, but I got the laces undone and slipped her feet out of the sneakers one after the other. I stood, embraced her for an infinite moment, just to feel her body against mine, and rocked her in my arms like a father holding his child. Her starched clothing began to annoy me, too, and I loosened the knot supporting her apron, expertly unbuttoned her dress, and swept these items down her flanks to the floor, there to join my V-necked T-shirt and my beautiful Fruit of the Looms. She regarded me with tender puzzlement, but did not scold me for returning us to the innocent nakedness of beasts and Minids. Instead she closed my eyelids with her fingertips and settled one gnarled fist on my heart.

I opened my eyes again. The hotel suite had rematerialized around my double bed, which I was sharing with Helen Habiline. Praise be to Ngai and the mysterious potion of Dirk Akuj!

. . .

"Mr. Kampa—Mr. Kampa, sir, may I go now, please?"

The face staring down at me was that of a matronly Sambusai woman with intensely bright eyes and a full, healthy mouth. Astonished, I slipped out from beneath her gaze and over the edge of the bed. The woman was dressed in white, the costume of a hotel maid. I tried to sort out the implications of her presence. Looking around, I saw Timothy Njeri unconscious on the floor beside my tea kettle—he was still in his skivvies, while I was buck naked—and Daniel Eunoto slumped in a corner sleeping the sleep of the sledgehammered. Monicah and Dirk Akuj were nowhere in sight. The sky beyond the picture window was a chastening blue.

"What are you doing here?"

"No one answer when I knock, Mr. Kampa." She gave me an apologetic smile. "I came in to clean."

"Before dawn?"

"Oh, no, sir. Much after. It's nearly noon."

A little more questioning revealed that she had been in my suite for almost two hours and that she was disastrously behind schedule. If I did not let her go, the manager would fire her, and she would have to return to a desolate mission outpost southeast of the Recreational Centre, where life was both hard and very dull. I wrapped a sheet about myself, gave her the equivalent of nearly fifty American dollars, and told her to catch up as much of her work as she could. I would protect her from the ire of the Sands management. The woman departed, thanking me.

I dressed and stalked about the suite trying to sort out my emotions. Dirk Akuj had hoodwinked us. His *ngoma* ceremony had been a cunning scam. Or had it? Timothy and Daniel would come round soon enough, I could tell by their breathing, but in the meantime I wanted to collect my thoughts without their help. Was it possible that for a moment—a brief moment, at least—my Helen's *ngoma* had inhabited the comfortable body of the hotel maid? In spite of everything, I felt pretty good.

Monicah had left me a note. It was written on the back of the birthday telegram from my mother:

Dear Daddy,

You can give me your permission to do this by not trying to bring me back, okay? We're crossing Lake Kiboko into Uganda in a motor launch, and if you want to catch us you probably can. I really, really hope you won't try. You had your turn, this is mine, and maybe one day Dirk and I can point everyone toward their tomorrow by stepping out of it back into today. Tell Grandma Jeannette and Aunt Anna I love them. Lots and lots o' love to you too,

Your daughter,
THE GRUB

I rode the elevator down to the lobby, then walked out to the marina in the strength-sapping heat. In spite of the heat several vacationers were out on the lake in paddle-boats; a light breeze fluttered the fringes on the colorful parasols beneath which these hearty tourists labored. Despite my daughter's note and her conviction that we could catch up with her if we tried, she and Dirk Akuj must have already reached the lake's western shore. Although it might still be possible to overtake them in the treacherous hinterland between Zarakal and Uganda, I was not going to blow the whistle on their escape.

In spite of this decision, I returned along the pierlike arm of the marina to the walk running north and south along the lakeshore. Here I turned north and made my way to the water-purification plant servicing the entire complex. My keys admitted me to the fenced enclosure surrounding the plant, and my status in the Zarakali government shortcircuited the objections of a pair of uniformed guards who clearly wondered what business I had in their little bailiwick.

I hiked through a maze of metal tubing, pressure gauges, and wheels to the clean sandy area where an immense water tower rose up into the desert sky. I climbed the narrow iron ladder on one of the tower's colossal legs and from the catwalk looked over Lake Kiboko after my daughter. The guards and several other plant personnel watched me ascend, dumfounded by my audacity.

Then I leaped out and caught a support rod with both hands. The plant personnel gasped. When I began a long slide inward, my feet dangling like window-sash weights, they cried, "Be careful, Mr. Kampa! Please be careful, sir!" Their shouts were reassuring hosannas. I slid the rod to an intersection beneath the tank, then hung there in the arid breeze gazing westward after Monicah. For the duration of my stunt, at least, I was a very happy man.

About the Author

Michael Bishop was born in Lincoln, Nebraska, in 1945 and spent the early part of his life as an "Air Force brat," living in many places throughout the world. Some of his experiences in Spain have served as background for part of *No Enemy But Time*.

Bishop received a master's degree in English from the University of Georgia and taught for several years at the USAF Academy Preparatory School in Colorado before turning to full-time writing following his early successes and recognition as one of the most talented new writers in science fiction during the early 1970s.

He has been nominated several times for the Hugo and Nebula Awards, and his first short-story collection, *Blooded on Arachne*, has just appeared in hardcover from Arkham House. It will be reprinted next year as a Timescape paperback. Bishop lives with his wife and two children in Pine Mountain, Georgia.

292